D0293074

ALSO BY ERIC BROWN

Novels
Weird Space: The Devil's Nebula
The Kings of Eternity
Guardians of the Phoenix
Necropath
Xenopath
Cosmopath
Kéthani
Helix
Helix Wars
New York Dreams
New York Blues
New York Nights
Penumbra
Engineman
Meridian Days

Novellas
Starship Fall
Starship Summer
Revenge
The Extraordinary Voyage of Jules Verne
Approaching Omega
A Writer's Life

Collections
Threshold Shift
The Fall of Tartarus
Deep Future
Parallax View (with Keith Brooke)
Blue Shifting
The Time-Lapsed Man

As Editor
The Mammoth Book of New Jules Verne Adventures
(with Mike Ashley)

First published 2013 by Solaris
an imprint of Rebellion Publishing Ltd,
Riverside House, Osney Mead,
Oxford, OX2 0ES, UK

www.solarisbooks.com

ISBN: 978 1 78108 092 4

10 9 8 7 6 5 4 3 2 1

A CIP catalogue record for this book is available from the
British Library.

Designed & typeset by Rebellion Publishing

Printed in the US

THE SERENE
INVASION
ERIC BROWN

SOLARIS

For Keith and Debbie Brooke

ONE

2025

CHAPTER ONE

ON THE DAY everything changed, Sally Walsh finished what was to be her last shift at the Kallani medical centre – though she didn't know that at the time – and stepped out of the makeshift surgery into the furnace heat of the early afternoon Ugandan sun.

The packed-earth compound greeted her with its depressing familiarity. A dozen crude buildings, looking more like a shanty town than a hospital, huddled in the centre of the sere compound, surrounded by a tall adobe wall. Beside the metal gate rose a watchtower, manned in shifts by a dozen government soldiers. When she began work at Kallani five years ago, it struck her as odd that a hospital had to be so protected, but after a few months in the job she had seen why: as fortification against rebel insurgents bent on kidnapping Westerners to hold hostage, to deter local gangs from raiding the hospital for drugs, and to stop the flood of refugees from over-running the centre in times of drought.

Last winter Sally had attempted to grow an olive tree in the shade of the storeroom; but the drought had killed it within weeks. How could she lavish water on the tree when her patients were so needful? Now the dead twigs poked from the ground, blackened and twisted.

Ben Odinga stepped from the storeroom, saw her and raised his eyebrows.

She shook her head.

"Have you finished?" he asked.

"I'm well and truly finished, Ben."

He looked at her seriously. "Come to my room, Sally. I have some good whisky. South African. You look like you need a drink."

She followed him across the compound to the prefab building that comprised the centre's residential complex. He held open the fly-screen door and she stepped into the small room. A simple narrow bed, a bookshelf bearing medical textbooks, a dozen well-read paperback novels and a fat Bible.

She sat on a folding metal chair by the window while Ben poured two small measures of whisky into chipped tumblers.

She took a sip, winced as its fire scoured her throat, and smiled at Ben's description of it as 'good whisky'. What she'd give for a glass of Glenfiddich.

He said, "The infection?"

She nodded. "There was nothing we could do, short of flying her to Kampala." Which, on their budget, was out of the question.

She went on, "I'm worried about Mary. They were close."

"I'll look in on her later, talk to her."

"If you would, Ben." She sighed. "Christ, I told her not to worry..." She looked up, then said, "I'm sorry."

He shook his head, smiling tolerantly. He had become accustomed to the frequency of her blaspheming.

A week ago a mother from a nearby village had brought in her malnourished daughter. Her complaint was not malnutrition, but a swollen abdomen. Ben had diagnosed appendicitis and operated, and all seemed well until, a couple of days ago, the five-year-old developed a high fever. Mary, a nurse six months out of medical college in Tewkesbury, had committed the cardinal sin of identifying with the kid.

Sally had long ago learned that lesson.

Ben said, "What's wrong?"

She looked up. "What makes you think...?"

"I've known you for years, Sally Walsh. I know when you have something on your mind."

She hadn't wanted to tell him like this; she had wanted to break it to him gently – if that were possible.

"I hope you won't think any less of me for this, Ben." She stared into her glass, swirled the toxic amber liquid. "I've had enough. I've had five years here and I've had enough. I'll be leaving in May."

She had expected his reaction to be one of disappointment, maybe even anger. Instead he just shook his head, as if in stoic acceptance. This seemed to her even more of a condemnation of her decision.

He said, quietly, "Why?"

She shrugged and avoided his gaze. "I'm burned out. I'm... perhaps I've come to understand, at last, that the reality here hasn't matched my expectations."

He said, "That is no reason to give in, Sally."

She looked across at him. He perched on the bed in his stained white uniform, a bony, whittled-down Kenyan in his early fifties, with disappointment burning in his nicotine-brown eyes.

"There comes a time, Ben, when we have to move on. I've had five years here. I'm jaded. The place needs someone new, someone with fresh enthusiasm, new ideas."

"The place needs someone like you, with empathy and experience."

"Please," she snapped, "don't make me feel guilty. I'm going in May and you'll be getting a replacement fresh from Europe, and after a few weeks it'll be as if I were never here."

"Don't kid yourself on that score, Dr Walsh."

She smiled. "I'll miss it – you and the others. But I've made my decision."

They drank in silence for a time. A gecko darted across the wall behind Ben. Cicadas thrummed outside like faulty electrical appliances. It was mercilessly hot within the room and Sally was sweating.

"Do you know why I became a doctor?" she said at last.

"You told me..." He waved his glass. "Wasn't it something to do with your Marxist ideals?"

"That was why I volunteered to work in Africa," she said. Ideals, she thought, that had long perished. What was that old saw: If you're not a communist when you're twenty, then there's something wrong with your heart; if you're still a communist when you're forty, then there's something wrong with your

12

head... Well, she was just over forty now and had lost her faith years ago.

"When I was fourteen, Ben, my mother was diagnosed with inoperable and terminal cancer. My father had died of a heart attack when I was two. I have no memories of him. When my mother told me she was ill..." She stared into her whisky, recalling her thin, pinch-faced mother, in her mid-forties, calmly sitting Sally down after dinner one evening and telling her, with a light-hearted matter-of-factness that must have been so hard to achieve, that mummy was ill and might not live for more than a year, but that Aunty Eileen and Uncle Ron would look after her afterwards.

She felt then as if she had run into a brick wall that had knocked all the breath from her body; and, later, a sense of disbelief and denial that had turned, as the months elapsed and her mother grew ever thinner and more and more ill, into an inarticulate anger and a sense of unfairness that burned at the core of her being.

An abiding memory from near the end of that time was when Dr Roberts came to her mother's bedside and simply sat with her for an hour, holding her hand. Perhaps it was this that persuaded Sally that she wanted to become a doctor. Not the cures Dr Roberts might have effected, or the pain she might have relieved, but the fact of the woman's simple humanity in giving up so much of her time to hold the hand of a dying patient.

Now she told Ben this, and he listened with that tolerant, amused smile on his handsome face, and nodded in the right places, and commented occasionally.

They finished their whiskies and he refilled their glasses.

"What will you do when you leave here, Sally?"

"Probably take up a practice in some leafy English village." How her younger self would have railed at her for admitting as much. She recalled, vividly, wondering how her fellow graduates could consider taking up practices looking after privileged English patients when men, women and children were dying of diarrhoea in Africa. What a sanctimonious little prig she must have been back then!

Ben broke into her thoughts. "So, Sally – and don't be offended when I say this – but you think that you have paid your dues?"

She said nothing, just stared down at the desiccated linoleum curling in the sunlight by the door. She felt terrible. She shook her head. At last she said in a whisper, "It wouldn't be so bad if I did feel this, Ben. It would be... understandable. The thing is, I don't feel I've paid my dues, and I probably would never think that I had, even if I stayed here for the rest of my life. My reasons are more personal, selfish if you like, than that. You see," she looked up, "it's just that I look at what's happening here and I despair."

He smiled. "Don't we all?"

"Do you know, Ben, in the five years I've been here, nothing, not one bloody thing, has got better. Nothing! The government is still corrupt, full of rapacious fat cats all sincere smiles one minute, and behind your back raking off profits that should go to help their people. And then the Chinese and the Europeans and Americans... using the continent like a gameboard. It makes me sick, Ben, what the Chinese are doing north of here."

"They've brought wealth, jobs, security for thousands," he said.

She stared at him. "You don't really believe that, don't you? You're not toeing the party line?" She held up her hand and counted off points on her fingers. "Eighty-five per cent of all profits made in Xian City go straight back to the mafia fascists in Beijing who still have the gall to call themselves communists. Ten per cent is raked off by Ugandan middle-men, and the rest goes to middle-class Africans who employ locals at slave labour rates. And have you seen the slums growing up around Xian, and have you read the reports of prostitution in the area? The Chinese are no better than all the other colonials who came before them – in it for what they can take out. Christ, Ben, you're Kenyan. You should know that!"

He was smiling at her, his calm face a picture of tolerance. "Anger doesn't help anything, Sally."

"I'm sorry... But do you know what angers me most, Ben? Me. I'm angry at myself for letting it get to me. I'm angry at myself for giving in."

He frowned, as if at a complex mystery. He whispered, "Then don't give in, my friend. Stay here."

She held back her tears and said, "I can't. I've made my decision."

With an acuity belied by his bland, smiling face, Ben said, "It's Geoff, isn't it?"

She looked at him, surprised by his deduction.

"Partly, but I was thinking of leaving before I met Geoff. So don't go blaming him."

She'd met Geoff Allen a year ago when he flew to Africa to cover the drought in the Karamoja region of northern Uganda. He'd impressed her with his naïve simplicity, his apolitical childishness: drinking with him one evening in her room, after she'd shown him around the Kallani medical complex, he had admitted that the reason he was a photo-journalist was that he hoped that by reporting the conditions of people less fortunate than himself, all around the world, the results of his work might provoke the citizens of Europe to do something about the poverty and injustice.

At first she had laughed at his political naivety, wondering where the hell to begin to put this big, handsome man right in his endearingly simplistic world-view. She had restrained herself, and after a few days in his company, as she toured with him around the various medical centres in the region, she had come to understand that his beliefs, no matter how misguided, were sincerely held. He believed that as an individual he could effect change at a higher level.

Perhaps, in Geoff Allen, she was reminded of the idealism and naivety she herself had possessed in her early twenties, which had now been eroded by cynicism and experience.

And as to what Geoff saw in her? After the first time they had made love, he'd held her and expressed his admiration at what she was doing here.

They'd seen each other just six times in the following year, and the last time – a snatched weekend in Kampala where Geoff was *en route* to cover the terrorist atrocities in Zambia – she had told him that she was leaving Uganda and returning to London.

"I'd be going back regardless of Geoff," she said now, "but when I get back we'll be buying somewhere together."

Ben raised his glass. "I sincerely hope that you find happiness. Geoff is a good man."

His approbation cheered her. Tomorrow Geoff was flying from London to Entebbe and making the long drive north – ostensibly to do another piece on the drought, in reality to see her. The thought made her a little drunk.

Ben raised his empty glass. "Would you like another whisky?"

She was wondering whether to accept the offer – despite the fact that she had an early shift in the morning – when the sound of gunfire rattled through the hot afternoon air.

HER FIRST IMPULSE was to rush to the door and see what was happening, and she was obeying the urge by the time common sense kicked in and suggested that it might not be the best idea. She stood in the doorway, staring across the compound. She saw the watchtower bloom in a sudden orange fireball, and a split-second later the sound of the explosion hit her. Three soldiers dropped from the tower, one by one, and lay twitching on the ground as they burned.

She watched with incredulity as another soldier ran towards his burning colleagues. He directed his rifle at them, and even as she watched she assumed that what he did then was an act of mercy: he unloaded a blast of bullets into each of the three flaming soldiers, instantly stilling their agonised spasming.

Then he moved to the gate, unbolted the locking mechanism, and hauled it open. A battered Ford utility truck, with a machine gun welded to its cross-bar, revved through the gate and into the compound.

Before she could move, the soldier turned, looked across the compound, and raised his gun at her.

She stared at him, uncomprehending. His name was Josef Makumbi, and she had chatted with him in the canteen during the periods when he was not manning the watchtower.

He yelled something at her.

Behind her, she felt Ben's hand on her arm, drawing her back into the room.

Josef fired. The bullets smacked into the timber above her head. He yelled again. "Here! Both of you!"

She stepped forward, sensing Ben behind her. She looked across at the corpses of Josef's colleagues. They were still burning. She had the absurd urge to ask him why he had killed his friends.

Ben whispered to her, "Be calm. Do exactly as he says. We will be okay, Sally."

Two men leapt from the cab of the truck. One was a Somali, and the other Arabic. A third terrorist, another Arab, remained on the flat-bed, manning the machine gun. He turned it on Sally and Ben as they moved across the compound towards the government soldier.

She caught his eyes. "Josef?"

The Somali and the Arab looked around the compound, spoke rapidly, and came to some decision. The Arab spoke to Josef in the local language. Josef nodded and twitched his rifle towards Sally and Ben.

"Get onto the back of the truck. Move! Do as I say or I'll shoot."

Sally stared at him. "Josef, how can you...?"

Ben's hand gripped her upper arm and urged her towards the truck. "Be silent!"

She allowed herself to be propelled along. She should have felt fear, then – she realised much later – but all she experienced at the time was bewilderment at Josef's treachery.

Ben assisted her onto the flat-bed. The machine-gunner swivelled his weapon and trained it on them. As they knelt on the corrugated bed of the truck, Josef ordered them to place their hands behind their backs. The Arab tied their wrists with twine, the cord digging into her flesh.

With a touch of sadism she came to see, later, as characteristic of him, the Arab prodded her between the shoulder blades. Unable to bring her hands up to cushion her fall, she fell face down and smacked the metal deck with her cheek. Ben fell beside her.

She wept, and rolled onto her side.

Josef grabbed her under the arms, dragged her across the flat-bed and propped her in a sitting position against the hot metal, then did the same with Ben.

Josef jumped from the truck, fastened the back flap, and stood in the compound watching the truck as it revved up, turned in a wide circle, and raced through the open gates. Sally fastened her eyes on the soldier's, hoping to cow him with her silent accusation, but his expression remained impassive as they drove away.

The Arab sat across from his captives, rocking with the bucketing motion of the vehicle as it accelerated along the sandy track. His face was thin, and running from his right ear to his hawk-like nose was a scar, a jagged wadi suppurating with some untreated infection.

The machine-gunner, a youth with a sickle-thin face and a milky left eye, stood with an arm slung negligently over his rattling weapon. He stared down at them, his expression contemptuous.

The direct sunlight was punishing. Normally Sally would have either rubbed high factor sun cream into her arms, face and neck, or ensured she was suitably covered. Now she felt her exposed skin burn.

They were heading north, she realised, into terrorist country.

She looked at Ben. His face was a mask carved from ebony. He whispered, "Try not to worry. They will make a ransom demand. We will be free in a day or two."

She said, "I have a bad feeling..."

The Arab kicked out, the heel of his boot gouging Sally's shin. "Be silent!" She pursed her lips rather than cry out at the pain.

They raced through the lifeless desert landscape, hitting potholes at speed. Sally rocked against Ben, his solidity reassuring. The metal ridge of the truck's side panel scored her shoulder blades.

They passed a village – Mullambi. They had

travelled over ten kilometres already. It struck her that she was in greater danger the further they travelled away from familiar territory. She felt the sun fry her head. She thought of her tiny room back at the compound and wanted to weep.

Across from them, the Arab closed his eyes, his head lolling. He appeared to be sleeping, his rifle propped across his lap.

"We will be fine," Ben said in a whisper. "We must do as they say, and do not question them. Whatever you do, Sally, do not argue with them."

"That," she said bitterly, "might not be easy."

"Just do not question what they are doing, okay?"

"Why? Because I'm a woman, and they don't like –"

He said impatiently, "Whatever the reasons! We should not antagonise these men."

She was silent for a time, then said, "They're going to kill us. I know it."

Ben turned to look at her. "That is not how these people work," he said patiently. "They will ransom us, makes demands for cash so that they can buy weapons."

The Arab opened his eyes and stared across at his captives.

Sally licked her rapidly drying lips and said, "Who are you?"

She felt Ben stiffen beside her.

The Arab stared at her, a potent distillation of contempt in his narrowed eyes. "My name is Ali," he said.

"I meant," she said, "which organisation do you represent?"

The man smiled. "Boko Haram," he said.

She wished she had never asked. Northern Uganda was plagued by competing bands of Islamic fundamentalists – each one a little more fundamental, it seemed, than the other. Originally from Nigeria, Boko Haram was the most hard-line of them all: bloodthirsty, uncompromising, and intolerant of everything Western.

"What do you want with us?"

Ben hissed, "Sally!"

The Arab said, "To... make example." He spat at her feet. "You come here, you fill my people with your ways –"

"Your people? Are you Ugandan?"

He said, "My people, my Muslim brothers."

"We're here," she said, "to help your brothers, to help your men, women and children. There is a drought, or haven't you noticed? Your people are dying."

"A drought? The drought is God's punishment. We do not need your help. You should go, all of you. Americans, Chinese, all of you infidels."

Anger rose within her. She wanted to argue with him, attempt to point out the absurdity of his argument, but knew that it would serve no purpose.

"Sally," Ben said again, almost inaudibly.

"Okay, okay," she said.

Smiling, evidently satisfied that his little speech had silenced the Western whore, the Arab closed his eyes and dozed.

They drove on, to the north. The sun was going down behind her head, affording her face a modicum of shade even as the back of her head burned.

They left the crude track an hour later, slogging through sand and along a dried-up river bed before coming to a sun-warped timber hut leaning so much that it resembled a parallelogram.

Ali dragged Sally from the flat-bed, and then Ben. She stood on the sand, her left leg paralysed with pins and needles. The driver climbed from the cab and moved into the hut. Ali gestured with his rifle. "Inside."

She limped away from the truck and stepped through the doorway, into the shade of the hut. The machine-gunner remained where he was on the back of the truck.

The instant shade was welcome – but the sight of what greeted them, when her eyes adjusted to the half-light, was not.

The room was empty but for three things.

A tiny camera mounted on a tripod, what looked like a butcher's chopping block positioned in the centre of the room and, propped up against the far wall, point down, a long, curved sword.

ALI PRODDED HER into a corner and ordered them to sit down. Sally squatted, her back against the wall. Just above her head a broken window allowed blistering heat to fall across her cheek. Glass crunched beneath her canvas pumps.

She glanced at Ben. He bowed his head and closed his eyes.

Ali and the other Arab stood behind the mounted camera, speaking in hushed tones.

Sally looked from the sword, to the butcher's block, and finally at the camera. It came to her that the most barbaric item of the three was the camera, because of what it denoted. The sword and the butcher's block she could almost understand, but the fact that their deaths were to be recorded, and ultimately broadcast, added a twist of voyeuristic sadism.

Ali and his colleague appeared to be arguing about the camera. Ali knelt and tinkered with it, speaking in rapid Arabic to the other. He flicked it with the back of his hand and stood, striding to the door and staring out.

He lit a cigarette and calmly smoked. He appeared bored, and Sally wondered how many other innocent Westerners he had casually slaughtered. There had been an aid worker kidnapped and shot a year ago, she recalled, and three Catholic nuns abducted from a mission in the west of the country earlier this year. Nothing had been heard of them since.

She had been well aware of the trouble in the area when she accepted the job, but assurances from her employers that the compound would be well guarded, and that not one medical worker had lost their life in the ten years that the Red Cross had been working in northern Uganda, had convinced her that any danger was negligible.

The second Arab was fiddling with the camera in mounting frustration.

She found herself saying, "What's wrong with it? Maybe I can fix it?"

Ben hissed, "Sally!"

Ali turned from the door, removed the cigarette from his lips, and said, "You are a woman. How can you know about cameras?"

"I am a woman, Ali, and I know many things."

He sneered. "You know nothing. You put Western drugs into our people, and also Christian evil."

She stared at him, restraining the urge to laugh. Soon she would be dead at the hands of this uneducated bigot, and her anger was overcome by despair.

She stared at the scar on his cheek. "I know, Ali," she said quietly, "that your scar is infected. If you don't get it treated, that there will be a possibility that the infection will poison your blood, and you will die. When... when you have finished what you are doing here, take my advice and see a doctor. You need antibiotics and antiseptic cream."

He stared at her. "Why are you bothered?" he asked.

She held his gaze. "When I trained to become a doctor, back in England, I swore something called the Hippocratic Oath. I swore to do all within my medical capabilities to save life..." She paused, then went on, "That's the difference between us, Ali."

He thought about this, then said, "No. The difference is that you are wrong and I am right. You are a Western infidel and I am..." he said a word in Arabic that she didn't catch.

She said, "And your god sanctions this taking of life?"

"God is great. What I do I do for God."

She closed her eyes and wondered what her Muslim friends back at Kallani would have to say about his corrupted, twisted form of faith.

She gestured to the camera with a nod of her head. "Untie me, Ali, and I will try to mend the camera."

Even if he consented and untied her, which she doubted, then what were the chances of her reaching the sword, or Ali's gun which he had lodged beside the sword, and using one of them before they retaliated?

The idea of being forced to act sent a wave of fear through her.

Ali appeared to be considering her suggestion, but a second later the Arab gestured to the camera and stood up. He spoke to Ali, who smiled at Sally. "It is working now," he said.

Beside her, under his breath, Ben was murmuring a prayer.

She said, "Why are you doing this, Ali?"

He said matter-of-factly, "We will kill both of you, and the film we will put on the internet to warn others like you, to say: Westerners, you are not welcome here. If you come, you can expect this, to be killed like pigs."

"And do you think this will stop people like me coming to help your people? It didn't stop me, Ali. Others will come, like me, and our governments, the Chinese, will search for you and eradicate you and others like you."

He said, "Chinese," and spat on the floor.

Ben whispered to her, "You're wasting your breath, Sally. They don't hear what you are saying."

"That's no reason not to say it," she said.

She closed her eyes. She thought of Geoff, probably in the air above northern Africa now and blissfully unaware of what was happening to her. She felt sorry for him, and almost sobbed as she thought of him hearing the news.

She hoped he would be spared ever seeing the film of her death.

She heard a sound from outside. The Somali appeared at the window and spoke to the Arabs. Sally looked up. The Somali tapped a big, old-fashioned silver watch on his thin wrist. She supposed he was telling them that they were wasting time talking. She found it suddenly impossible to swallow.

She was wrong about what the Somali was saying, however.

Ali picked up his rifle and stepped from the hut, followed by the other Arab. She heard the sound of their footsteps as they passed the window.

She pressed herself against the timber wall and pushed her legs so that she slid up the cracked timber planks. She twisted her head and peered out.

"What are they doing?" Ben asked her.

She smiled. "Praying," she said. "All three of them, praying..."

Ben began to laugh. "My Lord," he said. "Oh, my Lord..."

Sally allowed herself to slip down the wall. Something sharp bit into her buttock. She looked down and saw the broken glass around her boots.

"Ben," she said. "Ben, please stop praying and do something useful."

His laughter, then, sounded manic. "Like what, Dr Walsh?"

"Like grab a shard of glass and cut the twine around my wrists."

He stared at the shattered glass, then nodded shuffled on his bottom and turned so that his bound hands approached a long shard of glass. His fingers fumbled with it, blindly.

They manoeuvred so that they were back to back. Sally felt his fingers questing around the area of her wrists as he attempted to locate the twine.

"Whatever you do," she said, "don't slit my wrists. I don't want to bleed to death."

He grunted something. Sally wanted to weep and laugh at the same time.

She felt the glass bite into the twine, felt the up and down motion of the glass shard as Ben worked it patiently.

She tried not to hope. How long did Muslim prayers last? She thought back to her friends at Kallani, slipping out of the ward to the makeshift prayer room beside the surgery. They had always seemed to be gone an age, though she suspected they took the opportunity to sneak a quick cigarette at the same time.

The sword stood on its point against the far wall, its blade glinting in the sunlight slanting through the window. She was struck by its duality, now; a weapon existing in two mutually potential states, as the means of her liberation, or her death.

She tugged on her binds, attempting to assist Ben's cutting action. She felt a little give in the twine. She pulled harder; something gave again, the twine fraying.

Ben grunted. She tugged her wrists apart and the twine separated. She was taken by a quick panic. What to do now? Take up the sword and rush from the hut, and attack while they prayed? She turned and peered cautiously through the window, then swore under her breath.

"What? Ben asked.

The Somali was back on the truck, stationed behind the machine gun. The Arabs were standing, brushing sand from their faded military garb.

She turned and sat down quickly, placing her hands behind her back. She glanced at Ben. Great beads of sweat stood out like dew on his face.

The Arabs stepped back into the hut. Ali propped his rifle in the corner near the open door. He approached the camera, knelt and fingered the controls. Sally watched the other man move across the hut and take up the sword. He hefted it in both hands, assessing its balance. His face was expressionless as he concentrated on the weapon. He really does not feel a thing, she thought; we might indeed be pigs to the slaughter.

Ali was looking from Sally to Ben, as if trying to decide which one of them should die first. When his attention returned to the camera, she thought, she would make a run for the gun beside the door.

She had never in her life fired a weapon. Did the rifle have a safety mechanism, a catch that had to be switched before she could fire? Or could she simply aim the rifle and pull the trigger?

She decided to shoot the sword-wielder first, and then aim at Ali. She would keep him alive, tell Ben to order the Somali to jump from the truck and move away. She would like to keep Ali alive, deliver him to the authorities...

She smiled at the absurdity of the thought.

"You," Ali snapped, gesturing to Ben. "You first." He moved from the camera, reached down and took Ben's arm, dragging him towards the butcher's block. Ben caught her eyes, desperation and pleading on his face.

Ali pushed him into a kneeling position before the block, head down. The swordsman stepped forward, took Ben roughly by the scruff of his neck and forced his face towards the curved timber slab. He pushed down brutally. Ben's chin hit the timber, slid over the edge. His neck looked horribly exposed.

"Sally..." Ben sobbed.

The Arab stepped back, positioning himself with a fidgeting two-footed shuffle like a golfer addressing a tee-shot. He adjusted his hold on the hilt of the sword until he'd achieved a comfortable grip.

I must act, she thought; I must act now.

She screamed and launched herself forwards. She scattered the camera and tripod, caroming into Ali and knocking him off his feet. She reached out and grabbed the gun. Fumbling with the remarkably heavy weapon, she slipped her forefinger around the curved metal of the trigger.

She lifted the rifle, swaying, and pointed it at Ali and the other Arab.

Both men stared at her, frozen. Ali had picked himself up from the floor and was crouched, stilled by the weapon in her hands. The Arab with the sword was poised as if flash-frozen, his expression incredulous.

Before she thought what to do next, Ali's eyes

lifted, flicked behind her, and in that instant Sally thought: I should not have screamed...

Something slammed into the back of her head and she yelled in pain and fell to the floor, spilling the rifle.

Someone kicked her in the stomach – the swordsman – and the Somali who'd attacked her now dragged her in the corner and squatted over her, forcing the muzzle of his pistol against her temple.

She breathed hard, fighting the pain that throbbed in the back of her skull.

On the floor, foetal, Ben was sobbing to himself.

Ali was yelling at her, incoherent with rage, spittle flying.

The Somali said, "He says, you watch your boyfriend die, then your turn."

On the floor, Ben began to recite the Lord's Prayer.

Sally curled against the wall and stared at Ben, unable to close her eyes despite knowing what – thanks to her incompetence – was about to happen.

Ali picked up the camera and reassembled the tripod. He switched it on, caught Sally's eye and smiled.

The swordsman stepped up to the block for the second time, adjusted his footing, then his grip, and lifted the sword.

Sally wanted to cry out, vent her rage, but all she could do was cower into herself and sob.

The swordsman raised the weapon above his head, its blade catching the sunlight.

Sally looked away, biting her lip, steeling herself for the terrible sound of the sword as it hit the back of Ben's neck.

The moment seemed to go on forever.

Through the window, she saw something flash high in the sky. She looked up, experiencing the ridiculous hope that it might be a helicopter, searching for them. She saw nothing more than a glint of light high up, soon gone. The blue sky seemed to have dulled, as if a mist had descended.

She stared at the timber beside her head, holding herself tight, the point of the Somali's pistol still pressed, painful and hot, against the skin of her temple.

"...*for ever and ever, Amen...*"

Then silence.

She wondered if the swordsman was playing a vindictive game, delaying the inevitable so that Ben should suffer all the more.

She forced her gaze from the wall and stared at the swordsman. He stood, legs apart, sword half raised, a curious expression of puzzlement on his bearded face.

Ali yelled at him in Arabic.

Sword still poised, horizontal to his body above Ben's bared neck, the swordsman replied. He appeared faintly comical, frozen in position, speaking in a low voice.

Beside her, the Somali sniggered to himself.

Ali strode over to the swordsman, reached out and slapped his face softly, almost mockingly.

On the floor at their feet, Ben still murmured the Lord's Prayer with quiet dignity.

As she watched, the swordsman turned away from Ben and dropped the sword on the floor, and Sally could only assume that, for some reason, he had been unable to bring himself to murder Ben.

Yelling his disgust, Ali snatched up the sword, pushed the Arab to one side, and stood over Ben. He raised the sword, and this time Sally could not bring herself to avert her gaze.

When Ali had raised the sword so that it was at a right angle to his body, he paused. Or, at least, that was what it looked like to Sally. He held the sword at arm's length, directly above Ben's neck, and seemed unable to lift the weapon any further. He appeared to be shaking as if with suppressed rage.

From where he was leaning against the wall, in a state of shock, the watching Arab said something.

Beside her, the crouching Somali shouted at Ali. He turned to Sally and said, "They are cowards. Typical Yemenis." He spat something at them in Arabic.

Dazed, Ali backed from the chopping block until he fetched up against the wall, the sword dangling in his grip.

On the floor, Ben timorously looked up. He raised himself so that he was kneeling, and stared at his tormentors with nascent hope on his face.

The Somali swore, surged to his feet and crossed the floor in two strides. Before Sally could cry out in horror at what he was about to do, he raised the gun to Ben's forehead and pulled the trigger.

Or attempted to pull the trigger.

He stood with the pistol connected to Ben's sweat-beaded forehead, arm outstretched, an expression of ridiculous concentration on his thin face, like an infant attempting to perform a feat beyond his capabilities. He was convulsing, his whole body taken by a violent tremor.

No matter how hard he tried, the gun would not go off.

He cursed, flung the pistol aside, and grabbed Ali's rifle from where it lay on the floor. He swung the gun, inserted his finger into the trigger guard, and aimed at Ben.

The doctor closed his eyes, his lips moving in silent prayer.

As if released from paralysis, acting without fully knowing what she was doing, Sally pushed herself across the floor, grabbed the Somali's discarded pistol and stood quickly.

She held the weapon at arm's length, hands trembling, and directed it at the Somali. "Drop the rifle," she said in a voice that quavered maddeningly.

The Somali seemed to be caught in indecision. His eyes flicked towards the Arabs, as if seeking orders.

Ali moved towards her, reaching out.

Sally lifted the pistol, aimed above his head, and pulled the trigger. This time the weapon fired, deafeningly loud in the confines of the hut. The Arabs flinched and cowered back against the wall. The Somali dropped the rifle and stared at her.

The bullet had splintered the timbers in the ceiling, and a brilliant shaft of golden sunlight fell through like a spotlight, falling on Ben as he knelt in prayer in the centre of the room.

"If you move," she said, aiming at the terrorists, "you die..." Her voice trembled. She said to Ben, "Go out to the truck. See if the keys are in the ignition."

Ben rose to his feet and moved slowly, his arms

still bound behind his back, and walked towards the door. "Sally...?"

"Just get out of here!"

"Sally, don't shoot them, okay. Just don't shoot them..."

He left the hut.

She said to Ali, "Where are the keys?"

He licked his lips. "In the..."

He was interrupted by Ben's shout. "They're here."

Sally backed to the door, gripping the pistol in her outstretched hands.

Despite what the three had put her through, Ben's abjuration to leniency was redundant. She had no desire to exact revenge.

"If you move," she said, "I will shoot. Don't move until we've driven away from here."

She backed through the door, aiming at the cowering trio all the while, until she came to the truck.

She cursed Ben silently for not having the engine revving, then remembered that his hands were still tied. She reached behind her with one hand, found the door handle and pulled. Within the hut, the terrorists stood watching her, frozen.

She slipped into the driver's seat, expecting them to rush her at any second. Ben was beside her, sitting awkwardly in the passenger seat, knotted hands behind his back. With a surge of adrenaline she lodged the pistol between the dashboard and the windscreen and gunned the engine. The truck bucked, jolted, and surged forward.

She glanced back at the hut as she turned the truck and accelerated away. There was no sign of Ali or the others.

Ben said something over the roar of the engine.

"What?" Sally yelled.

Ben said, "My prayers were answered, Sally."

She looked up, through the windscreen. It was late afternoon, and the sun should have been bright above the distant tree line. All she saw was a diffuse blur where the fiery ball should have been.

She said, "Their guns jammed, Ben. We were lucky."

"You saw them, saw what happened. It was the work of the Lord. Their guns did not jam, Sally. They just could not bring themselves to kill us."

She shook her head. "I don't know what the hell happened. I'm just grateful..."

She brought the truck to a sudden stop, leaned through the window and vomited.

SHE FOLLOWED THE wadi to the road running north-south, and turned left.

She accelerated, residual fear pushing her to drive at speed. She knew the terrorists had no means of leaving the hut other than on foot, but it was as if what they had subjected her to was affecting her rationality. She half expected the men to leap out at them from behind the passing trees.

They came to a T-junction and Sally braked.

Ben said, "I know where we are. See, in the distance, the village of Moganda. We are perhaps one hour away from Kallani."

"Turn around, Ben, and I'll try to untie you."

She picked at the tight knot until she had worked the twine loose and pulled the binds free. He smiled at her, rubbing his wrists.

She gunned the engine and turned right. She checked the fuel gauge, smiled when she saw that it indicated the tank was a little less than half full.

The decision came upon her unexpectedly. She knew, once she arrived back at the medical centre, that she would locate Dr Krasnic and resign then and there. Krasnic would demur, tell her to take a break and think through her decision. But she also knew that she was never going to work at Kallani again.

She had given the place five years of her life, and that was quite enough.

They came to the outskirts of Kallani just under an hour later. A crowd surged along the high street. An almost palpable sense of excitement filled the humid late afternoon air. The attack at the medical centre was big news, in a place where for month after month nothing ever happened.

They edged through the crowds, drove through the centre of town, and minutes later arrived at the medical centre. The gates were open, and within Sally made out two Ugandan army trucks, a police car and a Red Cross jeep.

Crowds milled outside and within the compound so that their return, edging through the citizens and into the medical centre, was hardly commented upon.

The charcoaled bodies of the dead soldiers had been covered in dark green military tarpaulins. The watchtower still burned feebly, a mere blackened timber skeleton against the hazy sky.

Army officers, fat Ugandan policemen, and Red Cross officials stood about in small groups, conferring and consulting softscreens and speaking into wrist-coms.

Sally killed the engine, the truck just another vehicle amongst many. The engine ticked, cooling. She stared out at the activity in the compound.

A tiny African girl moved from a prefab ward and crossed towards the truck. She paused to turn and call something, and a dozen faces appeared at the windows. Sally opened the door and climbed out. The little girl ran to her, repeating her name and saying in Swahili. "You come back! You come back! Kolli, she says bad men took you."

"I'm back, Gallie. I'm back. Don't worry." Sally swept up the child, hugged her to her chest and carried her over to the prefab. Inside, twenty children were cowering in their beds, staring at her with wide eyes.

Mary, the nurse fresh out from England, hurried to her and said, "It's Dr Krasnic. You must see him. He's... he's in his office. He has a pistol. I tried talking to him, but..."

Sally transferred Gallie to Mary's custody, turned and hurried from the prefab. She almost collided with Ben on the way out.

"Sally?"

"Come with me!" she ordered. "It's Yan."

She feared what she might find as she ran across to Krasnic's office. His frequent depressions, allied to what had happened that afternoon at the complex, was a combination that did not bode well.

She came to the office and pushed open the fly-screen door.

Krasnic sat at his desk, looking like a statue carved from grey granite. He looked up when she entered. Ben stood behind her, a hand on her shoulder.

Krasnic said, incredulously, "Sally? Ben?" His eyes brimmed.

"We... got away, Yan."

Only then did she see the pistol lying on the table between his outstretched hands.

"I saw the carnage..." Yan said. "Mary told me you'd been taken." He shook his head. "I... I don't know what happened. I'd suddenly had enough, all I could take. So I filled my pistol..." He gestured to the gun on the desk, "raised it to my head and tried to pull the trigger. And nothing happened. So I tried again, yes? And... again, nothing. Was it God, telling me something?"

Sally opened her mouth to speak, but the words would not come.

She stepped forward, reached out and took the pistol. It was far heavier than she had expected, and cold.

"Yan, we need to talk..."

She was interrupted. Someone barged into the room, shouting. "Dr Krasnic!" The Ugandan orderly stared at Sally and Ben, then went on. "Dr Krasnic, amazing events in the south! You must come and see. The road is blocked!"

Before anyone could question him, he ducked back through the door and sprinted across the compound.

Sally looked out. The police car, the Red Cross truck and the army vehicle were rumbling in convoy from the compound.

Sally turned to Krasnic. "Yan, come with me."

She waited until he stood, like a tired old bear, and she took his arm. They crossed the compound to the terrorist's truck and all three shuffled along the front seat. Sally stowed Krasnic's pistol alongside the other above the dashboard.

Five minutes later they left the compound behind the slowly moving convoy and headed south.

Krasnic was the first to see it. He pointed, stirred from his suicidal fugue by what had appeared in the distance. Sally recalled the flash high in the sky earlier that afternoon and, later, the diffuse nature of the sun.

The convoy had halted in the road ahead, along with dozens of other vehicles, cars, motorbikes and bicycles. A crowd of perhaps two hundred citizens milled about at the end of the road – the end of the road because, spanning the patched tarmac that should have headed ruler-straight south without hindrance across the sun-parched desert, was what appeared to be a wall of glass.

Dazed, Sally climbed from the cab, eased her way through the crowd, and approached the silvery membrane. She could see through it, to the road on the other side, the dun African land stretching away to the horizon.

She looked up and stared in wonder at the concave expanse of diaphanous material that stretched high above their heads. It appeared that the town of Kallani was enclosed within the confines of a vast dome.

Krasnic was beside her. "What the hell...?"
Ben said, "It's a sign, Sally. A sign..."
She reached out and touched the sun-warmed membrane.

CHAPTER TWO

THE BOARDING OF the Air Europe flight from Heathrow to Entebbe was delayed for two hours due to a bomb scare in terminal six. Geoff Allen bore the hold up with customary patience. His job entailed prolonged travel, and these days delays were an inevitable part of the process. He unrolled his softscreen and spent the time editing a file of shots taken on his last assignment, a freelance trip to cover the aftermath of the bombings in Ankara.

A rainstorm was lashing the tarmac, and when the time came to board the ancient Boeing 747 the passengers were informed that, because of 'technical difficulties', the umbilical corridor leading from the terminal building was out of commission. As he dashed through the rain, he looked ahead to the sun of Africa and the week he was due to spend with Sally.

There was another delay, this time lasting thirty minutes, while the plane took its place in the take-off queue. He spent the time writing a short email to Sally and sending it as the plane climbed and banked over the dreary grey suburbs of south-west London.

See you in a little over ten hours. I can't wait. Work has been hell, I'll tell you all about it later. There I go again, complaining about my job, when yours... Anyway, things are just the same in England. Food-shortages and riots. Could be worse: look at France...

He went on in this rambling vein for another couple of pages, the epistolary logorrhoea a prelude to the oral: when he met Sally they'd talk non-stop, catching up on the mutual missed events of the past three months.

The plane flew west, out over the Atlantic and south over the Bay of Biscay, giving French airspace a wide berth. A nationalist terrorist group had brought down three planes in as many months over the south of France, in response to the number of foreigners flooding into the country. Airlines were taking no risks.

Allen lost himself in work, cropping images of bombed-out houses, the dazed victims in the streets of the Turkish capital. The country was paying the price for its acceptance of the West, its repudiation of 'traditional' values. Repression of dissidents, including Kurds and Islamists, had been severe and uncompromising, in the grand tradition of Turkish state heavy-handedness. The result was an anarchic free-for-all in which ideologically opposing terror groups, of every shade of political and religious persuasion, cut swathes through the country's innocent population.

A little while later he felt a tap on his shoulder. A woman peered around the seat behind him. "Do you think that's appropriate for children to view?"

"Excuse me?" Allen turned awkwardly to look at her.

The woman leaned to one side and indicated a small girl seated beside her. "My daughter saw what you were doing as she went to the toilet..."

His first reaction was to apologise – the typical English, deferential climb-down hardwired into every citizen of his class and age. His second, to tell the woman that her daughter should mind her own business.

He indicated the vacant window-seat beside him, "I'll move," he said, and did so.

In the aftermath, he wished he had said something caustic, along the lines of, "Perhaps you shouldn't shield your precious daughter from the realities of the world..." but on reflection he was relieved he'd not had the gall to do so; that would have started him on his hobby-horse, the sanitised, advertisement-led vapidity of the British news media these days, which was happy to report atrocities with lip-smacking gusto, but was prudishly reluctant to show the effects of bombings and similar attacks. Even the internet, once the bastion of *laissez faire* content, had been hamstrung by recent government restrictions.

The website and sister magazine he freelanced for was based in Germany, where restrictions were a little less draconian.

He worked on the photography for another hour, by which time a hostess was processing down the aisle handing out shrink-wrapped trays of fodder the blandness of which was calculated to offend the least number of passengers. Allen chewed on a cheese roll – the cheese the latest milk-free version, cheap, rubbery and tasteless – while staring through the window at the ocean far below.

They overflew a vast hydraulic wave-farm, a series of great metal platelets connected by tubular pistons the width of the Channel Tunnel. He'd covered a story down there a few years ago. The Spanish government had flown him to Cadiz, then ferried him out by hydrofoil, to witness an amazing sight. A hundred boat-people, refugees fleeing the revolution in Morocco, had set up camp on the back of one of the farm's great see-sawing plates, subsisting on fish and little else, until evacuated by the Spanish authorities.

The farm was free of inhabitants now, other than its skeleton crew of engineers, but he did see a tangle of wreckage and a sprawling scorch mark on one of the heaving pontoons: the result of a terrorist attack last year.

The last he'd heard, the Spanish government was thinking of closing down the farm on grounds of inefficiency, and building nuclear reactors to supply the nation's rapacious energy needs. Opposition voices pointed out the dangers of reactors prone to terrorism...

An elderly man hobbled down the aisle towards him, smiled and inclined his head, and walked on past. Allen responded with a vague smile of his own, wondering if he'd met the man somewhere recently.

His memory for faces, as well as names, was appalling, which was odd as he thought of himself as a visual person. He was endlessly fascinated by the appearance of things, of how reality presented itself visually – his degree had been in art history, and he'd been a photo-journalist for the past ten years – and yet he was forever unconsciously snubbing people because he failed to recognise their faces.

A little later the old man paused in the aisle beside Allen, cleared his throat and, when he had his attention, murmured, "I hope you don't think this impertinent of me, but I was wondering if you're Geoffrey Allen?"

The man had the diffident, old-school manners of a much earlier generation. Allen guessed he was in his eighties.

He smiled, wondering if the man had recognised him from one of the ID mugshots that occasionally accompanied his pieces in British colour supplements. He felt at once obscurely pleased and embarrassed.

He smiled. "That's right."

The man extended a frail hand. "James Cleveland. I worked with your father many, many years ago, and I once met you when you were *this* high. I've followed your career over the years." After they had shaken hands, Cleveland indicated the aisle seat. "You don't mind...?"

"Not at all." Though, truth be told, the last thing he wanted was to be pinned *in situ* by someone reminiscing at length about the greatness of his father – a situation he'd suffered on more than one occasion over the years.

"Your father was a wonderful politician, Geoffrey – I may call you Geoffrey, by the way?"

Allen smiled his assent and groaned inwardly.

"We were on the same back-bench committee many years ago, investigating police corruption. I have never worked with a finer mind…"

Cleveland continued in this vein, and Allen responded with nods and the occasional monosyllabic agreement.

The fact was that his father had been a great man, and that rare animal: a politician loved by the people, a reformer who worked tirelessly for his constituents. That he had rarely shown himself at home was a side-issue that few knew or cared about, outside of the immediate family, Allen himself and his younger sister Catherine. Perhaps it might not have been so bad if their mother had not also been a parliamentary politician, if not of his father's eminence, then certainly as hard-working. Allen was raised by a series of European nannies with, in the background, two distant figures called mother and father who he knew he should feel something for – as he had read about in books – but for whom he felt almost nothing other than resentment.

His parents worked hard for years, tirelessly for the people they represented… and where did it get them, he thought?

Now Cleveland said, "And I was so sorry to read about…"

"Yes," Allen interrupted, fearing what the politician emeritus might say next, "yes, it was a… terrible shock for all of us."

Tactfully, Cleveland changed the subject. "Well, I'm visiting my grand-daughter in Durban. She's just given birth."

"Congratulations."

"And you? Work, no doubt?"

"Actually, a working holiday. I'm visiting my fiancée."

"In South Africa?"

"Uganda. She's a doctor working with the emergency services in Karamoja."

Cleveland's rheumy eyes widened. "Not the most... stable, shall we say, area in the world. Your fiancée must be a remarkable person, Geoffrey."

Allen smiled. "She is," he said.

The old man patted Allen's hand like a beneficent grandfather. "Well, it has been wonderful talking to you. I hope you have a pleasant time in Uganda. Take my advice and visit Lake Edward in the south. Just the place for young lovers." With a smile he lifted himself from the seat and limped back along the aisle.

Allen glanced through the window and stared down at the brilliant blue, beaten expanse of the ocean, feeling obscurely troubled. It was always the same when he was forced to consider his parents, and their deaths.

He tipped back his seat, closed his eyes, and tried to fill his mind with other things.

HE WAS AWOKEN a little later by the sound of activity around him. He rubbed his eyes and looked around.

Passengers were releasing their folding trays, preparatory for whatever culinary delights Air Europe had prepared for dinner.

He ate a bland curry, overcooked dal and undercooked rice, followed oddly by a slice of polystyrene Victoria sponge, then glanced at the time on his softscreen, which he'd fastened round his forearm. It was five o'clock British Summer Time. Estimated time of arrival in Entebbe was a little after midnight, Ugandan time. He'd booked a hire car and would drive up to Kallani overnight. Time with Sally was precious and he didn't want to waste a second.

They were flying over the coastline of Northern Africa. The scalloped littoral of Morocco showed as a series of golden scimitars, the destination – before the revolution – of hordes of sun-starved northern Europeans and Chinese.

The plane thrummed inland, and an hour later the first of the Chinese mega-cities came into view.

It looked, he thought, like some kind of computer circuit board, a grid-pattern of prefabricated buildings and domes extending for tens of miles across the parched land. Monorails connected outlying towns which were rapidly being absorbed into the sprawling Cathay conurbation, eating up the terrain towards the Atlas mountains.

At first Allen had viewed with indifference the wholesale economic invasion of northern Africa. It struck him as the inevitable process of colonisation that the communist party of China had so vilified the West for in the past – the inevitable, rapacious rampaging of a regime turning from communism to capitalism.

Sally had set him right on that, listing a catalogue of abuses, both humanitarian and ecological, being committed by the fascist mafia, as she called them, of Beijing. She'd spent an hour telling him about specific instances of Chinese abuse, before relenting and changing the subject.

Afterwards, Allen had thought twice about suggesting ordering a Mandarin take-away.

He unrolled his softscreen and accessed the file containing the images he'd taken on his last trip to Uganda. He scrolled through shots of Sally beside Lake Kwania, looking tired and drawn after a shift at the medical centre lasting for three days with precious little sleep.

The pictures showed a thin-faced woman, not in the least photogenic, with a pinched expression and straggly hair. She was thin, pared down by a combination of a bad diet and overwork, constantly edgy and nervous and burning with the conviction of her political and humanitarian passions.

Allen loved her. For the first time in his life he had found someone he could trust, who he could talk to about his past, who listened to him and understood. As he gazed down at her thinly-smiling face, he realised that she was beautiful, and he felt a little drunk with the thought that in a few hours they'd be together again.

He noticed the first of the domes ten minutes later. He was staring out of the window, watching the rilled foothills of the Atlas mountains drift serenely by far below. They were flying over the southern slopes of the range now, and ahead was the vast stretch of the Sahara. He made out a flash of silver to the west, tucked into the foothills, and assumed it to be the glint of a river. Then he saw another, and another, and was surprised to note that they were domes, great silver hemispheres straddling towns and villages – perhaps a dozen in all, of various sizes, covering the centres of occupation along a winding road that snaked through the foothills.

Ahead to the right was a sizable town, and as the plane overflew it he had a closer view of the dome that arched over its entirety, encompassing its sprawling suburbs and two-storey central buildings like a vast snow globe.

Cleveland, making another trip to the loo, stopped in the aisle. "I suspect it's the Chinese again," he said, indicating the dome.

Allen frowned. "But why on Earth would they cover entire towns and villages?" he asked.

The old man shook his head. "They'll have their reasons," he said. "They always do, the Chinese – and you'll find that it will make absolute sense in the long term."

Cleveland shuffled on and Allen returned his attention to the silvery dome far below. The minute shapes of cars and trucks had halted on the road that appeared to run right into the sheer wall, and he made out what might have been tiny, ant-like crowds of people down there.

He unrolled his softscreen, accessed the net and was about to tap in Africa + Domes + Chinese, when the screen flashed a systems error and closed down. He strapped the screen round his forearm again, eased back his seat and stared out at the passing land far below.

THEY WERE FLYING over the Sahara an hour later when the plane stopped.

The first thing he noticed was the sudden, utter silence – startling after the constant thrumming of the engines. He looked out of the window. Five metres ahead of where he sat, the silver wing – which should have been vibrating ever so slightly – was absolutely still... and, more worryingly, the line of the aileron was unshifting against the arabesque of sand dunes of the distant desert. Startled, he peered directly down. They were passing over a road that cut from right to left through the sand, with a tiny truck on its tarmac'd surface. As he stared, the vehicle remained exactly where it was, unmoving in relation to the line of the wing.

Only then did he look up, across the aisle, and realise that his fellow passengers were likewise frozen. The woman across from him was lifting a sweet to her mouth, her fingers stilled an inch from her lips. Beyond her, a man was in the process of turning a page of the in-flight magazine. In the aisle, a smiling hostess was as immobile as a shop window mannequin.

Allen was about to stand up in alarm, attempt to see if everyone was similarly stricken with this paralysis, when an incredible rush of heat passed through his head and he was no longer aboard the plane.

He was flat on his back, seemingly floating in mid-air. He could feel no support beneath him. All was grey above. He tried to move his head, to look to either side, but was unable to do so. He wanted to cry out, but he could not move his mouth to articulate the words. He felt naked, though he was unable to look down the length of his body to see if this were so.

Later, he would wonder why he did not panic. It would have been a very reasonable reaction, given the circumstances. The fact was that he felt very calm, not in the least frightened. He felt a certain odd distance, a sense of remove he had once experienced when being sedated for a minor operation.

He recalled articulating the thought, *What is happening to me?* – and receiving a reply, as if in his head: *Do not be afraid.*

He wanted to laugh out loud but was unable to do so.

Seconds later he saw a bright light directly above him, dazzling. Silhouetted in the light was the outline of a human form, leaning over him. He felt only peace, as if he were in the presence of someone who, he knew, wanted only the best for him. The head-and-shoulders shape was dark, shadowy, there for a second and then gone.

He felt something ice cold on his chest, frozen pinpricks dancing up his sternum towards his head. His instinct to cry out in alarm was stilled by the strange conviction that all was well, that he had no cause to panic.

Even when he saw what was dancing up the length of his body, climbing over his chin, then his lips and nose, and progressing to his forehead, he did not attempt to cry out. He felt no dread or horror, even though what might have been a flashing, silver-limbed mechanical spider was squatting above his forehead and lowering an ovipositor towards his skin.

Later he would describe what followed as being like the sensation of a dentist's drill, accompanied by a high-pitched sound, felt rather than heard, a droning conducted through the bone which the ovipositor was presumably boring. Oddly he felt no pain.

A second later he experienced a blinding mental flash – which he could only describe, later, as feeling as if all his synapses had fired at once.

Then the spider, its job done, was dancing back down his face and body. He saw the human shape again, dark but benign, lean over him as if in inspection.

He was washed with a sensation of ineffable peace.

He blacked out, and an instant later was back in his seat on the plane.

He sat very still, sweating, and gripped the arm-rests. The engine was droning, the plane vibrating slightly. A glance through the window assured him they were in motion once again, the wing shaking, the desert passing by below. He glanced across the aisle: the woman was chewing the sweet that just seconds ago she had conveyed towards her mouth, and her neighbour was flipping through the magazine. The smiling air hostess approached, eyes flicking professionally over her charges.

She registered something in his expression and leaned towards him, her smile expanding in query. "Can I help?"

Before he could stop himself, he said, "Is everything okay? I mean... the plane...?"

She must have dealt with a thousand air-phobics in her time. She said reassuringly, "Everything is fine; no need to worry. We've lost on-line capability, but it should be up and running shortly. We will be arriving at Entebbe in a little over three hours."

"I thought..." He shook his head. "No, I must have been dreaming."

She smiled again. "If I can get you anything?"

"No. No, I'm fine. I'm sorry."

"Not at all," she said, laid a perfectly manicured set of crimson-glossed nails on his hand, then moved off down the aisle.

The aftermath left him feeling both embarrassed and frightened. What he had experienced was as real as everything else that had happened over the course of the past few hours: the plastic meals he'd consumed, his chat with Cleveland...

The plane had stopped dead in its flight, along with everyone aboard... except him. Then he'd found himself floating naked in a grey space, with a spider drilling into...

He gave a small involuntary gasp and reached up to touch his brow, expecting to feel the messy evidence of an incision there.

All he felt was a coating of clammy sweat.

He recalled the peace he'd experienced, the reassuring words in his head, exhorting him not to fear. The odd thing was that he had felt no fear then, while undergoing whatever had been happening to him, but now, looking back at the episode, he was overcome by a wave of retrospective dread.

Could some form of dream be held accountable? He thought not. Epilepsy, then? A brain seizure resulting in a hypnagogic hallucination? But the experience had seemed so damned real. He had seen his fellow passengers freeze... and yet they had experienced nothing.

He stood and walked down the aisle, scanning the seats for the ex-MP. He found the old man reading a Kindle. Cleveland looked up and smiled.

Allen said, "This might sound strange..." He paused, licked his lips, and was aware of Cleveland, and the elderly lady beside him, looking up at him expectantly. He went on, "You didn't happen to notice anything... *odd*, a few minutes ago?"

"Odd, dear boy?"

He wished he'd never asked the question. "I mean... did the plane seem to... No, I'm sorry... I must have been hallucinating. I must have dropped off... a nightmare."

Cleveland reached out, solicitous at Allen's agitated state. "Are you sure you're okay, Geoffrey?"

Allen smiled. "Absolutely. A dream, that's all. I'm sorry..."

Cleveland smiled his reassurance that it was no bother at all, and Allen returned to his seat.

He stared down at the distant desert and attempted to regain some measure of the sense of peace he had experienced during the hallucination.

* * *

ENTEBBE RUSHED HIM with its usual sensory overload of chaotic, over-populated, frenetic activity he should have been accustomed to by now – from his many visits to cities in Africa and Asia – but which always struck him anew.

The press of importuning humanity and the accompanying noise was a shocking assault. Crowds surged in the streets outside the airport, a morass of brightly coloured humanity seething even now, a little after midnight, under the glare of halogen floodlights. The constant babble of voices, blaring music, and traffic noise only confused the visual chaos – and, as if this were not enough, the stench of Africa, diesel, dung and cooking food, overlay everything. Even the humidity, he thought, was an unwelcome sensory burden.

Clutching his holdall, he pushed his way through the crowd towards the Hertz car rental office. A military convoy raced along the road, a phalanx of black faces staring at him impassively from the back of a troop-carrier. There seemed to be increased military and police activity in the streets around the airport, an atmosphere of tension in the air. There had been an attempted coup here just six months ago, and the situation was still pretty tense.

He made it to the office, presented his softscreen to the harassed woman at reception, and waited a minute for the transaction to be processed.

The women smiled at him and said, "And where are you heading, Mr Allen?"

"North. Karamoja," he replied, wondering at the question.

She beamed at him. "Travel north is not recommended, Mr Allen."

He immediately assumed she was referring to terrorist activity and felt a stab of alarm when he thought about Sally. "What's wrong?"

"The Chinese," she said.

He pulled a face. "The Chinese?"

She passed him his softscreen and the car key. "They are dropping domes on our cities, Mr Allen. Dropping them from the air. They started in the north and they are heading south. Soon Kampala and Entebbe will be covered." The pronouncement, imparted with the brazen confidence of the reliably informed, took him aback.

She glanced over his shoulder at the next customer in line, effectively dismissing him before he could question her further.

Bemused, he pushed through the press, exited the office and found his Volvo in the vast parking lot. He bought a bottle of chilled water from a vendor and sat in the driver's seat, took a drink of water and tried to work out what the woman had meant.

The domes he'd seen in the northern Sahara... He'd assumed them to be the work of the Chinese, but the idea that they were actively dropping them from the air, starting in the north and heading south, was absurd.

She had obviously got hold of a rumour, some anti-Chinese scare-mongering in the area.

He activated his softscreen and attempted to access the web, but connectivity was down. He tried to phone Sally, but the line was dead.

He took another long drink of water, consulted the map he'd pre-loaded on the 'screen, then began the long drive north despite the receptionist's alarmist warning.

HE WAS SOON out of Entebbe and the sprawling outskirts of Kampala, driving away from the conurbation on a motorway that for the first ten kilometres was well-lit but after that turned into a darkened road barely wide enough to contain two lanes of traffic. The only other vehicles he saw heading north through the sultry darkness was a convoy of military trucks – but the flow in the opposite direction was substantial. Trucks, cars and motorbikes jammed the road for kilometres, cacophonous with blaring horns and shouted curses. He wondered if these people too had heard rumours of the vile Chinese imprisoning towns under dropped domes...

Two hours later he was barrelling through parched grassland at a steady fifty miles an hour, and the flow of traffic heading south had dried to a trickle. There was no sign of any other military vehicles. He tried to find a news station on the car radio, but all he picked up were several music stations playing European rock classics and Baganda music.

A couple of hours later the sun came up with tropical rapidity to his right, revealing a seared landscape of stunted bushes stretching to the flat horizon. He reckoned he had another three hours to go before reaching Kallani and decided to find somewhere to stop for a rest and food.

He thought of Sally as he drove. She'd booked a five-day leave period, and said she'd take him west, to the Murchison Falls National Park. Zoologists there were working to reintroduce elephants back into the wild, and this was the reason his magazine had sent him out here. He'd spend the next few days catching up with Sally and taking a little time out to shoot the elephant story.

And in May, she had promised, she would leave Africa and come back to England, and they would set up home together somewhere in London.

The thought was still fresh enough to amaze him.

He was still thinking of Sally Walsh, half an hour later, when he saw his first dome from the ground.

It perfectly encapsulated a small town to the right of the road, perhaps two kilometres away. Its parabolic curve caught the light of the sun, its modernistic architecture striking him as bizarre out here in the African bush.

He decided to take a detour and turned along the sandy road that headed towards the town, steering around huge potholes in the approach road. Ten minutes later he braked suddenly and stared through the windscreen.

The wall of the dome cut across the road, effectively barring the way. A truck had halted before the sheer transparent wall, along with a couple of motorbikes and a battered police car. A dozen bewildered Ugandans stood before the rearing wall, staring through at the town.

On the other side, perhaps a hundred citizens, men woman and children, stared mutely out, imprisoned.

He opened his holdall, retrieved his camera, and took a dozen shots through the windscreen, then climbed out and approached the dome, stopping to take more shots.

He halted a foot from the glass – or whatever material it was – and found it to be perfectly clear, allowing him to see through without distortion. He reached out and laid a hand on the warm membrane, then knocked on it experimentally. It was not like knocking on a thin pane of glass – a window, say – but seemed much more solid, substantial. He looked down, then knelt and dug a trench in the fine sand at the foot of the dome. He reached the depth of a couple of feet, and still the membrane continued.

He'd thought the idea of the Chinese dropping them from the air ludicrous, but it seemed even more so now that he had seen a dome with his own eyes. And yet how to explain the phenomenon?

A young girl, perhaps ten years old, approached him on the other side of the glass. She stood mutely, watching him as he knelt beside the hole he'd dug. He reached out and splayed his fingers on the glass, and she laughed suddenly, silently, turned and ran away.

"Hello there!"

A portly Ugandan police sergeant was waddling across to him, smiling. "Good day to you, sir. You want to go to Morvani?" he asked, gesturing through the dome.

"Kallani," Allen said.

The sergeant shook his head woefully. "Bad luck, sir. Kallani just the same. All towns and villages north of here the same. All covered by these..." He reached out and slapped the glass.

Allen shook his head. "That's impossible."

"Not impossible, sir. Here they are. It has happened. Radio reports say that the Chinese dropped them on all our towns, but I tell you that is not so."

"No, of course not."

"No, my friend here saw what happened. Akiki!" he shouted towards the gathered Ugandans. A bare-chested old man in baggy shorts trotted across to them on stick-thin legs, bobbing his head at Allen. He clutched a malnourished brown goat on a length of twine.

The police officer quizzed him in the local language, and the man replied.

The sergeant translated, "Akiki says he was out here at dawn, looking for a goat that had escaped. He came into the bush, then turned to look back at his house. And he saw between himself and his house this thick glass wall. It appeared in seconds with no noise at all. In *seconds*..." The sergeant laughed. "And Akiki is most upset, for his wife said that his breakfast is ready and she will eat it if he does not return by noon."

Akiki gestured to a toothy, fat woman on the other side of the glass.

The sergeant said, "Akiki says that he has not eaten since midday yesterday, and he is starving. He says his wife does not need the food."

Allen backed away from the dome and stared up at the great rearing bubble. It stood perhaps five hundred metres high at its apex, and was approximately a kilometre in diameter. It appeared to contain the town neatly, as if positioned with care to include every building within its circumference.

The policeman called, "Akiki thinks it's a sign from god."

Allen looked at him. "And you?"

The Ugandan shrugged. "Who am I to know, sir? Perhaps Akiki is right."

Allen waved in farewell, climbed back into the car and U-turned. He rejoined the main road and continued north.

As he drove, he could not dismiss the fantastic notion – which had occurred to him while the policeman was speaking – that the arrival of the domes and his episode aboard the plane were in some way related.

Over the course of the next couple of hours he made out a dozen other domes, near and far, scattered across the face of the Ugandan bush. They were of differing sizes and shapes; some, like the ones he had seen from the air, were classically-shaped geodesics, perfect half-spheres, while others appeared lower and wider, more resembling watch-glasses.

Despite telling himself that there had to be some logical explanation for the sudden appearance of the domes, he could think of none. A one-off dome he might have put down to some elaborate and expensive art installation, though quite how it might have been achieved was beyond him. But this mass *endoming* of entire towns and villages, stretching from the Sahara in the north, thousands of miles south to Uganda...

Do not be afraid... the voice – no, the *thought* – had appeared in his head, along with the visions...

TWO HOURS LATER he arrived on the outskirts of Kallani.

It was a sizable town of some six thousand citizens, its population swelled by the influx of Red Cross and UN aid workers. It was also one of the poorest centres of habitation in an infamously poor region of the country. A collection of two story sand-coloured buildings, a mile square, comprised the town's centre, but a wave of slum dwellings constructed from flattened biscuit tins and hessian sacking extended south for a couple of kilometres.

A line of vehicles – Allen counted thirty before giving up – blocked the approach road. He tried getting through to Sally again on his 'screen and mobile, but the lines were still dead.

He left his car at the back of the queue, locked it and strode down the road towards the silvery wall of the dome.

Citizens were lined two deep around its southern circumference, and on the inside as many people were pressed up against the concave membrane. Husbands and wives, parents and children, lovers... all separated by a few inches of clear, impermeable membrane.

The silence was what struck Allen as strange. Normally such a gathering would have been attended by noise, chatter, laughter. But the people assembled here in their hundreds were absolutely mute, staring, some mouthing in the hope of being understood while others silently pressed palms to the glass, their gestures matched by partners and friends on the other side.

Allen left the road and walked around the curve of the dome, peering over the heads of the citizens gathered there.

Again, every building in the town had been contained. There were no outlying, individual buildings, no matter how small, not under glass. It was as if the positioning of the domes had been *planned*... he smiled at the absurdity of the idea.

He came to a section of the wall not thronged by citizens. On the other side, a gaggle of schoolgirls, in bright blue uniforms but barefoot, giggled out at him. He had an idea, unrolled his softscreen, summoned the word processing programme and tapped in twenty-four point font: *Dr Sally Walsh, Medical Centre. Can you please tell her that Geoff Allen is here.* He fished a twenty shilling note from his wallet and held it up beside the 'screen.

The girls read the message in an eager scrimmage, smiling all the time, then waved at him and ran off on the errand.

They were gone for what seemed like a long time. He chastised himself for his impatience. Sally might very well be working, pressed into service despite today being, technically, the first day of her holiday. It was an aspect of her job he found exasperating if understandable: the fact that she was on constant call, liable at any minute of the day or night to be summoned to minister to the need of her patients.

Twenty minutes later the girls returned, accompanied, Allen saw with alarm, by a khaki-uniformed police officer.

What followed was a ridiculous pantomime that might, in other circumstances, have struck him as comical.

The policeman approached the glass wall, accompanied by the schoolgirls, and peered through at him. Allen raised the screen again, probably needlessly, he thought. The officer read the words, nodded and regarded Allen with an odd expression combining unease with uncertainty.

Allen gestured, a pantomime shrug as if to say, "Where is she?"

The officer turned and spoke to a lanky schoolgirl, whose face expressed exaggerated alarm.

Allen rapped on the dome, attracting their attention. "What?" he mouthed at them.

The policeman shrugged helplessly, then said something, speaking slowly so that Allen might read the words.

He followed the man's lips, but the movements meant nothing to him.

A schoolgirl tapped the policeman on the shoulder, then dug around in her satchel. She produced an exercise book and a pencil, which the officer took with what Allen interpreted as a sheepish expression.

Tongue-tip showing in concentration, the officer wrote a line of laborious capital letters and pressed it against the wall of the dome.

Medical centre closed – Allen read – *attacked yesterday by terrorists. I will go and try to find out more.*

Allen nodded, a cold feeling of numbness spreading upwards from his chest.

The policeman hurried away.

Allen slumped to the ground and leaned against the sun-warmed wall of the dome, watched in silent sympathy by the schoolgirls on the other side.

CHAPTER THREE

JAMES MORWELL JNR. liked to think of himself as an altruist.

As a billionaire, his opponents and detractors liked to say, he could afford to be. But the fact was that many of his rich friends and colleagues hoarded their wealth like misers, pathologically opposed to giving away the odd few hundred thousand to good causes. Not James Morwell Jnr... He had a slush fund of five million US dollars which, every year, he dispensed with the largesse of a Victorian philanthropist, bestowing tens of thousands on charities and good causes around the world – tax deductible though it might be.

His father, who had risen from working-class obscurity in inner-city Toronto to become a multi-millionaire before the age of thirty, had insisted that James's philanthropy was nothing more than a sop to his conscience. "You're a lily-livered milksop, boy, and you don't like the darker side of what we do..."

Which was wrong, James had tried to argue to no avail. He had no qualms about the millions he invested in the arms industry, and certainly none about the millions he took from it in profits. War was a function of what it meant to be a human being, and always had been; if people were willing to fight, then Morwell Enterprises was more than willing to furnish them with the means to do so. And anyway, these days the arms that he supplied to various regimes around the world functioned often as a deterrent against military aggressors – so his detractors had no moral legs to stand on.

Not that the arms industry was the only arrow in Morwell Enterprises' well-stocked quiver. He owned, at the last reckoning, over a thousand companies worldwide which traded in everything from cosmetics to couture, oil to nuclear energy. He even owned three of the top ten sub-orbital airlines. But his abiding pride – perhaps because it had been the branch of Morwell Enterprises that his father had been least interested in – were the dozen companies which gave citizens the information they needed to make judgements about the world in which they lived and worked. He owned the world's largest internet newsfeed, TV channels in every continent, a thousand newspapers globally, and three of the biggest publishing companies in the West.

It was said, and Morwell was proud to quote the statistic, that on average nine out of ten individuals on the face of the planet digested news put out by some organ of Morwell Enterprises every day.

Little wonder that he was a personal friend of

the current US president, the Republican Lucas Blanchfield, and counted several of the British royal family as intimate acquaintances.

Even his father, a famous misanthropist who guarded his privacy with the same suspicion as he hoarded his millions, had not had anything like the degree of influence that his son, over the years, had carefully acquired.

Morwell Jnr. was young, healthy, and fabulously rich, and his greatest fear in life was losing what he had.

He was still in his early thirties – an age when the spectre of mortality was yet to appear above the mental horizon; he had rude good health maintained by well-monitored physical exercise and the country's finest doctors; and his business ventures had never been in better shape.

HE WAS IN his penthouse office when the dome appeared miraculously over New York.

He had just stepped from the gym where he kept a rubber effigy of his father, which he cathartically beat with a baseball bat every morning. In consequence he was feeling revitalised and ready for whatever the day might bring.

In thirty minutes, at eleven, he had an informal get-together with his team of advisers, specialists who kept him abreast of world events. He enjoyed these sessions, enjoyed listening to experts expounding. He had a keen analytical mind himself, and an ability to synthesise what he learned at these meetings and then recycle it, at swish Manhattan soirées, as his own original observations.

He crossed to his desk and was about to summon Lal, his personal assistant – or facilitator, as he liked to call the young Indian – when he caught a flash of something out of the corner of his eye. He turned and stared through the floor-to-ceiling glass wall. Something coruscated a matter of metres above Morwell Tower, the country's tallest building.

It looked, for all the world, like the inner curve of a dome seen from just beneath its apex. As if all New York had been placed under a mammoth bell-jar.

He noticed his softscreen flashing on his desk, and said, "Activate."

Lal's thin, keen face flashed onto the screen. "Sir, I think you should take a look through the window."

"So I'm not hallucinating, Lal. What in God's name is going on?"

"I... I don't know, sir. It happened around thirty minutes ago. I tried to summon you." Lal hesitated. "There have been other... ah, developments."

"Go on."

"I think it would be best if I were to show you, sir."

Morwell was in a mood to humour his facilitator. "Very well, Lal. We have a little time before the think-tank cranks in to action."

"I think they'll have a lot to talk about," Lal said cryptically. "I'm on my way."

While Lal took the elevator up from the seventy-fifth floor, Morwell turned to the window and stared out. He could see, in the distance, the great convex arc of the bell-jar sweeping out over Long Island,

and in the other direction over New Jersey... So what was it? Some vast and ingenious prank? A fabulous and daring work of improvisational art? Whatever it was, he reasoned, it was not real... in the sense that it not was a solid, physical thing, but more likely a projection of some kind.

"Sir."

Lal crossed the penthouse office and stood before the desk, his carob-brown eyes ranging over its surface as if in search of something.

Lal was in his mid-twenties and a direct beneficiary of one of Morwell Enterprises' humanitarian projects. Morwell funded schools and academies across the world, and from them drew the finest pupils to work in his many companies. Lal had been plucked from the slums of Calcutta at the age of fifteen, educated to a high standard and processed through the Morwell business empire. Five years ago James Morwell had installed Lal as a researcher in one of his newsfeed companies. In three years he'd worked himself up to become its editor, at which point Morwell swooped again and promoted Lal to the role of his PA.

Now Lal took up Morwell's stiletto letter opener and slapped his palm with its blade.

Morwell gestured to the bell-jar. "Any ideas?"

"I have people working on it, sir. But one thing is for certain – it's not an illusion, as I first thought. Reports are coming in from Long Island, sir. People are reporting that the dome is solid, a wall that has cut off the entire city of New York. But not only that, sir – the domes have covered all areas of population, no matter how large or small, starting in northern Canada and sweeping the globe. There are reports from every northern continent... every village, town and city is at present under a similar dome to this one. And as I speak, they are appearing over areas to the south of here."

Morwell sat down in his swivel chair.

Not likely, then, to be a daring work of art...

"You said there have been other developments?"

"That is right, sir. Observe." Lal placed his left hand flat on the table top and – before Morwell could stop him – raised the paper-knife and made to bring it down on his palm.

Morwell winced, then looked up and saw Lal's oddly comic grimace of effort. The man was shaking.

"Lal? What the hell...?"

"I... am trying... sir... to stab... my... hand!"

"Have you taken leave of your senses? I don't want blood all over my..."

Lal lowered the knife. "I cannot do it, sir. That is the thing. It is impossible. Reports from all across the northern hemisphere – acts of violence are no more. Boxing matches have ended in farce, with opponents unable to trade punches. Police report aborted bank raids and gunmen unable to pull the trigger..."

Morwell's first impulse was to laugh and accuse Lal of playing a practical joke. He glanced at the calendar, but it was April the 30th, not the first.

He stood quickly, crossed the room to the gym and slipped inside. He snatched up the baseball bat, strode across to the rubber effigy of James Morwell Snr., and raised the bat.

He had no trouble at all in beating the figure to hell and back.

He returned to the office with the bat, and Lal was staring at the carpet and pretending he hadn't witnessed his boss's little weakness.

"Sir?

Morwell approached Lal. "If you're pulling some kind of joke, Lal, you're gonna be awful sore in the morning."

Impulsively he raised the bat, meaning to swing it with reasonable force into the Indian's midriff.

He stood with the bat in mid-air, and tried to swing...

He was frozen, as if the impulse to act had lodged somewhere between brain and arm.

He strained in an attempt to swing the bat, but the only result was that his arm began a palsied tremor.

Sweating, and not only with the effort of the abortive exertion, Morwell slumped into his swivel chair and told Lal to get the experts in here, on the double.

CHAPTER FOUR

Ana Devi squatted on a girder beneath the footbridge at Howrah station and watched the Delhi Express slide alongside platform ten. She shared her perch with a grey-furred, red-bottomed monkey a couple of metres away, but that's all she was sharing with the devil. She clutched a banana to her ragged t-shirt, and the monkey eyed the fruit with greedy, beady eyes.

"*Chalo!*" she yelled at the animal. It remained where it was, watching her impassively. It would be a mistake to start eating the banana now, even though she was hungry, because the monkey would be incensed by the aroma and try to snatch the fruit from her.

And every fool knew that the station monkeys were diseased, and that one scratch or bite could spell a lingering, painful death.

Down below the train halted and disgorged a thousand passengers. The crowd flowed along the platform towards the exit and the stairs to the other platforms, and seconds later Ana heard the thunder of footsteps just above her head.

The cacophony of the pedestrians succeeded in doing what she had failed to do: the monkey pulled back its lips to reveal a set of wicked, curved incisors, gave a howl, and bounded off along the girder-work of the bridge.

Ana laughed, peeled the banana and wolfed it down.

The footfalls above her head diminished, the train eased itself with a hiss from the platform, and comparative calm settled over Howrah station.

Ana missed her brother, Bilal.

Most of the time she was fine. She had friends among the kids who made Howrah station their home, a gang of boys and girls fiercely loyal to each other because they had no one else. It was the only family she had ever known, though she had a vague recollection of the aunt and uncle who had looked after her and her brother when their parents died in the cholera epidemic of 2014. Then Ana's aunt had fled her uncle when Ana was six, and had been unable to fend for two hungry, growing children. Bilal, fifteen at the time, had taken Ana to Howrah station, where he had friends among the street kids who lived like monkeys in the rotting infrastructure of the old buildings. He'd lived with her there for a time, begging and stealing and making sure that she was provided for. Then, just as she was settling into life at the station, Bilal disappeared.

He'd gone to sleep with her one evening in the ancient goods truck they used as a bedroom, tucked up with her and a dozen other children like sardines in a can, and in the morning he was gone. There wasn't even a gap where he had been, because the other kids had shuffled up to let another child lie down. He'd owned nothing other than a pair of shorts, a t-shirt, and an enamelled metal cup, white with a blue rim, and much chipped. After a day of searching the station and the streets around about, she'd given up in despair.

Then Prakesh, a friend a year older than Ana, had dragged her along to platform fourteen and pointed down at the silver tracks. There, crushed flat and the enamel shattered, was a cup just like Bilal's. She'd jumped down, despite the danger, and retrieved it. On its flattened underside was the letter B that Bilal had scratched to make the cup his very own.

But Ana had refused to believe that Bilal had gone the same way as his cup, squashed beneath the merciless wheels of a train, because there was no blood on the oil-stained gravel between the timber ties, and when she asked a friendly chai-wallah if a street kid's body had been found that morning, he had shaken his head and told her no, only the bodies of a station monkey and a dozen rats.

So what had happened to her brother?

Ten years ago now... and Ana recalled the sense of desolation, of disbelief and loneliness, as if it had been just yesterday.

For years she had thought that one day he would return, fabulously wealthy, and whisk her away from a life of begging and stealing. And even now, at the age of sixteen, she still harboured a tiny hope that this might be so. But sometimes she gave in to despair, and wondered what kind of death her brother might have met.

She heard a sound behind her and turned quickly to throw the banana skin at the approaching monkey – but it was not a monkey, or at least not a furry monkey. Prakesh, whose protruding ears gave him the appearance of a little wise ape, swung onto the girder and hunkered down beside her.

"Station Master Jangar has just said the word, get out!" he reported, staring at her with alarmed eyes.

Ana produced a gob-full of spit and dropped it onto the tracks below. Dead shot! It hit the silver rail and sizzled in the midday sun.

She shrugged. "So, the bastard is always saying get out. That's his job."

"No, this time he means it. Lila and Sara and Bijay have left for the park, and Gupta and Sanjay are packing up."

Ana smiled to herself. Gupta and Sanjay, miniature businessmen in the making, had a shoe-shine box between them, a possession that legitimised their presence on the station, if only to themselves. It made no difference to Station Master Jangar when the word came down from the politicians to clean up the station.

"So if everyone goes, leaving only me, then they won't think I'm a street kid, will they? They'll overlook me and I'll just stay where I am, resting in the sun..." She stretched out her short length along the girder, placing her hands behind her head, then squinting up at Prakesh with one eye.

He looked alarmed – his default expression – at both Ana's reckless posture on the girder twenty metres above the rails, and at her defiance of Jangar's wishes.

"But Ana, he said that Sanjeev and his thugs are on their way! And you know what that means!"

His small hands were on her now, trying to tug her into a sitting position. Reluctantly she sat up, for mention of Sanjeev sent a cold jolt of dread down her spine.

Sanjeev was a fat thug and a bugger. He liked to corner boys and girls, smother them into submission with his great rolls of flab, then shove his greased and tiny tool up their bottoms. Those who protested too loudly he strangled and had his cohorts leave the bodies on the tracks for the trains to mangle in the night. If you bore the buggering in silence, you might live. Ana had survived a night with fat Sanjeev, thanked Kali that his cock was the size of a chilli pepper, and vowed never to be caught again.

"When are they coming?" she asked.

"Now!"

She scanned the length of the platform. "Where are they?"

Prakesh shook his head. "They started in the goods yard, moving west. I don't know where they might be now."

"Ah-cha, Prakesh. Let's get out of here, let's 'don our masks and fly with the night!'"

Prakesh grinned. He couldn't read, like so many of the other kids, so Ana often read to them from her comics. Her favourite strip was Superhero Salam and the Warriors of Dawn, who helped the poor and fought the rich and corrupt.

They mimed donning invisible masks, stood up and walked wobblingly along the girder to the timber signal box. From the underside of the footbridge they scrambled onto the sloping, slipping tiles of the box, crawled along the gutter, and shinned down the drainpipe.

They were on platform ten, in the very centre of the station, and from here they had to make their way to platform one and the unofficial exit in the fence.

They set off, zigzagging between commuters, earning curses from some and swipes from others. Ana just ducked and laughed and, a safe distance away, turned and pulled a disgusting face.

They raced up the steps and along the footbridge where, just a minute ago, they had concealed themselves from view. Two minutes now and they would be away from the station and across the Hoogli bridge to Maidan Park, a fine place to play cricket and watch the rich kids fly their kites, but nothing like the station for begging, stealing or finding a safe, warm place to spend the night.

They came to the end of the footbridge. Stairs descended to their right and left. They turned right, but Prakesh halted her headlong descent. "Stop! Look, Ana..."

The crowds on the steps were thinning now and Ana saw, staring up at them, the thin sly face of Kevi Nan, Sanjeev's one-armed minion. He let out a piercing cry and darted up the stairway. Ana and Prakesh turned and ran down the flight of steps at their backs.

Ana stopped. Ascending the steps, pushing roughly

through the commuters, was another of Sanjeev's greasy henchmen.

She grabbed Prakesh and they ran back up the steps, turned left and raced along the footbridge.

She was accustomed to running. Every day someone tried to catch her, arrest her, or chase her away. She was adept at flight – but usually there were only one or two people in pursuit. Now, it seemed, Sanjeev had mobilised his entire street army of pimps, crooks and hangers-on. She heard more than one cry from behind her, and from the stairways ascending to the walkway.

Ana found Prakesh's hand and pulled him close as they ran. "I know where to go. Follow me! They won't dare to come after us!"

The footbridge was enclosed in a shell of grey corrugated metal, the rectangular panels riveted together. Here and there the rivets had loosened, or been forced, and the corrugated panels flapped. Directly above platform three, Ana knew, there was a gap in the metal.

She dragged Prakesh through the crowd until they reached the metal cladding and ran along until they came to the vertical gap, little more than a slit between the panels. In one swift movement she knelt and forced the panel outwards, revealing a gap that gave onto a supporting girder.

"Follow me!" she said, and slipped through.

She was out on the girder high above platform three, standing with her back to the drop and gripping a perspex window ledge to stop herself from tumbling backwards.

Prakesh squirmed after her, grimacing as his t-shirt was snagged on a loose rivet. He pulled himself through, tearing his shirt and almost falling forward.

Ana reached down and steadied him. Wide-eyed with fear, he stood with his back to the drop and edged towards her.

"This way," she said, and stride by sideways stride made her way along the length of the footbridge.

Once before she had evaded a policeman this way, and her escape had become a legend among the kids of the station. The cop, a stick-thin youngster, had managed to squeeze through the gap in pursuit and follow her along the outside of the footbridge. He had gained on her, but he had reckoned without Ana's daring. They had been directly above platform two, with the train just leaving the station, and Ana had waited until the very last carriage was directly underneath. Then she jumped the three metres to its cambered roof, landed with a jarring impact and lay face-down and trembling as the train flashed beneath the bridge and away from the station, carrying her to safety. She had jumped from the train at its first stop and caught a night train back to Howrah and to a hero's welcome from her street kid family.

She hoped they would not be forced to jump onto the roof of a train this time.

She looked back along the length of the footbridge, but there was no sign of pursuit. Periodically they came to the grimy windows, and every time they did so Ana ducked and edged along beneath the window. As they approached the last one, however, she chanced a glance through. Kevi Nan was standing with his back to the window, smoking a bidi and shouting orders to his cohorts. Ana ducked.

"What?" Prakesh asked, fear in his voice.

"Kevi," Ana spat. "But he didn't see me."

"Ana..." Prakesh looked fearful, clinging to the ledge like a baby monkey. "How do we get down from here?"

"Don't worry. Follow me and do just what I do, ah-cha?"

They inched along the ledge, over platform two and approached platform one. At the end of the footbridge was a loose drainpipe, its metal streaked with slime, which descended to the platform. She had once climbed up this to reach the roof of the signal box – but the rickety section of the pipe was *above* the level of the roof, and now it would be the first section they'd have to negotiate on their descent.

A minute later they came to the pipe and Ana paused. She looked back at Prakesh and smiled. "We are doing well. They have not found us. Let's rest before we climb down, ah-cha?"

Smiling bravely, Prakesh nodded.

She scanned the platform. A train was due in, and platform vendors were preparing for the rush. Chai-wallahs jostled each other for the best positions, along with kids selling trays of biscuits, cigarettes and lighters.

"We'll wait till the train pulls in," she told Prakesh, "and climb down then."

Concealed by the crowds alighting from the train, they would squirm across the platform and through the gap in the fence. In Ana's mind she was already free, and recounting their escape to their friends in Maidan Park.

Two minutes later she heard a distant, mournful hoot and the Lucknow Mail eased itself into platform one. Doors sighed open and, amid a cacophony of vendor's cries, a thousand passengers surged from the carriage and along the platform.

"Follow me!" Ana cried.

She clung to the slippery drainpipe and slid down painfully, pausing at each joint to rest and look up. Prakesh was just above her, the corrugated soles of his feet gripping the curve of the pipe.

She set off again and looked down. The next section of the drainpipe was where it was loose. She looked up and said, "Prakesh, the pipe just below me will not take the weight of both of us. Let me go first, and when I shout up, you follow, ah-cha?"

"Ah-cha," he said, peering down at her.

She reached the loose section and slipped down carefully, feeling the pipe wobble with her weight. She reckoned she was about three metres above the concrete platform, and would have risked jumping but for the constant to-and-fro of commuters directly below.

She felt herself tip slowly and looked up in time to see the pipe come away from the joint just above her head. For a long second she was held in the perpendicular, like a monkey balancing on a pole, and then the drainpipe dropped outwards like a felled tree. Down below, Ana caught a glimpse of startled commuters moving to avoid her. She let go of the pipe and leaped, falling painfully on the soles of her bare feet and rolling. The pipe clanged down beside her, hitting the concrete like a tubular bell but missing her by a fraction. The crowd flowed around her, muttering their displeasure, but Ana was oblivious.

She leapt to her feet, looked up and down the platform in case her sudden arrival had alerted Kevi Nan and his men, then peered up.

Prakesh was clinging tearfully to the pipe high above, his descent halted. There was now a two metre gap in the drainpipe between the boy and the next section of pipe. He peered down at her, eyes wide and wet with tears.

"Ana," he called down pitifully, "don't go!"

"I won't!" she cried. "Listen to me – you've got to jump, ah-cha? I'll catch you."

"I can't!"

"You must. There's no other way, and soon Kevi Nan will be here! Jump and I will catch you."

Peering down in fear, he nodded.

"I'll catch you, Prakesh. After three. One... two... three!"

He launched himself, all flailing arms and legs, and Ana reached out and closed her eyes. He hit her and they rolled across the platform, Ana clinging to him despite the pain. The impact knocked the breath from her lungs, and her elbow throbbed when it struck the ground.

"Prakesh?"

"I'm fine, Ana! You caught me!"

She stood and pulled him to his feet – then yelped in fright as a hand gripped the back of her neck and squeezed.

She looked up, fearfully, into the fat face of Station Master Jangar, with his vast grey moustache and turban. The Sikh was jabbering to someone at his side, and she recognised the thin, rat-like squeak of Kevi Nan. She attempted to peer around and up, her movement restricted by Jangar's grip, and managed to see a hand slip a fifty rupee note into the Station Master's breast pocket.

Then Kevi Nan gripped her upper arm and half dragged her along the platform. She looked back at Jangar and Prakesh. Her friend had his fist crammed into his mouth, his eyes wide and tearful.

Ana managed a smile and a quick wave before Prakesh was lost to sight in the surging crowd.

She struggled, but Kevi Nan just increased the force of his pincer grip and Ana wept in pain. She hopped along as Kevi raced through the crowd towards the station's exit, holding her breath against his stench. Kevi Nan had only one hand, which he used for eating, and consequently his backside went unwashed. He tried to disguise the smell with rosewater, but for some reason this just made it worse.

He hauled her from the station and along a busy street, then down a quiet alleyway. From time to time when his crab-like grip seemed to slacken, Ana put in a token struggle – but Kevi Nan's one hand seemed stronger than two and he just sneered at her feeble attempts to get away.

At one point as they hurried down the alley, something flashed high overhead, and both Kevi Nan and Ana looked up. She saw a bright glint of light, like sunlight glancing off a pane of glass, but nothing else.

"Let me go!"

"And deprive Sanjeev his pleasure, Ana Devi?"

She was shocked that he knew her name, as if this, along with his grip, was another violation. "Sanjeev-ji has been watching you, Ana, watching you and waiting."

What was he talking about, she wondered. Sanjeev was so fat that he hadn't left his room for years, so how could he have been watching her?

"I have rupees," she said. "Twenty rupees. I'll give them to you if you let me go!"

Over the years she had managed to save a rupee here and there, and had amassed the grand total of twenty which she had concealed behind a loose stone in the outer wall of the station's Brahmin restaurant.

Kevi Nan laughed. "Twenty rupees? Sanjeev will pay me ten times that for your yoni, Ana!"

Something froze within her. Her yoni... Sanjeev was going to take her properly, this time, draw blood and deprive her of her virginity. She stared ahead, unseeingly, frozen at the thought.

Kevi Nan dragged her down a rat-infested alleyway, past slums where infants stared out with huge, kohl-black eyes. Some of the kids were older, perhaps her own age, and she hated the quick look of pity in their eyes as she passed.

They came to a high wall and a green-painted gate. Kevi Nan called out, and the gate opened just enough to allow them to squeeze through. He dragged her along a garden path overhung with a riot of unkempt trees and bushes, towards a familiar house painted as pink as a chunk of barfi. Ana felt her stomach turn as she recalled her first time here, years ago, and what Sanjeev had done to her.

They passed into the house, across a cool tiled hallway, towards a green double door. Kevi Nan called out, "I have the girl, Sanjeev-ji!" He eased open the door with his right foot and thrust her into the room.

The door closed quickly behind her. Ana stopped her headlong rush, regained her balance, and stood blinking in a room illuminated by a thousand flickering candles.

The heat was overpowering, along with the cloying scent of incense and dhoop.

When her vision adjusted to the glittery twilight, she gasped as she made out the figure ensconced in the corner of the room.

Sanjeev Varnaputtram was fatter than any fat man she had ever seen, and far fatter than when Ana had last seen him. He sat on a bed in the glow of the candles, naked but for a towel draped across his lap. The rolls of fat that made up his chest and belly were slick with either sweat or massage oil. His arms and legs stuck out at odd angles, forced apart by the amount of fat that encircled his upper arms and thighs.

His head, perfectly circular and absolutely bald, was a tiny thing perched on the mountain of his shoulders.

Sanjeev's appetite was prodigious. Rumour was that he consumed six take-away curries from Bhatnagar's – an expensive restaurant Ana had only ever dreamed of entering – every day. On the rickety table beside him a pile of a dozen ghee-coated silver trays suggested that the rumour might be true.

Now he was smiling, and a gold tooth – the tooth she recalled with horror from all those years ago, when he had tried to kiss her – caught the candle-light and winked.

She backed up against the door, pushing against it. The wood rattled but did not give, and she knew that Kevi Nan had bolted the door from the outside, just like last time.

"My, my," Sanjeev purred. "How you have grown. How, Ana Devi, you have blossomed from the vicious little she-cat you were, into a beautiful woman... Yes, indeed you are – a woman. Now..." he patted his lap, "come and sit down, Ana."

"No!"

He chuckled, as if delighted at her spirit. "In that respect you have changed little, Ana Devi. Still you are as feisty as you were... what, five, six years ago? You fought, then, if you recall, scratched like a lion cub. It made for even more enjoyment."

He gestured to the wall. "I have been watching you, Ana, watching you grow, mature, become the beautiful young woman you are now."

She stared at the wall beside the bed, and saw what he was talking about. Stuck to the wall was a photograph of her, taken very recently. She wanted suddenly to sob. It was as if Sanjeev had stolen a part of her. She wanted to take the photograph from him; that it belonged to Sanjeev seemed wrong.

"I have been waiting, Ana, biding my time. When I received the photograph..." He gestured with a tiny hand. "I knew that the time was right."

The actual photo was not the only violation, she

knew; someone had stalked her, sneaked up on her and taken the picture without her knowledge. What should have been her privacy had been despoiled. She felt sick. She was a street kid, but surely this did not mean that her life was not her own, a thing to be shared, abused, without her consent...?

"But if I may say, Ana, a beautiful woman such as yourself should no longer be wearing the apparel of a child. Look at that t-shirt! Filthy, and ragged, and doing little justice to the delights it conceals. Your breasts are those of a goddess, Ana Devi, and yet you choose to cloak them in rags! And your shorts..." He shook his head and tutted. "Are you aware of how wonderful you would look in new clothes, a sari, a shalwar kameez?" He pointed across the room to a table bearing a pile of folded, silken clothing.

"They are yours, Ana Devi. Please, take off those rags."

She stared at him and almost sobbed, "No!"

He chuckled, and the sound sickened her; it was the sound of privilege, and power, the sound of someone who knew full well that his desires would be satisfied.

He reached down, took hold of the corner of the towel which covered his midriff, and cast it aside.

She could only stare at his manhood.

His balls were huge, grotesque things, surely as big as coconuts, and by comparison his cock was tiny, really and truly like a small chilli pepper, apart from the domed, shiny thing at the end. It stood to attention above the coconuts, and Ana would have laughed had she not felt so terrified.

He reached out to a small bedside table, picked up a golden genie-lamp, and tipped it.

A thread of golden oil drizzled out, saturating his manhood.

"Ana," he said, "take off your clothes and come to me." And his voice was no longer tender, cajoling, but hard and forbidding.

He reached down and played with his oiled cock, coaxing it further upright. Its dome strained, empurpled.

"I said, come to me!"

The words to deny him would not form in her mouth, so she just shook her head and darted a glance around the room, searching for something she might use as a weapon against him.

She saw nothing, and anyway knew that resistance was useless: his leering cohorts were outside the room, very likely now laughing at what their boss was about to do to her.

She backed up against the wall, shaking her head.

"Very well, if you will not come to me..."

He called out, and instantly the door burst open, startling her. One-armed Kevi Nan and a rat-faced man strode into the room, staring from the naked Sanjeev to the cowering Ana.

"Shall we rip off her clothes?" Kevi asked, eyeing her.

"*Nai*!" Sanjeev said. "Here."

They hurried over to him, took his arms and hauled him to his feet.

Ana glanced through the door. Two other men stood there, big Sikhs with their arms crossed on their broad chests, barring her escape.

"*Chalo!*" Sanjeev shouted, shooing his aides from the room. They hurried out, closing and locking the door behind them.

Sanjeev faced her. His enormous gut had slipped. His erection peeked out from the fatty overhang, its oiled and swollen end shining in the candlelight.

He grabbed a stick from where it leaned against the wall and waddled towards her.

She had assumed the stick was a walking stick, but as he advanced he raised it at her and said, "Now, undress quickly! Quickly!"

She pressed herself against the wall, her arms tight across her breasts. He advanced, his flesh-rolls wobbling, his absurd cock bobbing.

He paused before her. His sudden closeness filled her with dread. If he were to reach out now he would be able to touch her. She made a feeble whimpering sound and was ashamed of her fear.

His face was drenched in sweat and he was shaking with lust.

He raised the stick again and said, "We can do this one of two ways, Ana Devi. You can come willingly to my bed, or I can beat you senseless. Either way, the end result will be the same. You will be mine, whether you like it or not."

She shook her head, mute and terrified.

"But if you come willingly," he said, "I will be gentle, and afterwards... the new, fine clothes will be yours, along with a hundred rupees. A hundred, Ana, think of all the things you could buy with a hundred rupees."

She began weeping then, despite her best efforts not to.

"Never," she cried, "never!"

"So you cannot be bought," he laughed, "with money, but I wonder..."

He towered above her, a giant mound of flesh. His tiny, greedy eyes gleamed. "But I wonder if you would be more amenable if I were to tell you about Bilal?"

She stared up at him. She had doubted she could be shocked any more, or frightened further. But the way Sanjeev said her brother's name filled her with fear.

"Bilal?" she said. "What about him?"

"You miss him, Ana. Oh, I know how much you miss him. My little spies... Rajeev, Kallif..." He smiled. "They tell me all about your dreams of the day when Bilal will return..."

She had wondered about Rajeev and Kallif, where they disappeared to for days on end, suddenly reappearing with rupees and bags of barfi.

"What do you know about Bilal?" she asked.

His eyes twinkled. "Take off your clothes, Ana, and let me see the perfection of your little body."

"Tell me what you know about Bilal!" she demanded. "Where is he? Is he alive?"

"Oh, he is very much alive, Ana, alive and prospering."

She felt hope beyond hope, even if it was being granted her from the mouth of a monster.

"How do you know this?"

"I have my spies, Ana, my informants."

"Where is my brother?" she demanded.

"He is alive and well, but he will have forgotten his little sister, long ago."

"No! No, Bilal would never forget me. Never..."

Sanjeev laughed. "Then why haven't your dreams come true, Ana? Why hasn't he returned to rescue you from a life of thieving and beggary?"

She shook her head, crying openly now, past all shame. "I don't know," she said in a tiny voice. "Please, tell me..."

"Bilal left Kolkata," he said, amazing her. "He was plucked off the streets by the representatives of an agency which educates street kids like yourself. Eventually, according to my sources, he left India and was taken to America."

But why didn't he come for me...? she wanted to ask.

"Now, Ana," Sanjeev wheedled. "Please take off your filthy t-shirt and shorts."

She pressed herself against the wall and shook her head.

"Would you prefer the stick, Ana? Would you like me to take you the hard way?"

She wanted to lash out at him, push his fat bulk so that he fell over and bashed his head on the marble floor, but she was paralysed with fear.

Sanjeev raised the stick and Ana winced and closed her eyes.

A second passed, then two, three...

An agonising eternity seemed to elapse.

She peeped out between her fingers, which she had raised to protect her face.

Sanjeev appeared to be frozen, the stick high above his head. His eyes bulged and his fat arm shook with the effort of attempting to bring the stick down. She wondered if he were having a heart attack.

To her left was a shuttered window. She summoned

all her courage and made a decision. She ducked beneath Sanjeev's raised arm, ran to the window and pulled it open, knowing that it would be barred. Her heart leapt when she saw not bars but a flimsy fly-screen. She reached out to steady herself – and her hand touched something soft on the table. The pile of expensive clothing...

As Sanjeev gasped behind her, wheezing as he turned and attempted yet again to hit her with his stick, she kicked out at the fly-screen and, as it shuddered and fell out from the window frame, she grabbed the clothing and leapt through the open window.

She was in the riotous garden surrounding the house. She hesitated, looking right and left. Sanjeev's strangled cry from inside the house galvanised her into action. She gained her bearings and stumbled to her left, through fronds and ferns towards what she hoped was the garden gate. Seconds later she came to the concrete path. To her left the front door of the house was still shut. She turned right and sprinted to the gate, reached it and hauled on the circular, wrought iron handle. She heard the door open behind her and an explosion of outraged cries.

The heavy gate opened slowly and Ana dived through, turned right down the alley and ran like the wind.

A minute later she came to the main road and the surging crowd, and with elation swelling in her chest she threw herself into the flow of humanity and allowed herself to be carried away to safety.

* * *

TWILIGHT CAME DOWN swiftly across the city and Ana made her way to Maidan Park.

She would lie low for a few days, allow perhaps a week or so to elapse before she returned to the station. Sanjeev would have his men on the lookout for her, eager to exact his revenge. To her knowledge no one taken into Sanjeev's lair had emerged without giving him what he wanted, and many a child had met their deaths by denying him.

Perhaps, she thought, she should leave the city altogether?

And what he had told her about Bilal? Had her brother really, truly left the city, been educated and taken to America? But why would Sanjeev have lied about such things? Why would he have told her that he had been educated and taken to America – unless it were true?

Perhaps, she thought, something had stopped Bilal from coming back for her. Perhaps, one day, soon, he would do just that.

She came upon a crowd of excited rich people pointing into the sky, where the light of the emerging stars seemed dulled, and the sun, on the horizon, was bloated to fully twice its size.

She thought of Prakesh, and hoped that Station Master Jangar had let him off with a warning and a minor beating, and thrown him from the station. She searched the park, but found neither Prakesh nor any of her friends.

She slipped into the shrubbery where a few months ago she had concealed a bedroll she had found in a skip. Now she curled up on it and, using the silken clothing she had stolen from Sanjeev's room as a pillow, settled down to sleep.

She was listening to the sound of the city, the roar of distant traffic, the tragic hoots of the trains, when suddenly all noise seemed to stop – and a sudden, eerie silence reigned. Above her, the branches of a tree, formerly moving back and forth against the moon, were still.

Then she was asleep, or assumed she was asleep, though it had come upon her suddenly, and she was visited by a strange dream – but not the usual one of vicious policemen and angry station masters.

She was lying on her back on... No, not *on* anything, but floating in a grey mist. She felt naked, and she thought she should be frightened, but a calming voice in her head told her not to be afraid. The odd thing was, the voice was not her own.

She tried to struggle, but she was paralysed. All she could move was her eyes; all she could see was the grey mist... and something in the distance, the head and shoulders of a man or woman, watching her in silence.

Then she felt something dancing on her chest, and swivelled her eyes to look down her body. What she saw sent a jolt of alarm through her. There was a big spider down there, on her belly and climbing slowly towards her head, a spider with long legs as silver as the cutlery in the Howrah station restaurant.

She wanted to scream, but could not make the sound.

The spider approached her, its limbs tickling her chest. Then it was crawling over her chin, her face.

It paused, pulsing slowly up and down, above her forehead.

She felt something touch the skin of her brow, as if the spider were applying a tikka mark to the centre of her forehead. She felt pressure then, and wondered if the spider was pushing something into her head.

She closed her eyes, and the voice in her head told her to be calm.

Seconds later she felt the spider skitter back down the length of her body. She tried to sit up but could not.

She awoke suddenly, and then did sit up.

She was in the bushes in the park, on the bedroll with the new clothes she had snatched from Sanjeev's room. She remembered what had happened there, how she had escaped.

Her thoughts were interrupted by something in the bushes to her right.

She turned, gasping. She made out a golden glow, and a shape that was in some way familiar.

A figure was seated in the bushes perhaps three metres from her, and she recognised its head and shoulders from her dream.

The figure was golden, and featureless, and its interior swam and pulsed with light.

It sat cross-legged, watching her calmly.

"Who are you?" she asked.

The figure – man or woman, she could not tell – stared at her even though its face did not possess eyes, and said, even though it did not have a mouth, "Do not be afraid, Ana Devi."

"How do you know my name?" She felt strangely calm. "What do you want?"

She had the impression that the golden figure was smiling.

"We want you," it said.

CHAPTER FIVE

FOLLOWING THE KIDNAPPING, Sally spent the night at Mama Oola's Guest House in the centre of town, a ramshackle Victorian building comprising bedrooms on two levels around a courtyard overgrown with bougainvillea and frangipani. Sally considered Mama's a bolt-hole, an oasis of tranquillity in a noisy town and, on a metaphorical level, from the stress of her job. She often booked into the guest house when she had a couple of days free, to allow Mama Oola to mother her and to feed her up on the Indian curries that were her speciality.

She slept late, dreaming of her ordeal of the day before. The scar-faced Ali haunted her sleep. Once she awoke screaming, convinced that the man had somehow entered the room.

Late morning sunlight slipped in through the slats of the louvered window, waking her to the realisation that she was no longer imprisoned by the terrorists. She crossed from her bed and flung open the window, letting in a blast of sunlight and the scent of frangipani. Overhead, the sun created a slick highlight on the meniscus of the dome, reminding her of a more enigmatic imprisonment.

She considered what had happened in the tiny hut, and the arbitrary nature of the event that had saved her and Ben. The thought sickened her.

She washed in the refreshingly cold water at the stained sink, dressed and hurried downstairs. She would go to the medical centre, see if she could be of any help there until Geoff arrived.

Geoff... She felt at once a wave of guilt at having forgotten him in the melee of recent events, and then a buoyant joy at the thought that soon they would be together. She dug her mobile from her shoulder bag and tried to get through to him.

The line was dead, not even a dial tone.

He was due to arrive at some point this morning. After checking in at the medical centre, she would go to the wall of the dome near the road south and try to find Geoff there when he arrived.

Mama Oola bustled from the kitchen and hurried across the courtyard towards her. She was a gargantuan woman resplendent in colourful traditional costume and gold bangles. She was in her sixties, but her big, round face was as unlined as a babe's.

"Sally! Sally!"

They hugged, and Mama's breasts wobbled against Sally like packets of mozzarella the size of footballs.

"I heard about the attack! I wept when I thought of you, then this morning Jenny told me you were safe and sleeping upstairs. You don't know how happy I was!"

She gripped Sally's hands, beaming at her.

"Strange things are happening, Sally. The dome. And..." She leaned close, drenching Sally in her rosewater and patchouli scent. "And this morning, Papa couldn't beat me..."

"Couldn't...?" Sally echoed. It was a relationship that Sally found incomprehensible. Mama Oola and Papa had been married for almost forty years, and it seemed to Sally that their conjugal day did not start well if Papa failed to attack her and Mama Oola didn't retaliate, giving as good as she got, with stentorian curses thrown in for good measure.

"Oh," Mama went on, "he was angry, he said his porridge was cold, so he came for me..." She stared at Sally, wide-eyed. "And he just stood there, mouth open, shaking uncontrollably." She laughed and slapped her ample thigh, then leaned towards Sally confidentially. "It was just like when Papa wants jiggy-tumble – he had the *urge*, but couldn't do it!" Mama shook her head, ear-rings the size of ladles dancing. "And the oddest thing was, Sally, I wanted to go for Papa, too – give him a good slapping round that silly toothless face of his! But do you know something, for all I wanted to slap him, I couldn't."

Across the courtyard, Jenny the house-girl appeared in the door to the kitchen and called across to Mama. She squeezed Sally's hand and shuffled away. "Come for coffee later, you hear? We have a lot to talk about!"

Sally promised she would and slipped through the flimsy metal gate that led from the courtyard.

As she made her way through the curiously deserted streets, she thought of what Mama had just told her, and considered Dr Krasnic and his abortive suicide attempts. And yesterday, the terrorists, unable to behead Ben, or pull the triggers of their weapons...

A cordon of soldiers and police stood before the fire-blackened gate of the medical centre. Dr Krasnic stood outside, in conversation with a tall Swiss woman Sally recognised as a Red Cross liaison officer.

When he saw Sally approach he excused himself and crossed to her.

"Sally, what do you think you're doing here?"

"I thought I'd see if I were needed."

"You booked five days leave, didn't you, and after what happened yesterday... Look, take some time off. You deserve it. We've enough staff to cover you, and anyway there's a relief team coming up from Kampala in the morning. I booked them after the raid, and before ..." He gestured into the sky, at the glistening dome overhead.

"A lot of good a relief team will be if they can't get in," she commented.

He shrugged. "Like I said, we can cover you. If we need help, I'll shout... I take it you're at Mama's?" He hesitated, then brought himself to look her in the eye. "Sally, what happened yesterday, when you found me..."

She interrupted. "That's between you, me and Ben," she said.

He shook his head as if in wonder. "I'd had a tough shift. After Kola's death, and Mary taking it so badly. And then the raid, the soldiers... and Josef, what he did..."

"What happened to him?"

"He fled, but didn't get far, of course. A unit of troops cornered him. They were seething with anger and wanting revenge. Only..."

"Let me guess. They couldn't shoot him dead, right?"

"Couldn't so much as lift a hand, though they tried, apparently. Lined up to shoot the traitor. They ended up escorting him to the police cells like a pickpocket." He looked at her. "What the hell is going on, Sally? I've tried to reach HQ in Kampala, friends in Europe. Nothing. We're completely cut off."

She shook her head. "All the violence, the soldiers shot dead. And then..."

He said, "Ben thinks it's a judgement from God."

She snorted. "And you know my reaction to that."

He looked up at the underside of the dome. "I don't know. It makes you wonder, Sally."

She made to leave. "If you're absolutely sure you don't need me..."

He shooed her away. "Go, go! Enjoy Mama's curries and have a beer on me."

She was walking down the street away from the medical centre when she looked up suddenly, alerted by what might have been a flash high above. She discerned a subtle shift in the quality of the light; the sunlight seemed suddenly *brighter*. She shielded her eyes and realised that the dome seemed no longer to be covering the town.

Heart thumping, she hurried to the main road heading south, along with what appeared to be the town's entire population. There was a carnival atmosphere in the air, and the reason was obvious: half a kilometre ahead, where yesterday the sheer crystal wall of the dome had blocked the road, the barrier was no more.

The two crowds, separated until seconds ago, now merged and mingled, embracing like survivors of some terrible natural catastrophe.

Someone called her name. "Dr Walsh!"

Sergeant Mesenevi was coming towards her, fighting his way through the tide of humanity. He gripped her hand. "Dr Walsh! Good news! Mr Allen is here. He thinks you are dead!"

"What?"

"I told him about the attack on the medical centre. Of course we didn't know if you were alive or dead."

"Just take me to Geoff, okay?" she demanded, emotion making her voice unsteady. She just wanted to hold him.

"Sally!"

And there he was, being dragged along by a posse of grinning barefoot schoolgirls, waving at her above the heads of the milling crowd.

She struggled through the press towards him and they collided and held on. She said his name over and over, inhaling the wonderful scent of his sweat, listening to his almost incoherent litany. "...told me about the attack... didn't know what the hell had happened to you... feared the worst. Christ, it's good to hold you!"

She gripped his hand and, watched by the beaming schoolgirls and the police sergeant, she dragged him back to the centre of town and Mama Oola's.

*   *   *

BY UNSPOKEN CONSENT they made love on the narrow, squeaking bed in the shadowy room, both of them weeping and murmuring almost incoherently. It was a more desperate and tender coming together than Sally had ever experienced before – the usual animal need of sexual desire and something more, some affirmation of life after so much death.

She switched on the ceiling fan and the downdraft laved their naked bodies, cooling.

She had not meant to tell Geoff everything that had happened to her the day before; had intended to downplay the kidnapping and her subsequent escape. But in his company, when they had shared so much, it seemed pointless to hold back on the experience.

"The attack...?" he began.

"They took me and Ben," she murmured. She pressed a finger to his lips. "I'm okay now. Don't worry. They... they didn't hurt me. They took us to a hut in the bush kilometres north of here."

Geoff's expression was set in stone.

"And when we got there..." She took a deep breath, her voice wavery. "Three things. A camera on a tripod, a chopping block, a sword..."

She wept, the tears coming in a heaving wave all of a sudden, unbidden, and she realised that she'd held in all the emotion, all the terror, until now, until she was safe with Geoff and could let it all out in a great cathartic damburst of retrospective fear.

He held her, kissing her sweat-damp hair, as she sobbed against him.

She took a deep shuddering breath, smiled up at him through her tears. "Oh, I was so frightened, Geoff. So disbelieving... that, that someone would do this to us. For ideological reasons. And film it, Geoff. I don't know where this is rational, but that's what horrified me more than anything else. Not the evil of their intent to kill us, but the callousness of their desire to film our deaths."

He kissed her eyes, her mouth. "How the hell did you get away?"

She thought about it, ordering the events. The incidents had an air of unreality, like a film watched a long time ago and imperfectly recalled. All she remembered, with crystal clarity, was how she had felt at the time.

Slowly, hesitantly, she told Geoff about her kidnappers' inability to kill her and Ben.

He said, "You were so lucky, Sally."

She shook her head. "No. No, Geoff. It... I know this sounds ridiculous... but it wasn't luck. Something was stopping the Somali from pulling the trigger."

Geoff said, "His conscience."

"No," she said, "because when I got back to the compound, I found Dr Krasnic..."

And, despite her promise to Krasnic that morning that his secret was safe with her, she told Geoff about the doctor's multiple suicide attempts. "And just this morning... Mama Oola told me that Papa had tried to beat her again, only he *couldn't*, and when she tried to hit him... she said she was unable to do it."

He reached from the bed, found his holdall and pulled out his softscreen. She watched him attempt to access the net, to no avail. "Still dead."

She stroked his face with her fingertips.

"When I was on the plane," he began, his eyes narrowing with recollection.

"Yes?"

He shook his head. "Nothing. It doesn't matter." He laughed. "I just recall thinking how much I love you."

Something rose in her chest, sadness and joy combined. "Whatever the hell happens, Geoff, whatever happens, we have each other."

They came together again and, gently this time, made love once more.

THEY TOOK A cold shower together in the communal bathroom at the end of the landing, then descended to the dappled courtyard where Mama Oola served them piled plates of vegetable pilau and ice cold lager. She winked at Sally when she presented the plates with a flourish, as if to say that after such lovemaking a hearty meal was necessary.

Geoff was quiet during the meal, which was unlike him. She had never met a more talkative person; he was usually forever telling her, during their snatched time together, about everything he had done since he'd last seen her. She sensed that his taciturnity now was due to more than just a lack of sleep.

She said, "You okay?"

He forked his pilau, looked up. "I was just thinking, we don't have to go to the reserve, if you're not up to it after..."

She reached out and gripped his hand. "I want to

get away from here. Anyway," she smiled, "you have work to do."

He nodded, and returned to his food.

"Geoff," she said a little later, "you began to tell me something earlier, about what happened on the plane."

He stared at her, smiling like a schoolboy caught out. "I didn't think you'd pick up on it."

"I can read you like a book," she said. "What happened?"

He had an expressive face, a way of pantomiming what he was thinking with exaggerated facial gestures. He frowned heavily. "I don't know. It seemed so real at the time, but now it seems like a hallucination."

She listened as he told her a fantastic story of reality coming to a halt, and how he had found himself floating in a grey void and being visited by a silver spider...

He stared down at his meal. "The thing was, Sally, it all seemed so damned real. And then what happened with the domes, and..." He looked up. "It occurred to me that it might in some way be connected."

She pursed her lips, considering. "I'd say... probably not. You've been working hard, and it was a late flight, and you hadn't slept." She shrugged. "And," she smiled, "you did once tell me that you're afraid of spiders."

He laughed. "Was. When I was a child."

She tilted her head and looked at him, dubious. "Thought you said tarantulas still gave you the heebie-jeebies?"

He smiled. "Touché," he said. "I remember when I was in Singapore –"

Jenny appeared in the doorway to the lounge, clutching the frame with both arms and hanging forward. "Sally! Come and watch! Mama! Mama! Come now!"

Mama Oola squeezed from the kitchen. "What now girl?"

Jenny was goggle-eyed. "Amazing! Come and see!"

She vanished inside, and Sally exchanged a look with Geoff and rose from the table. Geoff took his bottle of beer. Sally found his hand as they entered the shadowy lounge.

It was a long, low room, hung with drapes and furnished with multiple ancient sofas, opening onto a balcony at the far end. In the corner of the room, incongruous amid such genteel shabbiness, a vast flatscreen TV pulsed out garish images.

Sally sank into a deep sofa, Geoff beside her. Mama Oola eased herself into her own sofa, almost filling it. Jenny squatted before the TV, staring up at it with a houseboy and the girl who cleaned the rooms.

The TV was tuned to BBC World and a desk-bound reporter was saying, "...hope to be bringing you pictures and reports just as soon as they're available. To repeat, reports are coming in from around the world confirming what our reporter in London was just saying... In Laos, where the war with Thailand is in its third year, people are speaking of mass desertions from the armies on both sides of the conflict. In Botswana, our reporter on the ground has an eye-witness account of front-

Eric Brown

line troops being unable to operate their weapons... Now, this tallies with domestic news coming in from London and elsewhere."

Sally gripped Geoff's hand, tightened.

The reporter said, "One moment..." He touched his ear-piece, nodded and went on, "I'm told we can now join Rob Hudson in Alice Springs, Australia, where footage of a... vessel has just come through."

Sally sat forward, battling to free herself from the depths of the sofa. The scene switched to a reporter standing in the desert, staring up in wonder at the sky. The camera swung, showing a dizzy flash of bright blue sky and then, filling the entirety of the screen, a vast convex expanse of silver-blue metal, like a close-up shot of a mystery object the identity of which the audience had to guess.

The shot pulled out, steadied, and established itself.

On the sofa, Mama Oola rocked back and forth, clasping be-ringed hands to her ample bosom, her tearful eyes wide.

Beside Sally, Geoff swore under his breath.

An airborne vessel was moving slowly through the cloudless Australian sky. It was the only thing in the frame, so that its true dimensions were impossible to determine. Bull-nosed, splayed like a manta ray but much thicker, and silver-blue, it resembled some futuristic starship beloved of science fiction book covers.

Geoff whispered, "Foss..."

"What?" Sally asked, glancing at him.

"A cover artist, Chris Foss. It's just like one of his illustrations."

She said, half to herself, "But this is real, Geoff."

111

Then, sliding into view beneath the vessel, Sally made out the unmistakable shape of Ayers Rock – and the airborne vessel, as it moved over the sacred aboriginal landmark, was fully ten times the size.

"I don't believe it," she murmured.

Mama Oola was clapping her hands in delight, or in fright.

An awed voiceover was saying, "It appeared in the skies of Southern Australia just twenty minutes ago, heading north-west at approximately fifty miles an hour. It moved in absolute and eerie silence. I can confirm that jets from the Australia Air Force were scrambled to intercept, but that for some reason they were unable to leave the ground."

"It's beautiful," Sally said, "truly beautiful..."

She had never, she thought, seen anything quite as vast or magnificent in her life.

"And terrifying," Geoff said.

She looked at him.

He said, "Think about it, Sally. What happened yesterday. The domes, our inability to..."

She shook her head, slowly.

"It makes sense. What would an invading army do, if they had the capability? Somehow inhibit our ability to... to fight back."

She gestured at the slow, beautiful vessel. "This is a... an invasion?"

Geoff was silent, staring at the screen.

The scene shifted, returned to the studio. "Sorry to cut Rob off there... but we're getting reports, several reports from around the world. Okay, let's go over to Amelia Thirkell in Paris..."

"Thank you, Dan." A trim blonde woman in a stylish raincoat was standing before the Eiffel Tower, clutching a microphone to her chest and staring wide-eyed into the sky. "Just twenty minutes ago, twelve-thirty-one European time, a vessel identical to the ones that have been reported appearing in Australia, China, Argentina and elsewhere, manifested itself in the sky just north of Paris. Eye-witnesses, I'm told, say that it simply appeared as if from thin air. And then moved south slowly, as you see now..." The camera swung, and it was as if they were watching a re-run of the Australian ship's progress, only this time the backdrop was grey with rainclouds.

The beautiful, colossal ship was identical in every respect.

Jenny and the houseboy were shrieking with delight before the TV.

"I can confirm that, as in Australia, the air force scrambled jets to intercept, but that those jets could not, I repeat, *could not*, take off."

The shot lingered on the slowly moving vessel, occasionally swooping in for close-ups as if attempting to establish fine detail, decals or some other feature on the silver-blue tegument of the craft.

The superstructure, however, appeared featureless, as seamless as the surface of an egg.

It hovered over the Eiffel Tower, reducing the landmark to the size of a needle.

"...the strange thing is," Amelia Thirkell was reporting, "that the crowds massed here and on the banks of the Seine don't seem in the least phased by... by what we have here. And I can report myself that there is no sense of... of threat emanating from the ship."

"Angela," the anchorman back in London said, "sorry to have to interrupt there. We'll be back, but we have interesting developments here in London. With me in the studio are the physicists Dr Ed Danbridge and Dr James Chamberlain. Gentlemen, many thanks for coming here at such short notice. Now, you've both been doing calculations based on the vessels' trajectories..."

"That's right, Rob," Chamberlain said. "To remind viewers, the starships –"

The anchorman interrupted. "Now that's the first time we've used the s-word, but you think...?"

"The assumption is, Rob, that only an extraterrestrial intelligence could be behind the various odd phenomena reported over the past twenty-four hours. Anyway, the vessels appeared in the skies of Earth at precisely the same time all around the world, 11.31 Greenwich mean time. Interestingly, each ship is heading on a trajectory that we've plotted, Jim and myself, which will meet at some time in the near future, at a point a hundred kilometres north-west of the Malian city of Timbuktu in the Saharan Desert."

"Can anything be made of that, at this early stage?" the anchorman asked.

"I think it's too early to say yet. All we can do is watch and wait..."

"And speaking of watching, we can switch to David Runciman in Tanzania with reports of another starship..."

"Thanks, Rob. David Runciman here, in the Serengeti National Park, Tanzania, where as your studio guests reported, at 11.31 Greenwich mean time a vessel appeared in the sky above the park, heading slowly north-west..."

Geoff unrolled his softscreen from his arm, spread it on his lap and tapped the control bar.

Sally tore her gaze from the TV screen. "Geoff?"

"Just checking something..."

He brought up a map of Africa on the softscreen, zoomed in on Namibia, pushed the map north-west through Tanzania and Uganda, until arriving at the city of Timbuktu.

He said, "The ships are pretty amazing even on TV, Sally. Imagine seeing them in the flesh."

Her heart did a quick somersault. "You mean...?"

"If we get to the park before six," he said, "we'll be able to witness the ship's fly-by."

"Even if it *is* an invading ship?"

He squeezed her hand. "I can't miss an opportunity like this, Sal."

CHAPTER SIX

ALLEN SLAPPED HIS softscreen to the dashboard and kept half an eye on events unfolding around the world.

They left Kallani and headed west, in a couple of hours leaving the drought-stricken area of Karamajo far behind them. The terrain changed, became rolling and relatively green – not as sodden and fecund as the English countryside he'd left, but nothing like the dead, parched land of Karamoja.

"...and the outbreak of non-violence continues," said the London-based BBC anchorman. "LA is reporting its first day in living memory when there have been no reports of murders or muggings. The same is true around the world. Some governments have welcomed the phenomenon, while others have counselled caution. Meanwhile, world religions..."

He glanced across at Sally. She had drawn her hair back and tied it in a ponytail. She turned her head on the head-rest and smiled at him.

"Can you tell me, Geoff, why I don't feel... threatened?"

He'd been thinking the very same thing. Since his earlier suggestion that the 'outbreak of non-violence,' as the BBC had it, might be a prelude to alien invasion, he'd had time to reconsider.

"What happened to me aboard the plane," he said. "I know I wasn't hallucinating. It *happened*. It was real. And I know it was linked..." He gestured to the softscreen. "There was something I forgot to tell you earlier – about the experience. While I was flat out in the grey fog... before and after the silver spider did whatever it did to me... I saw a figure, a shape. Just the head and shoulders of someone. And I felt... I don't really know how to explain it... I felt reassurance in my head, and the words, *Do not be afraid*." He shook his head. "And I wasn't. I was suffused by peace."

"I thought you said, earlier, that the non-violence suggested invasion?"

"I know I did. And it does. Rationally, what has happened – our inability to fight, the arrival of the ships... it all points to an invasion. And yet the overwhelming sensation I received while they were doing whatever they were doing to me was one of peace."

She reached out and stroked his thigh. "Don't. That frightens me, the thought of their doing something to you."

He shook his head. "The odd thing is, Sally, that it doesn't frighten me in the slightest."

He felt her gaze on him, and when he looked at

her she was frowning. "You said it was a *human* head and shoulders..?" she said.

"That's how it appeared to me, and yet at the same time it felt... alien." He stopped himself there. "Or did it? I don't know. Maybe it's only in retrospect, after the arrival of the ships, that it occurred to me that the figure was alien."

They fell silent. On the softscreen, studio guests were debating the starships' arrival.

"Of course," a uniformed General was saying, "everything suggests that we should proceed with utmost suspicion. The fact that our military capability, worldwide, seems to have been compromised is an indication that the vessels' arrival is hostile in intent–"

"On the other hand," a scientist interrupted, "their preventing our ability to commit violence might be seen as a blessing, an endowment, and not necessarily as a precursor to hostilities."

"I am merely stating the need for caution," the General said.

The anchorman stepped in, "That's an interesting point Jim Broadbent makes there, General; we've been assessing what has happened in terms of potential threat. Perhaps we should take time to look at other possibilities..."

"Of course," Broadstairs said. "As a scientist I like to run a number of thought experiments, initially giving equal validity to all possibilities before dismissing them. One thing that has occurred to me is the nature of the starships' arrival here. They in no way seem to me the harbingers of invasion.

Look at the facts. They appeared simultaneously at eight locations around the world, and they seem to be making their way – if our calculations prove correct – to one of the most uninhabited regions on the planet. This, to me, is not the manoeuvring of an invading army."

The General said, "I merely counsel caution. If we are dealing here with... with extraterrestrials... then it would be dangerous indeed to attempt to second-guess their motivations."

The scientist was about to step in with a rejoinder to that when the anchorman said, "Gentlemen, I'm afraid we must leave it there for the time being, though undoubtedly we'll return to the debate as events unfold worldwide. In our Cambridge studio we have Xian Chen Li and Peter Walken, professors respectively in neuroscience and sociology... If I might begin with you, Professor Walken, and ask you what the long term consequences of this so-called outbreak of non-violence might be?"

"*If*, that is, the outbreak is indeed long term," Walken stipulated, "and not a temporary effect..."

Allen was listening to the broadcast while concentrating on the track ahead. They had left the metalled highway an hour ago and proceeded along a sandy track winding through hilly terrain. He calculated they were an hour from the park, with another couple of hours to go before sunset. The starship, if it kept to its current speed, was due to overfly the park at approximately six o'clock.

A while later, Sally said, "Geoff... You okay?"

He smiled reassuringly. "Fine."

"It's just..." She gestured at the screen, where the professors had given way to a reporter already in the Saharan desert north-west of Timbuktu. "What they were saying about our inability to commit violence..."

He knew what she was driving at, and he nodded. "Of course it... hurts," he admitted.

"I'm sorry."

"I mean, it's so bloody arbitrary." He glanced at her. "Take what happened yesterday, at the medical centre. The terrorists attacked, killed half a dozen soldiers, and took you and Ben..." He stopped, gripping the wheel at its apex. "It frightens me to think that if the attack had happened an hour earlier..."

He stared out at the rolling bush. Ahead and to their right a vortex of vultures swirled on a thermal. He went on, "And if the ships had arrived a couple of days ago, then the soldiers guarding the centre would still be alive. Like I said, so arbitrary."

She murmured, "And if they had arrived here three years ago..."

He smiled at her. "You're probably thinking me selfish that I'm viewing this, probably the most momentous event in human history, so personally."

"Of course not! It's entirely understandable, Geoff. I'd be looking at it in the same way."

He'd never spoken to anyone other than Sally and his sister about what had happened to his parents. He'd given her a sketched outline of the incident, and left it at that, not caring to describe his feelings at the time.

For some reason, now, he felt the need to unburden himself.

"The thing is that I almost understood why they did what they did. They were old and very, very ill. My father was eighty-nine, my mother a couple of years younger. My father's heart was rapidly failing, and my mother had terminal leukaemia. Their quality of life..."

"I understand. There were other ways of going about... ending it."

"The odd thing is that both my parents for all their lives had campaigned and fought – what a word to use! – for non-violence. So to end it like that was... shocking, somehow not right. What hurt me, and hurts me still, is that they didn't tell me or my sister about how they were feeling. I understand why – they didn't want to upset us. But they could have said something; we could have talked about euthanasia. It was a measure of their desperation, their extreme unhappiness, that they were driven to end it as they did. It was obviously a sudden thing, done on the spur of absolute despair. And thinking about their last few hours... that's what hurts so much."

Fortunately it was he who had found their bodies, not his sister Catherine.

He had taken to crossing London every other day, from his flat in Battersea to his parents' three story townhouse overlooking Hampstead Heath, to check on them, cook them a meal and chat about what he was working on at the moment. While they were slowly crumbling physically, mentally they were as alert as they'd ever been.

That spring morning he'd not visited his parents for a couple of days. He had phoned the night before, to apologise and say he'd be around in the morning – but had received no reply. He was not unduly worried, as both were half deaf and often missed his calls.

He let himself in with the spare key, called out that it was him, and ran up the stairs to the commodious, sunny lounge on the first floor.

They were seated together on the sofa facing the big bow window. At first he thought they'd fallen asleep while appreciating the spring morning.

His mother's head was resting on his father's shoulder.

He rounded the sofa and stopped dead in his tracks, shock pummelling his solar plexus.

The chest of his mother's white blouse was soaked in a bib of startling bright blood. Similarly, his father's waistcoat was stained. The pistol lay on his lap, his fingers loose around its butt.

Allen had staggered backwards, fallen into an armchair, and wept.

Later, when the bodies had been removed, Allen drove to Catherine's in Belsize Park and broke the news. He recalled little of the hour they spent together, other than telling her that *at least* his father had not shot his mother and himself through the head. It had seemed an important distinction at the time.

SALLY WAS STILL stroking his thigh, a while later, when they came to the road-block.

It occurred to Allen that it was an odd place to mount a road-block, on a flat stretch of land a couple of kilometres before the boundary of the national park. An ugly green military truck was drawn up by the side of the road and a dozen troops had erected a makeshift barrier consisting of two trestles and a length of red and yellow crime-scene tape.

The troops stood around in postures of boredom and negligence – always, Allen thought, a dangerous combination. They had rifles and machine guns at the ready, but oddly enough he wasn't encouraged by the thought that they wouldn't be able to use them.

Sally sat up. "What's happening?"

"I don't know. There's no reason for the road-block, as far as I can make out."

"How far are we from the park?"

"About two kilometres."

He slowed down as he approached the fluttering length of tape. Their arrival had galvanised the soldiers who approached the car and stood flanking it, staring in at Allen and Sally with sullen, almost petulant expressions. He glanced at their forefingers, hooked inside the trigger-guards of their respective weapons.

A sudden, alarming thought occurred to him. They were near the border with the Congo. Might these be Congolese troops, taking advantage of the arrival of the starships to cross the border to the relatively affluent Uganda in order to do a little pilfering?

He scanned the uniform of the sergeant, who had disengaged himself from his men and was striding over to the car, but he couldn't make out the soldier's insignia.

He murmured, "Keep your hands in sight at all times and don't make a sudden move." He smiled across at her. "And don't worry. We'll be fine."

He unpeeled the softscreen from the dashboard, set it on his lap, and kept his hands on the apex of the steering wheel. He smiled out at the approaching officer.

The sergeant halted a metre from the car and said, "Will you please climb out, sir, and the lady also."

He nodded at Sally, opened the door and climbed out. He felt conscious of being separated from her. The late afternoon sun beat down on his face.

The sergeant reached out. "Papers."

Allen tried not to smile at the anachronism. No one had papers these days. He proffered his softscreen. On the other side of the car, Sally was passing her ID card to another soldier.

The sergeant jacked a monitor into Allen's screen and, frowning, scanned the read-out on his own.

He said, "And why are you in Uganda, Mr Allen?"

"To cover a story in Murchison Falls park – the elephant breeding programme. I'm a photographer."

The sergeant looked over the top of the car. "And you, madam, why are you in Uganda?"

She told him that she worked for the Red Cross in Kallani.

"So you are based there?"

Sally nodded. "That's right. Yes."

"And why are you here?"

"Accompanying Mr Allen. I'm on holiday."

The sergeant looked from Allen to Sally, his gaze unreadable. "There is a state of emergency in the country now. My government has ordered that all foreign nationals must report to the Ugandan embassy for registration."

Sally made a sound of disgust. "But that's back in Kampala!"

"Nevertheless, you must report to the embassy, or you will be in breach of regulations."

Before Sally could argue, Allen said, "That's fine. We'll do that. We're due in Rangay before sunset, so if you would kindly let us past."

The sergeant stared at him, unmoving. "I must request that you turn back now, go back to the highway and head south."

Allen smiled and said patiently, "I have work to do in Rangay, a story to cover. We will head to Kampala first thing in the morning."

The sergeant stared him down. "Mr Allen, you will turn around now, head back to the highway and continue south. The country is under a state of emergency."

Allen nodded. "Very well."

The sergeant passed Allen his softscreen and he climbed back into the car. Sally slipped in beside him and slammed the door.

Allen started the engine. "So... what do we do?" He watched the troops mosey back to their truck.

The sergeant turned and stood watching him.

"What do you mean? I thought you'd agreed to the..."

"I mean, do we drive on, through the tape, ignoring the kind sergeant?"

Sally considered, smiling at him like a kid considering a dare. "Do you think they'd *try* to shoot if we did disobey them?"

"I very much doubt they'd risk shooting two foreign nationals..."

She nodded. "You've stirred the troublemaker in me, Mr Allen. Let's go."

He revved the engine and rolled the car forward through the tape. As it snapped and fluttered around the windscreen, he accelerated. He heard cries from the soldiers, saw them dash into the middle of the road behind the car. Sally swivelled in her seat. Allen kept his eyes on the road ahead.

"What are they doing?"

"The sergeant's pointing, giving orders. One of them is raising his rifle..."

Allen hunched in his seat, expecting the sound of gunshots at any second.

"And now?"

She laughed. "Nothing. The soldier's just standing there, aiming... The sergeant's yelling something. Right, he's aiming his own rifle..."

"If he aims at our tyres," Allen said, "does that constitute violence?"

"If he thinks of that, we might find out," she said.

It came to him, then, that the sociologists and philosophers would have a fine time trying to work out the parameters of intent, and how they pertained to the blanket proscription on violence.

"They're just standing there, Geoff. Not even coming after us..."

Allen relaxed, let out a long breath and finally laughed. "I don't think I've truly realised, until now, quite what this means."

Sally picked up his softscreen from where he'd

tossed it between the seats, fastened it to the dash and accessed the memory cache. "Listen," she said.

She found the broadcast of an hour ago. The neuroscientist and the sociologist were debating the embargo on violence.

Chen Li said, "What is even more fascinating is how the embargo – which we will call it until a better term presents itself – is facilitated. It appears, from reports, that individuals intent on committing acts of violence are *prevented* from doing so despite their desires. They are paralysed, frozen on the spot. They report a mechanical, a physical, inability to carry through the action their brain intends. This suggests that whatever agency is responsible for the... embargo... can effect change on some fundamental neurological level. This is both tremendously exciting, but also terrifying in its indication of the power of... of these visitors."

"What interests me," Professor Walken the sociologist said, "is the consequences of this intervention on both the individual and societal level. One thing is certain, if the embargo continues, then nothing, *nothing*, will ever be the same again on planet Earth. Violence will be a thing of the past... But, and it's a fascinating 'but', will our inability to commit violence, and our resulting repression of the act, have unforeseen psychological consequences on us as a race? Or will the fact that we cannot commit violence in time mean that we lose the desire, that the desire will be, as it were, bred out of us? That's the interesting question."

"And that, gentlemen, is where we must leave it,

I'm afraid," said the anchorman. "The debate will run and run, I'm sure."

One hour later they arrived at the national park.

THERE WAS NO one in the log cabin that served as the gatehouse to the park, other than a houseboy who told Allen that everyone was up at the 'hill' to watch the passing of the starship.

He showed Allen and Sally to their cabin, a small but comfortable three room dwelling on the edge of the lake. Sally found the refrigerator stocked with food, as per her instructions, and opened a couple of beers. Allen unfastened the French windows that gave onto a veranda overlooking the lake and stepped out, admiring the view. The sun was low in the west, smearing a gorgeous tangerine and cerise light over the bush. He looked south, but there was no sign of the approaching starship.

"I don't know about you," he said, "but I'd rather set up my stuff here than join the others on the hill."

"Me too. I don't particularly feel like company at the moment." She leaned against him, sipping her beer.

He set up his camera and checked his softscreen. He had one email from Wolfgang back at the London agency. He laughed and showed it to Sally. She read it out, smiling, "*Forget the bloody elephants and concentrate on the aliens!*"

"Will do, Wolfgang," he said.

He stuck his softscreen to the outside wall of the hut and set it running. The BBC was shuttling between their correspondents who were following the progress of the starships around the world.

According to their man in Africa, that continent's ship was passing over southern Uganda.

They stood on the veranda, arms around each other and gazing south. According to Allen's calculations the starship was three or four minutes away.

When it came, three and a half minutes later, he was surprised by his response.

He knew he would be awed, the visual artist in him impressed by the aesthetics of the experience, the brilliance of the silver-blue extraterrestrial vessel as it traversed the beautiful African sky, but he had never expected to be so *moved* by the event.

"But it's... massive," Sally gasped.

The ship slid over the southern horizon in absolute silence. Like all the others it was snub-nosed, splayed, a wedge that most resembled a manta ray. The dying sun caught its silvery tegument, giving it the lustre of a genie's lamp. Allen smiled at the not inappropriate metaphor: but what kind of genie, he wondered, might emerge?

It would not fly directly overhead, he saw, but between where they stood and the horizon. He raised his camera and took a continuous series of shots, pausing now and then to lower his camera and watch the ship's silent passage.

He calculated that the behemoth was perhaps five kilometres long, two wide from wing-tip – if they were indeed wings – to wing-tip.

To the west, silhouetted on the hilltop against the dying light, he made out a celebrating crowd, tourists and Africans alike. Their cries of delight and surprise drifted across the water. It was as if they were toasting the alien ship, welcoming it to planet Earth.

"Geoff, look..." She pointed to the softscreen on the wall. Evidently someone on the hill had a feed to the BBC, as the image of the starship above the lake was being beamed live online.

The announcer was saying, "And just in from Murchison Falls, Uganda, these images of the African starship."

It was at its closest now, directly opposite them across the lake. He tried to make out any sign of sigils or decals on its sleek flank, or seams and viewports. Even its bullish snout, where in a Terran vessel one would expect some kind of flight-deck or bridge to be positioned, was smooth and featureless. A technology beyond our ability to comprehend, he thought.

He marvelled at the privilege of being able to watch the arrival of the ship as it happened; it would be something he could tell his grandchildren.

"I remember the day the extraterrestrials arrived on Earth..."

He considered what had happened aboard the plane, the spider drilling into his head, and again he knew that, rationally perhaps, he should be apprehensive. Was it worrying, he wondered, that he was not?

He laughed aloud and pulled Sally to him, planting a big good-natured kiss on her temple.

"We're living in interesting times, girl," he said.

She looked up at him. "Isn't that a Chinese curse?"

The light diminished and slowly the starship slipped away to the north. When the vessel vanished from sight, Allen busied himself beaming his pictures back to London, then fixed a meal of salad, rice and chicken.

They ate on the veranda and then sat looking out over the lake with their beers, the softscreen playing at their side – a constant accompaniment.

At last Sally said, "I've been giving it a lot of thought, Geoff. Since yesterday, and what happened. I know I told Krasnic that I'd be leaving in May..."

He looked at her, recalling when she'd told him, last November, that she'd had enough of work in Africa and was coming home to London in May. His joy had been overwhelming.

Had she decided to stay, he wondered? Had the events of yesterday made her feel beholden to the medical centre, its staff and patients?

She turned to him. "But why wait until May, Geoff? I want out now. When we get back, I'll tell Krasnic I'll work till the end of the month, so he can find a replacement."

He reached out and took her hand. "I'm delighted, but you're absolutely sure?"

"I've never been surer of anything in my life, Geoff," she said. "I want to be with you in London."

He fetched two more beers from the cooler, and they toasted each other as the sun went down.

Beside them, ten minutes later, the tone of the announcer's voice made Sally sit up and pull the softscreen across the table.

"And there have been developments on the starship front. First, Bob Hudson in southern Spain..."

"Thank you, Sue. Yes. Just minutes ago as I speak the ship I've been tracking south across Europe suddenly disappeared, along with the seven other ships converging on the Saharan desert. We have footage here of the second it happened..." The softscreen showed the European starship moving slowly over Gibraltar when, in a flash, it was gone. "It just... winked out of existence..." the reporter concluded breathlessly.

"We must interrupt you there, Bob. We cross now, live, to Amelia Thirkell who has just arrived in the press encampment a hundred kilometres north-west of Timbuktu. Amelia, there have been developments..."

"There certainly have, Sue. If I can just set the scene here. We are – that is, the world's media – are encamped in a vast arc around what some of my colleagues have termed 'ground zero' – the locus where the starships will meet. The first people to arrive here reported that they could get no nearer than ten kilometres to ground zero, and seemed to be prevented by a... a force-field or barrier..." She pointed across the desert. "It's just a hundred metres in that direction, and surrounds ground zero in a vast circle."

Thirkell looked into the sky, an expression of wonder on her face.

"And then, literally minutes ago, just after the starships vanished, they appeared again over the darkening sands of the Sahara."

The image panned away from the reporter and lifted into the sky, where a strange and beautiful choreography of interstellar vessels was playing itself out.

Allen found himself gripping Sally's hand as they stared at the screen. Against the darkening skies, the eight identical starships approached a central locus, slowing as they came together. They hovered, silently, nose to nose, for all the world like the silver-blue petals of some vast intergalactic flower.

"Their nose-cones seem to be actually *touching*," Thirkell reported. "It's as if they're fitting together to form a vast pattern. Because of each ship's identical delta shape... they can join to form what looks like a great... snowflake."

The BBC camera looked up at the configuration at an angle of perhaps forty-five degrees, and from this viewpoint the eight starships no longer resembled so many individual vessels but one vast, interlocked shape, a great interstellar cartwheel lambent in the light of the setting sun.

Seconds later, a bright flash emanated from the hub of the configuration, a pulse of white light that spread in a concentric circle from the conjoined nose-cones to the outer edge of the ships. It did not stop there but fell, like a vast halo, towards the desert far below.

"It's coming down slowly, silently," Thirkell said in a wavering voice. "I... it looks as if it will land, or hit the ground... in the exact place where the invisible barrier or force-field prevented our forward progress..."

Beside him, Sally murmured something in wonder.

The halo of white light, perhaps a hundred metres high, reached the ground and settled. Three or four reporters – and then more and more – began to walk towards the effulgent light, their shapes silhouetted against the glow.

One or two reached out, touched the wall of light; the camera zoomed in, catching their expressions of wonder as they looked back and smiled.

Suddenly, the light began to lift. The cameraman followed its ascent to the circumference of the interlocked starships.

A chorus of cries greeted the ascent. Thirkell was saying, "I... I've never seen anything like it. This is miraculous! I don't know how to describe what has happened here in the middle of the Sahara, one of the driest, most inhospitable areas on the face of the Earth..."

The image on the screen showed the light settling around the rear of the ships and moving inwards, retracing its path towards the conjoined nose-cones.

The image, blurred, danced, as the cameraman panned down to show what was revealed on the ground.

Sally gasped, fingers to her lips, and Allen just stared in silent wonder.

The sands of the Sahara had been transformed. What before had been an undulating landscape of limitless sand was now a vast expanse of rolling green meadows, occasional oases, or lakes, with clusters of what appeared to be low-level domes occupying the glades and meadows.

The more audacious reporters, the same ones who had approached the white light earlier, now stepped forward and walked towards the margin of the paradise that had appeared as if by magic. Hesitantly, Thirkell followed them, tracked by her cameraman.

She approached the edge of the greening, rimmed by a circular silver collar that came to the height of her knees, and stepped over it. She climbed the gradient of a grassy knoll, staring about her in wonder, and when she came to the crest she turned and beamed at the camera.

"I don't know what to say. I'm sorry... This is the most amazing... Excuse me, I'm overcome by the most... I can only describe it as... as a feeling of optimism. I know that must sound crazy, even in the context of what has happened here, but..." She shook her head, words at last failing her.

The cameraman joined her on the summit of the knoll and panned, then zoomed in on the nearest dome. It was surrounded by what appeared to be a ring of cultivated land, where plants and shrubs grew in profusion.

And all around, hardened reporters were coming together and hugging. The image wobbled, showed a blur of Thirkell's blouse as she embraced her cameraman. She pulled away and looked into the sky, at the underside of the starships. "And as I stand here in this... this wonderland... I can't help but wonder when they might communicate with us..."

"And on that note," Sue said back in the London studio, "we'll leave it there. Let's stay with the images from the Sahara, the momentous images I might say, while we discuss recent events with my studio guests. Ladies, gentlemen, what is to be made of these developments...?"

Allen sat back in his seat, staring into the northern darkness where the incredible events were being played out.

Sally found his hand. "What's happening, Geoff?" she whispered.

He shook his head. "I don't know. But I do know that we'll find out, in time."

They sat side by side long into the evening, sipping their beers and watching events unfold on the softscreen.

It was after midnight when a wave of lassitude swept over him, a sudden incredible tiredness, and he tried to think back to the last time he'd slept. He'd snatched a couple of hours on the flight, and before that a few hours back in London.

He switched off the 'screen and they moved back into the hut.

They lay face to face on the bed, holding each other, and within minutes Allen was asleep.

SOMETHING WOKE HIM from a dreamless sleep.

He lay on his back, blinking up at the ceiling, and it was a few seconds before he became aware of the soft golden glow emanating from the adjacent lounge.

He sat up carefully, so as not to disturb Sally, pulled on a pair of shorts and moved to the open door. On the way he took the softscreen from where he'd left it on the bedside table, an instinctive action he was hardly aware of making.

He moved to the threshold of the lounge, and stopped.

Someone... *something*... was sitting on the edge of an armchair on the far side of the room.

Allen took a step forward, then another, and dropped into a chair opposite the figure.

It was humanoid and glowed with a golden lustre, its surface seamless and unmarked, but beneath its surface, *within* the creature, paler golden lights moved and roiled. It sat forward on the chair, its elbows on its knees, hands clasped, and seemed to be staring across at Allen. *Seemed* to be, for its face was without eyes or other features.

Allen thought of the head-and-shoulders shape that had stared down at him during his episode aboard the plane, and now, as then, felt an abiding sense of peace.

He surprised himself by asking, "Why don't I feel in the least frightened?"

The figure stared at him. He had the odd, inexplicable impression that it was somehow larger than the dimensions it presented here.

It replied, but he was unable to tell if he heard the words, or if they somehow simply manifested in his head.

"Because there is nothing to be frightened about, Geoffrey Allen."

"This... why you are here... it's about what happened to me on the flight out?"

"This is the corollary of that experience, yes."

"What do you mean?"

"We mean, I am here because of what we did to you then, Geoffrey Allen."

He sat back in the chair. He needed its support. He

took deep breaths and asked, "And what did you do to me?"

"We chose you," it said.

Allen nodded, as if this were a very reasonable explanation. "And why did you choose me?"

"Because you were deemed suitable."

"Suitable...?" he echoed. He glanced back at the bedroom door, slightly ajar, and considered Sally sleeping in there. Was this a hallucination, a hypnagogic episode brought about by lack of sleep and the excitement of recent events?

"Suitable for what?"

The figure did not answer at once, and the wait was almost unbearable.

"Suitable for what lies ahead, for the changes that will visit your race, your planet. We need people like you to present the human face of that change."

His blood felt as if it had turned to a slurry that his heart was having difficulty pumping around his body. He said, "Who are you, and why are you here, and... and what changes are you speaking of?"

"We are in the employ of the S'rene, or the Serene, as you will come to call them."

"But... but you're not one of the S'rene yourself?"

The figure inclined its featureless domed head. "I am a self-aware entity in the employ of the S'rene," it said.

"And the S'rene? Who are they? What are they?"

"The S'rene are a race that hails from a star known as Delta Pavonis. They are peaceable, and benign."

"And the reason you, they... are here?"

A pause. Then, "To help you," it said.

"To help us?" he echoed, with the first stirrings of excitement.

"To help you, before you destroy yourselves," said the golden figure.

"That would be inevitable?"

The figure, the self-aware entity as it called itself, inclined its head again. "That would be inevitable. The S'rene have seen it happen before, to other races, before they were in any position to help."

"Other races...?" Allen said, his mind spinning.

"Hundreds..." It paused, then went on, "The galaxy teems with life, with civilisations, a concordance rich beyond your imagining."

His cheeks felt suddenly wet. He realised he was weeping.

"And how will you help us?"

"We have started already," it said. "But that is only the start. Much work lies ahead, much change. The world, life as you know it, will alter for you out of all recognition."

Allen nodded. "And how can I help?"

The figure stood suddenly. When seated, it had given no indication of its true dimensions. Standing, it appeared at least seven feet tall, as proportionally broad, and it reached out a hand to him now.

"Your softscreen..."

He fumbled with it, standing before this towering giant, and held out the softscreen. The golden figure touched it, then dropped its hand to its side.

"That is all?" Allen asked.

"You will go to Entebbe at eleven in the morning. Present your 'screen at the information desk in terminal two. A vessel will be waiting to take you to the Nexus."

"The Nexus?"

The figure gestured to the screen in Allen's hand. It flared, startling him. Upon the screen, he saw, was an image of the conjoined starships above the greened Sahara.

"The Nexus," said the figure.

"And there?"

"There, you will learn how you and others like you will help to bring about the change."

Allen sat back down again, or rather slumped, and when he looked up he saw that the figure that had stood before him, so imposing and dominant, had vanished.

He was aware of another figure on the edge of his vision.

Sally stood, naked, in the doorway to the bedroom.

"Geoff... I heard you talking, and when I..." She came to him. He stood quickly and hugged her to him, needing her reassurance.

"Christ, Sally..."

"What happened?"

"You didn't see...?" He gestured to the opposite chair.

"I saw you talking to yourself. You seemed agitated, overcome with emotion. I saw you stand, and then you held out the 'screen, and moments later it suddenly flared, and you gasped."

He stared into her eyes in the semi-darkness of the room. "Sally," he said, "they are the Serene, and they have come to help us."

She took his hand and led him gently back into the bedroom.

"Come to bed," she said, "and tell me all about it."

THEY LEFT THE park at first light and drove south-east to Entebbe.

"Apprehensive?"

He thought about it for all of three seconds. "Oddly, no. Like last night, that figure... had someone said beforehand that I'd be confronted by an extraterrestrial... self-aware entity, as it called itself, I would have thought I'd've been scared to death. As it was..." He shook his head. "They instil reassurance in us, Sally. We have nothing to be apprehensive about."

"It's a lot to take on trust."

He agreed. "It is." But how to explain the sensation of benignity that the representative of the Serene had emanated last night?

They arrived at Entebbe fifteen minutes before eleven and parked in the shadow of terminal two. Allen had no idea what to expect as he entered the airport and approached the information desk, Sally at his side.

A smiling Ugandan woman took his 'screen, scanned it and passed it back. "If you would like to make your way to departure lounge three, there will be a representative waiting."

They crossed the busy concourse and hesitated before the check-in.

"So much for a week's quiet holiday together," she said.

They stood facing each other, Geoff began to speak, then fell silent.

"What?" Sally asked.

He laughed. "Oddly, I don't want to go, Sal. I don't want to leave you."

She pushed him playfully. "Don't be silly. You've got to go."

"I know. It's just..."

They kissed.

"I'll be in touch just as soon as..." he shrugged, "as it's all over."

"I'll go back to Kallani," Sally said, "settle a few things there, then take the first available flight to London."

"I'll tell Catherine you're on your way. She'll give you the spare pass key to my place. And then..." He smiled and drew her to him. "Why do we always have less time together than we want? If it's not work, it's blessed extraterrestrials!"

They laughed, then kissed farewell.

He presented his softscreen at the check-in, turned to wave at Sally, and passed through.

He was alone in a vast lounge. A sliding door at the far end, giving onto the tarmac, opened and a figure stepped through. A tall, dark European woman, in her thirties, strode through and fixed him with a professional smile. "Mr Allen, if you would care to follow me."

They left the lounge and stepped into the blistering sunlight, and crossed the tarmac.

"Are you...?"

"I was hired by an agency to meet you and your colleagues."

"My colleagues...?"

If she heard him, the woman gave no sign.

They paused before a silver, corrugated hangar, and the woman indicated a sliding glass door.

Allen stepped through. When his vision adjusted to the shadows within, he saw a sleek, jet black delta-winged plane in the centre of the hangar.

He looked behind him. The woman was nowhere to be seen.

He crossed to the plane. At his approach, a ramp extruded. He hesitated at its foot, peering up into the vessel's darkened interior.

He climbed.

Again his vision took time to adjust as he ducked through the plane's entrance. The interior was furnished with four seats, two to a side, facing each other. Three of the seats were occupied. He made out a tall African woman, a young man of Asian origin, and a middle-aged woman who might have been Arabic.

As he stared at each of them in turn, he realised that they were unconscious.

The fourth seat was empty.

He moved forward, hesitated, then sat down.

Instantly a luxurious lassitude engulfed him. He wanted to laugh out loud at the wondrous sensation as he descended towards oblivion.

He felt a subtle vibration – the plane, moving? – and then lost consciousness.

CHAPTER SEVEN

SALLY HAD AN aversion to using bribery to get what she wanted – aiding and abetting a system that was responsible for much that was at fault in the continent of Africa – but in this instance it was the only way to achieve her goal.

It cost her one hundred US dollars, slipped into the cold palm of the desk sergeant, to be allowed into the holding cell at the Kallani police headquarters.

She was taken to a tiny concrete room, divided by floor-to-ceiling bars, with a plastic bucket seat positioned on either side of the bars.

She sat down. A minute later the door in the other half of the cell opened and Josef Makumbi, shackled hand and foot, shuffled through.

He looked sullen, and his eyes widened fractionally when he saw her.

He slumped into the seat and stared at her.

"Hello, Josef."

He stared at his lap, then looked up at her. "What do you want, Dr Walsh?"

She looked at the man who had cold-bloodedly taken the lives of at least four of his colleagues. She was tempted to ask him why, but restricted herself to the reason for her visit.

She said, "Three days ago I was taken, along with Dr Ben Odinga, by three men who drove us north and held us prisoner. One of the men was named Ali." She hesitated. "Who was he, Josef?"

He stared at her with bloodshot eyes, and surprised her by asking, "Why haven't they beaten me, Dr Walsh? They brought me here, locked me up, and then one man, a big sergeant, he comes in with a baseball bat... I could see the look in his eyes. He wanted to kill me, Dr Walsh. He wanted to punish me for what I did." He shook his head. "And he tried to. He lifted the bat, tried to hit me, but something stopped him."

She said, "I want you to tell me the full name of your accomplice, Ali, and where I might find him."

"Will they kill me, Dr Walsh? I know they want to, for what I did."

She shook her head and ran a tired hand over her face. She felt the sweat and grime of her long drive north. She said, "Please, tell me Ali's full name and where I might find him."

He stared at her.

She returned his gaze, looking into the eyes of one of the last men on Earth, she realised, to commit the act of murder. At any other time she would have been curious to know what had motivated the man to turn on his colleagues – but all she wanted now was to confront the man who had tormented herself and Ben, to hear his side of the story.

"Well?" she said.

"If I tell you, they will not beat me to death?"

She inclined her head. "I promise."

He nodded, licked his lips. "His name is Ali al-Hawati, and he is from the village of Benali. He has a wife there, but no children. He works as a fisherman on the river."

The village was a hundred kilometres east of Kallani, on the border with Kenya. It would be a long, hot drive, with no guarantee at the end of it that she would be able to find and confront the man who would have willingly taken her life and filmed the process for all the world to see.

She would never have had the courage to attempt to track down her tormentor, normally. But, with the coming of the Serene, things were very different.

She stood. "Thank you, Josef."

"You will make sure they will not beat me to death, Dr Walsh?"

She stared down at him. "You have nothing to worry about on that score," she told him, and left the cell.

EARLIER THAT DAY, after arriving at Kallani from Entebbe, she had met Yan Krasnic and told him of her decision to leave Kallani and return to England. She offered to work until the end of the month, but Krasnic smiled and said, "No, you can go now. The relief team arrived yesterday, and since the coming of the starships... well, we can concentrate on treating victims of the drought, of famine. No more do we have to contend with the casualties of war and bush skirmishes, though for how long that might last..."

"And you?" she asked.

He looked through the window of his surgery. Krasnic was in his early fifties. He looked about seventy. "I'm okay... After what happened the other day, I too have decided to return home, to Croatia. It's a beautiful country, Sally. I miss it. I think I will retire."

She hugged him before leaving, then found Ben Odinga and said goodbye.

"God is great," he said, smiling at her. "I will miss you."

She returned to Mama Oola's, packed her scant belongings, and said a tearful goodbye to the matriarch, promising to return one day.

Then she had made her way to the police headquarters and bribed the grinning desk sergeant.

She left Kallani at one o'clock and drove east. While at Entebbe that morning she had booked a flight to London on a plane leaving Uganda at noon the following day. That would leave her with enough time to do what she had to do, for her peace of mind, and return to Kampala in the morning.

As she drove through the drought-stricken, sun-pummelled land, a hellish landscape devoid of life, where even the trees stood stark and leafless like charcoal twigs in the parched earth, she considered her motives in confronting Ali al-Hawati.

What did she want? For that matter, what did she expect?

She did not want to know of his motivations, for she could guess them. He was politically driven, or religiously driven – they were one and the same. He wanted his worldview to prevail, and saw her and her fellow aid workers as legitimate targets in the war against decadent Western liberalism.

She had no illusions that she would gain his forgiveness; he would hate her now – if not more so, given her escape – as he had hated her the other day.

No, what she wanted was to look him in the eye and tell him that his chance had come and gone, that, with the coming of the Serene, the opportunity to get what he and his fellow believers wanted was a thing of the past. She wanted to tell him that he had lost the war, and that everything would be very different, now.

She wanted to tell Ali al-Hawati that no longer did she fear him and his kind.

Then she would smile, and turn her back on him, without flinching at the thought of attack, and walk away.

As she drove through the punishing afternoon heat, she turned the car radio to Uganda FM and listened to the latest reports from around the world.

She would have liked to have had Geoff's softscreen with her now, despite her frugality and anti-materialism that had never allowed her to indulge herself. For the past few years she had made do with a cheap wind-up radio to provide her with news of the outside world.

Republicans in America were encamped outside the White House in protest at their government's inability to confront the extraterrestrials. Shares in arms manufacturers around the world had tumbled, and in the States the gun lobby and pro-hunting groups were vociferous in their complaints about having their rights violated by the aliens. The President had gone on live TV last night to demand a meeting with the leader of the 'alien invasion.'

Sally smiled to herself and tuned into a music station.

Three hours later she came to the river and the village of Benali, its inhabitants stirring in the cooler hours of late afternoon. Women washed clothes in the river and children played with tyres in the dusty streets. It was a scene, typical of Africa, which had changed little in a hundred years.

She made out a large number of Yemeni men and women among the Ugandans. After the Israeli strikes on Sana in 2019, displaced Yemenis had fled south, settling in Ethiopia, Somalia, and even as far as Uganda. They were largely fisher-folk, drawn to the coastal regions or, in this case, the wide river on the border with Kenya.

She braked on the crest of the road overlooking the village and the river. The shanty town looked impoverished, a series of corrugated metal huts, patched with multi-coloured polythene sheets – where Islamists must have found eager recruits among the poor, displaced Yemenis.

She wondered if al-Hawati had been lured into terrorism by the promise of riches, or the reward of a martyr's place in paradise. Would she despise him any the less had his motivations been the former?

Her arrival caused a commotion amongst the village children. They flocked around her car, keeping a safe distance, watching her with big eyes, mistrustful yet curious.

She climbed out and smiled at the children, African and Yemeni, and singled out the tallest – a boy clutching a deflated vinyl football – and said, "I am looking for Ali al-Hawati, a fisherman. Do you know where he lives?"

This provoked an intense and noisy debate among the crowd. The boy with the football shouted loudest, then looked at Sally. "He lives beside the river. Come with me."

She followed the boy, followed, in turn, by the ragged posse of village children, chattering among themselves.

A few days ago, she thought as she hurried down the sandy track after the boy, she would never have dared enter a Yemeni village known to harbour terrorists. Even now she experienced a residual fear at what she was doing, tempered by the knowledge that no one, now, could harm her physically.

Nevertheless, as they turned a corner and came to a line of huts fronting the river, her heart set up a laboured pounding.

A Yemeni woman in a stained shalwar kameez and a half niqab veil sat before the second hut, mending a fishing net. She looked up and stared at Sally, her brown eyes massive above the fabric that covered her mouth and nose.

The young boy said something to the woman, and without a word she stood and hurried into the hut. Behind Sally, the children stopped as one and watched in silence.

Seconds later a man, wearing only shorts and a ripped vest, stepped out.

He stopped dead when he saw Sally, and she was gratified at the expression of shock on his thin face. The jagged scar that ran across his cheek was red raw; he had declined her advice to seek medical help.

In English he said, "What do you want?"

"I came to see you, Ali."

His eyes narrowed, flicked beyond her to see if she were alone.

"Why?" he snapped. "What do you want with me?"

Behind him, the woman – presumably his wife – ducked from the hut and stood watching them.

Ali turned and, with surprising vitriol, shouted at the woman. Her gaze fell from Sally, as if in shame, and submissively she scurried back inside.

"I came, Ali, simply to talk."

Her words discomfited him; his sneer faltered. He looked beyond her at the gallery of watching children, and he gestured with anger and yelled at them in Arabic.

When Sally turned, she saw that every last one of them had fled.

She wondered at the power this man had wielded in the village, and if the reason for the anger that manifestly simmered beneath the surface of his superior demeanour was that he realised, with the coming of the Serene, that his ability to command fear, and therefore respect, would in time diminish.

They stood in the late afternoon sunlight, facing each other, and Sally felt as if they were the only people in the world.

"I came to tell you," she began, "that what you did the other day, when you attacked the medical centre and kidnapped me and my colleague, made me more fearful than I had ever been in my life. I feared what you were going to do to me. And at the same time I was angered by my powerlessness to do anything to prevent what you were doing. To you, I was nothing – I, who had for years helped Ugandans and Yemenis, was less than nothing in your eyes. You would kill me and film my death, and show it to the world... and that filled me with anger and hatred and fear."

He spat, "You are all the same, Westerners, men and women, you bring your ideas here and we do not want them!"

Sally smiled. "And that's where you're very wrong, Ali. You see, we are not the same at all. It's convenient and easy for you to think that we are all the same, but unlike you and people who think like you, we, my colleagues at the centre, are all very different in our opinions and politics, our beliefs or non-beliefs. I work with Muslims and Christians and atheists, with many nationalities... We are all very different, but we work together for the common good." She shook her head. "But I could talk to you for a million years, and I would never make you understand the values by which I live."

"I despise your values!"

She smiled at him, and said softly, "But you do not know my values, Ali. You do not know who I am, or what I believe." She waved, as if to dismiss all this, and went on, "But the reason I came here is to tell you, Ali, that I no longer fear you. Everything is different now, with the coming of the aliens. They have brought a truth to our planet which you, in your ignorance, will have to come to terms with. Perhaps, in time, you will learn peace, and look back and see the wrong you did. I hope so. But..." she smiled at him, radiantly, suddenly overwhelmed with a feeling of liberation, "I want to tell you that I no longer fear you, and nor do I hate you."

She reached into the breast pocket of her shirt. "I have brought you something, Ali."

She held it out.

He stared at the small tube of antiseptic in her hand.

"For your infection. It needs treatment."

With great deliberation, he filled his mouth with phlegm and spat in the sand at her feet. "I do not need your Western medicine!"

She shrugged, returned the tube to her pocket, and turned to leave. This was the moment she would turn her back on him, fearing nothing, and walk away.

He said, "What now?"

She hesitated. "What do you mean?"

"You have told the police about me, where I am?"

"I've told them nothing," she said. "But I think Josef Makumbi might. He is in jail now, and in time he will be questioned by the police, and in fear I think he will tell them everything."

She smiled at the sudden flare of alarm in his eyes, and it filled her with satisfaction.

He stepped towards her, his intent obvious. She held her ground, did not flinch as he came within half a metre of her and tried to raise his arm.

His inability to carry through the action that his will dictated, the thwarted expression on his face, was almost comical to behold. He began to shake.

She peered at him. "Go on, Ali. Try it. Hit me. That's what you would like to do, isn't it?" She shook her head. "The days when you could dominate with violence are gone, Ali. Goodbye."

She turned, a feeling like jubilation swelling within her, and walked away.

She was halted by another cry, but this one was not from Ali.

His wife had emerged from the hut, a plastic carrier bag clutched in her right hand.

She surprised Sally by saying in English, "You are leaving Benali?"

Sally nodded. "I'm going to Kampala."

The woman hesitated. Ali stared at her, a look of terrible realisation dawning in his eyes.

At last his wife said, "Please, take me with you. I wish to leave."

Ali shouted something in Arabic, took a step towards his wife. She flinched, cowering and bringing her arm up to protect her face. Ali stood over her, frozen, and tears tracked down his face, trickling into the runnel of his scar.

Slowly, Sally stepped forward and took the woman's arm. "Come with me," she said softly.

Silent, eyes fixed in fright on her husband, the woman nodded. Sally drew her away, along the track from the river towards the road and the hill where her car was parked.

Behind them, Ali cried out. He was giving chase, calling out almost incoherently. His cries drew an audience of faces which emerged from the huts on either side and stared at him, which enraged him further.

They reached the car and Sally opened the passenger door and the woman, clutching her scant possessions to her chest, slipped inside.

Ali stood beside the car, ranting now, attempting to reach out but each time finding his movement restricted like a puppet whose controller was suffering a fit.

Sally climbed in behind the wheel and started the engine. Beside her, the woman pulled down her veil and spoke quietly to her husband through the open window. Ali opened his mouth to reply but, this time, no words came.

Sally looked at Ali, and their eyes met. He spat, "You will not win!"

"This is not about winning or losing," she said. "It is not a contest."

They left the village of Benali and headed south.

They were silent for a time, and then Sally asked, "What did you say to him?"

The woman stared ahead. "I simply told him that I have never loved him, and that every day with him I dreamed of escaping," she said, then went on in almost a whisper, "Four days ago he told me what he was going to do to the people he took from the medical centre – to two doctors. He was proud and boastful, but when he came back here yesterday he was quiet, and he said nothing about what had happened."

"We escaped, my colleague and I."

The woman smiled. "Escaped, like I am doing now."

They drove on in silence, and a little later Sally asked, "You have money? Will you be okay in Kampala?"

"I have saved a little. I will be fine. In Kallani I trained to be a secretary. I can use a computer and many programs, though for many years I have mended fishing nets and suffered my husband's beatings."

Sally slowed down and held out her hand. "I'm Sally," she said.

The woman smiled and took her hand. "I am Zara," she said, "and I am very happy to be leaving."

Sally smiled. "I know exactly what you mean, Zara," she said.

She accelerated, heading south towards Kampala, and smiled as she considered the new life awaiting her in England.

CHAPTER EIGHT

ALLEN CAME AWAKE instantly. He knew exactly where he was and experienced no sense of dislocation. He looked across the aisle at the two facing seats, and then at the one beside him. They were empty. He wondered if the others had been awoken one by one so that, for whatever reasons, they could not confer.

A golden strip pulsed on the floor before him, the only light in the darkness. He stood and followed it, stepped from the plane and found himself in an identical darkness, illuminated only by the golden strip that extended for perhaps five metres before him. He followed it, walking steadily. The odd thing was that, as he went, the length of the strip remained the same; he had the peculiar sensation of walking on a treadmill.

Another odd thing was that he was not in the slightest apprehensive or even overawed. He was aboard an alien starship, he told himself, experiencing that which no human being, other than those who had accompanied him aboard the plane from Uganda, had experienced before. Yet he felt only an intense curiosity. He wondered if the Serene were responsible for this state of mind, too; they had the capability of inhibiting the act of violence in human beings, after all. Perhaps they were dictating his feelings now... and what about his thoughts?

That way, he realised with a smile, lay madness.

He must have been walking for five minutes. He stared into the darkness but could make out nothing, and the glow in the floor revealed nothing of his surroundings either. He realised, then, that although he had carried his holdall aboard the alien plane, he had left without it.

A minute later the glow stretching out before him became shorter, then vanished. He came to a halt in the absolute darkness and waited. Again he felt no fear.

Seconds later he felt something touch the back of his legs; some slight force applied pressure behind his knees; quickly, and involuntarily, he fell into a sitting position. He was caught by something soft and accommodating, like the world's most comfortable armchair. He sat back, his head against softness, his arms outstretched on some kind of rest.

Then the darkness lifted slowly.

He was seated in what might have been some kind of vast amphitheatre created from the soft, black substance which cradled him – cradled him, he saw, and thousands of others. To either side, and above and below, he made out men and women of all races. Like him, they were staring around in awe.

His nearest neighbour, a young Indian woman, was perhaps three metres away, a distance sufficient to make casual conversation difficult. She caught his eye and smiled briefly, and Allen smiled and shook his head in complicit wonder.

The amphitheatre swept around in a vast ellipse, dotted with representatives of humanity ensconced in the sable padding.

He felt an immense emotion – joy and privilege – swell in his chest.

Only then did he turn his attention to the well of the amphitheatre. A glow resided there, like a pool of molten gold, and he knew where he had seen it before: emanating from the nose-cones of the conjoined starships. He guessed, then, where he was; the amphitheatre was somehow formed from the front sections of each of the eight Serene starships.

The Nexus?

As he stared down, the glow swelled from a flattened disc to a pulsing globe, and from it strode a number of golden figures identical to the one which had presented itself to Allen back at Murchison Falls.

He counted a dozen figures ranged in a semi-circle and facing the massed representatives of humanity, and he knew that they continued all around the amphitheatre, hidden by the spherical golden glow. The one before Allen's section seemed to hover in mid-air, staring directly at him.

Behind the figures, the golden glow diminished, sank, became again a disc. Then that too vanished, to be replaced by an aerial view of the verdant paradise created in the Saharan desert. As he watched, the oases appeared to be increasing in size, growing ever outwards.

A voice, issuing from the golden humanoid before him, said, "The new city continues to grow, and will soon cover the entirety of what was once the Saharan Desert."

Allen heard a collective gasp from those around him.

"The city is the first of many we will grow around the globe," the figure – or rather all the figures around the amphitheatre – went on. "In two days we will move on, first to central China, then India and Siberia, followed by Alaska, Brazil, Australia and Borneo."

Further around the amphitheatre, someone stood up, a tall, southern European woman, who said, "If I may ask: why are you doing this?"

"We are creating the cities as the second phase of the programme to assist humanity in its growth towards stability and continuance. An immediate need for much of humanity is a number of sustainable mass living areas, integrated urban units where millions can live and work without fear of poverty, starvation, violence, political subordination or intimidation."

"And who will govern these cities?" the same woman enquired.

"They will be self-ruled by elected representatives of each city's population."

"And the governments in whose countries these cities are situated?"

"In time," came the reply, "the function of national governments will be a thing of the past. Nationalism will fade, along with concepts such as national borders and boundaries."

A murmur of comment swept around the amphitheatre.

A human voice, belonging to someone on the far side of the vast chamber, said, "You've created this... this city in the Sahara, one of the most desolate, inimical regions on Earth... but how will it be sustained? What about things like energy, water...?"

"We are in the process of creating desalination plants to convert sea water," came the reply, "and as for energy... The Serene possess the technological wherewithal to beam limitless energy to the surface of your planet. We have solar converters, machines which transfer the energy of your sun – and others – to wherever in the galaxy we require it."

Allen smiled at the very idea, then laughed aloud.

The woman who asked the original question stood again. "If I may say this – my original question has not been answered. Why are you doing this?"

There was a pause, then the figure spoke. "We are intervening here on Earth because your race has, in the past few hundred years since what you term your industrial revolution, grown exponentially, a growth fuelled by a fatal combination of political greed and lack of foresight. What is even more tragic in your situation is that many of you – both on an individual level and on that of institutions – know very well what needs to be done in order to prevent a global catastrophe, but cannot enact change for the better because power and vested interest rest in the hands of the few."

Allen sat back and closed his eyes, and wished that Sally was here to hear what the Serene were saying; she would be unable to restrain her tears of joy.

The voice went on, "No shame should accrue in light of these facts; no individual is really at fault. The process was vastly complex and incremental, a slow-motion, snowballing suicide impossible to stop. A hundred, a thousand races across the face of the galaxy have perished in this way, before we had the wherewithal to step in and correct the aberrant ways of emerging races."

A ringing silence greeted the words, before someone asked, "And how many races have you saved from themselves?"

"Approaching one hundred."

"And did they ask for your intervention?" It was a rhetorical question.

"That was impossible, as you well know, for they did not know of our presence until our arrival, just as you did not know of the Serene until recently."

"And they welcomed your actions to save them?"

"There are always, among the races we assist, those individuals and organisations who oppose our intervention, for they have much to lose: namely, power and wealth. However, these people in time come to realise the rightness of what we are doing."

Someone nearby stood up, a small Oriental man who asked, "And what say will the human race have in how these changes will be instituted?"

"That depends on the nature of the changes in question: some, like the creation of the green cities, the institution of solar energy – and the concomitant cessation of the production and use of current, polluting forms of energy – are non-negotiable, for they are fundamentally necessary for the safe continuance of the human race. Other changes, political changes, will be in your hands, though guided by our suggestions and expertise."

An African woman stood and said tremulously, "You... you have banished violence from the planet. I... I would like to know how long will this last? Did you do it so that we could not oppose you with our armies, or...?"

The golden figure spoke. "We have assisted you to achieve the state of non-violence – which several of your philosophies have been advocating for centuries – not so that you would be unable to oppose us, which would have been impossible, but so that you can live now without fear of violence, either individual or state. This is not a temporary measure, but ever-lasting."

A gasp raced around the amphitheatre. Someone said, "But... violence is something inherent in the psyche of the human race, an action and reaction hardwired into us on some fundamental, chromosomal level, surely..."

"Violence has been inherent in the evolution of the human race, just as it has been and is in the animal kingdom. But there comes a time when the urge to violence needs to be outgrown, when the consequences of violence threaten the very chances of racial, global survival."

"But surely there will be... psychological, not to say societal, consequences of our inability to commit violence?"

The golden figure pulsed. It spread its arms in an all-encompassing gesture. Allen saw the other golden figures, arced around the amphitheatre, do likewise. "You are correct, there will be consequences, and some of them will be adverse... But none will be as destructive or damaging as the continuance of your ability to conduct violence upon each other would have been. We will ease you through the transition, be assured of that."

Someone said, "You said you have intervened with other races? And these have managed to overcome their species' violence?"

"All races are different, as you might imagine. Some fare better than others in their periods of... readjustment. We know that the human race will thrive and prosper."

A silence grew, before the next question. The small Indian girl next to Allen stood up and said, "This must have taken a... a long time to set up. How long have you been... watching us?"

Allen had the impression then that the golden figures around the chamber were smiling. "We have been aware of the human race for centuries," they said. "When the time was right, we applied ourselves to the study of your particular problem. We have been closely monitoring developments for the past two hundred years, and working to intervene for the past one hundred."

"You saw us develop nuclear weapons," someone said, "and use them... and yet you did not see fit to step in then?"

"But when," said the figures reasonably, "would have been the right time to step in? Appalling though nuclear weapons are, they are responsible for fewer deaths than the invention of the simple sword. Should we have intervened then? No, the time was right when two factors concurred: when you became technologically capable of wiping yourselves out, and when you had the intellectual capability to understand your place in the universe and the rightness of our need to intervene."

A silence lengthened, and Allen found himself standing. "Why," he asked, "are we here? Why have you chosen *us* to tell all this to?"

He sat back down, frustrated that he had not asked more – like, what had happened aboard the plane, with the silver dancing spider; just what had the Serene done to him and, presumably, to everyone else in the amphitheatre?

"You were chosen," said the golden figure before Allen, "because the Serene need human representatives to assist with the many changes that will affect Earth over the coming decades. You were chosen, all ten thousand of you, because you were assessed and found to possess the attributes required by the Serene."

Someone asked, "Which are?"

Again Allen gained the impression that the figure before him was smiling. It gestured with an outstretched hand and said simply, "Chief of all, you posses humanity, an empathy with your fellow humans, a common decency. You are, if you like, representatives of your race."

Allen stood again. "But what *exactly* do you want with us?"

The figure inclined its head, a gesture he recalled from the figure which had visited him back in Uganda. "One day a month, maybe two, you will be required to work for the Serene, to travel the world and, in time – when we have established settlements on other planets of the solar system – to those too. You will liaise with people working in various positions on the many projects we are establishing to bring change to the world, whether these projects are political, technological, scientific, social... For the duration you are working for the Serene, you will be unaware of what you are doing. Those days will be, as it were, blank; you will have no memories of what you did, who you met, or what you talked about."

Someone objected, "But that's wholly unreasonable!"

"But necessary," said the golden figure. "There will be those amongst your kind who are opposed to the Serene and the changes we are instigating. If you retained awareness of the work you do, you could be compromised, endangered. It will be safer, for yourselves and for the success of the various projects undertaken, for you to work in ignorance. However," the figure went on, "those amongst you who do not wish to lend themselves to our ends, who feel they cannot work within this remit, are free to absent themselves from proceedings."

Seconds elapsed. Allen considered what they had been told, thought through what he was allowing himself to do, and did not demur. He swept his gaze around the auditorium. Here and there he saw figures disappear, absorbed back into the padding which cradled them. Someone nearby was thus retracted, his place taken by a seamless black void.

The golden figure went on, "Very well. Thirty of you from a total of ten thousand have decided not to take part in what lies ahead. They will be returned to their lives without prejudice, but without any knowledge of what occurred here today."

"And the rest of us?" someone asked.

"Shortly, you too will be returned. You will retain memories of what happened here, and in a little under a month you will be contacted."

"And will we be... compensated for the work we do for the Serene? Many of us have jobs which..."

The golden figure interrupted. "You will not be paid, as such, to work as representatives of the Serene; however, nor will your work situations be prejudiced." The figure spread its arms. "In time, the nature of work as you know it will change, as your society changes. With limitless energy, with advanced computer systems, with much production automated, you will find that you have increased leisure time... which in turn will bring its own demands."

A silence developed, and then someone asked, "Why should we trust you? Why should we take on trust everything you have said? For all we know, you might be the front for some hostile alien invasion."

"I assure you that that is not the case, as you know..." And, again, the intimation that the figure was smiling. And the representative of the Serene was right: Allen knew, somehow without knowing quite how, that the invasion was wholly peaceable.

The African woman stood up again. "You said that there are other races that you've helped, out there in the universe... But when will we meet them? When will the human race be allowed out of the solar system to mix with these other races?"

He looked across at the woman, admiring her foresight.

"It will happen in time," the golden figure said. "You are not prepared, quite yet, but that will change. One day you will meet beings similar to yourselves, and many wholly dissimilar, which inhabit the breadth of the galaxy."

Allen looked at the African. Her mouth was open in wonder.

The golden figure finished, "Shortly you will meet individually with us, and any last questions will be answered."

Seconds later the golden figures fade from sight. The panoramic view of the Saharan city vanished, to be replaced with the golden glowing disc, and suddenly it felt as if he was being absorbed into the very fabric of the padding around him.

He was back in darkness, with a golden strip glowing on the floor before him.

He was eased into a standing position, and stepped towards the lighted strip. He followed the light, but this time walked only a few paces before he found himself once again taken up by the padding. He sat, waiting, and a second later a golden figure manifested itself before him.

As earlier, in the lounge back at the national park, Allen made out flashes and pulses of light within the body of the figure, and again he wondered at the nature of this 'self-aware entity'...

The figure reached out towards Allen's right hand. It held something – a band of gold the identical colouration of itself – and slipped it over his hand. Allen looked down. A slim bangle sat on his wrist, warm to the touch. As he stared, it seemed that the band was absorbed into his flesh. Seconds later it had vanished.

The figure spoke. "Mere monitoring devices. Do not be alarmed. They also allow us to communicate with you."

Allen said, "You said that you'd answer any final questions?"

The figure inclined its head. "That is so."

"In that case, what happened to me, and presumably to the others out there, when time seemed to stop and I saw a silver...?"

The figure raised a hand. "It was not as you assumed. You saw what you thought was a spider, felt it *invade* you... This was your mind, making sense, as it were, of sensual inputs which were beyond its comprehension. It merely substituted images, sensations, that you could readily comprehend."

"Then what *did* happen to me?"

"Your mind was audited," the golden figure told him. "Your identity was accessed, recorded, and found suitable. The exact process of what we did would be beyond your scientific comprehension."

"And... and how you managed to stop the entire human race from committing violence? Presumably that, too, would be beyond my puny intelligence to comprehend?"

"Intelligence does not come into the equation," it said. "Rather, you – and I speak here of 'you' as the human race – you do not have the required scientific knowledge to understand the process whereby the Serene facilitated *charea*, as we term it, a word allied to the Hindu concept of *ahimsa*. Suffice to say that on a level of reality beyond the sub-atomic, there are fundamental particles – which you call strings – which are accessible and are... the only word I can find that remotely suggests the term we use, is 'programmable.' Through this readjustment of fundamental reality, the Serene brought about *charea*."

"The domes...?" Allen began.

"The placement of the domes was necessary in order for the Serene to bring about the successful implementation of the *charea*."

"And the Serene?" Allen asked. "You are their... their acceptable face, perhaps? What are they like in reality? Why don't they show themselves?"

"They are humanoid in appearance... not dissimilar to yourselves."

"And not monsters, repellent to our senses?"

"By no means."

"Then why don't they show themselves to us? I take it they are somewhere aboard these ships? Would it be possible to meet one...?" The very idea of it, he thought; to meet the aliens responsible for the salvation of the human race...

The figure hesitated. "There are no Serene aboard the *kavala*, the eight ships. They are few in number, and spread wide throughout the galaxy. We do their bidding, in their absence."

Allen wondered whether he should be put out, on behalf of the human race, that the Serene did not see fit to be present during the momentous changes taking place on his planet. He said, "The golden figure I met earlier, in Uganda... it said that it, you, were 'self-aware entities'... But what does that mean? Are you... robots, androids, or something my puny intellect cannot comprehend?"

"We are living, biological beings, self-aware, individual, conscious – but grown, as it were, and programmed with the... desires, is the right term... of our mentors, the Serene."

"And have you yourself ever met a member of the Serene?"

The figure gazed at him. "That honour has never befallen me, but several of my contemporaries have had the privilege."

"And what are the chances that I might one day meet a Serene?"

He sensed the being smile. "As a selected representative of an uplifted race," it said, "the chances I would assess as... *good*."

Allen smiled, then laughed. "If I'd been told about any of this a few days ago..." he began.

The golden figure said, "And now, if you have no more questions..."

"I have about a million, but it'd take a year to think of how to phrase them."

"There will be time enough in the years ahead, my friend. Now, you wish to be transported to London?"

He stared. "How could you possibly know that?"

The figure inclined its domed and pulsing head. "The Serene know so much," it said, and faded from view.

The padding around Allen flowed, returned him to an upright position. He followed the golden strip-light on the ground, and minutes later found himself aboard the alien plane. He was the first human of four to take his seat, and the second he did so he slipped into unconsciousness.

SPRING HAD COME to London, sunlight replacing the grey drizzle he had left just days before – but that was not the only change. The ad-screens plastered across the walls of buildings as he came into Victoria monorail station no longer flashed with tawdry advertisements. Every one of them showed the eightfold coming together of the alien starships over rural China, and the growth, on the parched land far below, of a second green city.

He noticed a change among his fellow Londoners, too. There was a collective air of excitement about the place, a buzz he had experienced only in times of momentous events – the outbreak of war, or Great Britain's victory in the 2022 World Cup. Everyone was discussing the arrival of the aliens – the fact that they were called the 'Serene' was not public knowledge yet – and it appeared that even now, in the early days of the *charea*, some subtle change had come over the citizens of the capital. Was he imagining it, or were people more polite to each other, more respectful? As if, concomitant to the blanket ban on violence, individuals were wary of showing even such nascent signs of violence as bad temper or irritability with their fellow man.

He wondered how long it might be before a more unconscious psychological response manifested itself? Denied the cathartic release of violence might some individuals, the psychotic and unstable, suffer increased mental conflict? And what about citizens who never thought of resorting to violence? Would the very fact of violence being denied have some effect on society as a whole? No doubt, over the days and weeks ahead, the newsfeeds and TV channels would be bursting with pundits expounding their views at length.

On the way from Heathrow he read on his softscreen that the very first official communiqué from the alien ships had been received at the UN headquarters. The Visitors – as the news media had dubbed them – had announced that they would broadcast their intentions to the world at three that afternoon, Greenwich mean time.

Just as he was about to alight at Victoria, and take the underground to Notting Hill – where Sally would be awaiting him – he heard a couple of businessmen discussing in anxious tones what the aliens might have planned. One invoked the old film *Independence Day*, another *The War of the Worlds*, and both agreed that the end was nigh... Nursing his knowledge like a privilege, Allen felt like telling them that they were foolish and that there was nothing to worry about.

He left the carriage and took the packed escalator down to the Tube, and as he made his rattling journey west to his apartment and Sally, he saw his first case of 'spasming,' as it came to be known.

A dozen school kids were arguing in the aisle. In the general verbal to and fro, one particular insult was taken badly and a youth moved towards another, anger on his thin face. He pulled a knife, drawing gasps from nearby passengers, then stopped suddenly, his face twitching, his entire body convulsing as if in the grip of some autonomic malaise.

"He's spasming! Spasming!" the others taunted, dancing around the stricken youth.

Allen stepped from the train at Notting Hill, thinking that the display of spasming and the resulting taunts were eminently preferable to the violence that had been circumvented.

HE UNLOCKED THE door to his flat and stepped into the hall, the pleasurably tight pressure of anticipation within his chest. He heard a sound from the lounge, dropped his holdall and waited for Sally to emerge. She appeared in the doorway in faded blue jeans and a white cheese-cloth blouse. She stopped there, her breath caught, then rushed at him. He lifted her off the floor and it came to him that the heft of her in his arms, her reality, was far more meaningful, far more emotionally resonant, than his recent encounter with the extraterrestrials.

He carried her into the lounge and collapsed on the settee; they kissed and hugged, pulling away frequently to look at each other.

She appeared far more beautiful than he recalled her ever being in Africa; her face was fuller now, no longer taut and stressed, and she'd had her hair cut and styled, shortened to shoulder-length.

"You look... incredible."

She laughed. "It's great to be back. I can't believe the range of food. I forgot what London was like... I'm eating well. I've put on pounds!" She patted her perfectly flat stomach and laughed.

"All the more to love," he said.

She tugged at his shirt, and they undressed and moved to the bedroom.

Later, lying face to face in the sun that slanted in through the bay window, she stroked his arm and murmured, "Tell me all about what happened on the alien ship."

"The Serene," he said, "hail from a star twenty-odd light years from Earth, a star we call Delta Pavonis."

He told her about his experience aboard the nexus of alien ships, the amphitheatre containing ten thousand fellow human representatives, and what the 'self-aware entities' had said.

He seemed to talk for a long time, recounting his impressions, his feelings.

"And they chose you," she said, as if in awe.

He laughed. "For my humanity, my empathy."

She whispered, "Which is the reason I fell in love with you, Geoff Allen."

"Thank you. But enough of me. What have you been up to?"

"Well..." she began, then told him about the encounter with her kidnapper in the village of Benali.

"And... how did he react?"

"With anger, especially when I offered him antiseptic for his face... He came for me and..."

He said, "There's already a term for it." He described the youths he'd seen on the Tube earlier. "It's called spasming."

"That's exactly what happened when he tried to attack me. He stopped dead, taut, and... *spasmed*."

She was silent for a while, thinking back. He said, "It must have been... satisfying."

She nodded. "Yes. Yes, it was. But then... then something happened, and I don't know whether I did the right thing, or..."

"What?"

She sighed. "Ali had a wife, Zara. It was obvious from how he spoke to her that... that he treated her like an animal, to be blunt. When I was about to leave, she ran from their hut and asked to come with me. I... I don't know whether what I did then was a sadistic impulse, done to get another one over on my enemy... or done out of altruism. I said she could come with me, and we made for the car, Ali following in distress and anger, and spasming as he tried to prevent Zara from leaving him."

She fell silent, shaking her head.

She murmured, "She told me about her life as I drove down to Kampala. You wouldn't believe it, in the twenty-first century. She was little more than a slave. Ali wanted a son, but Zara fell pregnant twice and both times with a girl, so he forced her to terminate the pregnancies. And he beat her, abused her. She's an educated woman, not that that makes the slightest bit of difference to the reprehensibility of his attacks. But she was clever enough to know that she deserved more. And then with the coming of the Serene... this gave her the courage to act."

He thumbed a tear from her cheek. "Sally, you did the right thing. Don't browbeat yourself trying to scrutinise your motivations."

"But one's motivations are important, Geoff. They're who we are, after all."

He smiled and shrugged and wondered why some people tortured themselves like this, needlessly examining their actions and reactions and the reasons for them.

"You're a good person, Sally."

She looked momentarily unhappy, then said, "Don't you question yourself, Geoff? Analyse your motivations?"

"I don't know. Sometimes, maybe..."

She smiled, reached out and stroked his cheek. "That's one of the things I love about you, you know, you're so..."

"Go on, say it. 'Simple'."

She laughed. "Uncomplicated."

He remembered something, looked across the room at the wall clock and said, "It's a quarter to three. The Serene are broadcasting an announcement on the hour. We could go down to the King George and watch it there?"

"Let's do that," she said, jumping out of bed and dressing hurriedly. "I could kill a G&T."

On their way to the pub, arm in arm, they discussed the ramifications of the Serene's *charea*.

"So much will change, Geoff. It'll take us a long

time, and much soul-searching, to adjust ourselves, our psyches, to the consequences. I was reading yesterday about suicides, or potential suicides. They can't kill themselves, though dozens have blogged about trying to find inventive, non-violent ways to do so... Intentional 'accidents', by whatever means – but they all fail."

"Which will have its own psychological fall-out," he said. "The shrinks will have a field day."

"Have you seen the coverage from America? The Republicans are up in arms – well, they would be, if..." She laughed. "They're demanding action from their government – as if the government could act! It's nice to see the all-powerful demon rendered impotent for once." She smiled. "The gun lobby refuse to believe it's not some temporary thing that will go away so they can go back to the good old days of being able to shoot each other with the slightest provocation."

"Well, they can still bear arms, as per the Second Amendment... They thankfully just can't use them."

"You obviously haven't heard the latest. I don't know if it's any more than a rumour – but I wouldn't put it past them. Apparently some arms manufacturer is looking into developing something called Random Factor Weaponry. It's based on the theory of intended or unintended consequences. If you pull a trigger, they say, and the obvious consequence is that it will result in the death or injury of someone, then the act is rendered impossible thanks to *charea*. But if there were some randomised factor built into the pulling of the trigger, or the pressing of the button... so that the action *might not* result in death or injury, then, according to the theorist, this could be a way of getting around the Serene's proscription on violence."

Allen shook his head. "I sometimes despair..."

"The delights of capitalism for you."

For a Saturday afternoon, the streets of London were preternaturally quiet; he put it down to the imminent announcement from the Serene. Everyone was at home in front of their televisions, awaiting the most momentous broadcast in history.

Sally said, "And your golden men, the 'self aware entities', have been seen all over the place."

"They have?"

"Reports have come in from around the world. Citizens have seen them standing on rooftops, on mountainsides, just standing there, absolutely motionless and silent, just watching..."

They pushed through the entrance of the King George, and Allen was surprised to see that the main bar was only half full. A flatscreen TV played in the far corner. He ordered a pint of Fuller's best bitter and a gin and tonic, and carried them to a table before the flatscreen.

They clinked glasses. "Here's to the Serene."

"To the Serene."

They stared up at the screen, which showed an aerial shot of the eightfold arrangement of starships over China, and the expanding green city far beneath. Seconds later the image switched; the murmuring of fellow drinkers ceased and a sudden silence fell across the bar.

A golden figure, swirling with interior light, stared out of the screen.

It spoke – its tone, Allen realised for the first time, neither male nor female.

Beside him, Sally reached out and gripped his hand.

"We are the Serene," said the figure, "and we have come to aid the people of planet Earth."

CHAPTER NINE

JAMES MORWELL COWERED in the corner of the bathroom, naked, as the woman – also naked – advanced on him.

Every Friday morning at nine o'clock Cheryl, a statuesque mulatto hired from a very discreet escort agency, visited him at his penthouse suite for a little recreational rough and tumble. Today they had started in bed, where Cheryl usually warmed up with a few well aimed slaps preparatory to a barrage of fists. This morning, however, she could not even manage the slaps. She straddled him, lifted a hand, and spasmed.

He glanced down at his flaccid member, knowing that it would only respond when the first blow landed. Even closing his eyes and thinking of past times, Cheryl drawing blood from his lips with her jabbing uppercuts, failed to stir his quiescent libido.

He'd rolled off the bed, shouting at her to follow

him, and retreated to the bathroom. This, usually, was the culmination of the session and the high point of her visit. His father had once, and only once, taken a bat to James in his fourteenth year, and far from shying away from the pain, Morwell Jnr. had relished it.

As with most things in his life these days, he thanked, and blamed, his father.

"Hit me, for chrissake!" he yelled, curled like a foetus between the bath and the toilet bowl.

Cheryl picked up the baseball bat and advanced, a look of determination on her beautiful face. She raised the bat, paused, and froze in that position like some perfect statue of Amazon power.

"Do it!" Morwell yelled.

She strained. The muscles of her upper arms spasmed.

She lowered the bat, sobbing. "I... I'm sorry. It's impossible. I can't..."

Damn the Serene, he thought. Not content with undermining his business ventures, their *charea* injunction had brought an end to one of the few pleasures he had left in life.

He stared up at her as she towered over him.

"Jesus... Okay, take a piss. You can do that at least, can't you?"

With luck, a little golden shower might retrieve the situation.

Cheryl lodged a bare foot on the toilet cistern, squatted above him, and obliged.

*   *   *

LATER MORWELL SLIPPED Cheryl a cheque for a thousand dollars, showered, and took the elevator down to the boardroom.

Yesterday, just after the Serene had addressed the world, he'd called in the heads of his various corporations. The earliest they'd been able to gather had been eleven this morning, and Morwell had spent a tortured evening fretting about the collapse of his empire; not even Lal's honeyed words of reassurance had helped him this time.

He stepped into the boardroom and looked around the oval table. Everyone was present, and a gallery of more terrified faces he'd never seen. Terrified, he thought, for the most part; though one or two cocky bastards looked almost smug – no doubt relishing his predicament.

He sat at the head of the table, Lal at his side, placed his fingertips together, and said, "Right, no beating around the fucking bush this morning. Let's have it. As usual, from my left. Jennings?"

Ralph Jennings, the CEO of Morwell Media, an organisation spanning the globe and encompassing TV channels, online sites and a thousand newsfeeds, was a bulky, tanned Texan who exuded confidence. He, of everyone around the table today, appeared the least concerned.

"I know the coming of the Serene is a double edged sword, but in terms of Morwell Media it's proved a helluva draw. Viewing figures across the board are up seventy-three per cent and advertising revenue has consequently rocketed by some seven billion, total. Of course, that was before yesterday's announcement."

"Of course," Morwell said with bitterness. He looked along the table at Raul Nader, the smug European bastard in charge of Morwell Energy. "So... give me the bad news, Nader."

Nader cocked an impeccably plucked eyebrow. "To employ an Americanism, Mr Morwell, we are going down the john. We're stuffed. When the Serene announced the limitless flow of solar energy... our shares plummeted even further than they had been doing. Not that we're alone in this–"

Morwell leaned forward. "I couldn't give a shit whether we're alone or not. All I want to know is how Morwell Enterprises is affected, okay?"

Nader gave one of his smug smiles. "I would have thought the larger picture, the vaster scheme of things, is the only way to approach what's happened over the past couple of days. Merely concentrating on our own performances..."

"Go on."

"...is pointless. We might as well admit that nothing will be the same again. Everything is changed, now. You heard what the Serene said."

"I heard the fuckers very well, and I want to salvage what I can."

The bastard had the temerity to laugh in his face. "Salvage what? This is the end of everything as we know it. Capitalism, as such, is history. You might as well face it, sir: Morwell Enterprises is dead in the water."

What hurt so much, Morwell thought, was to hear the truth from such an arrogant slime-ball as Nader.

Composing himself, he looked down the table

at Valery Rasnic, the Serb who headed Morwell Defence, the arms division of Morwell Enterprises. "Valery?"

The slab-faced Serb looked grim. "Our shares were wiped off the board overnight, sir. They're valueless. We can't even sell our holdings at a ninety per cent loss."

"We could," Nader put in silkily, "always start producing ploughs..."

Rasnic glared at Nader.

"There was a little hope in the hours before the announcement," Rasnic said. "Perhaps the non-violence was only a temporary measure. But..." he spread his hands. "That's not to be. We are dealing here with a race so far in advance, technologically, of ourselves..."

Morwell turned to Lal. "You've been looking into how the Serene effect what they call *charea*?"

Lal said, "I have experts in a dozen fields working on the problem, sir. The first reports should be with me in a matter of hours."

"To what end?" Nader asked. "You saw their ships! Christ, they're *growing* cities in the deserts out there with technology we can't even dream about. They've stopped every citizen in the world from committing acts of violence. Let's be honest with ourselves, we have no way of comprehending how the Serene are doing what they're doing."

A silence greeted his words. Morwell regarded his conjoined fingers. He looked up and said, slowly, "You sound, Nader, as if you think this... *invasion*... is a good thing."

Nader pursed his lips, rocked his head in that insufferably arrogant manner of his. "You want my opinion, the planet was stuffed until the Serene came along. Global warming, resource depletion, wars and terrorism... The end was in sight. Only a fool could oppose what they've done."

Morwell pointed a finger at him. "That's where you're very wrong, Nader. We at Morwell are proud of our optimism... You don't think I was sitting back and doing nothing, for chrissake? Look at the billions I sank into clean fusion, the atmosphere clean-up technology... I had experts, futurologists working around the clock..."

"To come up with solutions that might ameliorate global conditions minimally, just as long as they didn't impact on increased Morwell profits."

Morwell made a pistol of his fingers and said, "Nader, you're..."

The bastard climbed to his feet, smiling. "Save your breath, Morwell. I resign. Not," he added, as he strode away from the table, "that there's much left to resign from."

He closed the door quietly behind him as he left the room.

Lal leaned towards Morwell and murmured, "I'll have Nader's deputy fly in and meet us. He's an able man."

Morwell nodded, distracted.

He looked around the table at the half-dozen silent men and women, heads of his chemical division, advertising, mining and the rest...

They were frozen, frightened of saying a damned

thing lest they incur his wrath. The hell of it was that he understood something which they had so far failed to grasp: his wrath was worth jack-shit now. He was powerless, and he knew it. Perhaps it was sheer disbelief, or lack of imagination, which kept them looking to him loyally for all the answers.

He nodded, and one by one the rest of his team gave their bleak reports: they all said pretty much the same, that shares were plummeting, the market was moribund, that a hiatus existed until the Serene made their next announcement and the restructuring of world markets and global industry commenced.

Towards the end of the meeting he said, "I, along with every other head of industry in the US, have been summoned to the White House tomorrow to meet our illustrious, but impotent, president. Apparently we're meeting with 'representatives' of the Serene, and there we will learn what the future holds for us, if anything. Word is that the existing infrastructure will remain, though altered, with experts in place to ease us through the interim period of... adjustment."

He looked around the table. He was met with understanding nods, the occasional timid smile.

"Very well, that will be all. I'll convene a meeting in five days to go over what we've found out. Thank you all for coming."

As the boardroom emptied, he turned to Lal. "Fetch me a coffee. And then there are one or two further things we need to discuss."

*   *   *

"SO WHAT'S THE story with these sightings of so-called golden men?"

He sat before the floor-to-ceiling window, cupping his coffee in both hands, and stared out down the length of Manhattan. Nothing at all seemed to have changed out there; life went on as usual. It might have been a week ago, with no one dreaming of the Serene...

"There were rumours at first. People reported seeing tall, silent golden figures. They were stationed in elevated positions, staring out, unmoving. Then footage started coming in."

Lal tapped his softscreen and routed the image to the wallscreen. Morwell swivelled his chair and stared at the scene. A cityscape, somewhere in America, and on a tall building a golden figure, staring down with authority, a certain silent majesty.

"They remain in position for up to six hours," Lal said, "then simply fade away. People have tried to get near them, but can only approach to a distance of a couple of metres, then they come up against a... some kind of barrier, sir. An invisible, irresistible force." He tapped the screen again and the image changed. The next one showed a young man approach a golden figure on a hilltop. He reached out, his outstretched hand hitting something solid, then patted his way around the figure like a mime-artist.

"Okay," Morwell said, "I get the picture."

"I have our best people looking into the manifestations, sir," Lal assured him.

Morwell nodded. "And what's the situation with the random factor weaponry you told me about?"

Lal cleared his throat. "There have been... developments, sir," he said, and tapped his softscreen.

"I had Adams in weapon technology and Abrahams in computing put their heads together and they came up with something. The basic idea is to utilise the idea of unintended consequence, or accidental ramifications, to develop an effective weapon that would circumvent the Serene's *charea*."

He tapped his screen again and the image on the wall showed a young man garbed in what looked like a prison uniform. He was seated in a chair with a skull-cap fastened to his shaved head. The man's eyes looked dead, or drugged.

"We found a volunteer from a local psychiatric institute. He has a long history of suicide attempts and self-mutilation, occasioned by manic depressive episodes. He also happens to be terminally ill. We cleared it with the family's lawyers, and agreed to pay out a generous compensation package." Lal smiled. "The young man was the perfect guinea pig, as it were."

Lal indicated a computer terminal to the left of the image. "What we have here, sir, is the working end of the device. It's basically a computer system that randomises the results of certain initial inputs."

"In plain English, Lal."

On the screen, a white-coated figure swung a keyboard on a boom so that it hovered before the seated young man. The image froze.

"Put simply, the subject presses one button on the keyboard before him. Now, this command initiates over a thousand possible results. The initialisation begins a sequenced command cascade, the majority of which subsequent commands will result in the electrodes in the subject's skullcap failing to work. However, just one command in the millions generated will result in the desired effect – the electrodes firing and bringing about the subject's death." Lal smiled. "It works on the principle that an action taken might, somewhere down the line, result in an accident – and accidental deaths are not proscribed by the Serene."

Morwell frowned. "But doesn't that mean the subject will have to hit the command millions of times to achieve the desired result?"

Lal smiled. "No. The single command initiates a million such commands within the system's program."

"I see," Morwell said, leaning forward. "Ingenious. And?"

Lal tapped his screen and the still image unfroze.

The young man leaned forward, reached out and attempted to tap a key on the board before him. His hand froze and he spasmed.

Morwell grunted. "But did the subject know what he was trying to do?" he asked.

"That's the worrying thing, sir. He didn't."

"And yet he was stopped by the Serene, by their *charea*, from going through with the action...?" He shook his head. "The Serene have got that one covered, too."

He sipped his coffee and turned to the view over Manhattan. He recalled something Lal had told him late last night. "And what about these 'representatives' of the Serene? They're human, I take it?"

Lal sat side-saddle on the desk. "Apparently, yes, sir. I've been collating reports from around the world and it appears that an unknown number of humans have been selected, randomly, to facilitate the work of the Serene on Earth. As of yet, the identities of these people are not known – we only know of the 'representatives' because a few individuals spoke of being approached by golden figures and being told of their selection, though they have no recollection of being 'deselected,' as it were – these memories have only been recovered later when these people became suspicious of 'lost' hours and underwent hypnotism. It appears that the Serene are keen to keep their representatives incognito."

Morwell leaned back in his chair and considered what Lal had just told him.

He pointed at his Indian facilitator. "Lal, I want you to start an investigation. This is priority. It's important to know who these 'representatives' of the Serene are, what the exact nature of their work is, and why they were chosen. Work on it."

"Yes, sir. Is that all?"

Morwell nodded, and Lal hurried from the boardroom.

Alone, he contemplated the events of the morning, one of the most disastrous business meetings he'd ever chaired.

Still, not everything had gone wrong.

When Cheryl had copiously urinated over him that morning, he'd managed to achieve a brief erection.

CHAPTER TEN

DAWN WAS LIGHTENING the skies over the Bay of Bengal when the midnight train from Delhi pulled into Howrah station.

Ana Devi, dressed in the shalwar kameez she'd stolen from Sanjeev, and a new pair of sandals bought from her savings, jumped from the last carriage, squeezed through a gap in the corrugated iron fence, and made her way quickly across the goods yard to where her friends would still be sleeping. She high stepped over the rusty tracks, lifting the leggings of her shalwar so as not to dirty the bottoms.

She was still trying to come to terms with what had happened to her over the course of the past day.

She, dalit Ana Devi, an orphan street kid with no education, little money and few prospects, had been selected by an alien race known as the Serene to act as a representative, along with thousands of other people from around the world...

She had even stood up in the vast gathering of the representatives and found herself asking a question. Later, one to one with a golden being, she had asked further questions, and found out much more.

For one or two days every month, she would be called upon to travel the world and liaise with those working for change; before then, however, the Serene had given her a specific task to accomplish.

Everything had changed now; nothing would ever be the same. She thought of the people who had made her life a misery, starting with the low-lifes like Sanjeev Varnaputtram and Kevi Nan, then the various station workers and the corrupt policemen, right up to the scheming, greedy politicians... No longer would they be able to wield their power, backed by the threat of violence, that had made her life, and those of many others, a living hell for so long. The rich had a shock coming; the poor could anticipate poverty no longer.

She wondered what her friends might have to say when she told them that she was taking them away from the station and the hazardous, hand-to-mouth existence they had become accustomed to for years?

The goods yard was quiet, the silence broken only by the distant, familiar cannonade of dull successive clankings as engines buffered wagons together on the far side of the yard. She had often been awoken at dawn by the noise; she wondered if she would miss it.

She came to the wagon that doubled as the station kids' bedroom. She stood on the cracked wheel below the sliding door, reached up and hauled it open. A gap of six inches allowed a shaft of sunlight to fall across perhaps twenty sleepy children, squirming like piglets and calling out in feeble protest at being woken.

Someone looked up, saw her and cried out, "Ana! It's Ana!"

She climbed into the wagon and hugged her friends, tearful at her reception.

"But where have you been?"

"We thought you were dead!"

"We heard you'd got away from fat Sanjeev..."

"You been gone for days!"

Everyone was wide awake now and crowding around her, eager to hear her story.

She stared around at the wide-eyed, expectant faces.

"Kevi Nan took me," she began. "Jangar caught me and Prakesh, and Kevi Nan paid the bastard for me. He took me to fat Sanjeev and the bugger tried to fuck me." She stared around at the circle of faces, looking for Prakesh.

"Dalki told us you'd got away," a tall boy called Gopal said. "He said you flew through the window and lost yourself on the crowds on Moulana Azad Road."

"But that was two days ago, Ana. Where have you been all this time?"

"Why didn't you come straight back to us?"

She raised a hand to silence the questions. "I got away from Sanjeev because of what the aliens, the Serene, have... have done to us, the human race."

Danta, a six-year-old boy and the youngest of the group, held up a flattened, melted water bottle. "I put it on the chai-wallah's brazier, Ana, and made my own spaceship!"

She smiled. The melted bottle did slightly resemble a Serene starship. She was always amazed at her friends' imagination and ingenuity.

"No more can anyone harm us," she said. "Sanjeev tried to hit me with a stick, but he couldn't do it, so I jumped through the window and ran. After that I went to the park and slept in the bushes, and then..."

She stopped, staring around at the expectant faces. "And then I had a dream, and I was visited by a golden figure, someone who works for the aliens, and he told me to go to Delhi airport where a plane would take me to Africa."

She had expected cries of "Liar!" or at least looks of disbelief, but all she saw on the faces of her friends were expressions of amazement.

She looked into their eyes, one by one. "The plane took me to the aliens' starships high above the new city they have made in the African desert, and there I saw many other people from around the world who have been chosen to work for the Serene."

They stared at her, comically open-mouthed. At last a little girl said, "You, Ana Devi...?"

She nodded, and was suddenly aware that she was weeping. "Me," she said, "Ana Devi... They want me to help them bring peace and prosperity to *everyone* in the world."

She dashed away her tears; she had to appear brave in front of her friends. She told them about the day or two every month when she would travel the world, working for the aliens. "But first," she said, "the Serene asked me to do something very important. We are leaving the station," she went on, raising her voice above the babble of excited chatter, "and travelling south to a new home."

A tumult of questions greeted her words. Ana silenced them and said, "Gopal, what did you say?"

"But how will we leave Kolkata? We have no money!"

Anan reached into the pocket of her kameez and pulled out thirty silver tickets. "I have these," she said. "We will leave on the eight o'clock train to Cochin, and get off at Andhra Pradesh in the middle of India."

"Why there?" more than one child asked.

"Because that is where the Serene want us to live."

"But *how* will we live?" someone else asked. "Will we steal and beg and sell lighters as we do here? And is there a big station there where we can make our home?"

Ana shook her head. "We will be given houses," she said, "and we will work in proper, paid jobs."

She saw flattened palms pressed to cheeks, wide astonished eyes, open mouths and many tearful eyes.

She looked around the group again; Prakesh was not among her friends.

She said, "Prakesh?"

Someone replied in a small voice, "When you got away from Sanjeev, he sent Kevi Nan for Prakesh, who was in Jangar's office polishing his boots and cleaning his leather belt. Kevi Nan paid Jangar and took Prakesh to Sanjeev."

Ana felt anger swell in her chest. "And he has been there ever since?"

Everyone nodded.

She thought about what to do, then said, "We cannot go without Prakesh, so together we will go to Sanjeev's and free him! Do not be afraid. Remember, fat Sanjeev and his men can no longer harm us, ah-cha?"

She turned without a further word, jumped from the wagon and marched across the interlaced tracks. She paused before the iron fence, and only then looked behind her. She had expected perhaps three or four followers – but smiled when she saw that everyone, even little Danta, had crowded after her.

She led the posse through the fence, across the car park and down the warren of alleys towards fat Sanjeev's house.

Five minutes later they came to the timber gate in the high wall. Gopal and three others had picked up a split railway tie from the goods yard, and now they used it to great effect. They battered the timber against the lock, and after three blows the gate shuddered open.

The kids surged in, led by Ana.

She ran up the overgrown path, through the open front door and into the tiled hallway.

Kevi Nan and the two big Sikhs sat crossed-legged on the floor, smoking a hookah. They looked up, surprised, when Ana appeared on the threshold, bumped forward by those behind her.

Kevi jumped to his feet, followed by the Sikhs. "What do you want?" Kevi said.

"Where is Prakesh?" Ana asked.

The Sikhs moved, stationed themselves before the door to Sanjeev's room. Ana found Gopal and whispered, "Follow me."

She hurried from the hallway and turned right, forcing her way through the shrubbery. They arrived at the shuttered window, and Gopal did not have to be told what to do.

He and a friend launched the battering ram at the shutters and they flew apart like kindling.

Ana climbed through the window, recalling when she'd escaped from here two days ago. Now she jumped down from the sill and stared around the glittering, candle-lit room.

Fat Sanjeev sat upright on his bed, naked and glistening with oil. Lying on his belly beside him, also naked but sound asleep, was Prakesh.

Sanjeev glared at Ana. "I thought, as violence failed to give me what I wanted with you, I would be gentle with the boy. But..." His gaze slipped to the sleeping child. "But it would seem that even peaceable pleasures are denied me. Take him!" Ana crossed to the bed, knelt and stroked Prakesh's short hair. "Prakesh," she whispered. "It is me, Ana. Wake up." She shook his shoulder, gently.

His eyelids flickered and he stared up at her drowsily.

"Prakesh," she said, "I have come to take you away from here."

He sat up on the edge of the bed, and Ana found his shorts and t-shirt on the floor and dressed him.

Sanjeev said, "He might be a little unsteady on his feet, Ana Devi, as we shared a little Bombay rum."

She averted her eyes from the fat man and tried to shut her ears to his words. She pulled Prakesh to his feet. He swayed against her, and Gopal took his arms and together they walked him across to the window.

Outside, twenty faces peered into the room, staring at Sanjeev with fear and hatred in their eyes.

Ana helped Prakesh over the sill, then climbed out herself. She paused and turned, staring into the room illuminated like a stage.

Sanjeev was smiling at her. He even lifted a hand in farewell. "Until next time, Ana," he said.

She shook her head. "We are leaving Kolkata," she said, "and never coming back. I hope I will never see you again, Sanjeev Varnaputtram."

She had the sudden urge to reach back into the room and upset a candle so that it set fire to the curtains... but something stopped her – and she did not know whether it was the *charea* of the Serene, or her own conscience which made her turn and hurry from the open window.

They returned to the goods yard and Ana ordered everyone to gather their scant belongings. As they were about to set off for the station, Ana cornered Rajeev and Kallif and said, "You are coming too?"

The pair of ten year-olds regarded her suspiciously. "You said..." Kallif began.

Ana interrupted, "I am not sure I want to take two little spies along with me."

They stared at her in silence, their big brown eyes regarding their bare feet.

Ana said, "Why did you tell fat Sanjeev all about me, hm?"

On the verge of tears, Rajeev said, "He made us spy on you, Ana. Then he asked many questions. He said that if we didn't tell him all about you... he said he would hurt us again."

"So you told him all about me, and he gave you sweetmeats and barfi in payment for your treachery..."

Kallif began blubbering. "But we did share them, Ana."

"Can we come with you?" Rajeev begged. "Please don't leave us behind!"

How could she, in all fairness, leave them here to suffer at the hands of fat Sanjeev?

At last she nodded. "But from now on, no spying, ah-cha?"

They beamed at her. "Thank you, Ana! Thank you!"

THEY MADE THEIR way to platform six, where the Cochin Express was steadily filling with passengers for the long cross-country journey.

She found carriage C, the rag-tag gaggle of street kids on her heels. A liveried attendant barred her way. "The train is full!" he snapped. "Everyone is heading south to see the alien starships. Go back and watch the show on television. *Chalo!*"

Smiling, Ana withdrew the tickets from her pocket and waved them at the man. "I have tickets for my twenty-three friends and myself, with six to spare."

He took the tickets, examined them with incredulity, and shook his head. "Where did you steal these from, girl?"

At the end of the platform, a whistle sounded and the guard shouted, "All aboard!"

"Allow us to board the train like all the other passengers with valid tickets," Ana demanded.

"You are thieves and dogs–" the attendant began.

Ana squirmed past him, pulling Prakesh after her. The others followed quickly. The attendant cried out and tried to stop the snaking street kids. They evaded his grasp with practised ease, and he stepped forward and raised a hand to lash out at them.

Ana turned to see the mortified attendant spasming, and her friends filing past him with verbal taunts and their own mimicry of the man's galvanic, puppet-like spasms.

She led the kids to their seats and eased Prakesh down beside her. The other passengers were staring at Ana and her friends, some with distaste and others with tolerant amusement. Ana smiled back at them, defiantly. Minutes later the train pulled slowly from the platform.

She stared through the window at the decrepit station sliding past. She saw the buildings and advertising hoardings that she had known for years, the familiar faces of the station workers. She looked up, at the footbridge high above, and saw a grey-furred monkey staring down at her. The odd thing was, she thought, that she felt not the slightest regret at her departure.

His head on Ana's shoulder, Prakesh murmured, "Where are we going, Ana?"

As the train slid from the station, she told him.

GOPAL WAS THE first to see the Serene starships.

They had been travelling for hours when Ana fell asleep, tired from staring out of the window at the passing countryside, the farmers toiling in the fields, identical stretches of dun-coloured land passing by without variation.

Gopal's cry woke her in an instant. She sat up quickly, then worked to control her panic. She no longer had to fear being awoken in the dead of night by someone's alarmed cries, ready to run from whoever had a grievance against her and her friends.

"There!" Gopal pointed, pressing his face against the window. Ana peered and made out, high in the distance, the ellipse of the eight conjoined starships. At this distance and angle they presented a discus-shape hovering over a green blur of land on the horizon.

"What did the Serene look like?" Danta asked.

"Were they green?"

"Did they have big eyes and claws?"

"Were they monsters?"

Ana smiled and said that she had not seen the Serene aboard the starships. The golden figure had explained that they were few and far between, and were not monstrous but humanoid.

"But who are the golden figures?" Gopal wanted to know.

"They work for the Serene," she replied.

"Like slaves?"

Ana laughed. "No, more like... like servants."

Of course, she thought, the golden figures might not have been telling the truth: what if the Serene looked like monsters, like big hairy spiders which human beings would find horrible to look at; what if the golden figures were just human-shaped in order to set human minds at rest?

She realised that, even if this were so, it did not really matter. The Serene had brought peace to the Earth for the first time in living memory.

Two hours later the train drew to a halt at the town of Fandrabad and Ana led her little tribe out into the sweltering midday heat.

They left the station, along with a thousand other pilgrims, all chattering excitedly at what lay ahead. Ana came to a sudden halt on the steps of the station and stared in amazement at the sight that greeted her.

On the edge of the small town, a great shimmering wall of white light stretched away on either side for kilometres. If she stared hard she could see through the veil of light. She made out a stretch of green land, dotted with domes and other buildings, but faint as if seen through gauze.

It seemed as if every TV and satellite station in India, and beyond, was gathered at the foot of the shimmering light, along with crowds of curious Indians and even a few Westerners. In many places the crowd stood five deep, attempting to see what lay beyond the veil.

"What now?" Prakesh asked.

She looked around at her group. "Now we go to the light," she said. "Follow me closely."

She gripped Prakesh's hand and led her band towards the noisy crowd. The hubbub of chatter increased as they drew nearer. Food vendors had set up stalls around the light's perimeter, and big pantechnicons belonging to the satellite companies blocked the road. Ana led the way around the truck, and past reporters holding microphones and talking about the wondrous extraterrestrial visitation.

The crowd was thick before them, eager pilgrims pressing up to the white light and peering through. Ana watched as the occasional daring individual reached out and touched the light, then turned and excitedly reported that it felt *solid*...

Ana recalled what the golden figure aboard the starships had told her.

She looked back at her gaggle of rag-tag street kids, clad in torn shirts and shorts, most barefoot, some with flip-flops. "Now everyone hold hands so that we're all linked together," she instructed.

Like this they moved around the circumference of the light, Ana attempting to find an area where the crowd was not so thick. Their passage aroused much comment and the occasional insult. "What are these little animals doing here?" one fat Brahmin called out. "Cannot the police do their job for once?"

"Get back to the slums, harijans. There is nothing out here for you."

Ana ignored the shouts, heartened that the name-callers were often shouted down by their fellows: "Show the children some respect, ah-cha? We are living in a time of peace."

At last the crowd thinned before the wall of light, and Ana led her children towards an area where a line of citizens only three deep stood gazing through the light.

She stopped, turned and addressed her friends. "Make sure that we are all together and holding hands. Follow me, and do not stop walking as we approach the light..."

Prakesh stared at her. "We're going *through* the light, Ana?"

She grinned. "Wait and see."

"But someone said that the light was *solid*!"

"Just trust me, ah-cha?"

She stepped forward and tried to ease her way past the cordon of curious individuals. "Excuse me, please. Can we come through...?"

The crowd parted with reluctance, one or two people muttering at the kids.

Ana paused before the wall of light and looked up. It rose high into the sky, and to the left and right. She stared through the light and made out a rising stretch of green, like the brightest lawn she had seen on the softscreens in the restaurants along Station Road.

She turned to her children and said. "Remember, hold hands, and do not let go. Now follow me!"

People laughed. "And where do you think you're going, slum-girl? Do you think you and your kind will be allowed into paradise?"

Hardly daring to hope that the next few seconds might make these people eat their words, she closed her eyes and stepped forward, into the light.

She heard gasps from behind her, then startled cries. She walked through the light and felt the ground beneath her feet change from sandy soil to soft, springy grass.

She opened her eyes and stared around her. The rest of the children had passed through the light with her, hand in hand, and stood about in mute startlement. Ana looked back through the light and made out faces pressed up against the barrier, staring at the street kids with envy and incredulity.

Before them, a great town spread out to the horizon, bright green grass and silver domes, tubular silver towers and other, similar-shaped buildings, but these ones laid out flat along the land.

She looked up and gasped. High above was the great conjoined disc, like a shield in the sky, of the Serene starships.

Ana led her children up the gentle incline towards the nearest dome.

THEY WERE MET by a tall Westerner who called himself Greg and led them further into the town to a building which, he said, they could call home. The low, brick-built dwelling was divided into several rooms, with a communal dining room, a lounge overlooking a vast garden, and bedrooms to the rear.

Greg introduced Ana and the children to an Indian woman called Varma, who called herself a supervisor and said that over the next few days she would instruct the children on life in the new town. First, they were to rest in their rooms, and in three hours meet in the dining room for a communal meal.

Ana selected a room, between Gopal's and Prakesh's, stepped over the threshold and moved to close the door behind her. She found that she was unable to complete the action, and something caught in her throat. She had lived for years with no idea of privacy, had slept every night packed tight with the other street kids – and now she could not bring herself to shut out her friends and family.

There was a narrow bed in the room, and a bedside table and a chair, and a window that looked out over the rolling green land.

She moved to the bed and sat down, bouncing a little to test its springiness.

She had shared a bed with her brother many years ago, at the age of five, when she had lived with her aunt and uncle, but she had forgotten quite how soft they were.

For the first time in sixteen years she had a room and a bed of her own.

The comfort would take some getting used to.

She lay down on the bed, rested her head on the pillow, and tried to relax. She opened her eyes and sat up. There was something wrong. She felt alone. She moved to the open door, stepped out and almost collided with Prakesh, who laughed and jumped back.

They grinned at each other.

"What do you think, Ana?" he asked.

She shook her head. "I don't know." She took his hand on impulse and drew him into the room.

Lying on the bed, side by side, they began giggling uncontrollably and suddenly she no longer felt alone.

They ate at a big communal table at five o'clock, a simple meal of dal and chapatis, followed by bananas.

It was the best meal Ana had eaten in years.

Later, as the sun went down, Varma took the children on a tour of the garden, and explained, "We are self sufficient here at Fandrabad, or soon will be.

You will be given a plot of land on which to grow the food you will consume, and every morning you will attend school classes."

A buzz passed around the group.

Varma said, "How many of you can read?"

Of the twenty-four children, only Ana and Gopal raised their hands.

Varma smiled. "In a year from now, all of you will be able to read and write."

Later the children sat around a patio area before the garden, staring up at the starships directly overhead. A circle of blue light marked the centre of the eightfold arrangement where the starship's nose-cones came together. From the centre of the light, a broad, blue beam fell to Earth, connecting the land on the horizon with the joined starships.

Ana saw Varma in the garden, picking beans, and stepped from the patio to join her.

She gestured to the starships and they both stared upwards. "The light," Ana asked. "What is it?"

Varma smiled. "Energy," she said. "The concentrated energy from other stars. It is being beamed to Earth to supply the planet's needs in the years to come."

Ana smiled, not sure that she fully understood Varma's words.

She reached out and found herself hugging the woman. She pulled away, hesitated, then looked into Varma's deep brown eyes. "Are you human," she murmured at last, "or are you really a golden figure?"

The women smiled, then reached out to stroke Ana's hair. "What makes you think that, little wise one?" she said, but would say no more.

Ana had one more surprise in store for her that evening.

There was a wall-mounted softscreen in the lounge, which the children could watch if they wished. When she stepped inside on her way to bed, she saw that Gopal and Prakesh were watching a news programme.

She stopped and stared at the bright images. The screen showed crowds in America and Europe, protesting against the arrival of the Serene. Ana listened to the voiceover in English, but did not understand much of what was said.

Then the scene changed and a reporter said, "And from New York a spokesman for Morwell Enterprises had this to say..."

A handsome Indian man with a thin face, a ponytail and trendy ear-stud faced the camera. "That is correct. I can confirm that James Morwell is in negotiations with other businessmen and heads of state around the world in an attempt to formulate a united opposition to the regime imposed upon us, without our consent I might add, by the Serene..."

The scene switched, showing a meeting of politicians in Europe. Gopal called out to her to join them, but Ana just shook her head and hurried to her bedroom, stunned.

She lay down in the semi-darkness and stared at the ceiling, unable to believe what she had seen.

She was in no doubt. Ten years might have passed, and he had changed a lot, but she recognised the young Indian man on the softscreen, the spokesman for Morwell Enterprises.

It was her brother, Bilal.

TWO

2035

CHAPTER ONE

SALLY SAW HER last patient of the day, finished writing up her notes, then turned off the softscreen and pushed her chair away from the desk. She turned to face the picture window and stared out on a scene that never failed to fill her with delight.

The mellow Shropshire countryside rolled away to the south in a series of hills and vales, softened by the late afternoon sunlight. Here and there she made out villages and small towns – revitalised since the coming of the Serene – and the manufactories that were run almost exclusively by robots, the factories' aesthetically pleasing silver domes concealing the ugly subterranean industry which plumbed the countryside in places to the depth of a kilometre. To the south was the Malvern Energy Distribution Station, an array of silver panels as wide as a couple of football pitches. Twice a day a great pulse of energy was beamed to the EDS from an orbital relay station, the last leg of a journey that had seen the energy transmitted light years through space from stellar supergiants around the galaxy. On grey winter days the bright golden pulses lit the land like falling suns in a display that always cheered Sally.

Between the EDS and the small town of Wem where Sally lived and worked was a network of farms producing the food which fed the nation. She had read somewhere that since the changes wrought by the Serene, forty per cent of Britain's landmass was given over to food production – which was low in comparison to some countries. Uganda, for instance, was almost seventy per cent cultivated, and many other African countries even more so.

Frequently over the past few days – the tenth anniversary of the Serene's arrival – she had thought back to her time in Uganda, contrasting her life then to what she had now. It was only in retrospect that she realised that, for much of her time while in Africa, she had been desperately unhappy. She would never have admitted as much at the time, convincing herself that in working in a country sorely deprived of medical aid she was not only helping others but fulfilling some deep-seated psychological need of her own, but now she could see that she had been sublimating her own desires and needs by losing herself in good deeds. It was a time in her life she was pleased to have experienced, perhaps had *had* to go through in order to grow, but she was glad that it was over.

First Geoff Allen had come into her life, and then the Serene... She often wondered if she would have

turned her back on Uganda if the aliens had not
arrived and promised to make things better – and was
honest with herself and realised that she would have
done. She had planned to get out before the coming
of the Serene, anyway – and her kidnap at the hands
of terrorists had been the final straw. Strung-out, a
nervous wreck and jaded with the stultifying routine
of treating preventable diseases month after month,
she had had to leave for the sake of her sanity. She
sometimes felt pangs of guilt – which Geoff, with his
easy-going approach to life, often jibed her about
– when she realised that the Serene had made her
decision that much easier.

She had so much to thank the extraterrestrials for.

She activated her softscreen on impulse, tapped
into her favourites, and seconds later routed the
image to the wallscreen.

She sat back, smiling, and stared at the scene
showing the main street in Kallani – though a street
vastly changed since Sally had last been there.
Then it had been an unmade, dusty road flanked
by crumbling concrete buildings and stunted trees,
thronged by impoverished locals on the verge of
malnutrition.

Now the road was metalled and the buildings
largely replaced by poly-carbon or synthetic timber
structures, and the people walking down the street
appeared well-fed. North and south of Kallani, all
across the Karamoja region which a decade ago
had been a drought-stricken wilderness, the land
had been revitalised and given over to farms run by
locals. This was the pattern that existed across all

Africa, in fact across much of the world – deserts reclaimed, wildernesses turned into either sources of food production or sanctuaries for native wildlife. The industries that had threatened vast areas of the world, principally mining and logging, had been wound down, redundant now that abundant stellar energy was online and synthi-timber was such an easily manufactured commodity. The Serene had given humanity the technological wherewithal to venture out into the solar system and mine the asteroids for metals, both relieving a tired Earth from the need to give up these resources and eliminating the resultant pollution.

She instructed the image to pan down the main street and turn left. She swung the view to focus on the building that nestled between two carbon fibre A-frames. Mama Oola's was one of the few old concrete buildings remaining in the street – Sally could well imagine Mama's objections to having new premises foisted on her – and little seemed to have changed over the years. The façade was still crumbling and distressed and adorned with bountiful bougainvillea, and occasionally Mama Oola herself could be glimpsed bustling to and from the local market. She'd appeared, the last time Sally had seen her, as ageless as ever.

Now Sally moved the focus along the street and across town to the new medical centre – no longer a tumbledown compound of aging prefabs and corrugated huts. A white carbon fibre complex, all arcs and stylish domes, occupied the old site. And Sally knew that the treatment that went on there was very different to that of her time; gone the cases of malnutrition, preventable maladies and the victims of violence both domestic and political. She suspected that the day to day cases that presented in Kallani would be little different to those she treated here in Wem.

Dr Krasnic, whom she emailed from time to time, had decided to stay on at the centre in Kallani, but Ben Odinga had moved to a practice in Kampala. She smiled to herself, killed the image and not for the first time thought how good it would be, one day, to return.

She was about to leave the office and walk home when her softscreen chimed.

She was tempted to ignore the summons and sneak off, suspecting that her manager wanted to see her before she left. Guilt got the better of her and she accepted the call. The image of a woman in her mid-fifties expanded into the 'screen and it was a few seconds before Sally recognised her.

"Kath?" she said, surprised and delighted. "My word, where are you?"

"Would you believe here in Wem? In fact, about half a kay from where you're sitting." Kathryn Kemp raised a glass and Sally saw that she was beside the canal in the garden of the Three Horseshoes.

"Wonderful. Look, I've just finished work. I have a couple of hours before I'm due home. I'll be with you in a few minutes."

Kathryn laughed. "I'll get you as a drink. Leffe?"

"As ever."

"I'll get them in," Kath said and cut the connection.

Sally locked the office, took the open staircase to the sun-filled atrium, and stepped out into the warm summer afternoon. She hurried through the surgery's garden and took the path along the canal.

Kath Kemp was her oldest friend. They'd met nearly thirty years ago as medical students in London, hit it off immediately and stayed close ever since. Kath was grounded and serious, a private person who let very few people into her life; she had never married, never – as far as Sally was aware – had a boyfriend or girlfriend, and as Kath seemed reluctant to broach the matter of intimate relations, Sally never pressed her on the subject.

Despite their closeness, she had to admit that Kath was something of an enigma. They spoke at length, and at great depth, about their work, the world, politics – and Kath was happy to listen as Sally opened her heart and poured out her troubles, or her joys. But Kath never reciprocated; Sally had been piqued in the early days of their relationship, and then come to accept this as merely a facet of Kath. Sally loved the woman for her warmth, her empathy; she trusted Kath more than anyone else in the world, except perhaps Geoff, and enjoyed basking in her sheer... there was no other term for it... *humanity*.

It had been to Sally's great joy that Geoff, when he'd first met Kath nine years ago, had formed an immediate rapport. "She's a remarkable person, Sal. She exudes empathy."

Their careers had diverged after graduation. While Sally had specialised in tropical medicine,

Kath had practised psychiatry. She'd worked first in London, and then five years ago moved to New York, specialising in the treatment of recovering drug addicts and alcoholics.

They kept in contact with regular emails and online chats, and caught up in the flesh perhaps once every couple of years when Kath returned to London on business.

The Three Horseshoes dated from the sixteenth century, a former coaching inn with bulging walls, a twee bonnet of thatch, and a magnificent beer garden. She and Geoff had spent many a quiet early evening here in the summers, before their daughter Hannah's arrival on the scene; Sally liked to watch the seven o'clock pulse of energy drop from the troposphere and plummet beyond the inn's thatch, marvelling at the contrast of ancient and ultra-modern.

She stepped off the canal path and ducked beneath a strand of wisteria, knocking a bloom and inhaling the wonderful scent.

There were few people in the garden; Kath sat beside the well-stocked fishpond, facing Sally with a welcoming smile on her broad, homely face.

She stood and held out her arm. "And look at you!" Kath said. "Motherhood obviously becomes you."

They embraced, and as always Sally had the odd sensation of hugging her own mother, dead these past thirty years.

They sat down, toasted each other, and Sally took a long drink of sharp, ice cold Leffe.

Kath Kemp was short, a little stout now in her early fifties, with a cheerful face that exuded good will. Sally had no doubt that she was loved and trusted by her patients.

"What a lovely surprise. But you said nothing about coming over! How long are you here for?"

"A last minute decision to attend a conference in Birmingham. I arrived in London this morning, but the conference doesn't start for a couple of days."

Sally reached out and gripped her friend's hand. "You're staying with us, and no arguments. You've not booked in anywhere?"

"I was about to try here." She indicated the inn at her back.

"Don't be silly. I want you to see Hannah."

Kath beamed. "Can't wait. She's five now? She must have grown in the past two years..."

"It's really that long?" Sally shook her head.

"And Geoff?" Kath took a sip of her orange juice.

"He's very well. You know him – Mr Imperturbable. He never changes. He's in Tokyo at the moment, covering the opening of a big art gallery, then moving north to shoot the opening ceremony of the latest arboreal city."

"He certainly gets about."

Sally smiled. She had told no one about the fact that Geoff liaised for the Serene; she suspected that Kath knew but was too diplomatic to mention the fact.

"I'll cook you something tonight and I'll take tomorrow off. Let's go for a long walk."

"Just like old times."

In their student days they'd gone on jaunts along the Thames to Richmond, and spent hiking holidays in Wales and Scotland. Sally squeezed Kath's hand. "It's great to see you again."

"It's nice to come home," Kath said, smiling around at the idyllic setting.

"You still think of England as 'home'?"

"For all the greening of New York and Long Island, it will never be my 'green and pleasant land'." She smiled. "Anyway, how's work?"

"I'm still enjoying it."

"And still general practice."

She nodded. "We got away from London over a year ago. I don't know... perhaps I was getting old, but I couldn't hack city life. I saw this post advertised, and the thought of rural Shropshire..."

"'Westward on the high-hilled plains, Where for me the world began...'" Kath quoted, and Sally laughed.

"Housman, right? He always was one of your favourites." Another odd side of Kath's nature was her love, her adoration, for old poetry. Sally suspected that much of what she quoted were lines from obscure English poets.

"And you're settled here?"

Sally nodded emphatically. "Very. Hannah's taken to it like a fish to water."

"And Geoff?"

Sally laughed. "I often think he'd be happy anywhere, just as long as he had me and Hannah and a good pub." She looked at her friend, a suspicion forming. "Why do you ask?"

Kath considered her orange juice. "Well... I'm recruiting good people, doctors in all fields, for a new project. I'm putting out feelers, testing the water with certain people I know and trust."

"A new project?" Sally echoed.

"Before I talk about the project, Sally, I'll tell you about what I've been doing."

Working with recovering drug addicts and alcoholics, Sally thought – and in the US at that. It was everything she considered anathema and contrary to the life she'd built for herself and her family here in Shropshire.

"About six months ago I changed jobs," Kath said. "Nearly a decade ago a Serene-sponsored think-tank was set up to look into humanity's response to all the changes. Recently they began recruiting for more staff. The offer was too good to refuse."

"I thought you'd be working with your reclamation projects forever."

"Do you know something, the incidence of alcoholism and drug dependency has decreased by something like seventy per cent over the course of the past ten years."

Sally looked at her friend. "Since the arrival of the Serene."

"That's right. Drug and drink dependency was always, largely, a class and income linked phenomenon. Cure poverty, joblessness, give people a reason to live, and the *need* for an opiate is correspondingly reduced. Since the coming of the Serene, and the societal changes they've brought about... Well, my job became little more than a sinecure. I was bored. I didn't feel in the least guilty for leaving the post."

"Good for you. Wish I could say the same about Uganda."

"Still beating yourself up over that?" Kath admonished.

Sally smiled ruefully. "Not really. I was washed up..." She waved. "Water under the bridge, Kath. I've bored you with all that before. Anyway, the new post..."

Kath drained her orange juice and set the empty glass down on the condensation ring it had formed on the wooden table top. "For the vast majority of the human race," she said, "the coming of the Serene has been a beneficial thing. No one can argue against that. Look at the changes – the reduction of poverty, famine, not to mention the fact that wars and violence of all kinds have been banished to the..." She stopped and laughed, "to the 'dustbin of history'! Listen to me, Sally. I'm sounding like a textbook!"

Sally smiled and pointed to Kath's empty glass. "I don't know about you, but I could kill another one."

Kath nodded. "And while you're at the bar I'll try to work out what I'm going to say without recourse to tabloid platitudes... Hey, recall those?"

"Platitudes?"

"Tabloids. Another vestige of a long gone era."

Sally picked up the empty glasses. "I'll get those refills."

While she was at the bar, she looked at her friend through the mullioned window and thought about relocating Geoff and Hannah to the faraway USA. No matter how good the offer, how rewarding the work, she thought, I'm not going to do it.

She returned with the drinks and took a mouthful of lager.

"Where was I?" Kath said.

"'For the majority of the human race'..." Sally recapitulated.

"Right. Well, in the early days there was lots of opposition. And understandably, on a superficial, knee-jerk reaction level. Some people, especially those in power and the rich, had a lot to lose. Everything was changing. All the old certainties were gone. For decades, centuries, we in the West had turned a blind eye to the inherent unfairness of how the world worked. We led easy, affluent life-styles for the most part, and who cared if that meant that the good life was at the expense of millions, billions, in the so-called third world whose poverty subsidised our greed?"

Sally interrupted mildly, "Well, a few of us did object, Kath."

Her friend nodded. "Of course we did. But we were – if you don't mind the phrase – pissing in the wind. We had too much against us. The combined might of government with vested interest and economic institutions that feared an upsetting of the status quo. But then the Serene come along and sweep everything aside."

"And...? Where is this leading, Kath?"

"Sorry. I'm waffling. Right, so in the early days there was opposition, and a lot of it, which died off as the years progressed and the average citizens could reap the benefit of the changes. Who cared about a few powerful politicians, generals and fat cats who were no longer powerful or rich?" She paused, then went on, "The opposition didn't vanish entirely, though – it went underground, developed an intricate, complex nexus of secretive cadres and cells made up for the most part of politicians, former tycoons, military leaders and their ilk. They assumed new roles in the new system – their expertise in many matters was considered valuable – but they remained discontented and..."

"But surely they're no threat to the new system?"

Kath frowned. "Not as such, but they're still a... a worry."

Sally regarded her friend, sure that there was something Kath was holding back. "So what has this got to do with your new post?"

"Right. Well, I was contacted by a consortium of politicians, backed by the Serene, to trace and keep tabs on these people. I know – it sounds like something from a bad espionage novel. But when you think about it, it makes sense. My specialism is in psychiatry, and my early studies were in the field of power structures in industry. Anyway, for the past year I've been seconded to certain enterprises headed by former tycoons who, ten years ago, were vocal in their opposition to the Serene, and who still hold these views."

Sally regarded her drink and let the silence stretch. At last she said, "Right. I understand. What I fail to see is how I can be useful in all this."

"I'm not trying to inveigle you into some undercover spying network, Sally. I've told you all this to explain that the people I work for are close to the Serene, the so-called 'self-aware entities' we've all seen around. As an aid to my current work I've been asked to sound out a few professionals, mainly in the area of health care, and see if I could lure them into new posts. You wouldn't be working with the old, recalcitrant tycoons, might I add."

Sally took a long drink, then asked, "So... what would the new post be?"

Kath shrugged. "Very much like the job you hold here, general practice in a small, rural community."

Sally sat up. "So not in New York?"

Kath smiled "No, not in New York."

"But in America, right?"

"Wrong, not in America."

Sally laughed with exasperation. "Kath! Will you please tell me... where on Earth is this small rural community, then?"

Kath held her gaze, silently, across the table. "That's just it, Sally," she said, "it's not on Earth. It's on Mars."

Sally blinked and lowered her glass. "Mars?" she said incredulously. "Did I hear you right? You said *Mars*?"

Kath nodded. "Mars."

Sally shook her head. "Impossible. Do you know what conditions are like on Mars? An unbreathable atmosphere made up of carbon dioxide..." She tailed off as she saw Kath staring at her.

"What?"

Kath murmured, "Not anymore."

"You mean...?"

"The Serene. They have terraformed the planet,

made it habitable. It's a new, pristine world. A garden world. It's... dare I say it?... a paradise."

Sally laughed. "So that's what all the reports about 'clandestine work' on Mars was all about?"

Kath smiled. "That's right. And we – they – are looking for colonists."

"But..." Sally was aware that she was not thinking logically as she asked, "But doesn't it take years to get there? I mean..."

"Think about it, Sally. The Serene are from Delta Pavonis. They can travel light years in weeks. The jaunt to Mars takes their ships a few hours, and that's the slow way."

Sally stared at her. "What do you mean, the slow way?"

Kath shrugged. "They have other technologies, apart from their starships. But I really shouldn't be talking about that. Anyway, a decision isn't required immediately, of course. I'll give you a few days to think about it. When does Geoff get back?"

Sally shook her head, still dazed. "The day after tomorrow. But... but Geoff, he..." She stopped herself.

Kath was smiling. "I know what Geoff does, Sally. It's been cleared with the SAEs who control him."

Sally looked around her at the beer garden, the rolling hills beyond. Mars, she thought. It still sounded unrealistic, some kind of practical joke.

"If... if we did go. Then how often would we be able to return?"

Kath shrugged. "How about every couple of months?"

Sally shook her head. "But, I mean... why Mars? Why leave this planet? It's not overcrowded, is it?"

"Planet Earth eventually will be. The Serene are looking at things long-term. And by that I don't just means decades or centuries, but millennia. They see Mars as the first step on the long outward push from Earth, an inevitable start of the human diaspora."

"But what will it be like? I imagine red sands, desolate, bleak..."

"Forget about everything you know, or thought you knew, about the red planet. The Serene have changed all that, as they have a habit of doing. Imagine rolling countryside not dissimilar to Shropshire, vast forests, great oceans... A temperate world that will easily accommodate two billion human beings."

"This is... staggering."

"I know. Hard to take in at first. That's how I felt when I was told."

Sally looked at her friend. "You'll be going, too?"

She nodded. "Eventually, perhaps in a year or two, when my work finishes on the current project. Look, talk it over with Geoff when he gets back, give it some serious thought. I'll leave you a few e-brochures, for your eyes only. I'll call in again in a few days, on my way back from Birmingham, and we can all discuss it then."

Sally nodded, "Yes. Yes, of course."

Kath smiled. "Now, did you say you're cooking dinner tonight? Mind if I give you a hand?"

Sally laughed. "I'd love it, and no doubt Hannah will join in too."

They left the garden and Kath said that she'd hired a car in London. "I'll drive you back."

"It's not far, about half a kay on the edge of town overlooking the vale."

"Sounds idyllic."

"It is," she said, and thought: too idyllic to leave. But Mars... what an opportunity!

They walked from the pub garden to the quiet, tree-lined road that led into town. As they walked towards the car, parked a little way along the road, Kath asked, "Why Shropshire?"

"As ever, there was a job advertised. I grew up just a few miles south of here, so it was like coming home."

Kath stepped into the road and moved towards the driver's door. She looked at Sally over the curving, electric-blue roof, and smiled. "'That is the land of lost content, I see it shining plain'..."

"Meaning?"

"One can never go back, Sally. Only onwards..." She smiled again.

Sally would recall that smile for a long time to come.

The truck seemed to appear from nowhere. Sally saw a flash of movement in the corner of her eye as it swept past from the right. She heard a short scream and screamed herself as Kath was dashed away, rolled between her car and the flank of the speeding truck and deposited ten metres further along the road.

Sally ran to her friend and dropped to her knees, taking Kath's limp hand to feel for a pulse but knowing what she would find.

Kath lay on her back, wide open eyes staring at the sky. She seemed physically uninjured, at first inspection; at least there were no wounds, no blood...

But the oval of her skull was misaligned, her jaw set at an odd angle, and the lack of pulse at her wrist confirmed everything Sally had feared.

She screamed, then scooped Kath into her arms and rocked back and forth, sobbing.

She looked down the road for the truck, but it had sped away as fast as it had appeared.

She fumbled with her phone, rang the emergency services and then just sat at the side of the road, holding Kath's dead hand. There was no one else about, for which she was thankful. She did not want her grief intruded upon. It would be bad enough when the police and ambulance arrived, without the spurious sympathy of bystanders.

Memories flashed through her head, images of her time with Kath. They went back so far, had shared so much. It seemed so cruel to the girl and young woman Kath had been that, all along, her arbitrary end had awaited her like this in a future country lane.

What seemed like only minutes later an ambulance pulled up and two paramedics leapt from the cab and hunkered over Kath's body. A police car pulled in behind Kath's rented car and a tall officer climbed out, took Sally firmly by the shoulders and led her away from Kath.

Stricken, Sally watched the paramedics lift her friend's body onto a stretcher, cover her face with a blue blanket with a finality she found heart-wrenching, and slide her into the back of the ambulance.

* * *

THE POLICE OFFICER was young, and seemed even younger in his summer uniform of light blue shirt and navy shorts. He indicated the pub garden and said, "You need a stiff drink, and I'll take a statement. Did you see the vehicle that...?"

Sally shook her head. "Just a flash, then it was away."

He nodded and moved to the bar. Sally chose a table well away from the fishpond. She slumped, dazed, still not wholly believing what had happened. She thought of the dinner they would have prepared together...

She gulped the brandy the officer provided, then almost choked as the liquid burned down her throat. She took a deep breath. The young man was speaking, asking her questions. She apologised and asked him to repeat himself.

She told him Kath's name, her occupation. No, Kathryn Kemp had no living relatives, no next of kin. The only people to contact would be her employers... and at the thought of this Sally broke down.

The officer offered to drive her home, but Sally said she lived just around the corner and that the walk would help to clear her head.

She sat for a while when the officer departed, staring across the lawn at the fishpond.

She gazed at the bulbous koi, breaking the surface for food. She recalled something Kath had said, when they had met in London not long after the arrival of the Serene. They had strolled to a newly opened gallery, toured the exhibition, and later sat at an outdoor café beside a well-stocked fishpond. They had discussed the changes wrought by the aliens, and Sally had wondered about the changes that would affect the world's economy.

Kath had indicated the fish cruising the pond and said, "A crude analogy, Sally. The Earth is a fishpond, with finite resources. The fish would survive for a while without intervention, eating pond life, but eventually their food resources, their economy if you like, would break down. But humans kindly feed them a few crumbs, sustain them..."

"So you're comparing the human race to fish?" Sally had laughed.

"I said the analogy was crude." Kath shrugged. "The Serene come along, save an ailing world, pump energy into the system. Our economies will collapse, but they were corrupt anyway, and will be replaced by something much better. We were in desperate need of the crumbs the Serene are throwing us."

Sally recalled Kath's smile on the sunny London day nine years ago, and all of a sudden she felt very alone. She wanted to go back to the house and have Geoff hold her, comfort her.

She left the beer garden. Instead of going by the road, which would have been the quickest route, she took the canal path behind the pub and cut across the fields on the edge of town. As she walked, she was aware of a sudden brightening in the air above her head, and looked up.

An energy pulse lit the heavens, dazzling. She looked away as the entire sky brightened and the pulse fell towards the energy distribution station to the south. A few crumbs... She laughed to herself, then wept.

She approached the house through the gate in the back garden, then stopped and stared across the lawn. The house was a rambling Victorian rectory, cloaked in wisteria, a little shabby but in a comfortable, homely way. The garden was typical 'English cottage', loaded with abundant borders and strategically placed fruit trees, pear, apple and cherry. At the far end of the lawn Hannah played on a swing, pushed by Tamsin, her child-minder. Sally leaned against the yew tree beside the gate and watched for a minute, preparing herself like an actor about to step on to the stage.

She fixed a smile in place and breezed into the garden. Hannah saw her, launched herself from the swing, and ran across the lawn. Sally picked her up and smiled at Tamsin.

The young woman stared at her. "Sal," she murmured. "You look like you've seen a ghost."

Sally lowered Hannah to the grass and she ran off. "I... I've just heard that a good friend has died." She could not, for some reason, tell Tamsin that she had witnessed the accident. "It... it's a hell of a shock."

"I'll stay, Sal. I'll put Hannah to bed. It's fine, I've got nothing on tonight."

"No you won't, Tamsin. But thanks anyway. I'll be okay, honestly. Get your bag and go home."

"Hannah's eaten." Tamsin looked at her, concerned. "Look, it would be no trouble for me to stay."

Tamsin took some persuading, but Sally was adamant. She wanted to be alone with Hannah tonight, read her a story before bedtime. Geoff might be away, but normality would be achieved with the daily routine of putting her daughter to bed.

When Tamsin had reluctantly departed, Sally started the familiar bedtime process. Pyjamas, brushed teeth and washed face, toilet and snuggle down in bed. She asked Hannah about her day at school, an enquiry which as usual was stonewalled with a child's innate reluctance to vouchsafe any information she regarded as solely her own.

She read a few pages of Hannah's current schoolbook, kissed her and said goodnight, feeling guilty for the perfunctory performance as she turned off the light and left the room.

She stood in the middle of the lounge, crammed with bookcases, old chairs and sofas, the walls hung with pictures and prints. Kath had never seen the house, and Sally would have enjoyed giving her a guided tour. On top of one bookcase was an old photo of Sally and Kath in their college days, picnicking beside the Thames. Sally picked it up and stared at the twenty-two year-old Kath laughing at something she, Sally, had said or done.

She ran to her study, activated her softscreen and tapped in Geoff's code. The time here was eight, which meant that it would be five in the morning in Japan – but would Geoff have finished his work for the Serene yet? Even though Geoff had told her what time he was due to complete what he called his 'shift,' for the life of her she could not remember what he'd said.

The screen remained blank and a neutral female voice said, "Geoff Allen is unable to take your call at the moment. If you would like to leave a message after the tone..."

She held back a sob and said, "Geoff. Something awful... Hannah's fine and so am I. It's Kath. There was an accident. I saw it." She wept, despite her best intentions not to. "Oh, Geoff, it was awful, awful... Please ring me back as soon as you can. I love you."

She cut the connection and sat staring at the blank screen.

She emailed her manager at the practice, told him that she wouldn't be in tomorrow due to the sudden death of a very close friend, then moved to the kitchen and made herself a big pot of green tea. She thought about eating and vetoed the idea. Food, at the moment, was the last thing she wanted.

She curled up in her chair by the picture window, as the sun lowered itself towards the hazy Shropshire hills, and sipped the tea. Somehow the picture of herself and Kath was in her lap, though she had no recollection of carrying it into the study.

A thought flashed across her mind and would not go away. What a stupid, stupid death... A death that someone like Kath did not deserve. She was exactly Sally's age, fifty-three, far too young to die when she had so much life ahead of her, so much important work to do, so much to see... She thought of Mars, and how wonderful it would have been to walk together across the meadows – or whatever! – in the shadow of Olympus Mons.

Always assuming, of course, she and Geoff had agreed to the move.

And what of the job offer now? Should she

relocate to the red planet, leave behind all that was familiar, merely because the Serene had suggested it? Without Kath there to shepherd her through, it seemed unlikely.

Lord, but she missed Geoff on his days away. It was only for two or three days a month, but it always seemed much longer to her. In between his work for the Serene, he worked from home editing the photos taken on his previous trip, and was away for two days or so on commissions for the agency, which somehow never seemed as long as his Serene work.

They had discussed this, and wondered if it was something to do with the fact that there was an unknown element about the Serene commissions. For half of the time he was away he was unconscious, his body a puppet of the Serene, to do with as they wished. Perhaps, she thought, it wouldn't be so bad if she knew exactly what kind of work he was doing.

She finished her tea and made her way to the bedroom in the eaves of the house.

She lay awake for a couple of hours, her head full of Kath – flashing alternative images of her friend in her college days, and the smile she had given Sally across the top of the car as she'd quoted Housman just seconds before...

She slept badly and awoke, with a start, at seven when Hannah – a ball of oblivious energy – sprinted into the bedroom and launched herself onto the bed.

They had breakfast together and Tamsin arrived at eight-thirty to tidy up and take Hannah to school. Sally told Tamsin to take the day off – normally on Thursdays she came back and did the cleaning and washing, but today Sally wanted to lose herself in the routine of housework.

"If you're sure..."

"I'm not going into work, Tamsin. I need to fill the time with something."

At ten to nine she accompanied Hannah and Tamsin outside and waved them off as Tamsin pulled her electric car from the drive. She sighed, standing alone and hugging herself in the bright summer sunlight, then returned inside.

A strong coffee, housework...

An insistent pinging issued from her study, and her heart kicked. Geoff, getting back to her.

She hurried through the house and accepted the call.

The screen was briefly blank, then flared. The image showed a woman in her early fifties, smiling out at her apprehensively.

Kath...

Sally sat back in her chair as if something had slammed into her chest.

Then she knew what had happened. Kath had called the previous afternoon, and the message had been delayed.

"Sally, I know this will be something of a shock."

Blood thundered through her head, slowing her thinking.

"Sally, it's me, Kath. I'm sorry for doing this. Perhaps I should have come round to the house in person, in the flesh..."

Her voice croaked, "Kath?"

Her friend's expression was filled with compassion, understanding. She said, "Sally, what happened yesterday... I'd like to come around, see you and explain."

Sally managed to say, "But you were dead. I saw it happen. I saw it... *You were dead*!"

"I'll be around to see you in a few minutes, Sally." Kath smiled one last time and cut the connection.

Sally sat very still, hugged herself and repeated incredulously, "But you were *dead*..."

CHAPTER TWO

As the train pulled into Howrah station, Ana Devi had no sense at all of coming home.

She had assumed, on the long journey north across the Deccan plain, that she would feel a certain identification with the place where, from the age of six to sixteen, she had spent all her life. She had a store of memories both good and bad – with the good, oddly enough, outweighing the bad. She supposed that that was because she had not been alone here, a street kid scraping a living on an inimical city station, but had been surrounded by a makeshift family which had shared her experiences. She had transplanted her family to central India, and the fact that they had taken on good jobs and prospered meant that, despite their harsh upbringing, they had prevailed.

The station was a strange mixture of the old and the new. Much of it she recognised with a throbbing jolt of nostalgia, and then her recollections would be confused by the position of a new poly-carbon building or footbridge. As the train slid into the station, they passed the goods yard and the rickety van where she and twenty other kids had slept at night. The yard was surrounded by containers and new buildings, and she hardly recognised the place. The train eased to a halt on the platform, and Ana smiled as she stared across at the Station Master's office. She wondered if Mr Jangar still ruled Howrah with a rod of iron.

She stepped from the train and allowed the crowds to drain away around her until the platform was almost deserted. She glanced up at the footbridge, where she had spent many an hour as a child watching the trains come and go, and caught a fleeting glimpse of a darting figure up there on the criss-crossed girders. She caught her breath, at once dismayed that children still haunted the station and alarmed at this individual's daring. The girder was almost twenty metres high, and one wrong step would send the kid tumbling to the tracks below. Then the figure halted suddenly, squatted and stared down at her – and Ana laughed aloud. It was not a street kid but a slim grey monkey.

She looked around the platform, seeking out the nooks and crannies where, ten years ago, she would have seen evidence of the street kids – or the 'station rats' as Mr Jangar had called them – but only commuters occupied the platform, awaiting their trains. Of course, she told herself, street kids were a thing of the past, now. Her generation had been the very last.

She pulled the silver envelope from the side pocket of her holdall and crossed to the station master's office.

A secretary sat before a softscreen. He looked up enquiringly as Ana entered.

"I am looking for the station master, Mr Jangar," she said. "I have an appointment with him at three o'clock."

The young man referred to his screen and nodded. "Ana Devi?" He indicated a door to Ana's right. "Mr Jangar will see you straight away."

She hurried through the door and found herself in a small waiting room. She approached a door bearing the nameplate "Station Master Daljit Jangar," and knocked.

A deep voice rumbled, "Come in."

Ana pushed open the door, suddenly a child again, her heart thudding at the thought of meeting the feared Jangar after all these years.

She stepped into the room and he rose to meet her, the very same barrel-bellied, walrus-moustachioed, turbaned Sikh she recalled from her childhood, only a little fatter now, a little slower.

They shook hands and he indicated a seat, then sat down behind his impressively vast desk and stared at her. "Now what can I do for you, Miss...?"

"I am Ana Devi," she said, "and I am the senior food production manager at the Andhra Pradesh wilderness city."

He nodded, peering at her closely. "If you don't mind my saying, Miss Devi, your face is very familiar."

She smiled. "And so it should be, Mr Jangar. You made the lives of myself and my friends a constant misery."

He shook his head in confusion. "I don't quite understand..."

"As a child I lived here on the station. I begged and stole, played on the girders beneath the footbridge, slept in the van in the goods yard."

"Ah, a station rat. You were a nuisance, I will say that much. The trouble I got from the police superintendent to clear the station of kids." He chuckled, as if reflecting on good times.

Ana said, "We had nowhere else to live, Mr Jangar. Oh, sometimes we slept in the park, but it was a dangerous place. At least here there was food to be had, and shelter, and crowds to hide among."

She glanced across the room to the stick propped in the corner, Mr Jangar's dreaded lathi. She remembered one occasion, when she was seven or eight, and a ticket collector had caught her stealing biscuits from the station canteen and dragged her kicking and screaming to Jangar's office. She had half a mind to remind him of the beating he had dealt her then, but restrained herself.

"You no longer have occasion to use your lathi?" she asked.

"Oh, I threaten dilatory workers with it from time to time, Miss Devi, but gone are the days when..."

She said, "Thanks to the Serene."

He stared at her. "There was something to be said for a little constructive punishment, in the right place."

Ah, she thought, so that's what it was, that beating and others that had left her black and blue and unable to walk properly for a week: constructive punishment. Would it have pained her any less, she thought, to have known that as a tiny seven-year-old?

Jangar cleared his throat. "But I take it that you did not come here merely to reminisce, Miss Devi."

She smiled. Part of her motive for delivering the letter – which might as easily have been sent by email – was to visit the station again and impress upon Jangar how she had overcome her lowly origins.

She slid the silver envelope across the desk and watched him slit it open and read the letter.

He harrumphed. "From the wilderness city director himself," he muttered.

"And as the letter states, he is not impressed by the continual lateness of the Kolkata trains, Mr Jangar. We depend upon punctuality in order to maximise the distribution of our produce, as I'm sure you understand."

"Quite, quite..."

"This could have been sent by email, Mr Jangar, but Director Chandra wanted me to stress the importance of the matter, and to say this: if things do not improve, Mr Jangar, then the matter will be presented to the city council."

Jangar looked up, but could not bring himself to look her in the eye. "I will have my transport manager look into the matter forthwith, Miss Devi."

"Excellent." Ana stood, reached out and shook Jangar's hand. "It has been a pleasure to talk of old times," she said, and swept from the office as if walking on air.

One demon from her past confronted and exorcised, she thought.

She booked into a new hotel complex across the road from the station, showered and rested on the bed for an hour before leaving the hotel and strolling through the busy streets.

Everything changed, she had once read somewhere, but India changed more gradually than anywhere else. She saw prosperity on the streets, where ten years ago she had seen poverty – families living in the gutters, maimed beggars on street corners, kids trapping rats and birds in order to provide their only meal in days...

Now she saw well dressed citizens promenading, and stalls selling fruit and vegetables – she felt a sense of pride in this – and new poly-carbon structures nestling alongside ancient temples and scabbed buildings. Tradesmen still plied their crafts beside the roads: cobblers and shoe-shiners alongside hawkers selling freshly-pressed fruit- and sugar-cane juice. But gone was the grinding poverty that had once given the streets an air of hopeless desperation.

She made her way to Station Road and stood outside Bhatnagar's restaurant where, as a girl, she had pressed her nose against the window and stared at the ziggurats of gulab jamans, the slabs of kulfi and dripping piles of idli, and beyond them to the fat, wealthy diners filling their faces with food that Ana had only dreamed of eating.

Now she stepped through the sliding door –

metaphorically taking the hand of the timid girl she had been – and was met by a liveried flunky who bowed and showed her to a table beside the window.

She ordered a vegetable pakora starter followed by a dal mushroom masala, then finished off with barfi and a small coffee. She glanced through the window, half expecting to see hungry faces pressed to the glass; but the children she did see out there were clutching the hands of their parents and did not spare a glance at the diners beyond the wondrous piles of sweetmeats.

As she was about to leave, Ana caught the eye of an old waiter and said, "Do you know if a gentleman by the name of Sanjeev Varnaputtram still orders food from this restaurant?"

The old man appeared surprised by the enquiry. "Varnaputtram has fallen on hard times. No longer can he afford to dine on food from Bhatnagar's."

"So he's still alive?"

"So I have heard, but he is old and very ill these days."

"And do you happen to know where I might find him?"

The man laughed, showing an incomplete set of yellowed teeth. "Where he is always to be found. His house on Ganesh Chowk. He is so fat, Miss, that no one can move him!"

Smiling, Ana tipped the waiter, settled her bill and left the restaurant.

She made her way back towards the station, then turned from the main street and paced down the narrow alleyways to the house where Varnaputtram still lived.

She had tried to look ahead and guess what her feelings might be when she made this journey back into her past, and this specific walk down Ganesh Chowk to confront the monster who was Sanjeev Varnaputtram. She had assumed she would feel fear – a vestige of the dread from all those years ago – and also apprehension, but the surprising truth was that she felt none of these things: what she did feel was anger.

She came to the familiar gate in the wall and pushed it. To her surprise it was not locked – Gopal's doing, she thought, and it had not been repaired in a decade.

She was confronted by an almost solid wall of vegetation, through which she could barely make out the narrow path. She ducked along it, batting fronds and branches from her face, and came at last to a pair of pink doors, flung open to admit the slight evening breeze.

She stepped into the tiled hallway, expecting to be stopped by Sanjeev's lounging minions, Kevi Nan, the Sikh double-act and other hangers-on. But the hall was empty, and as she crossed the tiles towards the pink-painted timber doors to Sanjeev's inner sanctum, she heard a querulous voice call out, "Datta? Is that you?"

She reached out, pushed open the door, and stood on the threshold.

She had assumed that Sanjeev might have shrunk over the years – following the rule that all things returned to in adulthood appear smaller – but she had assumed wrongly. Sanjeev might no longer dine on Bhatnagar's finest take-aways, but he had evidently found an alternative supplier. He was vast, with gross rolls of fat overflowing the narrow charpoy. A towel – made tiny by comparison to his splayed thighs – covered his manhood.

A bald head sat atop the mound of his body, and tiny marble eyes peered out. He was sweating, and he stank.

"Who are you? What do you want, girl?"

She remained on the threshold, staring at her erstwhile tormentor.

"I said what do you want?" Sanjeev shrilled. "And where is Datta?"

She stepped into the room, pulled up a rickety chair, and positioned it before the bed. She sat down in silence, never taking her gaze from the appalling specimen of humanity before her.

She said quietly, "Where are your henchmen now, Sanjeev?"

His eyes, deep in their pits of flesh, stared at his with incomprehension. "What do you mean?"

"Kevi Nan, the Sikhs, the other thugs you paid to abduct street kids from the station and bring here. Where are they now, Sanjeev? Left you, moved on?"

"You haven't heard? Kevi is dead, fell under the Delhi Express years ago. The others..." He waved a tiny hand and Ana was reminded of a seal's twitching flipper. "I am an old man, and ill, and they have left me like the vermin they were. Only Datta remains, in the hope that when I die he'll get the house."

Ana felt a strange emotion somewhere deep within her, and fought to suppress it.

She said, "You have really no idea who I am?"

He peered at her. "Police? Or from the council?"

"I am Ana Devi, and ten years ago I lived at Howrah station. Six years before that, Kevi Nan captured me one day and dragged me here, and you ripped the t-shirt and shorts from my body – the only clothing I possessed at the time – and dragged me onto..." She stopped, her voice catching, and worked at withholding her tears. "Then you buggered me all night with your pathetic, tiny cock..."

She stared at him, attempting to discern the slightest sign of remorse in his features.

She said, "And then, ten years ago, just as the Serene arrived, you had me dragged back here, and again you tried to rape me, only this time..." She smiled at him. "This time, the Serene had arrived and I got away."

He pointed with his ridiculous flipper hand. "I remember you!" He wheezed, his breath coming unevenly. "You escaped through the window. The beginning of the end! Only it was not quite the end..."

She said, "Kevi Nan abducted my friend, Prakesh, and you plied him with rum and..."

Sanjeev chuckled. "And you and your station rats came and carried him off and that, sadly, *was* the very end."

She shook her head. "The end of the abuse?"

He lifted his fat fingers and tapped something on his upper arm. Ana stared at the square protuberance of an implant, as Sanjeev explained, "Six months after the aliens came, the authorities arrived here, burst in and issued a warrant. I had to go to court! Me, Sanjeev Varnaputtram! It was the very last time I left this room."

"And you were found guilty, and your punishment was..."

"This! Chemical castration, they call it. Do they realise what they did to me, do they? Me, Sanjeev Varnaputtram!"

She stared at him, and that earlier, incipient emotion – pity, it had been – was washed away as she realised that he had no comprehension whatsoever of the depravity of his crimes.

She said, "It was the least you deserved. Some would say you got off lightly."

"Get out!" he spat. "I said, get out."

She remained sitting on the chair, staring at him.

"Before I go," she said softly, "I'd like to tell you about some of the boys and girls you victimised over the years." She paused, took a breath and said, "Gopal Dutt is now a train driver in Madras, with a wife and three children. Danta Malal is a botanist working with me in the Andhra Pradesh wilderness city; he is to be married later this year. Prakesh Patel is a biologist in the same place, and the father of three boys. And I... I am a senior manager working in food production in the same city." She smiled at him. "We have survived our childhoods, we have overcome the poverty and abuse, and every one of us has moved forward and prospered."

She stood and moved to the door, then turned and stared at him. "And you, Sanjeev Varnaputtram, what have *you* done?"

She hurried from the room before he could muster a reply, and only when she reached the sanctuary of the alleyway did she break down and weep.

SHE LEFT THE hotel at ten the following morning and strolled across the city. She sat at a café, ordered a sweet lassi, and watched the passing crowds.

At the far side of the square the Serene obelisk rose, sheer and jet, into the dazzling summer sky. At first the arrival of these singular towers in all the major cities of the world had divided aesthetic opinion. Experts opined that they were the height of architectural ugliness, others that they were in their own way things of severe beauty. Ana tended to agree with the latter school of thought: she never looked upon an obelisk without being reminded of the good that the Serene had brought to Earth, and she thought of these towers as monuments to that good.

She sometimes found it hard to believe that she had been working for the Serene for ten years now. The time since leaving Kolkata seemed to have flown. So much had changed in the world – change, she realised, that sequestered with her work in the wilderness city she had hardly noticed. It was only when she fulfilled the needs of the Serene once a month, and found herself waking up in various locations around the world, that she came to realise the extent of the changes. She had seen cities transformed, slums giving way to new poly-carbon developments, impoverished citizens replaced by well-fed and well-dressed individuals; and, most of all, pessimism receding on a wave of optimism.

She had visited every continent on Earth now, and at least a hundred cities – though, over the course of the past five years, those visits had been restricted to the cities which contained the obelisks. She wondered why this was so. Every time she came to her senses, she was in the vicinity of a jet black tower. There had to be a link, though one to which she was not privy. Yet another enigma of the aliens who had changed the world.

In the early days she had found herself fearing coming to her senses in these strange and far-flung places, and she would flee to the airport and wait until the sleek Serene jet was ready to take her back to India. She was allowed a day or two to herself in these exotic cities – a reward, she supposed, for whatever work she did for the Serene while unconscious. Over a period of time, as she gained confidence, she remained in the cities and explored a little, knowing that physically she could come to no harm. She had experienced other cultures, other ways of thinking, other foods – strange, at first, after her staple diet of curry in India – and met people of all colours and creeds.

A couple of years ago it came to her that she was, truly, a citizen of the world. She had learned to speak English, was learning French, and had a smattering of Italian and German. She wondered what the ignorant girl she had been, ten years ago, would have thought of this sophisticated woman she had become, who wore Western clothing and could order food in three or four different languages.

She looked at her watch and smiled. Kapil was late, which was not unusual. Despite his many excellent qualities, punctuality was not one of them. He often kept her waiting – up to two hours on one occasion! – and he blamed it on having a mother and father who had both worked for the Indian railways, where good time-keeping was a given. He said he had grown up despising the tyranny of the clock, though Ana teased him that he was making excuses.

She had met Kapil Gavaskar at the Andhra Pradesh wilderness city two years ago when he had flown in from America on a fact-finding mission. Ana's city had just achieved record levels of fruit production, and the world was lining up to find out how.

She had been immediately attracted to the tall, slim Indian-American, who spoke Hindi with an odd twang and professed a dislike of Indian food. She had set about remedying the latter by taking him to her favourite restaurants, and even tutoring him in how to pronounce certain Indian words without a Texan vowel extension.

They tried to see each other once a month, which sometimes didn't happen. When their itineraries proved impossible to match – like last month – Ana felt bereft, but it only served to make their next meeting all the more exciting.

They had not talked of marriage, yet, though Ana often considered life with Kapil on a permanent basis. She had yet to meet his parents – old-school Brahmins, who would doubtless turn up their noses at her lowly dalit origins.

She jumped as she felt hands on her shoulders – then relaxed as he kissed the top of her head. "Ana," he murmured, "I've been watching you for the past minute. You were miles away."

She clutched his hand as he took a seat at the table. "I was thinking about you."

"Flatterer!"

"It's true." She stared at his face, drinking him in. "Oh, it's so good to see you!"

He ordered a coffee and sipped it as he stared at her. He was thin-faced, handsome, with humorous eyes and a quick smile.

He frowned. "Are you okay? Is something wrong?"

She had told Kapil about her childhood shortly after they'd met – thinking that it was best to get the truth out of the way early on, so that he could leave her without breaking her heart. One of the many things that made her love him was that he had listened to her admission in silence, then kissed her on the lips and said that if it was her upbringing that had made her who she was, then he could not fault it.

But she had never told him about Sanjeev Varnaputtram, and what he had done to her and countless other street kids.

She did so now, choosing her words with care, and finished by recounting their encounter yesterday.

"The bastard!" he cried. "I'll have him arrested!"

She smiled. "He is already chemically castrated, which is punishment enough. And he is old and ill." She shrugged. "But it was so good, Kapil, to tell him that his victims are all now prospering. I felt... empowered."

He took her hand and kissed her fingers.

She said, "How long do we have?"

"Until the morning. I must leave for China at ten tomorrow. I'm advising them on their sustainability program."

"One whole day!" she laughed.

"I haven't been to Kolkata for at least fifteen years. I was thirteen, and my parents were taking me to see an ancient aunt before we left for America."

"Perhaps I could give you a guided tour – show you Howrah station, the streets I played in, Maidan Park where I watched the rich kids flying their expensive kites."

He looked reflective. "I might have been one of them..."

She drained her lassi, and he his coffee, and they strolled from the square hand in hand.

They spent the day wandering around the city, visiting the sites of her childhood, the station and the park, the once mean streets between them, and Ana relived memories of her childhood, but told him only of the good ones.

She took him to Bhatnagar's that night, and she feasted again. Kapil, thanks to Ana's expert tutoring, had come to appreciate the cuisine of his home country. They finished the meal and strolled through the warm night, bought ice creams and promenaded along the revamped sea front, watching the liners and cruise ships leave the port and head off into the Bay of Bengal.

On the way back to the hotel they passed a store selling softscreens and other hi-tech goods, and the window was a flickering panoply of visually discordant images. One caught Ana's eye and stopped her in her tracks. Kapil stopped too and glanced from screen to screen, unable to discern which image had arrested her attention.

Ana stared, open-mouthed, at the Indian with the long ponytail and ear-stud, who was mouthing silently to the camera.

"Ana?"

She pointed.

"Ah... handsome, no?" he said.

She dug her elbow into his ribs. The young man vanished on the screen, replaced by sports news.

Ana walked on in silence, lost in thought. That was only the third time in ten years she had seen Bilal on television, and always the sight of him touched some deep regret within her.

"Well...?" Kapil prompted.

She stopped and faced him in the moonlight. "I've never told you this, Kapil. But I had a brother... I mean, I have a brother." She pointed back to the shop-front. "That is him. Bilal Devi. He ran out on me when I was six."

He guided her to a coffee house, sat her down at a quiet table, and demanded the full story.

She told him how Bilal had protected her from local children, made her cheap kites from newspaper and twine – and how, when she was almost seven and Bilal sixteen, he had vanished without a trace.

"Ten years ago I found out... from Sanjeev Varnaputtram, of all people, that he had been taken up by a philanthropist, and educated, and then selected to work for a big American corporation."

"But he never contacted you?" Kapil asked.

She shook her head. "Never. Nothing. Not even a letter... For a long time I thought he must be dead, and I sometimes wished that it were so. Then I wouldn't have to live with the knowledge that he deserted me and never thought to get in touch."

He gripped her hand. "And you've never thought to try and contact him?"

She shook her head. "And the thing is, I don't know why. Fear, perhaps. A part of me so much wants to see him again. But... but what if he spurns me, doesn't want anything to do with me?" She shrugged. "How would I cope with that?"

He walked her home, murmuring that she had him now, and back in their room he undressed her slowly and they made love.

Afterwards, as always, she pressed her lips against his chest and wept.

He stroked her hair and whispered, "Why, Ana? Why do you always cry?"

She laughed through her tears, reached up and caressed his cheek. She wanted to say, "Is it not little wonder? But you would never understand..."

He left for the airport at seven the following morning, and they parted before the hotel with kisses and promises to see each other in one month.

Later, back in her room as she was preparing to leave and catch the train to Andhra Pradesh, a familiar soothing voice sounded in her head.

"*Ana, a flight to Tokyo at eleven, and then tomorrow a fact-finding tour of the Fujiyama arboreal city...*"

She smiled to herself. She had not visited Tokyo for years, and she had read a lot about the arboreal cities.

She contacted her manager at the wilderness city and arranged for her deputy to cover her shifts, then packed her holdall and took a taxi to the airport.

CHAPTER THREE

JAMES MORWELL SAT in the penthouse office of Morwell Towers and stared down the length of Manhattan. Not that the tower was strictly speaking Morwell Towers any more; the lower stories had been taken over by other concerns, and only the top two floors remained in the control of the organisation. The tower resembled a block graph, with the gradual leasing out of floor after floor to other companies representing the diminution of the once great empire of the Morwell Corporation. Within days of the arrival of the Serene, shares in the arms and energy branches of the corporation had plummeted, while across the board his other enterprises had suffered almost as much. The only section of his business empire to have survived, after a fashion, was his various media outlets.

Now James Morwell was effectively little more than a manager overseeing the smooth running of his news networks, with control but little power. He likened what had happened to the emasculation that might have taken place in the old days, if some communist dictator had assumed control and put an immediate end to all forms of free enterprise. Everything, now, was in effect under state control – that state being the hegemony of the alien Serene.

He was little more than a party functionary giving orders to others who did the real work. Gone were the days when his decisions, along with that of his board, could add millions to the price of Morwell shares, bankrupt a country or bankroll the rise to power of friendly politicians in far-flung corners of the world.

Not that he was accepting what had happened without a fight. Ten years had elapsed, and he might be the powerless puppet figurehead of a once proud business empire, but Morwell still harboured dreams of returning the planet to its pre-Serene days.

It might have been no more than a futile gesture of resistance, but not long after the coming of the Serene he had started a website devoted to the promulgation of ideas opposing the pacifist regime of the extraterrestrials. He had expected the website to be closed down summarily, but that had never happened. A decade later the website – rousingly entitled The Free Earth Confederation – boasted more than ten million subscribers worldwide. They ranged from disgruntled individuals whose lives and livelihoods had been affected by the changes – boxers and self-defence experts, anglers and hunters and many more – to former dictators and high-up military personnel, as well as free-thinkers and scientists from various fields. He had realised, early on in the campaign, that it was important to get big-name thinkers and philosophers on his side. He had contacted those with known Republican sympathies, the so-called climate change sceptics and the libertarian mavericks who, years ago, had opposed the liberals on ecological issues, and sorted out those who had done so through genuine belief from opportunists who had been bought by government research grants and funding. He had organised forums, seminars, and gathered every dissenting voice together on his website.

He genuinely believed that there was a groundswell of public opinion growing for the restitution of the old way of life.

He genuinely believed that when the Serene had imposed – without consent – their *charea* on the people of Earth, humanity had been robbed of something fundamental. Not for nothing had mankind evolved, by tooth and claw, over hundreds of thousands of years. We became, he reasoned, the pre-eminent species on the planet through the very means that the Serene were now denying us. It was his opinion, and that of many eminent social thinkers and philosophers, that the human race had reached the peak of its evolution and was now on an effete downward slope, little more than the pack-animals of arrogant alien masters.

Violence was a natural state. Violence was good. Violence winnowed the fittest, the strongest, from the weak. The only way forward was through the overthrow of the Serene and the subversion of the unnatural state of *charea*.

Of course, these were fine words. The reality was that the Serene were so far in advance of humanity in terms of science and technology that it was analogous to a band of Cro-Magnon spear-carriers taking on the might of an elite Delta Force.

With the added complication being that the Serene were an enemy which did not show itself. And its minions, the golden figures, were as elusive as they were enigmatic. Not one of his sympathisers had ever been able to open communications with the so-called self-aware entities.

His softscreen chimed, pulling him back to the real world, and Lal's face flared on the screen. "A little more information regarding the representatives, sir."

"Fine. Come on up."

He had first set Lal the task of tracking down these 'representatives' ten years ago. In the early days he had not even been certain of their existence – from time to time, as Lal's searches got nowhere, he thought the notion of humans in the employ of the aliens was no more than a rumour – but Lal through persistence and ingenuity had come up with occasional pay dirt. He had identified individuals who did move around the globe with erratic and seemingly motiveless purpose, individuals from all walks of life in whom the Serene should have no interest. But just as soon as Morwell hired people to apprehend and question these people, they vanished as if spirited away.

A knock sounded on the door and his facilitator

Lal Devi, who'd stood by him through thick and thin since the coming of the Serene, slipped into the room, as sharp as ever with his silk suit, ponytail and air of optimistic efficiency.

He set his own softscreen on the desk top and tapped it into life.

"Two suspects, sir. The first..."

A face appeared on the screen, an African women in her fifties. "Chetti Bukhansi, 53, from Chad. An engineer. We've been tracking her for a month, on a tip-off from one of our sympathisers. I gave the order for a mole to be introduced, and the insertion was successful but came up with nothing substantial. Bukhansi travels a lot with her work, and it might not be the 'cover' of a representative."

Morwell frowned. "So in effect a big fat blank."

Lal nodded. "Just so." He tapped the screen again and the African face was replaced by that of a European in his twenties. "This is Markus Dortmund, 28, from Germany. An artist. His girlfriend is a Free Earth Confederation member and contacted me via the website. We put someone on his trail..."

"And?"

Lal shrugged his slim shoulders. "The jury is still out. He travels a hell of a lot, but then his line of work calls for it. That's the difficulty we face, sir – we just cannot be sure with any of them when they're doing their own legitimate work, and when they might be working for the Serene."

Morwell said, "But surely..."

"It's impossible to be with the subjects twenty-four seven, sir, impossible to attend all their meetings.

It's quite possible that when they're conducting seemingly casual meetings with other individuals, work for the Serene is taking place."

Morwell nodded his understanding, impatient though he was.

"Very well. Keep tabs on this individual, Dortmund, and for chrissake don't get too close. We don't want to spook the Serene and lose him."

"Understood."

"And anything further on the idea that the Serene have been amongst us for longer than the ten years since their obvious arrival?"

It was a schizoid French philosopher who'd first posited this theory, and Morwell still didn't know how seriously to take it.

The philosopher argued that for the Serene to institute the changes in the infrastructure of the economy of the planet in such an apparently short time, thousands of 'operatives' must have been in place pulling various strings and laying the ground-work for the revolution. Businesses had gone under overnight, only to be resurrected days later; banks had been run dry and then re-capitalised... And then there had been the logistical, organisational changes that had taken place: entire industries had vanished – meat farming among others – and yet within days all workers had been allocated other jobs. Such a smooth and painless transition pointed, so the philosopher argued, to careful planning and the placement of experts in a hundred different specialisms.

Now the Indian stroked the line of his jaw. "I've had investigators checking the backgrounds of more than a hundred individuals, and they have unearthed certain anomalies. People whose life histories seem to have started from nowhere in their mid-twenties or -thirties; people without family or friends whose background has proven impossible to trace, as if they just popped out of nowhere ten, twenty, thirty years ago." Lal shrugged again. "But the exasperating thing is, sir, that these anomalies might be caused by nothing more than incomplete or inefficient records. I'll keep my team investigating and report when we come up with anything more conclusive."

They chatted about other matters for a while, then Morwell dismissed Lal and returned his attention to the view of sprawling Manhattan.

He spent hours like this, he realised, staring out at the city but in reality thinking back to a time very different from this one. A time when he worked an eighteen-hour day and made a dozen vital decisions every hour; a time when he courted politicians and had them know that a vote the right way, or a bill passed in favour of a certain policy, could mean the difference between their party gaining millions in funding and getting nothing. Nowadays the world seemed to be run by a bunch of liberal bureaucrats whose favour could not be bought for love nor money. All the more ammunition for the mad Frenchman's idea that they had been amongst us for centuries, Morwell thought.

His softscreen chimed again and the beautiful young face of his latest escort, as he liked to call these women, smiled out at him. What was her name? Suzi, Kiki? She was new – had been recommended to him just last week – and knew how to satisfy his needs.

"James... I'm here." She blew him a kiss.

He smiled. "I'll have security send you up to the penthouse. And you'll find five bottles of Perrier in the cooler."

She pulled a pretty moue. "*Five?*"

"Just drink them and I'll be up in an hour, okay?"

She pulled a face, hit the deactivate key with ill-grace, and vanished from the screen.

HE WAS ABOUT to leave the office and indulge himself in one of the few activities he enjoyed these days – even though his sex-life, since the coming of the Serene, had been diminished – when he noticed something in the corner of the room.

He turned quickly in his swivel chair and stared.

Something was flickering in the angle created by the two plate-glass windows, and at first he thought it an effect of the light on the glass. As he watched, however, the flickering light intensified and resolved itself into a standing blue figure.

"What the fuck–" Morwell kicked off and launched his chair across the room away from the figure. He fetched up against the wall and exclaimed again.

The figure was tall, well over two metres high, and composed of a swirling blue light. It seemed to contain azure spiral galaxies that rotated and shifted as he stared.

It stood with its arms at its side, totally silent, and

gazed directly at him – though its face was the same swirling blue as the rest of its body, and featureless.

He managed, "What do you want?"

Some envoy of the Serene, come to end his opposition? His heart began to beat faster and he realised he was sweating.

The figure spoke – or rather its words sounded in his head. "Do not be afraid."

"Wh-what are you?"

"We are the Obterek," said the figure, still unmoving, "and my time here is limited."

Morwell eyed the door, four metres away. He wondered if he could reach it before the figure moved to stop him.

"What do you want?"

A beat, then the figure said, "We desire the same outcome as you, James Morwell."

His heart skipped. "You... you're nothing to do with the Serene?"

"We oppose the Serene; we oppose everything the Serene are doing to your planet and to your people. The Obterek are ancient enemies of the Serene."

Morwell nodded slowly, taking all this in. "And you are here because...?"

"Because we believe you can help us in our opposition of the Serene."

He stared at the figure, smiling to himself. "You appear here out of nowhere, a figure of pulsing light. You've obviously travelled light years to reach Earth and possess technologies we have yet to dream of... And you think *I* can help *you*?"

"We do not have the time to explain fully, James

Morwell. Also, your understanding of the terms we use would be insufficient. Suffice to say, we the Obterek can insert ourselves into the reality of your solar system for brief periods only, for scant minutes every month. The Serene are vigilant, and watch for us, and we can compromise their surveillance only temporarily; likewise, we can breach their *charea* only briefly."

He pounced on this. "You can breach the *charea*?"

"With extreme care and a great expenditure of energy, yes," said the figure. "But to answer your question: you can help the Obterek undermine the Serene, and return the planet and its people to the Natural Way, because you inhabit this reality in a way that we do not. Together we can bring an end to the regime of the Serene on Earth."

Morwell gained confidence. He moved his chair closer to the figure and said, "And how might I accomplish this? And why me, of all..."

The blue figure interrupted. "You maintain an opposition, feeble though it is, to the Serene. You have contacts, a network of agents working to your ends. One of these: to locate the Serene's human representatives."

Morwell nodded. "That is so, yes."

"We, too, are interested in these people. We, the Obterek, believe they hold the key to what the Serene are planning in this system. The Serene are using them in ways we cannot quite fathom. To capture a representative, to find out from these people how they are being used, will mark a step change in our opposition to the Serene."

Morwell nodded. "We have been attempting to trace these people, which is easier said than done. We have leads, suspects. But when we get close..." He snapped his thumb and forefinger, "they go to ground."

"In that, James Morwell, we can assist."

For the first time the figure moved. It took a step forward, and then another, and there was something startling about the strength of purpose it exhibited, as if battling against a gravity greater than that to which it was accustomed.

It stood before his desk, pulsing, and from just a couple of metres away Morwell could feel the heat radiating from its body.

The figure reached out a hand, and opened it.

A shower of what looked like sparkling blue coins – the same shade and make-up as the body of the Obterek – spilled across the desk.

Morwell stared at the dozen discs as they glowed on the desk-top.

He looked up at the figure. "And these are?"

"What they are called does not matter, nor how they work. I could not explain their mechanics in any way that you would understand. Put simply, though erroneously, they transmit the content of a sentient's mind to us through a breach in the space-time continuum. This explanation is imprecise, but will suffice."

"And you would like my agents to...?"

"When you apprehend a suspect, one of these attached to that person will be enough to begin the transmission process."

He stared at the discs. "And just how do we attach them?"

"By simply placing a disc against the skin of a suspect. The disc will do the rest, will insert itself instantly under the skin of the suspect, who will feel nothing. One hour later, however, the subject will die – an unavoidable consequence of the transmission."

"Die..." Morwell said to himself. He gestured towards the discs. "But I can handle them with... impunity?"

"You will not be harmed."

He was silent for a time. At last he asked, "And how do I know I can trust you? How do I know that these... these discs will do what you say they will?"

He had a dozen more questions, but these would do to start with.

The figure said, "The fact is that you do not know, for certain. You must merely trust. And hope, James Morwell. And hope is a commodity of which you have had little over the course of the past ten years." The figure paused, pulsing beautifully, and went on, "We have read your manifesto. We have studied your online pronouncements. The Serene, too, are aware of you, but in their complacency they allow you to conduct your opposition, such as it is. But that is the difference between the Obterek and the Serene: if you were opposed to the Obterek, we would have no compunction in carrying out your summary extermination."

Morwell almost smiled with the thrill of hearing such threats. He was thirteen again, and his father was approaching him with a baseball bat...

He leaned forward and said, "And after the Serene have been vanquished, and the Obterek rule, what then?"

The figure standing before his desk began to fade. Its last words sounded in his head: "Then you, the human race, will be alone again, such is the Natural Law..."

"But –" he began, meaning to ask what the Obterek would gain from a return to the old ways.

A second later the blue figure vanished.

Morwell leaned forward and touched the closest disc. It was warm, and pulsed against his fingertips. Smiling, he reached out and trawled the rest towards him like a gambler scooping his winnings.

CHAPTER FOUR

ALLEN HAD TWO hours to wait before the monotrain was due to leave Tokyo and head north to the Fujiyama arboreal city, so he sat in the plaza outside the station and sipped a coffee.

The city skyline was dominated by a thousand-metre-tall obelisk, jet black and slightly tapering towards its summit. It was one of a dozen identical buildings gifted by the Serene, along with the eight 'wilderness towns', the hundred-plus littoral domed cities, and the arboreal cities, numbering in their thousands, that were springing up all around the world. The difference with the black obelisks was that they were the only Serene buildings placed within already existing cities, and they were the only constructions not purposefully created for human habitation. In fact, no one knew why the obelisks had appeared simultaneously five years ago in the centres of twelve of the largest cities on Earth.

Since their arrival Allen's monthly missions, as he thought of them, were always to the cities occupied by the obelisks. The routine was always the same. He would be alerted by a golden figure's calm voice in his head telling him to make his way to London Airport, where he would board a Serene plane and instantly lose consciousness.

The next thing he knew it would be one or two days later and he'd be sitting on a bench near one of the obelisks. In the early days the same routine would transpire, and he would come to his senses in various far-flung cities around the world. He would check his softscreen and more often than not find he had a photo-shoot appointment the very same day somewhere not far away. For the past five years, however, every time he regained consciousness he was close to an obelisk – leading him to assume that his 'missions' and the obelisks were in some way linked.

A few months ago he'd taken the monorail into London with Sally, and after a morning spent in the National Gallery Allen had suggested a stroll to Marble Arch. There they, along with thousands of other curious sightseers, walked around the base of the obelisk, marvelling at its seamlessness, its lack of features, the faint pulsing warmth it gave off.

The media had not been slow in suggesting what the towers might be: they were, opined a respected international newsfeed, where the Serene themselves dwelled, looking out with sophisticated surveillance apparatus at the doings of the human race. More bizarre suggestions included the idea that they were the very engines that maintained the Serene's regime of non-violence across the face of the Earth, that they were the physical essence of the extraterrestrials themselves, or that they were alien prisons where malcontents from across the galaxy were suspended and stored.

Allen subscribed to none of these theories. The obelisks were, he surmised, meeting places where summits between fellow representatives like himself gathered to conduct Serene business – fulfilling much the same role as did the amphitheatre in the conjoined starships a decade ago.

Of course, quite what business he and the other representatives were conducting was another mystery.

He sat back and watched the crowds of Japanese workers and shoppers pass back and forth across the plaza. Visually not much had changed in the populated centres of the world. The scene here ten years ago, before the coming of the Serene, would be much the same as this one, other than the minor changes of fashion, advertisements and some architecture. The changes were on a more substantial, psychological level, he thought – which had an effect on the people of the plaza. There seemed to be a more carefree atmosphere wherever crowds gathered now, a realisation that the threat of violence, however remote, was no more, so that individuals were no longer burdened with the subconscious fear of their fellow man. It was the same wherever he went, a joyful absence of fear which promoted, in turn, a definite altruism: he was sure he'd seen, over the course of the last few years, acts of kindness, generosity and selflessness in a larger measure than before the arrival of the aliens.

He considered his own life over the past ten years, and smiled to himself as he realised that perhaps the greater difference made to it had not been the coming of the Serene, but the arrival of Sally Walsh and his daughter, Hannah.

He often experienced a retrospective shiver of dread at the thought that he might never have met Sally Walsh. He had been in the right place at the right time: a photo-shoot in the drought-stricken region of Karamoja where, just an hour before he was due to pack up and leave, Sally had arrived in a battered Land Rover to treat seriously malnourished tribespeople.

He'd liked the look of the thin, washed-out doctor instantly, and had made an excuse to extend his photographic session.

Their life together in England since then had been little short of idyllic.

He missed Sally and Hannah on his days away, and when he worked in locations around Britain between missions for the Serene, but he counted himself fortunate that he had the majority of every month – perhaps twenty days – to get under their feet while he ostensibly did the housework.

Thoughts of Sally made him reach for his softscreen. It would be the middle of the night in England, but she might have left a message.

He smiled as he saw her name at the top of the list, and accessed her call. A second later he sat up with alarm as his wife's distraught face filled the screen. "*Geoff. Something awful...*"

His heart jumped sickeningly, but her next words reassured him on that score: "*Hannah's fine and so am I. It's Kath. There was an accident. I saw it."* Her face crumpled, and Allen wanted nothing more than to hold her. *"Oh, Geoff, it was awful, awful... Please ring me back as soon as you can. I love you."*

He checked the time of the message: she had left it over three hours ago.

He called back immediately, realising that Sally was likely to be sound asleep. There was no reply, so he left a message, whispering urgently into the screen, *"Sally... I got your call. I'll be home in around ten, twelve hours. I don't know what to say. I'm so sorry. I'm thinking of you. I love you."*

He signed off, aware of the inadequacy of his words, and stared unseeingly across the plaza.

A TALL, TANNED, dark-haired woman in a short yellow sun dress had turned on her seat a couple of tables away and was watching him. She was perhaps in her mid-thirties, with the poised elegance of a film star or ballerina. Her face was hauntingly familiar, and he wondered if that was where he'd seen her at some point, on screen or stage.

Her gaze persisted and she smiled, and Allen, being English and unused to the attention of glamorous women, looked away and felt himself colour maddeningly.

He was aware, peripherally, of her uncrossing her long legs, standing and striding across the plaza towards his table.

Only when her shadow fell across him did he look up. His smile faltered.

She said, in Mediterranean-accented English, "I never forget a face."

"Then you have the advantage of me," he said, "because I do. Forgive me, but have we met?"

She touched the back of an empty chair with long fingers. "Would you mind...?"

"No, please."

She sat down, signalled to a waiter with the air of one accustomed to attracting instant attention, and ordered an espresso.

She offered her hand. "Nina Ricci, and we have not met. But, ten years ago, we did attend the same gathering, and I have seen you once or twice since."

"I'm Geoff," he said, and only then did the belated penny drop. "Ah," he said, relieved. "The Serene starships..." The tall, Italian-sounding woman who had been the first person to ask the Serene a question.

"That's right. We were among the few who asked questions back then. I think most people were petrified by fear, but not we..."

He wondered why she had come to speak to him. He said, "For the ten years I've been a representative, I've never met another one."

She sipped her coffee and smiled dazzlingly. "Ah, but I think that is because you have not been looking, Geoff."

"And you have?"

"I am by nature a curious person. I want always to know how, what, why, when, who..."

"You'd make a fine journalist."

"That is what I am, Geoff. A feature writer for the *Corriere della Sera,* Roma. I'm here to cover the opening of the arboreal city in Fujiyama."

"Snap. That's where I'm going." He patted his bag hanging from the back of his chair. "Photographer."

"But of course" – she pierced him with her olive-dark eyes – "that was not the principal reason we were brought here."

He smiled. "Of course not. And your journalist's curiosity would like to know why?"

In reply, she turned in her seat – the graceful torque of her back suggestive again of a ballerina – and pointed a long finger at the sable obelisk towering over the plaza.

She said, "Have you made the connection, Geoff?"

"That for the past few years we always wake up close to an obelisk? Yes, it had occurred to me."

"And do you wonder what we do in there?"

"So... you think that we actually enter the obelisks?"

"I do, and so do the other three or four representatives I've met over the years."

He shook his head. "Anyway, as to your question: pass. I've no idea."

She pulled a mock-shocked expression. "No? Surely you must have? An intelligent Englishman like yourself?" She was baiting him.

"My wife would disagree about the intelligent bit," he said, pleased for some reason that he'd mentioned Sally. He shrugged. "I don't know... We're conducting Serene business. So... I assumed in the early days we were meeting business people, heads of state, the powerful movers and shakers of the world. I see no reason why we're not still doing that. Maybe... maybe we're passing down the wisdom of the Serene."

She was looking at him askance. She had a repertory of practised facial expressions, like an actress forever anticipating the close-up shot. "Do you really think this, when the Serene have in their service a legion of the so-called 'golden figures'?"

He thought about it. "I might be wrong, but I always thought the self-aware entities manifested themselves only to us, the representatives – and in the early days stationed themselves on high rooftops and mountain summits, of course."

She considered him for a few seconds, then said, "Reality check, Geoff. The golden figures are amongst us."

He stared at her. "They are?" He made a show of looking around the plaza and finding none. "Strange, but I don't see a single one."

She leaned forward, elbows on table, pointed chin lodged in her cupped palm. "That is because, unobservant Englishman, they are in disguise."

"Ah..." he said, and pointed at her. "But if they are disguised, then how could I be observant enough to spot them?"

She nodded. "Point taken. Perhaps I am lucky, because once I observed an accident."

He finished his coffee. "I'm afraid you've lost me." He smiled, intrigued by this beautiful, inquisitive Italian.

"I one day was walking down the avenue in Barcelona when I saw a man run over by an automobile. Splat! Dead and no doubting the fact. Only, a day later I saw the *same* man walking as large as life down the street a mile or so away... I never forget a face, as I said. So, being the curious type of girl, I accosted the man and asked him how, since I saw him die pretty messily the other day, he was now as fit as fit can be and showing no signs of his injuries."

"And he told you?"

"He smiled and said my name, and took me to a quiet park nearby–"

"You should be wary of men who suggest quiet parks."

She smiled. "But you see, I knew then that he was not a man, I mean a real man." She waved a hand. "And then, when we are quite alone in the park, he becomes a golden figure and tells me that there are hundreds of thousands of his kind passing as human – and, moreover, have been for many, many decades."

She stared at him with large eyes as much to say, "So, what do you think of that?"

"Amazing," he responded on cue. "What else did he say?" He thought of the self-aware entities going among the human race for decades, doing their good work...

"Not a lot, other than if I were to try to broadcast what he had told me, or write about it for publication, I would find myself unable to do so. I would... what is the English word...? spasm."

"But I take it it's okay to tell an audience of just one?"

She shrugged her bare shoulders. "Evidently. Anyway, do you see me spasming?"

He recalled her original question. "So... because there are a legion of golden figures working amongst us, you think that the reason we... we gather in the obelisks is not merely to hand down the wisdom of the Serene, liaise with the powerful and such?"

She pointed a pistol finger at him. "Exactly so, Geoff."

He nodded. "Intriguing. So... what do you think we do in there?"

She pulled a glum face. "Ah, now – I was hoping that you might be able to shed some illumination on that."

"Sorry to disappoint, Nina. I've no idea. But what about the other representatives you've met?"

She made a carefree gesture. "Oh, they too do not know."

"But do you have a theory? Come on, an intelligent journalist like you..." he said mockingly.

She smiled. "Of course. I think they are studying us."

"Studying us?"

"I think, like in a horror movie, once we are inside the obelisks they take us apart atom by atom and see how we work."

He tried not to laugh. "Funny, when I leave the obelisks – always assuming, of course, that I enter them in the first place – I feel pretty well for a man who's been deconstructed atom by atom. I don't suppose you have any valid reason to think this?"

She shrugged her tanned shoulders again. "Just, as you say, a hunch."

He shook his head. "A wild hunch, if you don't mind me saying. The Serene have had plenty of time to study us, take us apart, before they came here – if what you say about the SAEs being here for ages is correct. At this stage I'd say it was pretty late to be studying us."

"Well, what is *your* hunch?"

"I don't have one. Sorry, but in this instance I think speculation is useless. We couldn't have guessed at the capabilities of the Serene before they came here, so trying to second guess their methods now is futile."

"So you're happy to be their tool, and ask no questions?"

He thought about it. "Yes, I am. The Serene have rendered the human race incapable of committing acts of violence. That's a pretty magnanimous gift. I'm happy to do their bidding in return." He looked at her. "What about you?"

She nodded. "I think what the Serene have done here is wonderful."

"Did you listen to the nay-sayers in the early days? The right-wingers and libertarians who foresaw the end of the human race as we knew it?"

"I listened, and thought them wrong. You?"

"I heard what they said and hoped they were wrong, but feared they might be right."

The newsfeeds and internet had been rife with doom-mongers in the first couple of years after the Serene intervention in human affairs. They forecast that such a radical alteration in the mechanism of the human psyche – the total abnegation of an individual's ability to carry through acts of violence – would have dire psychological consequences. So-called experts stated that violence was a safety-valve which, if not allowed to blow from time to time, would store up untold mental pressure which would in time burst with catastrophic results.

Now Nina said, "I always thought they were wrong, Geoff. Okay, so if everyone on the planet committed acts of violence every day, day in day out, then they might have had a case. But think about it – how many acts of violence did you perpetrate before the coming of the Serene?"

He shrugged. "Not many. In fact... I can remember defending myself against a bully when I was twelve, and once or twice *wanting* to hit someone, but never carrying out the urge."

"There you are then. I am the same, along with the majority of the people in this square, I think. The nay-sayers, as you call, them were wrong. Violence is not a pre-requisite of being human, just a nasty side-effect of social conditions. And violence is certainly not a *right*, as some would claim it is."

He smiled. "I think you're correct there. Nina."

She pointed to his empty cup. "Would you care for another coffee?"

"I've had two already. Another one and I'd be hyper." He looked at his watch. "Our train is in forty minutes. Tell you what, a beer would go down nicely. For you?"

"Do you think they have Peroni, Geoff?"

He asked the waiter, but the only foreign lagers available were Leffe and Red Star. She said she would prefer Leffe, and he ordered two glasses. "My wife's favourite," he said.

"And what does she make of being married to a representative of the Serene?"

The beers arrived and Allen took a refreshing mouthful. "I think she's... proud, and intrigued."

She cocked an eyebrow. "Proud to be married to you, because the Serene picked only the best?"

He looked at her. "Did they? I never claim that."

"When I was chosen, Geoff, I asked the golden figure who was shepherding me: why me? It replied that I was selected because of my humanity."

He nodded. "I recall being told something similar. But there are millions of others out there with just such qualities who weren't selected." He shrugged. "Sally, my wife, was a doctor in Africa before the Serene arrived. She had a... a deep-seated need to help others, which I suppose came from being the daughter of dyed-in-the-wool socialists. I don't know. My wife is just as good a person as I am, if not better."

Nina nodded without replying and watched him as she sipped her drink. "Can you think of any negatives to the coming of the Serene?" she asked at last.

He had to think about that. "Personally, no. I know that some evolutionary biologists have argued that the Serene intervention has steered our race away from the course on which it was set..." He shrugged. "But then who's to say that that course was in anyway sacrosanct, or the right one, so to speak? It's an argument that has raged in politics since the days of colonialism – should 'super-powers' dabble in the affairs of so-called lesser or undeveloped nations, even if for their good? The Serene are here. That's a fact, and in my opinion the world is a better place because of it." He sipped his beer and added, "Of course, some religious fundamentalists still claim the Serene are in league with Satan."

She waved that away as if swatting a fly. "Nut cases and cranks."

He smiled. "The world's religions have taken something of a battering, thanks to our alien friends," he said.

"The *traditional* religions. Do you know how many religions have sprung up over the past few years, *inspired* by the Serene?"

He'd heard of the phenomenon, and said, "Half a dozen, or even fewer?"

She shook her head, smiling. "Would you believe over five thousand?"

"No. Five thousand? Where did you read that?"

"I actually wrote a feature for my paper on the new religions. For some deep-seated reason, the human race needs to believe in a god-like figure, a deity, and in the eyes of many the Serene amply fill that god-shaped hole."

"But five thousand?"

She shrugged. "And these new religions span the globe, from east to west, north to south, supplanting the old religions and gaining strength."

"I wonder how the Serene regard them?"

She made a rosebud of her lips, then said, "My guess is that they despair." She smiled. "The Serene strike me as supremely rationalist."

"Another of your hunches?" he asked.

She laughed. "Maybe so."

"Well, I suppose if the Serene come here and perform

miracles, they can't be surprised at the reaction of some of our more credulous cousins." He tipped his head back and forth. "They certainly fit the bill. Our saviours, who set us on a new moral course..."

She squinted at him. "I never had you down as a religious type, Geoff Allen."

He smiled at her. Her familiarity, her assumed knowledge of him, he might have found discomfiting in one less affable than Nina Ricci, but she made her personal pronouncements with an easy, almost mocking candour that he found at once charming and disarming.

Only then did he wonder how she knew his surname, for he was sure he had introduced himself only as 'Geoff'.

He asked, "What other Serene-related stories have you worked on recently?"

"The big one was an investigation into how the Serene have been 'assisting' some of our biggest drugs companies."

He smiled. "Before their coming, I would have said that the drugs companies certainly needed 'assisting'," he said with sarcasm.

"Of course, the Serene have changed everything to do with the business model of the pharmaceuticals," she said. "Now instead of working for their share-holders, like every other company before them, they are working for the people. My investigations uncovered the fact that many of the newly released drugs of recent years have their origins off-planet. I spoke to experts who assured me that they were derived from chemical bases that did not exist on

Earth." She shrugged. "Which would go to support the fact that in the last decade human life-expectancy, worldwide, has increased by an average of a little over twelve years."

He thought about it. "I suppose the resulting increase in population will be sustained by the limitless supply of energy and the vast new cities... But even so, the planet is finite."

She was smiling at him.

"What?" he asked.

"Would you like to hear another of my hunches?"

"Do I have a choice?"

"No," she said. "My hunch is this: I think soon the Serene will take us off-planet, away from Earth, to colonies in the solar system..."

"Nice idea," he said. "Imagine living on a moon beneath the rings of Saturn..."

"You mock me, but I am deadly serious. As you say, the planet is a finite system, and the population is increasing dramatically. So where will we go, but off-planet?"

He shrugged. "You might be right," he said. "If the Serene can bring other forms of life here, then I see no reason why they can't take us... elsewhere."

"'Other forms of life'? Oh, you mean the arboreal cities?"

He nodded. "I'm looking forward to seeing them. I'm told they're the eighth wonder of the world."

"But shouldn't that be eleventh, coming after the eight joined starships, the greening cities, and..." – she pointed a crimson lacquered nail at the towers across the plaza – "the obelisks?"

He laughed. "I don't know. I've lost count."

He'd read online accounts of the arboreal cities, and the mammoth trees from Antares II which made terrestrial giant redwoods seem like saplings in comparison, and when his editor had suggested he do a photo-shoot of the Fujiyama arboreal city – as he would be visiting Japan anyway – he had jumped at the chance.

He checked his watch. "But speaking of arboreal cities... our train leaves in ten minutes."

They finished their drinks and crossed the plaza to the station, had their softscreen reservations scanned, and strolled the length of the platform to the second carriage. Allen relaxed in a luxurious window seat and minutes later the torpedo-train slipped from the station.

Nina Ricci sat opposite him, silent as she regarded the reforestation projects north of Tokyo.

Allen stared through the window, noting the new sea defences that had been erected along the coast after the tsunami of 2018. They slid past a vast energy distribution station just as a beam of concentrated light fell to Earth like a meteor, dazzling him and the hundred other passengers who 'oohed' and 'aahed' like school children.

As the train sped around the bend of a bay he closed his eyes, feigning sleep, and considered Sally and her distraught message.

CHAPTER FIVE

SALLY FOUND A post-it note and wrote: *I'm in the back garden. Take the side path to the left and I'll see you there.* She tore off the yellow rectangle, stuck the note to the front door beside the big brass knocker and retreated to the back garden.

For some reason she didn't want to open the front door and confront Kath – or whatever it was that Kath had become. She did not, she thought, want to be confined in the house with her. It was not a thought she could rationalise, and part of her felt guilty for having it. But it came to her that she needed to meet this new, resurrected Kath in the open, in the sunlight, so that she could run if she needed to.

She was still in a state of shock. She recalled the dazed disbelief she had experienced just after the coming of the Serene. This was similar, only intensified a hundredfold. She felt abstracted from reality, as if she were moving in a bubble secluded from everything, her every sense retarded.

She crossed the garden and sat on the wooden bench beneath the flowering cherry tree. From here she could look back at the house, and the wicket gate to the side path through which, in a matter of minutes, Kath would walk. Kath Kemp, whom Sally had watched die yesterday...

It was an idyllic scene, with the sun shining and the wisteria giving off its heavy scent which wafted to her across the garden. The mullioned windows winked in the sunlight, and the borders were abundant with blooms. It was a scene that might be a hundred years old, so little had changed here in the past century.

The gate beside the house squeaked open and Sally sprang to her feet with a sharp, indrawn breath.

Kath Kemp paused, holding the gate open. She was perhaps twenty metres away from Sally and smiled that familiar smile at her.

Sally took a step forward, and then another. She felt like an invalid, learning to walk again after a terrible accident. She was aware of a pain in her chest and shortness of breath.

Kath too began walking, slowly, and they met in the middle of the lawn, drenched in sunlight, for all the world as if they had never met before.

Sally stared at the woman before her, stared at her broad, smiling face, her swept back hair. Her skin was flushed, alive; she exuded, as she had yesterday, a radiant compassion that Sally found impossible to describe or to quantify: it was who Kathryn Kemp *was*, an identifying signature, which filled Sally whenever she thought about her friend in absentia.

Kath reached out a small, broad hand, tentatively, as if unsure how she might be greeted.

After a second, Sally took it, almost gasped at its warmth, its... humanity.

She knew, then, suddenly, what had happened.

The Serene had somehow, with the superior technology they possessed, brought Kathryn Kemp back to life. They had deemed her too valuable a person in their schema to allow to die. This was essentially the same Kath as before, but new, remade.

Kath squeezed her hand and said, "Shall we sit down?" She indicated the bench beneath the cherry tree. They crossed the lawn and sat side by side in the dappled shade.

Sally turned and stared at her friend. "I saw it happen, Kath. You quoted Housman, and then... then the truck came around the corner and..."

"I'm sorry," Kath said. "I can't imagine what you must have gone through."

Sally smiled to herself. That was Kath, the compassionate: she had died, and been brought back to life, and she apologised for the hurt that this had occasioned.

"I have a lot to tell you," Kath said in a soft voice, "to explain."

"I... I think I know what happened. You are important to the Serene, Kath. And they're so powerful. I mean, look how they've banished human violence. What is it to bring the dead back to life?"

Kath stared at her with wide eyes.

Sally said, "I'm right, aren't I?"

Kath shook her head. "No," she said gently.

"I don't understand. You're the same Kath I've always known. I saw you die, and here you are, alive... The Serene must have brought you back to life. You were *dead*, Kath!"

"I was dead, and the Serene did resurrect me – I am the same Kath Kemp you have always known, but the truth of it is that I am not, and never was, human."

Sally felt dizzy. Had she not been sitting down she would have slumped into the seat. A hot flush cascaded across her face.

"Then what?"

"I am what you call a self-aware entity."

Sally shook her head in a mute negative, unable to find her voice. At last she said, "No. No, that can't be right, can it? I mean... I knew you before the Serene arrived. I knew you at college. We were twenty. That first meeting, in the canteen and we both reached for the last..."

"Vanilla slice."

"And we were friends from the start, best friends, and that was years and years before the Serene arrived... And I remember you saying – I remember it clearly! You said you didn't believe in UFOs and little green men. You called it all..."

"A wish-fulfilling delusion..." She nodded, smiled. "Yes, I did."

Sally took a deep breath. She felt as if she were about to faint. She fought to remain conscious. "Then... in that case..."

"I am and always have been a self-aware entity," Kath said.

Sally sprang to her feet and ran off down the garden, hugging herself tightly, her thoughts in turmoil.

She stopped before the swing, brought up short by its ridiculous, meretricious essence. The swing made her think of Hannah, and what she might be doing now. Break time – so she would be chomping on her health bar, sipping apple juice.

Sally knew that when she turned around and looked at the bench beneath the cherry tree, it would be empty. She had hallucinated the meeting with Kath, was suffering hysteric delusions brought about by the shock of her friend's death last night.

She turned around.

Kath Kemp sat on the bench in the shifting, dappled sunlight, gazing across the lawn at her.

Sally hugged herself, as if protectively, and stared across at Kath Kemp, or at whatever Kath Kemp was.

A self-aware entity?

The idea was impossible.

Slowly, hesitantly, she retraced her steps and paused before the bench, staring down at her friend. Kath looked up, squinting against the sunlight.

She found her voice at last. "But you look so human, Kath." You *are* so human, Kath...

"Of course." Kath smiled. "I had to pass for human." She patted the bench. "Please, sit down."

Sally obeyed, then said, "But everything we shared, the friendship. You were... my best friend, Kath. We shared everything. I told you..." She stopped, staring at Kath. She had told Kath *everything*, had opened her heart to the woman... and Kath had listened, taken it all in, and for her own part had reciprocated... *nothing* about herself.

Had that been, Sally thought, because she had nothing human to say about herself?

"But I am still your best friend, Sally. I might not be human, but that doesn't mean that everything we shared is invalidated. I am an empathetic, thinking, feeling, being. I have emotions, emotions that over the years of interacting with your kind have flourished, become almost human. Your friendship means everything to me. This... my death, your learning of my true nature, should not come between us."

Sally sat in silence, trying to order her thoughts. At last she said, "A self-aware entity..." She shrugged. "It means nothing really, does it? Surely everything sentient in existence is a self-aware entity?" She stopped, staring at her friend, and asked softly, "Just what are you?"

Kath took a deep breath, as Sally had seen her do on a thousand previous occasions when preparing to answer a complex question. "I will give you my history, Sally, and see what you make of it."

Sally had the ridiculous impulse, then, to ask Kath, to ask this self-aware entity, if she would care for a cup of tea. She restrained herself.

Kath said, "I am an organic somatic structure grown around a programmable sentient-core nurtured to term in a vat on the planet of Delta Pavonis V, twenty light years from Earth." She paused, then went on, "I am partly organic, partly artificial. I am what you humans describe, crudely, as a cybernetic organism. In the Serene system, I am accorded full citizen's rights; I am beholden to no one. I have what you call free will."

"But you said you were programmable."

"My sentient core, in infancy, was programmable – but then you could say the same of a human baby's brain. It is programmable, and *is* programmed, by its environment, by its parents and peers. It is a question, I suppose, of defining one's terms. Because I was programmable does not *de facto* make me some soulless machine in the employ of the Serene."

"But you work for them?"

"Through choice, yes. Because I perceive what the Serene are doing, here and elsewhere, as a wholly beneficial and *good* endeavour."

"But... you were programmable. Therefore, you were programmed."

"In my early years, yes. I was programmed with the knowledge of what the Serene were doing. But, later, I was given the choice of whether to serve them, or not."

A silence came between them, and at last Sally asked, "And you are... immortal?"

Kath smiled and shook her head. "I will live for a long time, perhaps a thousand years, before my mind and body... degrades, and I die."

Sally stared at the entity she had thought of, over the years, as her best friend, and something struck her. She asked in almost a whisper, as if afraid of the answer, "And how old are you?"

Kath tipped her head, closed one eye, and looked at Sally. How familiar that semi-amused expression

was! How many times had Sally seen it in the past?
A hundred, a thousand?

Kath said, with a twinkle in her eye, "I am a little
over two hundred years old."

Sally nodded, as if it were perfectly acceptable to
have one's best friend inform you that she was over
two centuries old.

"And before you came to Earth... you lived on
Delta Pavonis V?"

"For a hundred years," Kath said, "while in
training for my assignment on Earth."

"So... so you have been on Earth for more than a
hundred years?"

"A little over one hundred, in various guises."

Sally took a breath, her heart racing. She felt as if
she were hyperventilating, and tried to assess what
she was thinking, feeling.

She had always assumed that she had been Kath's
best friend – as they had shared so much in the past
– and to find out now that Kath had had a previous
incarnation, or many incarnations on Earth, gave
her an obscure sense of being let down, of not being
unique in Kath's estimation.

Ridiculous, she knew.

She said, "A hundred years? So the Serene have
known for that long that one day they would come
to Earth and... change things?"

"For much longer than that," Kath said.

"And they sent you here to...?"

"Initially I was sent here on a fact-finding mission,
to gather and collate information and send it back to
our home planet."

"And then?"

"And then, along with other self-aware entities, I helped to smooth the way, to create benevolent institutions, create an intellectual atmosphere wherein the very notion of the *other*, the alien, could be discussed, accepted."

"You had a different guise? You were not always Kathryn Kemp, of course?"

"Of course. I was a male for many years, then female, and then a male again."

"And... how many of your fellow self-aware entities were there, and still are?"

"We numbered, in the early years, in our hundreds, and then fifty years ago in our thousands. Now... there are perhaps a million of us on the planet."

A million, Sally thought.

"And you were never found out? There were never accidents like last night, when you might have been hospitalised, examined and discovered?"

"We are similar, physiologically, to yourselves. A surgical examination of our bodies would reveal nothing – only a neurological scan, or neurosurgery might give away the lie, but we had means of ensuring we never compromised our identities."

She smiled at Sally, then surprised her by saying, "I don't know about you, Sally, but I would love a cup of tea..." She gestured to the house. "Let me go and potter about in the kitchen, while you sit here and think about what I've said. Earl Grey?"

"My favourite."

"I know..."

Impulsively, both Sally and Kath, human and Serene

self-aware entity, came together in a hug. Sally held on and closed her eyes, and told herself that it really didn't matter that her friend was not human.

Kath moved into the house and Sally sat in the shade, watching her as she moved back and forth behind the kitchen window.

Kath was Kath, she told herself – the friend she had had for more than thirty years. Did it matter, really matter, that she was alien? Perhaps if Kath had befriended Sally back in their college days with some ulterior motive in mind, then Sally would have cause for unease. But as far as she could tell they had come together spontaneously, drawn to each other by that inexplicable personal chemistry that attracted human beings to each other... or in this case humans and self-aware entities.

Unless...

A thought struck Sally as she watched Kath ease herself sideways through the back door bearing a tray.

Sally drew up a small table and Kath poured two cups of Earl Grey.

They sat side by side and Kath said, "I hope this doesn't change things between us, Sally. I value our friendship."

"So do I, of course. But there is something I'd like to know."

"Go on."

"Our friendship... Why? I mean, when we met, I was instantly attracted to you. It was spontaneous." She looked at her friend, then away across the garden. "What I'd like to know is... was it planned on the part of the Serene, for some ultimate purpose?"

She took a breath, and voiced her fear: "Were you aware of what would happen, with Geoff being a representative...?"

"Do you mean," Kath asked, "can we see into the future?"

"I suppose I do mean that, yes."

"Well, of course not. The Serene are powerful, that I will admit, and much of our science might seem to you like magic, but there are some things that are even beyond the remit of the Serene."

"So our friendship?"

"Is nothing more than friendship, and nothing less. A coming together of like souls, if you will. We... are encouraged by our overseers to *inhabit* our lives as humans, to live and think and feel as you do. Part of that is to experience what makes being human so often rewarding, to share friendships and..."

"And love?"

Kath nodded. "That too, occasionally."

Sally asked, "And you have known love?"

"Not this time, Sally. For the past thirty years I have been so busy with... with laying the groundwork, that I have had little time left for affairs of the heart. But in a previous life...yes, I loved a woman."

Sally sipped her tea and regarded her friend. "That must have been hard."

"In some ways it was, but in others it was not. We were together for twenty years. We self-aware entities are... developed with an aging capability, for want of a better expression. I grew old and watched my lover grow old too, and I felt sadness that her time was so brief while mine, comparatively, was so extended. To watch her die was painful, but an experience, I told myself, that was essential in order to fully understand what it is to be human."

Sally looked at her friend, wondering at her past lives. "When was this?"

"In the middle of the last century. My guise was that of a British diplomat working at various postings around the world. I met and fell in love with a wonderful woman, a novelist whose work I still keep, and read. It's a comfort to have her voice to hand."

They drank their tea in silence for a time. A slight wind stirred the boughs of the cherry tree, and its scent descended like a balm.

Sally said at last, "I would have thought, when you 'died' this time, that... I don't know; that the life you had would have ceased and you would have started a new incarnation."

Kath nodded. "It sometimes does happen like that, Sally. It's a 'natural' transition, so to speak. But not this time. I have important work which it is essential I continue in my guise as Kathryn Kemp."

"And I suppose you can't tell me of this work?"

"I'm sorry, I can't. The work is sensitive and confidential."

She looked at her friend, who was holding the small china teacup in both hands before her wide lips and smiling across the garden, considering who knew what memories? Sally said, "But you need not have told me all this, Kath. You could have been resurrected, and gone back to your life and our paths might never have crossed again."

What did she hope would be Kath's reply? That their friendship meant so much that she, Kath, could not continue living without telling Sally that she had not in fact met her end in a leafy English lane?

Kath was nodding. "I could have done that, but I would have been uncomfortable, both on a personal level and on a more fundamental, logistical level. I, Kath, your friend, would have been distressed at your pain, your grief – quite apart from the fact that, one day, our paths might have crossed... and I am human enough to envisage the hurt this would have caused you." She reached out and squeezed Sally's hand. "Also, I wanted to tell you what really happened last night."

"What really happened? But I saw what happened? The speeding truck..."

Kath was regarding her earnestly. "Didn't it occur to you that the truck came out of nowhere rather fast?"

"Well, yes, but..."

"And the rapid response of the ambulance and the police? They arrived in minutes after your call – a world record, wouldn't you say?"

"I... I don't know. I was in shock. Numbed. I lost all track of time." She stared at her friend. "But I don't understand. What do you mean?"

"The ambulance and the paramedics, the young police officer who questioned you, they were all, like me, self-aware entities."

Sally said tentatively, "Yes, that makes sense. When one of their own dies, I can see that it's best that they respond to the incident themselves."

"That's true, and we do institute such procedures, but in this instance there were... special circumstances, is perhaps the best way to put it."

Sally repeated the phrase.

Kath paused for a second or two, regarding her tea. She looked up. "This is what I, we, wanted you to know. You, and people around the world like your husband Geoff, the special representatives of the Serene, are essential to our regime on Earth and beyond. It is only fair that we share with you the facts of the situation."

"Now you're sounding like a character from a bad spy novel."

They both laughed. Back in their twenties, in their student days, as a relief from course work Kath had taken refuge in spy novels of the fifties and sixties, often reading out lurid passages to Sally over breakfast.

It was one of the many hundreds, thousands, of memories Sally had of her friend which she would be forced to reassess, in light of recent revelations. Why was an alien self-aware entity reading cold war spy novels? As part of her deep cover guise, as an attempt to understand the machinations of human politics?

She shook her head, clearing her thoughts, and asked, "And what are the facts of the situation?"

Kath regarded her half-empty cup. It was a while before she spoke. "The Serene, in what they are doing here on Earth and elsewhere, have opposition; enemies, if you like."

"Enemies?"

"The universe is vast. This small galaxy alone

has at least a hundred sentient, space-faring races, though only two as evolved as the Serene."

"And one of these...?"

Kath nodded. "I'll spare you the lurid details, but the Serene and our opponents have been pitched against each other for millennia."

"And they oppose what you are doing here on Earth?"

"One day, Sally, when I have more time, I will tell you the history of our mutual opposition, our mutually exclusive philosophies of species evolution. Suffice it to say that they will do everything to halt our progress here on Earth and across the solar system."

"And last night – how did they manage to...?" She thought of the truck, and what Kath had said about it appearing from nowhere.

"Sally, our opponents are not here, physically. That eventuality would be a disaster – but they infiltrate our ranks on a virtual level, let's say."

"I'm not sure I understand."

Kath nodded, and paused to consider her explanation. "The way the Serene have turned the human race against violence is to... manipulate reality on a quantum level. To use a crude analogy, they re-program the 'strings' that are the fundamental building blocks of reality. Now, on occasions, our opponents are able to get past our defences and infiltrate this virtuality, re-program events to their own desires. Last night was one small, and very insignificant example – but they are becoming more frequent of late and what we fear is that they are a precursor to a greater, more sustained attack.

Last night's incident and others like it was our enemy testing the waters, so to speak, stretching the parameters of our defences. My death was trivial, but we fear what they are building up to."

Sally finished her tea and set the cup on the seat beside her. "Geoff and I... over the years we'd lie awake and stare out at the stars, and do you know what? We'd speculate about the Serene... what was out there, what the Serene were doing. I think Geoff even surmised that the Serene must have enemies, political, if not military."

She looked at her friend. "I believe that the Serene are working for the best interests of humanity, Kath." She shrugged and smiled. "I suppose I have to believe that, don't I? I have only the evidence of my experience, limited though that is, and the parameters of my prejudice. But, really, what as human beings do we know?" She thought of the fishpond analogy and said, "We are like fish being fed crumbs by vastly superior benefactors. We know nothing, really, of what lies beyond our pond."

"I can only tell you what you would expect to hear from the representative of the Serene," she said, "and that is that we have the best interests of the human race at heart. You are destined for great things; please believe me when I say this, and that your destiny lies beyond the bounds of your home planet, and will be determined by the success of the Serene in defeating the objectives of our enemy."

"Which is why you told me about the push to Mars?"

"And beyond. We will move from Earth, terraforming and inhabiting the planets, first Mars, then Venus; we will set up colonies among the asteroids – vaster and more complex than the mining outposts that exist out there now – and then you will colonise the moons of Jupiter and Saturn, and beyond."

"And one day, the stars?"

"Not for a long, long time, Sally," Kath said. "There is much to be done before then, much to prepare the human race for. There is work to be done in the solar system itself."

"Work?"

"One day, when we are on Mars or beyond, it might be safe to confide in you. For the present, and especially after last night's events, I must be wary."

"So... your enemies don't know of your ultimate objectives?"

Kath smiled, then laughed. "It is always unwise, and dangerous, to underestimate the knowledge of one's opponents. I sincerely hope that they are unaware of what we plan, but who can tell?" She stood. "I mentioned an e-brochure last night, about the colonisation of Mars. I have it in the car. I'll fetch it and then, maybe, it would be nice to prepare lunch together, yes?"

"That would be wonderful."

Kath set off across the lawn, and Sally called after her. "Kath, be careful..."

Her friend turned and beamed her a wonderful smile. "I'll do my best."

Sally sat in silence in the shifting sunlight and realised that she felt an odd, lazy contentment; Kath, her best friend, was back from the dead, and the Serene were leading the human race towards its destiny...

And, tomorrow, Geoff would return.

Kath was back minutes later with the brochure. "In a couple of days I'll drop by and we'll discuss everything," she said.

"And when Geoff gets back I can tell him about last night?"

Kath nodded. "Everything."

They passed into the house and, together, prepared lunch.

CHAPTER SIX

THE FUJIYAMA ARBOREAL city occupied the entirety of the coastal valley basin and the hills on the far side. It appeared on the horizon as the monotrain rounded a long bend, and a murmur of appreciation passed through the carriage. Allen stared, attempting to make sense of what he saw. He had expected a large forest of trees similar to sequoia, but each one tall and broad enough to house thousands of citizens, set in an idyllic garden vale.

What he saw was a series of silver-grey skyscrapers, each one several kilometres high, tapering to points. Located at intervals on the flanks of each tower were what looked like platforms, similar to bracket fungus, and above each platform an array of silver antennae that sprouted from the side of the tree and terminated in large crimson globes.

It was a sight eerily alien, he thought.

"It's not what I was expecting," he admitted to Nina Ricci.

She looked at him. "You haven't seen pictures of them before?"

He shook his head. "I wanted to come to this project fresh, with no preconceived views of what I was about to see. It sometimes helps me to see things from a new, fresh angle."

"Well, what do you think?"

"I'm not sure. It's visually arresting. Very alien. I wonder what it'd be like to live in one of those things?"

"That's what I hope to find out when I interview the first people selected for the honour."

He glanced at her. "And who are they?"

"Coastal farmers, mainly, and fisher-folk. The people who lost everything in the last tsunami."

"Makes sense. But with the proscription on fishing...?"

"The Serene found occupations for everyone in a profession hit by the *charea*. The fisher-folk became farmers, along with many of the world's formerly unemployed."

He looked at the bristling city of alien trees. "And they farm what...?"

"See the vast green area at the base of each tree?" She pointed. "From a distance, the arboreal city appears closely packed, but in actual fact there is something like a kilometre between each one. This makes for a lot of land to farm. Also, see those platforms climbing the towers in a helical formation?"

"I was wondering what they were."

"Well, I suppose you might call them fields, though it would be something of a misnomer. They grow micro-protein spores that are processed into a high protein food – each platform provides sufficient food to supply its section of the tower's inhabitants all the year round. Not that this is what they solely live on. Much of the processed spores are exported – I'm sure you've eaten it at some point."

"And these spores are alien?"

She nodded. "But tailored to our metabolisms."

The monotrain eased itself into a station unlike any other Allen had experienced. It was as if the train had come to an unscheduled halt in the country. He looked through the window at a greensward rolling away from the train, planted with regimented flower-beds and crossed by raised timber walkways. Only a sign, 'Welcome to Fujiyama Arboreal City,' told him that this was where the journey terminated.

They left the train and Allen found that many of the passengers were, like Nina and himself, accredited journalists and photographers. They were divided into small groups of four or five individuals and allotted a smiling, punctilious Japanese guide.

The plan was to tour the fields between the towers first, have a light meal in an *al fresco* cafeteria, and then visit one of the towers itself.

Allen was already shooting, then pausing between shots to marvel at the city. It was as if he'd been transported to the surface of some planet light years away. The trees towered overhead, taller than any structure he'd experienced, diminishing to vanishing points in the blue, cloudless sky.

The base of each dwelling tree was surrounded by a margin of garden, beyond which the farms proper began. The guide conducted them on a tour of the farms, transporting them on the raised timber walkway in small electric buggies. She gave a running commentary, detailing crop yields and growing patterns, which Allen recorded on his softscreen.

They motored above the level of the fields, passing human workers and automated pickers, silver spider-like robots with busy, multiple appendages.

"Each worker is required to put in a shift of four hours a day," their guide said. "The rest of their time is free to do with as they wish. Each city tower is equipped with recreational facilities, schools, art colleges, etcetera, as you will see later."

There was only so much he could photograph from the buggy. What he was cataloguing here was no more than what every other photo-journalist was getting; he decided that at some point during lunch he would slip off and snap some unofficial shots.

"There are more than two hundred city trees in the Fujiyama basin," their guide explained. "Each tree is inhabited by approximately ten thousand citizens, though such are the dimensions of each tree that living accommodation is more than spacious."

In a whispered aside to Nina, Allen said, "I thought studies done in the last century concluded that high-rise living was far from beneficial?"

She whispered in return, "I think that was due more to socio-economic factors than to the actual type of habitation, Geoff. If you put poor people in a confined space anywhere on Earth, with inadequate amenities and low employment... well, what would you expect the conditions to be like?"

He nodded. A cursory examination of the workers in the fields – along with what the guide had said about the living regimes here – suggested that conditions in the arboreal city were far preferable to the lives these people had led before they were relocated here.

The buggy arrived at a covered circular area between four rearing tress. Allen made out people eating at low tables and realised that he was hungry.

He, Nina, the guide and the three others in their group left the buggy and strolled across to the cafeteria. They sat cross-legged at a low table and scanned the menu.

They ate a surprisingly good seaweed salad with *yadha* – the local name for the spicy processed spores – accompanied by another local speciality, a sweet beer again derived from the alien spores.

Allen finished his beer and was about to tell Nina that he intended to slip off to get some 'local colour' shots, when she restrained him with a hand on his arm and said, "I have seen a friend over there–" she indicated a nearby table "–I would like you to meet. She too is a representative of the Serene."

Allen nodded, a little impatient at the delay. Nina rose from the low table, crossed the cafeteria and spoke to an Indian woman in her mid-twenties. The Indian rose with the sinuous grace of an uncoiling cobra and followed Nina back to Allen's table.

She sat down and smiled at him as Nina made the introductions. "Geoff Allen, this is Ana Devi, from India."

Ana Devi gave him a dazzlingly white smile and they shook hands. "Delighted to meet you, Mr Allen," she said.

The woman had a curiously handsome face that might, in other circumstances, be seen as beautiful. He saw strength in her eyes and line of jaw, a certain rawness that spoke to him of lowly origins and a hard childhood.

Nina murmured, "Geoff, too, is a representative."

Ana laughed and said to him, "Why am I not in the least bit surprised, Mr Allen? Nina makes it her duty to collect us, for some reason – is that not so, Nina?"

"Well, in the interest of possible future stories..."

"You will one day write about us, no?" Ana asked. "My story would fill a book, and maybe even two. Oh, some of the tales I could tell you!"

Allen looked at Nina. "How many others have you traced?"

She pursed her lips. "Perhaps a dozen. It's not that difficult."

Ana rocked her head in amazement. "Do you hear her? 'Not that difficult'! But Nina has probably told you that she has a photographic memory, and can recall the face of everyone she saw ten years ago when we came together in the Serene's starships."

"So all I have to do now is keep a close eye out for those faces when we come to our senses after our 'missions'," Nina explained.

Ana looked at Allen. "You are a photographer, no?"

Allen told her something about his life and work, and Ana stared at him with massive brown eyes and said, "Ah, Shropshire. I would one day love to visit that county. Wasn't there a poet...?" Her wide brow corrugated in concentration.

"Housman," Allen supplied, wondering why the recollection of the old poet should bring him a fleeting sense of melancholy.

"Ah, yes, Housman. *A Shropshire Lad*." She beamed. "I have visited London, of course, but never even left the capital. Is that a disgrace, Mr Allen?"

He murmured, "Of course not," and asked her what she was doing here.

"I am on an official visit to the arboreal city as I work in one of the wilderness cities. Mine is in India, and I supervise the city's food production. I am here to see how things are done on a much larger scale, and maybe pick up some useful tips. Also, I am looking into the feasibility of growing the alien spores at our commune, too."

"A remarkable foodstuff," he said.

She laughed. "I think it would go very well in curries, Mr Allen!"

They chatted for a further five minutes and, when Ana was talking to Nina about her life back in India, Allen excused himself and slipped away.

He left the cafeteria and strolled between a long row of fruit canes. In the distance, reduced by the perspective, a Japanese worker plucked raspberries from the canes with incredible speed and dexterity. He took a dozen shots, one of her blurred hands, high up in the cane, against a backdrop of a distant arboreal tower.

He thanked her, finding himself mirroring her repeated bows, and moved on.

He left the quadrant of soft fruit and came to an area where melons grew on abundant vines. Here, silver robots danced at speed, plucking full, ripe melons from the bushes and loading them into buggies affixed to their torsos.

They skipped around him while he took dozens of photographs. Later, in the peace and quiet of his study, he would take his time and crop the images, selecting the best to send to London.

He came to the end of a row and turned, brought up short by what he saw there.

A tall golden figure, intimidating in its immobility, stood upright with its arms at its sides, staring straight ahead. Allen stopped in his tracks, took an involuntary breath, and stared at the figure.

It was the first one he'd seen, at close quarters, for many years, and he was struck anew by the sense of peace that emanated from its swirling, lambent depths. He wanted to ask it what it was doing here, but the question for some reason seemed ridiculous, and he held his silence and just stared in fascination.

It remained unmoving, pulsing with an inner illumination that held Allen's attention as if he were hypnotised. At last, smiling at the figure, he backed off and returned to the cafeteria. He felt oddly refreshed, even renewed, by the unexpected encounter.

AFTER LUNCH ALLEN, Nina and the others took the buggy back to the arboreal city and commenced a tour of the soaring alien tree.

"The city trees," said the guide, "are living entities with a cellulose basal structure. They achieve great material density through having evolved on a high gravity planet, Antares II, and such height because Antares II is covered by low level cloud, necessitating the growth of the trees above the cloud level. This tree is of average size, being a third of a kilometre in diameter at its base, and a little short of five kilometres high."

They were on the ground floor of the city tree, in a vast cavity like a concert hall. The guide explained that the length of the tree was filled with air pockets – like cinder toffee, Allen thought – which provided living space for families. Elevators, using thermal energy, carried citizens to the higher levels.

"We will ascend to the mid-point of the city tree," their guide said, "and examine a spore garden."

They crossed the echoing atrium and entered an elevator. Ana Devi had joined their group on Nina's invitation, and she marvelled at the cell structure of the walls as they rose smoothly on the elevator platform. The material of the trees, on closer inspection, reminded Allen of the cross section of a sponge.

They emerged in another, though slightly smaller, chamber, this one given over to various sports. Allen saw people playing tennis and baseball on purpose-built courts and diamonds, and reckoned that this cavity was perhaps two or three hundred metres in diameter.

Their guide led them across the cavity towards a great arched window, into which was set a series of doors. She stood aside and invited them to pass through.

From the ground it had been hard to assess the size of the spore gardens, and Allen's fear had been that when he stepped out onto the platform he would be overcome by crippling vertigo. They were, after all, now almost three kilometres above the surface of the world, level with an armada of cirro-cumulus clouds.

As he followed Nina Ricci through the archway, he realised that he had no reason to fear the elevation. The platform was vast – not the narrow, flimsy structure he had thought it might be from the ground – and gave the impression of solidity. He could easily believe that he was on *terra firma*, strolling across a patio given over to the cultivation of some exotic alien fungus.

The platform was the size of two football fields laid side by side, but red rather than green, and comprised of hundreds of metre-square trays bearing the alien spores. On closer examination the crimson growth resembled bloody lichen and gave off a pungent, peppery aroma.

Their guide knelt, plucked a small wad of the stuff, and popped it into her mouth.

"Please help yourself," she said. "I think you will find it rather delicious."

Allen watched Ana Devi sample a mouthful, and nod in agreement. "It reminds me in texture of paneer, Mr Allen, perhaps flavoured by turmeric. I think it would go down well in India."

He tried some, agreeing that the spongy, spicy food was not at all unpleasant.

"One of the marvellous things about the spores," their guide went on, "is that, quite apart from their protein content and adaptability to human cuisine, they grow from mycelia to maturity in a matter of days."

The group broke up and strolled across the platform. A guard rail ran around the circumference of the perimeter. Determined not to let his fear of heights spoil his appreciation of the view, Allen strode down the aisle between the spore cells and came, hesitantly, to the rail. He reached out, gripped its upper spar and, only when he was satisfied that his hold was secure, leaned forward and peered down.

He stepped back, dizzied by the view.

He gripped the rail with greater force and laughed at his cowardice. Not, he told himself, that he had any conscious control over it. A wave of nausea swept through him at the sight of the vertiginous drop... but even so he stepped forward again and stared down at the ground almost three kilometres below.

There were even, he saw, strings and scraps of cloud floating by *below* where he stood. He made out the much reduced radial gardens, the toy-like cafeteria and, off to the right, the thin thread of the monorail line.

It was almost like looking at the world in a satellite photograph, he thought, then remembered himself and took a series of shots he hoped would convey the sense of immense, god-like elevation.

"You look like a seasick cruise passenger, Geoff," Nina Ricci said as she joined him, Ana Devi at her side.

He smiled queasily. "I feel like one. Have you looked over?" He stepped back from the rail and gestured.

Nina smiled and leaned over daringly, peering down and laughing out loud. "Why, it's wonderful!

Look at the view! I've never seen anything like it! Come and see, Ana."

The Indian smiled at Allen with complicity. "I think I will not get too near the edge," she said. "As a child I climbed the footbridges of Howrah station like a monkey, but I am no longer so daring."

"Glad I'm not alone," he muttered. He glanced at Nina and wished she'd move away from the edge. He almost reached out and dragged her back, but resisted the impulse.

As he stepped back towards the centre of the platform, meaning to investigate and maybe even taste a section of the spores coloured a shade deeper than the rest, he felt a tremor beneath his feet. He put it down to the vertigo affecting his balance, and paused to steady himself.

The tremor continued and behind him Ana Devi gave a sudden, small cry of alarm.

He felt a strong hand grip his upper arm, and looked around to see Nina dragging both himself and Ana across the platform towards the arched entrance. The guide was ushering the others back inside too. Something plummeted in Allen's gut as another tremor shook the platform. He staggered and almost fell.

As they passed into the tower, relief flooding through him, Allen glanced over his shoulder. He could not make sense of what he saw. The platform, far from shaking as he'd expected, was undergoing a strange visual transformation. He wondered, fleetingly and absurdly, if this were some form of Serene safety mechanism.

The guard rail where he'd stood was no longer the barred silver barrier; it had taken on a grey and pitted aspect, almost as if its atomic structure were decaying and crumbling before his eyes. The decay crept little by little across the platform, eating up the spore trays and approaching the tower itself.

Someone screamed. In the panic that ensued, Nina Ricci, still gripping Allen and Ana, pushed them across the chamber towards the lift entrances set into the far wall. They ran.

Allen heard a sound at his back, like the crepitation of encroaching fire. He looked back and saw not the expected flames but the entire far wall transform from a curving, mural-covered surface to a grey decaying concavity which threatened at any second to crumble into nothingness.

Then, in the blink of an eye before Nina pushed him into the lift, he saw the first of the electric-blue figures.

He gave a strangled cry as the lift-door whisked shut and the elevator plummeted. As horrific as the grey-decay had been, the sight of the electric-blue men filled him with dread. They suggested an intentional agency in whatever was happening here, not just some accidental dysfunction of the fabric of the tower.

He was packed tight into the elevator with Nina, Ana, and a dozen others. He stared at Nina and asked. "What was that? I saw..."

Ana said, "Blue figures? I saw them too. A glimpse. They appeared out of nowhere." Her brown eyes rounded on Nina. "What were they? What is happening?"

The Italian shook her head, unable to mask her fearful expression.

Allen looked up, almost expecting to see the ceiling of the lift turn grey, a blue man peering through vindictively...

The electric-blue figures, he thought, were identical in every respect but one to the Serene's golden self-aware entities.

The lift dropped at speed. Allen closed his eyes, willing the elevator to reach the ground. He would feel immeasurably safer, then.

He thought of Sally, and his one wish was to be back home with her.

Someone said, "The platform was eaten up from the outer edge. I saw a couple of people fall..."

Allen felt sick. He recalled old footage of the jumpers from the World Trade Centre, and felt the same gut-wrenching shock at the thought of what those victims must have experienced.

Three kilometres, he thought. With luck, they would be unconscious through oxygen deprivation, caused by the speed of their descent, long before impact.

He tried to clear his head of the images.

But what if the decay reached across the chamber back there and ate into the mechanism of the elevator? They still had a long way to fall...

The elevator gave a sudden lurch. He closed his eyes. This is it, he thought, futilely gripping a handrail.

But Nina was urging him forward with a shouted command, and he opened his eyes to see that the elevator door was open and the people before him were rushing out. He followed Ana Devi, Nina's hand still painfully gripping his upper arm, and all three ran across the ground-floor cavity towards the yawning exit, along with hundreds of other alarmed citizens.

He felt another wave of relief – a sense of having achieved some small degree of sanctuary – when they emerged from the tower into the dazzling afternoon sunlight.

Something other than Nina's grip on his arm, and her urgent shouts, kept him running, and he was assailed by a new fear.

What if the tower fell while they were still running, crumpled vertically so that its debris spread in an even, radiating shock wave, felling everything in its path?

He sprinted. At one point he found Ana Devi's hand in his as they ran side by side, and all three now left the flower garden surrounding the tower and ran down an aisle between rows of low-lying vegetables. Courgettes – he realised with dreamlike inconsequence – Sally's favourite.

Ahead, a crowd of people had come to a halt, turned to face the tower, and were pointing.

Nina turned, forcing Allen to do the same. He looked back at the tower and saw what had arrested the attention of the crowd.

The city tree was not falling – neither crumpling vertically nor toppling like the tree it was – but gradually vanishing. From its distant, cloud-wreathed summit down, it turned deathly grey, pitted and atomised – a creeping decay which ate down the length of the tower until it reached its midpoint. Allen looked up, towards the summit... or rather towards where the summit should have been.

It was no longer there, and as he stared, disbelieving, the rest of the structure, from its mid-section down, turned grey and gradually vanished from sight.

Nina Ricci stared with massive eyes and said, "Oh, no..."

Allen looked at her. There was something about the doom-laden timbre of her words which suggested more than just the horror of the tower's disappearance.

"Nina?"

She shook her head as if in disbelief. "They've compromised the reality-structure paradigm," she whispered, and Allen suddenly wanted to shake her and ask what the hell she was talking about.

At that second Ana Devi gave a startled cry and squeezed his hand. "Look!"

She was pointing to her right. In the distance Allen saw another city tower deliquesce from the top down. From this one, too, crowds of citizens were flooding out, fanning from the entrance in panic and taking refuge in the fields.

"And look," Ana almost whispered, staring across at where the tower they had just left once stood.

A dozen electric-blue figures were spreading out from the tower's footprint with malign purpose.

They had weapons, what looked like rifles, and they were using them. From time to time they stopped walking, raised their rifles, took aim and fired. They never missed. Blue lances of laser light vectored across the fields, cutting down men and women as they ran. Allen looked away, repulsed, unable to move for several seconds until Ana tugged at his hand and yelled, "Run!"

"This way," Nina said, leading them through the vegetable fields towards the more substantial cover of the fruit sector. He sprinted with Ana and felt a measure of safety when they were hidden from sight by the melon vines, though he knew the idea was absurd. He had no doubt that he, Nina and Ana could be seen through the foliage, and all it would take was for one blue figure to take aim and fire.

He heard the crackle of the laser blasts, the cries of the fleeing citizens, along with the sound of a stampede as others beside himself attempted to escape the slaughter.

They must have put a couple of hundred metres between themselves and the blue figures when a pain in his side brought him up short. He wondered, for a second, if he'd been hit – then knew that the sharp pain was no more than a stitch. He gasped and kept running. Nina had raced ahead, and Ana had released her grip on his hand and joined her. Allen, giving them both several years and at least thirty kilos, struggled in their wake.

Ana turned and exhorted him to keep up. He would have gladly replied with some sardonic quip, had he the breath to do so.

Ahead was a poly-carbon shack. The women darted behind it, and when Allen turned the corner he saw that they'd ducked inside. He staggered after them and pulled the door shut behind him.

The women were crouching at the far end of the hut, peering through a horizontal slit window. He joined them, glad of the respite, fell to his knees and stared out.

"What the hell," he gasped, "is happening?" He stared at Nina as if she should know the answer.

"They've compromised the nexus the Serene had in place," she replied.

Allen nodded. "Fine. Now, first of all, who are 'they'? And second, what the hell is the nexus?"

Before answering she paused to look through the window. There was no sign of the advancing blue figures, though the sound of their handiwork carried through the humid air. Allen heard the regular sizzle of lasers, followed almost instantly by the abbreviated cries of the slaughtered.

"'They' are the enemy of the Serene, the Obterek. And the nexus is the *charea* paradigm the Serene set in place around the planet. I'm pretty sure the Obterek couldn't have compromised the *charea* worldwide, just locally. At least I hope so."

Allen stared at her. "How do you know all this?"

She shook her head, as if to say that here and now was neither the time nor the place to tell him.

"Do you think we are safe here?" Ana asked, staring at the Italian with big, frightened eyes.

Nina bit her lip. "As safe as anywhere," she said. "I'm pretty sure the Serene will be working to seal the compromise. It can only last for a matter of minutes."

But, to Allen's ears, she didn't sound so sure.

Through the slit window he saw movement beyond a row of shrubbery. Seconds later a striding blue shape crashed through the foliage, shouldering its laser and firing. Ten metres to the figure's right, a second figure emerged, and beyond that another one.

They ducked beneath the level of the window and Nina hissed, "When they pass the hut, we get out of here."

Allen's heart was pounding in fear. "Where?" he asked, not sure if her plan to leave their hiding place was a good one.

She thought about it, but before she could reply the hut disintegrated around them. Allen yelled and rolled with the impact of something hitting him from the right. He fetched up on his back metres from the wreckage of the hut.

He saw Nina scramble from the shattered poly-carbon rubble and take off, heading for the cover of the melon vines. She never made it.

Beyond the collapsed hut, a blue figure turned and took aim at her. Allen, watching, had the urge to cry out in warning – but self-preservation stopped him. He played dead and stared at the blue figure as it fired.

The laser beam lanced out and cut Nina down. He saw a wound bloom in her torso and heard her startled cry as she fell.

The figure turned and marched away. Raising his head from the ground, Allen looked around for Ana. He saw her seconds later, cowering in the ruins of the hut, her slim body covered with what remained of the poly-carbon door. It had effectively saved her life, shielding her from the attention of the blue figure which had accounted for Nina.

Their eyes met, and Allen raised a hand in a gesture for her to stay where she was.

He knew that, lying on his back in the open field, he was terribly exposed. Should one of the figures –

what did Nina call them, the Obterek? – return this way, or simply look back the way they had come, then he was dead.

Without conscious thought he rolled onto his belly and scrambled back towards the ruined hut. There were sufficient scraps and shards of poly-carbon remaining to afford him minimal cover.

He reached the hut and put the ruin between himself and the line of blue figures. Ana grasped his hand and he held onto her warm fingers as if for dear life.

He thought of Sally and Hannah, and felt a flash of terrible dread at the possibility that he might not survive what was happening here.

Ana's grip tightened on his hand. "Look, Mr Allen..."

She was staring, open-mouthed, across the ground to where Nina's body lay, bloodily butchered by the laser fire.

Beyond the body, emerging from the shattered foliage, was a golden self-aware entity. Allen watched it as it approached Nina's corpse and, in a bizarre act at once intimate and brutal, fell on top of it.

Ana gasped. Allen stared, disbelieving. Where Nina's body had lain, there was now only the golden self-aware entity, its pulsing outline mimicking the posture the Italian women had assumed in death. For a few seconds the golden figure remained perfectly still, face down, and then it slowly rose into a crouched position, like a sprinter, and took off at speed towards an advancing phalanx of blue figures.

And where Nina had sprawled, she was no more.

"What... happened?" Ana managed at last.

Allen shook his head, lost for words.

"Look," Ana said, pointing.

More golden figures had appeared as if from nowhere and confronted the Obterek, whose lasers seemed ineffective. Each blast directed at the golden figures' torsos merely halted them in their tracks, briefly, before they surged on as if having absorbed the energy and gained extra momentum from it.

The self-aware entities gained on the blue figures. Just as Allen was wondering how they might conduct the imminent fight, instead of slowing down to confront the killers the golden figures ran into the blue men and absorbed them. The golden entities pulsed brightly for a brief second, halted and stood foursquare, rocking slightly, as if the absorption of their enemies was taking its toll.

From the direction of the now vanished tower, more blue figures were striding forth, lasers poised but inactive as the human populace had either fled the scene or been killed.

From behind where Allen and Ana cowered, a second phalanx of golden figures passed and strode forward in line to confront the advancing Obterek.

The blue men raised their weapons and fired, their barrage doing nothing to halt the golden figures' advance.

Allen was dazzled as something coruscated to his right. Belatedly he realised that it had been a laser beam, and only when Ana gasped his name did he turn to see her slump back, a bloody hole opened in her chest.

He cried aloud and reached out for her hand. Before he could complete the action, he felt a lancing pain in his lower back. He yelled and turned in time to see his attacker, a blue figure not five metres away, swing its weapon towards an advancing golden figure. The Obterek fired, to no avail, and seconds later was taken into the corporality of the self-aware entity.

Allen lay on his back, gasping. The beam had skewered his flank, slicing through his torso, and the pain was indescribable.

He turned his head. Ana was propped beside him, eyes open in death, blood leaking from between her small breasts. He wanted to cry out at the injustice of what had happened, protest at his approaching end.

He felt something slam into him. It was like a jolt of energy, a blast of pure force that seemed to lift him off the ground with its momentum. He realised that he was on his feet, surrounded by what felt like a cocooning flow of energy. He felt at once petrified and exhilarated, and heard a familiar voice in his head. "*Do not be afraid...*"

Then he was moving. Or, rather, he was moving not under his own impetus but under that of his saviour. He was aware of his legs working, describing the motion of running, though he felt neither the impact of the ground nor the exertion of the act of sprinting. He was being carried through the air, he realised, *inside* the body of a self-aware entity.

They were leaving the Fujiyama arboreal city at great speed, outpacing his fellow humans who were still running from the scene of carnage. He was aware of the cessation of pain in his flank, and a consequent dulling of his senses. Seconds later he passed out.

He came to his senses an unknown time later, and he was still running, or rather the self-aware entity was running, tearing like an express train through hilly terrain. Trees flashed by, then buildings; the sense of speed, of forward motion, was incredible, and yet Allen felt nothing, no rush of air, no jarring impact with the ground. He was anaesthetised to all sensation and travelling like the wind.

He passed out again, and when he came to he saw that he was no longer in the countryside. He had no notion of how long he had been travelling, or how far he had covered. City blocks flashed by in a blur, and citizens around him appeared to be frozen, motionless.

Ahead, he saw a familiar sight, and could not bring himself to believe what it meant.

He was in Tokyo – but how could that be?

Directly before him was the rearing sable façade of the Tokyo obelisk.

They were heading towards it, accelerating, and Allen willed the golden figure to slow down before they impacted.

But the golden figure did not slow down – if anything it gained speed. The looming face of the obelisk rushed forwards to meet them.

Allen blacked out.

CHAPTER SEVEN

ANA FINISHED HER shift in the administration dome early and, on her way back to her rooms, dropped in to see how Prakesh was getting on in the labs.

Prakesh was supervising his team of biologists who were researching the genetics of a form of wheat seed donated by the Serene. The idea was that the extraterrestrial wheat might, when crossed with a Terran variety, produce a hybrid with a higher yield than anything grown on Earth to date.

She passed through the airlock and peered through the window at the clean area. Half a dozen white-suited scientists worked at long benches, while to the right Prakesh was bent over a softscreen.

He saw her and waved, then crossed to the window and switched on the intercom.

"Any progress?" she asked.

He lowered his face-mask and smiled. "It's slow.

We're only just putting the markers down. It might be another day or two yet before we have results."

She nodded. "Fine. Keep me posted, would you?"

She made to leave.

Prakesh said, "Ana, would you be free later? Since getting back from Japan, you've been..." He hesitated. "I was wondering if everything's okay?" He looked, in his concern, like the young boy she'd known all those years ago.

She smiled. "I'm fine. Just very, very tired. I'm having an early night. And then... Look, I'll be away for a few days, taking a break. But I promise we'll have time to catch up when I get back, ah-cha?"

He nodded, but looked unconvinced. "Have a pleasant break, Ana."

"I'll be in touch." She switched off the intercom and stepped from the dome.

The sun was going down slowly, but in the east, dropping like an accelerated sun, was the golden glow of the evening energy beam falling towards the distribution station a hundred kilometres north of Madras.

The sight of it never failed to fill Ana with reassurance.

She made her way to the residential block where she had a comfortable second floor apartment overlooking the fields which stretched, without interruption, to the horizon.

She sat on her bed, activated her softscreen, and summoned the library of images.

She scrolled through various media shots of her brother, Lal Devi as he was known now, which she had downloaded and stored over the course of the past few days since arriving back from Japan.

What had happened at Fujiyama had changed things.

She unbuttoned the front of her blouse and stared down at the smooth coffee-coloured skin of her chest. She touched the place where the laser had impacted and tried to recall the intense, shocking pain. She relived the mental anguish of knowing that she was about to die, and recalled her exact thoughts: *Twenty-six years, and this is how it ends...*

And then the breathtaking impact of something vital and strong slamming into her body and taking her over, raising her to her feet and carrying her at speed from the carnage...

And then she had awoken to find herself on the train heading south to the Andhra Pradesh wilderness city.

Not long after arriving home her thoughts had turned to her brother, and what she had told Kapil about not wanting to find him.

Well, the events at Fujiyama had changed her mind on that score.

She had been so close to death – had perhaps even died for a second – and the thought that she was mortal had hit her, later, along with the thought that had she died at Fujiyama then she would have left so much undone.

Earlier in Kolkata, before taking the Serene jet to Japan, she had faced her fears and approached both Station Master Jangar and Sanjeev Varnaputtram. She had confronted both men and in doing so had realised that the reality had not been as terrible as she had expected it to be.

She had learned a lesson from that and, with the knowledge that she was mortal and must do now what she would not always be around to do, had resolved to track down her brother and, eventually, confront him too.

In her free time over the past few days she had googled the company he worked for and the address of their head office in Manhattan. Yesterday she had booked a berth aboard the sub-orbital leaving Delhi for New York and arranged to meet Kapil on the evening of her arrival.

She slept badly that night, her dreams full of rampaging blue figures lasering down innocent humans; she relived her own death, and woke suddenly in the early hours drenched in sweat.

She rose, showered, then packed her holdall and took an electric cab to the train station.

The journey north to Delhi, through the flatlands of the Deccan changed now out of all recognition from the parched farmland of just ten years ago, gave her time to look ahead to her meeting with Bilal. He would be shocked, of course, when she turned up – a ghost from a past he thought he had left behind. But she would not accuse him, would not ask why he did not contact her – or at least say goodbye. To accuse him would be to risk alienating and angering him, and she feared that, after having waited for so long to be reunited, he would walk out on her and refuse to see her again.

They would talk, catch up on the lost years. She

would tell him about growing up without him – though without censure – and recount what had happened to her since the coming of the Serene. Only if he was willing to talk about his past would she probe and ask what had happened to make him leave her without saying goodbye.

As field after field of alternating rice and corn sped past, she stared through the window and smiled to herself.

She caught the midnight sub-orbital shuttle from New Delhi airport and slept peacefully, untroubled by nightmares. She awoke to dazzling daylight outside the circular window, with a startling view of the New York coastline and the glittering length of Manhattan far below. Minutes later they were decelerating towards the airport on Staten Island, and thirty minutes later she passed through customs and was riding the monotrain across the bay to Manhattan.

Kapil met her at TriBeCa station and whisked her back to his apartment in Little Italy, where she showered, changed, and enjoyed a long, leisurely meal of strong coffee and croissants.

At one point Kapil asked, "But what made you change your mind?"

She had refrained from telling him about the events of Fujiyama. When she'd spoken to him briefly the other day, she had still not come to terms with what had happened there. She had trawled the newsfeeds for mention of the attack, but found nothing. Obviously the Serene were imposing a news blackout on the event.

Now, little by little, she described the afternoon, the

wonder of the arboreal city, the other representatives she had met... and then the attack. As she spoke, she recalled new details she had either forgotten or repressed: seeing Nina Ricci lasered almost in half before her very eyes; a mother and child mown down mercilessly by a dispassionate blue figure... And then her salvation thanks to a Serene self-aware entity.

They held hands across the table, Kapil too shocked to speak for long minutes, until, "Well, all I have to complain about is a razor cut yesterday morning..."

She laughed and swiped his head.

"And after that..." She frowned. "I knew I had to contact Bilal." She smiled at him. "None of us live for ever, Kapil, and I knew I had to act sooner rather than later. Did you...?"

He nodded. "I contacted his PA and explained that we had business interests in common, and my recent links with China which might prove beneficial to the Morwell Corporation."

Ana bit her lip. "And?"

"Your brother is a very busy man, but I arranged an appointment for eleven this morning, but I could only get fifteen minutes."

"That will be fine, to start with."

"Then, as you instructed, at nine this morning I had my secretary contact his PA and tell her that, due to illness, I wouldn't be able to make the meeting but would be deputised by my assistant. You're going under the name of Sara Ashok, so remember that."

She leaned across the table and kissed him. "Thank you so much, Kapil. This means a lot to me."

"I'll come with you as far as Morwell Towers. After that you'll be on your own." He gave her one of his lovely smiles. "I'll wait for you, then we'll go for a coffee and you can tell me all about it."

She looked at her watch. Ten-thirty. "We'd better be setting off."

As they left the apartment, Ana tried to quash her sudden apprehension at the thought of meeting her brother. She told herself not to be so stupid. She had faced down Sanjeev Varnaputtram after all, so what did she have to fear from Bilal?

SHE RODE THE elevator to the fortieth floor of Morwell Towers, her anxieties mounting in proportion to the rate of her ascent. Kapil had left her outside the building with a kiss and the assurance that he would be waiting for her – and that she had nothing to fear. Nevertheless she did feel fear: fear of an outright rejection from her brother, or an inadequate reason for his not saying goodbye all those years ago.

The lift doors swished open and she found herself in a plush carpeted corridor with a pulsing softscreen on the opposite wall. A name appeared on the screen, Lal Devi, underlined by a flashing arrow indicating that she should turn right. Hesitantly she stepped out and walked down the corridor, reading the nameplates on the doors to right and left as she went.

She came to the door bearing the name Lal Devi and stopped, her breath coming in ragged gasps. She took a deep breath and checked her watch. She was a couple of minutes late.

She knocked, and when she heard a voice call, "Enter," opened the door and stepped inside.

The first thing she noticed was the opulence of the office. It occupied a corner site, with two great plate-glass windows looking down the length of Manhattan. Behind a big silver desk, shaped like an arrow-head with its point directed at the door, was a slim man with a thin, handsome face. He wore his hair long in a ponytail and sported an amethyst stud in his right ear.

She stared, comparing this slick, besuited businessman with the malnourished urchin she had last seen twenty years ago.

He hardly glanced away from his softscreen as he gestured her to take a seat at the point of his desk. "Ah, Miss... Ashok. I'm sorry I couldn't meet your superior, Kapil Gavaskar, but illness knows no social boundaries."

She forced herself not to dislike her brother for his opening words, as he rose and took her hand in a limp, perfunctory shake.

"I'm Lal Devi, James Morwell's right hand man, as you no doubt know." He gestured to the screen. "And we're interested in what you have to offer as regards your Chinese links."

She said, "Bilal..."

He looked up and frowned. "Now, no one has called me that for a long time."

She stared at him, this slick, fast-talking, high-flying aide to a one-time billionaire tycoon. How did you come to this, she thought?

She found her voice and said, "Do you know who I am?"

He glanced at his screen, his face quirking with a quick frown. "Miss... Ashok. I don't believe we've met before."

"You don't recognise me?"

He looked mystified, then a little annoyed. But was it any wonder that he didn't recognise her? She had changed so much in appearance from the ragged street kid she had been.

Her heart laboured as if pumping treacle. She felt a hot flush rise up her face as she said, "We last saw each other, Bilal, many years ago. On Howrah station, the day before you disappeared."

He stared at her and shook his head, and Ana wasn't sure if he was totally confused or had realised who she was and was denying the fact.

Then he whispered, "Ana?"

She held his startled gaze. Despite her earlier resolutions not to intimidate him with accusations, she found herself saying, "Bilal, why didn't you say goodbye? Why did you just leave like that? There one day, gone the next..."

He shook his head. "I..." he began, lost for words.

He reached out, tapped his softscreen, and said, "Amanda, cancel my appointment at 11.30. I'll be free again at midday."

He sat back in his swivel seat, the cushion squeaking, laid back his head and closed his eyes.

She had hoped his reaction would be one of joy at their reunion. She had foreseen tears, maybe, and apologies, and had expected him to move around his desk and embrace her.

He did none of these things, just lay back with

his eyes closed, the expression on his aquiline face unreadable.

"Bilal, I have come a long way to see you. All the way from India."

He opened his eyes and looked at her. "Ana... This is something of a shock, to say the least."

"A pleasant shock?" she asked. "Or...?"

"An unexpected shock."

They stared at each other, Ana trying to hide her pain at his response. She said, "I just... I just wanted to know why you didn't contact me before you left, why you didn't say goodbye. You can't imagine how I felt." She reached into her handbag, pulled something out, and slid it across the desk to him.

He picked it up and turned the flattened enamel cup.

"I found this... on the tracks. For a long time I thought you might be dead, only no one had reported a street kid's body on the tracks, so I hoped... Oh, how I hoped! But the years went by and there was no word from you." She stopped, took a breath, and asked, "So, I would just like to know why you never said goodbye."

He turned the flattened cup over and over, and said as if to himself, "I left it on the track, to be destroyed... A symbol, if you like, of my leaving."

She repeated, "Bilal – why didn't you tell me you were going?"

"Ana... it was a long time ago," he said, as if this somehow excused his actions.

"What do you mean by that?" she snapped.

He gestured, spread his hands, and smiled disarmingly. "Twenty years, Ana... I hardly recall?"

"What happened?" she almost cried.

He shook his head.

She went on, "It was the day after Holi. We'd had so much fun throwing paint powder at commuters... How we laughed! We went to the sleeping van late that night, and in the morning when I woke up you were no longer beside me. That wasn't unusual. Remember, you often got up at dawn and went out looking for food... But this time it was different. You never came back. And the following day I found your cup, squashed flat on the tracks... So what *happened*, Bilal?"

He nodded, as if in acknowledgment of all she said, and reassurance that he would come up with an adequate response. "Ana... a few weeks before Holi I met a man. A Westerner." He waved a hand. "No, it was nothing like that. He wasn't like Sanjeev Varnaputtram. Remember him?"

She felt a flare of anger. How could she forget Varnaputtram?

He went on, "This Westerner worked for a corporation in the States which ran schools and colleges in India. He wasn't out scouting for pupils – our meeting was quite by chance. You know how I always loved reading the *Hindustan Times*, the *Times of India* – anything I could get my hands on, left by commuters on the trains. One day I was riding between stations, begging, when I picked up a paper and began reading. I was sitting across from a tall, pale American. We got talking. We discussed politics, and

I think I – I don't mean to sound arrogant here, Ana – but I think I impressed him. He was working in the city and would be there for a couple of weeks. He invited me to his apartment, where we talked and talked, and it was as if I'd found a teacher, someone who filled me with knowledge and respected me, a street kid."

How wonderful for you, Ana thought.

"He told me who he was, what he represented, and asked if I would care to sit an entrance exam–"

"Why didn't you tell me this?" Ana asked, fighting back the tears.

Bilal shrugged. "I... I honestly don't know, Ana. I was so excited. The college was in Madras, and graduates were promised places in a business college here in New York."

"But you could have told me! You could have said what was happening, told me where you were going, said goodbye!"

He shook his head. "It all happened so quickly. I sat the exam and a couple of days later the Westerner, Paul, he told me I had passed, and that the following day I should accompany him south to Madras."

She stared at him. "Why didn't you come and say goodbye?"

He looked down at his desk and said, "Because I didn't want to hurt you, Ana. Also... you would have begged me not to leave, pleaded with me. I loved you... I didn't want to see you hurt, upset. Because, don't you see, I had to go. I had to get out of there. The opportunity was too great to pass up."

"But you left me there, left me to scratch a living on the station, begging, stealing..."

Was she being unreasonable, she wondered? She tried to see the situation from his point of view. He was right in that she would have been devastated, and pleaded with him not to go, but even so she could not help but feel a sense of betrayal.

"I know, I know..." He shook his head. "Don't you think it pained me? I was plagued with guilt for years and years. I thought of you every day..."

"But you never tried to get in contact with me?" she asked incredulously.

"Of course I did..."

"But?" she pressed, leaning forward in her seat.

"One day, perhaps five years later, I was in India on business. I went to the station, looked for you. I asked around, asked Mr Jangar, a couple of porters. They said they hadn't seen you for weeks and weeks... So I gave up and the following day came back to New York."

She took a little hope from this. Five years after Bilal vanished, she would have been eleven. For a couple of months she and Prakesh and Gopal had ridden a night train to New Delhi to see what the living was like at the railway station there. But the street kids had been feral, hostile, and had repelled the invaders with stones and broken glass bottles. They had tried other stations along the line to Kolkata, but had found nowhere like Howrah, and had eventually returned.

She told him this, and said, "You tried *once*. Once in twenty years. If only you'd gone back, tried again..."

He nodded. "I'm sorry, Ana. You're right. I should have done. But... but after that time, I feared the worst, feared that you were dead, and I threw myself into my work. Try to see this from my point of view."

She gave a long sigh, at once despairing and conciliatory. Of course, how much of what he said was true? He'd changed a lot over the years; he was a businessman, adept with words, with twisting meanings. He could easily be – what was the phrase? – spinning her a line so that he came out of the encounter with his pride intact and his actions justified.

She looked around the office and said, "You've done very well for yourself, Bilal. I bet you have a wonderful apartment, expensive things..." She almost broke down then, for some reason she could not fathom.

He smiled. "I do okay. Mr Morwell is very generous. Though I must say I do work hard for the Corporation. And things have changed a lot since the arrival of the Serene. Ten years ago the Morwell Corporation was worth billions. Our annual turnover was greater than the GDP of many sizable countries. We had real power; we were powerful movers, not just the effete, emasculated facilitators we are today."

She stared at him and said, "You sound as if you resent what the Serene have done for us?"

He rocked his head from side to side. "I can see that in some ways, some people might think that we are better off for the apparent largesse of the Serene. But the fact is that the Serene have taken something away from us that was very important."

She stared at him. "You mean," she said with heavy sarcasm, "the ability to kill and torture and maim each other?

"That is only a part of it, a symbolic part, if you like. The Serene have taken away our evolutionary future and imposed upon us their own regime – their own, if you like, evolutionary game plan. And," he went on, as if warming to his theme, "has it ever occurred to you that for all their largesse, the Serene have never made manifest why they are doing this for us, what their larger, grand plan might be?"

She interrupted, "I would have thought that that is obvious – that preventing the human race from destroying itself is reason enough."

He smiled, somewhat smugly, and shrugged. "We have only the word of the Serene that we were heading for extinction. The point is debatable."

She would not let him have the last word. "Even if it is debatable, what is not in contention is that millions of innocent lives have been saved by the Serene intervention. So much misery has been avoided..."

He shrugged again, a smug gesture she found insufferable. "The history of humanity, the history of the world, is one of mutual violence – the law of the jungle. It got us to where we were ten years ago – the pre-eminent species on the planet. It made us what we were, an independent, intelligent race questing ahead in the field of science and technology, forging our *own* way forward. Now..." He smiled sadly. "Now we are nothing more than the puppets of the Serene, jerking on the strings of unknown and unseen masters whose motives are opaque to us."

She allowed a silence to develop, and then said quietly, "I see that our opinions are diametrically opposed, Bilal, as I have wholeheartedly embraced the coming of the Serene."

That patronising smile again as he said, "You always were ruled by your heart, not your head, little sister. But tell me, what makes you think that the way of the Serene is the right way for the human race?"

"They have eliminated violence from the world," she said, "and in so doing have banished fear. The powerful, the hostile powerful, no longer hold sway. The world is fair, equitable. There is no more poverty. Everyone has food, and a roof over their heads."

"And we are in thrall to aliens whose *raison d'être* remains unknown."

"The Serene," she found herself saying, "are wholly good."

He raised a supercilious eyebrow at this. "Oh, and you would know that personally, would you?"

She took a breath and said, "A week ago I was in Fujiyama when there was... a breach in the *charea*. The Obterek – other aliens, enemies of the Serene – attacked."

He leaned forward. "I heard nothing of this."

"Well, you wouldn't have. The Serene imposed a news blackout."

He said, "Typical of our oppressors..."

She went on, "I saw killing on a mass scale. I was killed myself, lasered here." She smote the area between her breasts. "Only... a self-aware entity absorbed me, is the only way I can describe it, took me away from the slaughter and healed me."

He stared at her, evidently wondering whether to believe her. He said, "And this makes the Serene wholly good? They save your life, so therefore..."

Exasperated, she interrupted. "I know the Serene are good. I have worked for them for ten years, and though the nature of the work is not known to me... something has... *filtered* into my consciousness, and I know the Serene are working for the good of humanity."

He leaned back in his chair. "That's a grand claim to make, isn't it? Working for the Serene?"

She said proudly, and despised herself for it seconds later, "I am a representative of the Serene. Myself and thousands like me, selected ten years ago on the day the Serene came to Earth..."

It was a boast that, she was pleased to see, had silenced this arrogant man who was her brother.

At last he said, "So... I see that we obviously have our differences. But I can't see why this should mean that we can't get along in future like brother and sister..."

Despite herself, despite some deep dislike of the person Bilal had become, Ana found herself smiling. He was after all her big brother, who for many years had protected her, and maybe even loved her.

He got through to his secretary and had her fetch them coffee, then sat back in his chair and said, "Enough of the Serene, Ana. Do you recall the day I saved you from a beating by Mr Jangar?"

Ana looked past the slick businessman he had become, saw the scruffy street urchin with tousled hair and food around his mouth, who had caused a diversion in Mr Jangar's office, allowing Ana to slip past the station master's bulk and escape onto the crowded platform.

For the next hour they chatted about their old life on Howrah station.

CHAPTER EIGHT

ALLEN AWOKE AND found himself on a train in the middle of the English countryside.

To his fellow passengers it must have appeared that Allen had surfaced from a troubled sleep, but all he could recall was the jet façade of the obelisk rushing to meet him. He wondered how long had elapsed. He looked at his watch. It was eleven in the morning on a beautiful sunny summer's day, and the train was pulling into the stop before Wem. His watch also told him that it was the 10th, the same day he had visited the Fujiyama arboreal city – so given the time difference he had made the journey from Tokyo to where he was now in a matter of an hour... Obviously his calculations were way out, but he felt no urge to work through them again. What mattered, after the nightmare of slaughter at Fujiyama, was that soon he would be home.

He sat up, recalling the events in the fields around the vanished city tower, and touched the place just above his right kidney where the laser had skewered him. There was no pain, no sensation at all. He recalled that a golden figure had seemingly absorbed Nina Ricci. And he too had been taken, saved, by the self-aware entity.

He wondered then if the black obelisk in Tokyo was some kind of medical centre, where he had been taken for surgery. But the surgery must have been swift if that were so, and he recalled the cessation of pain on the way from Fujiyama and reasoned that the golden figure had effected physical repairs then.

On the luggage rack above his head was his hold-all, and wrapped around his right forearm was his softscreen. The Serene, or their minions, had thought of everything.

He considered contacting Sally and telling her that he would soon be home – hours earlier than expected – but decided to surprise her. He imagined her in her study, or perhaps sitting beneath the cherry tree in the garden, catching up on the latest medical advances on the various softscreen feeds she subscribed to. The thought warmed him.

He considered her message of the day before; the accident in which her friend Kath had died. He would do what little he could to comfort her when he got back, rather than launching into an account of the horrors he had experienced.

Ten minutes later the monotrain pulled into Wem and Allen alighted. He left the station and walked along the high street, and after the impersonality of

Tokyo he was cheered by the familiar faces of the locals who were out and about. He realised that it was a scene that had changed little over the years – apart from the absence now of once-familiar company names that had made every town and city the same. Gone were the chains, Macdonald's and KFC and their like, which had force-fed a willing populace a diet of low quality food laced with addictive fats, salts and sugars. He wondered if this was not merely an obvious consequence of the Serene's restructuring of the world's economy, but a follow-on from their *charea* injunction. Did the Serene, in their wisdom, consider what the food industry had perpetrated on their customers a form of protracted and insidious violence?

Gone too were the butcher's shops, of course. Only the occasional tiled frontage remained, showing euphemistic scenes of contented cows grazing bucolic meadows. Healthfood outlets, fruit and veg shops, proliferated, along with privately run family concerns prospering under the fiscal aegis of the alien arrival.

A few weeks ago Sally had mentioned the health benefits that had accrued from the changes. In her line of work, as a country GP, she saw fewer cases of obesity and heart disease, fewer cancers and stress-related maladies. All, she said, attributable to the Serene in one way or another.

He wondered at the die-hard few who opposed what the Serene were doing, and that led him to reflect on the attack at Fujiyama, and the motives of the Obterek.

* * *

HE CROSSED TOWN and took the canal path to the outskirts, and five minutes later came to the back gate that led into the long garden.

He paused for a second and stared at the idyllic scene, the lawn and the trees and the mellow, golden stone of the house. Sally was not sitting beneath the cherry tree, but she must have been in the kitchen because, as he pushed through the gate and walked down the lawn, she emerged from the back door and dashed to meet him.

They hugged for a long time, and when she pulled away she was beaming.

"I got your message," he said. "I'm sorry–"

She shook her head. "It's okay... Look, it's hard to explain. I know I said I saw Kath... there was an accident, as I said. I saw her *die*." She shook her head and laughed, and Allen stared at her.

"Sally?"

She tugged his hand. "Come. We'll talk over a cup of tea. There's a lot to tell you about."

Bemused, he followed her into the house and sat at the kitchen table.

She made two mugs of Earl Grey and sat next to him. She took a deep breath, shook her head, and laughed again. "I honestly don't know where to begin." She reached out and stroked his cheek. "Geoff, you look so young when you pull that mystified expression."

"You're talking in riddles, Sal."

"I'm sorry, but it's been a strange couple of days. Look, Kath, my long-time friend Kath Kemp, is not what she seems. You might find this hard to believe, Geoff, but she's a self-aware entity."

He had a flash vision of Nina Ricci telling him about the man she had met in Barcelona...

He nodded. "And when you saw the accident, and you thought she'd died...?"

"Oh, it was horrible, horrible. She *was* dead. No pulse. You can't imagine what..." She hugged her tea cup, then went on. "An ambulance came, whisked her away. And then... the following morning, she called me and arranged a meeting. She came over and told me she was a self-aware entity and had been here, on Earth, for a little over a hundred years."

He stared at her. "Small, dumpy, mousey, homely Kath Kemp? A self-aware entity?"

"I know, I know... But somehow, it made sense. And, you know what? I see her still as the same person. Still a friend... My friend, the alien entity."

"And did she tell you what she was doing here?"

"Not everything. A little. I think the best description would be that she's a facilitator."

He interrupted. "Don't tell me. That accident... it wasn't an accident, right?"

She was watching him closely. "No. No, it wasn't, but how...?"

He told her about Fujiyama, the dissolution of the tower and his hairs-breadth escape, then the attack of the blue figures.

"They're called the Obterek," he said, "according to a journalist I met. Aliens who oppose the Serene. They... I can't recall exactly the phrase she used, but the Obterek somehow reconfigured the reality of the arboreal city area and undermined the Serene's *charea* injunction. Then they set about killing as many humans as possible."

Sally said, "But there was nothing on any of the news channels..."

"I suspect the Serene imposed a blackout." He paused. "I said the blue figures began killing humans... and they succeeded, but... I don't really know how to explain this – but the golden figures, the self-aware entities, brought them back to life. I saw the journalist die. Then she was absorbed by a SAE..." He stopped, pulled the flap of his shirt from his trousers, and twisted to peer down at his midriff.

Sally slipped from the table and knelt beside him. "You? You were hit?"

His fingers traced where the laser had impacted. The skin was smooth, unblemished.

"It hit me here, and the pain..." He shook his head in wonder.

She took his hand and kissed his knuckles. "What happened?"

"I felt the impact, the pain..." As he spoke, tears came to his eyes. He dashed them away and went on, "And I thought I was dead. I... do you know something, I thought of you and Hannah, your grief..."

She sat on his lap and they hugged. "It's fine now, everything's okay."

"Then something else hit me, a physical force, and I was... somehow *inside*... a self-aware entity. It left the area at speed. I passed out, and the last I recall was heading towards the obelisk in Tokyo, and I felt panic at the imminent impact. And then I woke up on the train ten miles south of Wem." He looked up at her. "What's happening, Sally? Fujiyama? Here? The Obterek? Did Kath say anything?"

She frowned. "A little, but not much more than I've told you. But she's calling in tomorrow on the way back from Birmingham. She has something she needs to discuss with us."

"I'm not sure I like the way you said 'something,' Sal."

She looked up at the wall clock. "Three fifteen. Tell you what, let's take the canal path to the school and pick up Trouble. I have something to tell you on the way."

She stood up and fetched her handbag.

"That 'something' again." He smiled. "Don't you think you've told me enough already?"

They left the house and Sally locked the back door. As they strolled hand in hand along the canal path, with insects buzzing in the hedges and waterboatmen skimming the still surface of the water, she said, "How would you like to live on Mars?"

He peered at her. He went for levity. "Well, all things considered, I'm pretty settled in Shropshire, and I've heard property prices there are astronomical."

She feigned pushing him into the canal. "I'm serious."

"Kath, right? That's what she wants to talk to us about tomorrow?"

"She told me a little about it. They, the Serene and the SAEs, have terraformed Mars, and they won't stop there. They're pushing outwards, through the solar system... and they need colonists."

"Us? Me and you and Hannah?"

She nodded. "I'm a medic, and in demand. You're a representative —"

"Whatever that means."

"Kath was serious. They want colonists to settle Mars first, and after that..."

He thought about it, about a terraformed Mars; it was the stuff of boyhood dreams. He considered strolling in the foothills of Olympus Mons and laughed aloud.

Sally nudged him. "What?"

He told her. "Hannah would miss her friends. But I suppose kids are adaptable..."

"You're already considering it?"

"No, not really. Let's wait to see what Kath has to say, okay?"

They collected Hannah from school, tired and rosy-cheeked from a long day. She ran on ahead, skipping and shouting with a couple of friends. On the way back, Geoff suggested they pop into the Three Horseshoes. "I could kill a pint."

They sat at the table by the fishpond while Hannah lay on her belly and poked a finger into the water. The fish broke the surface, staring up at her. On his way to the bar, Geoff wondered what the koi made of the giant being whose pink finger promised, but did not deliver, food.

He carried two pints of Leffe and a fresh orange juice from the bar, and they sat in the westering sun and watched their daughter play with the fish. Sally said, "Mars..."

He smiled at her, and it struck him anew that his wife was quite beautiful.

He laughed. "Mars indeed!" he said.

* * *

HE SPENT A troubled night, his dreams plagued by images of Obterek blue men lasering down defenceless humans.

He woke around five, the room light despite the drawn curtains, and listened to the sound of Sally's breathing. He reached out and slipped a hand across the small of her back, reassured by her warmth.

Hannah, their alarm clock, burst into the room at seven-thirty and woke Allen from a light slumber. She chattered constantly until breakfast, where a bowl of Weetabix shut her up. They walked her to school along the canal path and returned silently, each lost in their own thoughts.

"Tea?" Sally asked when they got back.

Allen nodded. "What time's Kath due?"

"She said around ten."

He looked at the clock. Nine-twenty. "Not long then."

He was feeling curiously apprehensive, and he could not really say why – whether it was due to the idea of Mars, or of meeting, face to face, a self-aware entity in human form.

They sat on either side of the kitchen table and sipped their tea. At last Allen said, "How would you feel about moving to Mars, if it's really on?"

She pursed her lips and rocked her head, considering. "I honestly don't know. I suppose it would depend on the job, and the type of people we'd be with. I know, I know, we wouldn't know about the latter until we got there. But I suppose I could adapt to living almost anywhere, so long as I had you and Hannah, a decent job, and we were surrounded by good people."

"We have all that here, Sally."

She nodded. "But even so, the idea of Mars. The experience. A part of me feels we'd be foolish to pass it up, while another..."

"And you accuse me of being a stick-in-the-mud."

She smiled. "Well, I'm very happy with what I have here, thank you very much."

"And so am I, but I know what you mean. The thought of Mars..." He slapped his leg with the flat of his hand. "But let's wait until we hear what your self-aware entity friend has to say, hm?"

"All those years, the times we spent together..."

"How does it make you feel, the knowledge of who – what – she is?"

"I've thought about that a lot over the past couple of days. At first, I don't know... but I felt as if our friendship had been somehow... devalued. As if for all those years Kath had been living a lie. But then I realised that was stupid. She wasn't out to get anything from me – other than what every human being wants from someone, friendship, loyalty, understanding, being there when it matters... We shared all those things. So the fact that she's also an alien, a self-aware entity... In a way, it doesn't really alter anything."

"And yet."

She laughed. "And yet it does alter everything. I think now I can never be as... as open with her, I suppose. I'll always be wondering about her motivations in being here, always wondering if she really understands me, or if it's just simulating a response." She waved. "I'm sorry, I'm expressing it badly."

"I think I understand," he said. "One of your best friends has turned out to be something other than what she purported to be, so of course you have every right to reassess your relationship with her."

"And forge a new relationship with her, built on that new knowledge," she said. She cocked her head, listening. "That's the side gate. It must be her."

Seconds later Kath's head and shoulders passed the kitchen window and she knocked on the slightly open door.

From where he sat at the table, Allen watched the two women come together on the threshold and embrace. He had always been struck by the differences between these two good friends: whereas Sally was tall, elegant and – though he admitted bias in this – beautiful, Kath was small, thick-set and plain. She exuded a matronly bonhomie that he found endearing, and which people warmed to. And it was all, he reminded himself, a construct, a fabrication to humanise what was in fact an alien being.

He rose and crossed the kitchen towards Kath. He always found greeting women a little awkward – a handshake or a chaste peck on the cheek: one too formal and the other too intimate – and he ended up stooping a little to give her a hug.

"Geoff," she said. "It's lovely to see you. It's been more than two years."

"How about we sit in the garden?" he suggested. "Tea all round?"

While Sally ushered Kath into the garden and arranged a table and a spare chair beneath the cherry tree, Allen made three cups of Earl Grey, opened a packet of locally made shortbread, and carried them outside.

They sipped tea, nibbled biscuits, and traded the usual pleasantries for a few minutes – commenting on the weather, the fine state of the garden – though Allen was aware of the incongruity of the charade.

At last Kath paused and looked up from her tea. "I take it Sally told you all about what happened the night before last?"

"In detail," he said, "and I filled Sal in on the events at Fujiyama."

Kath pulled a quick frown at this, murmuring, "Ah, yes..." She looked from Sally to Allen, and said, "That was a breach we could have done without, but you'll be pleased to know that no lasting damage was done, despite the appearance of initial conditions. Everyone 'killed' at Fujiyama was saved by the SAEs."

"I was shot in the torso," he began, shaking his head.

"My... colleagues melded with the dead and dying, imbued them with our life-force, and affected such repairs as were needed. On a quantum level, it was a simple procedure."

"But the other evening? Couldn't you have saved *yourself*, then?" Sally asked.

"It was a very different form of attack, Sally. Far more... lethal. I needed help, from my colleagues, in order to effect recovery."

Allen said, "And the Obterek? Who are they? Why are they attacking you?"

Kath nodded, balancing her tea cup on her knee. "They are our opponents, or enemy, from the sector of the galaxy from where we hail. We are ideologically opposed, I suppose you could say. The history between us is long and complex. Anyway, they compromised the *charea* program we had in place – only locally, I'm glad to say, and staged a minor offensive."

"Minor?" Allen queried. "It appeared rather major to me. The destruction of a couple of towers, the slaughtering of dozens, hundreds, of humans..."

"Believe me, Geoff, it was a minor incident. As the Obterek meant it to be – not so much the first stage of a concerted offensive, but a warning shot. It was a breach which told us that they were capable, given the opportunity, of much greater damage. Their attacks have been increasing of late, and although we are confident that we can counter everything they have to throw at us, the incidence of their attacks is nevertheless worrying."

Sally leaned forward. "But what do the Obterek object to, Kath? Who can possibly oppose what the Serene are doing here?"

"The Obterek can. They are a military race, evolved in conditions far different from any you might be able to imagine. Their rise to eminence in their solar system, and the neighbouring ones, is a bloody catalogue of conflicts won and lost, the brutality and barbarity of which is hard to envisage, or believe. They are responsible for the annihilation of more than a dozen innocent races, and they see what we are doing as against the natural law. That is their great phrase – translated into English, of course – Natural Law, the edict of the universe which no race should contravene."

"But surely," Sally said, "a purely subjective idea?"

"Of course," Kath said, "but try telling the Obterek that."

"How long have the Serene and the Obterek been at loggerheads?" Allen asked.

"Would you believe over two hundred thousand Terran years?"

He shook his head at the very idea.

Kath went on, "The conflict exemplifies a typical pacifist-aggressor paradigm: what does a peaceful people, who live by rules of non-violence and respect for all life, do when attacked by a force who does not hold to such ideals? In the early years our people were split. There were those who said we should counter like with like, and defend ourselves by attacking. There were others, whose view thankfully prevailed, who maintained that we should abide by the ideals that had made our race what it was: humane, tolerant, compassionate. We inhabited many worlds by this time, and on one we set about working on a means of peaceable defence."

Sally opened her mouth in a silent, "Ah..." She said, "*Charea*?"

Kath nodded. "And for forty thousand years, with frequent interruptions, *charea* has worked."

A silence developed, each contemplating their own thoughts, until Sally asked, "You said that the incidence of Obterek attacks are increasing, but does this mean that one day they will prevail?"

"We certainly hope not. You must understand that to subvert, or compromise, the quantum structure of the *charea* requires such energies as you would find hard to conceive. And the Obterek simply do not have the resources to reconfigure more than a fragment of the basal structure of reality at any one time. Granted, they may attempt to take the life of a self-aware entity from time to time, or even stage a more daring attack like that at Fujiyama, but as I stated earlier these are, we think, merely warning shots. We live in preparation of the Obterek upping the stakes, of developing ways of countering the *charea* that we cannot foresee."

"And if one day the Obterek prevailed, destroyed the *charea*? What then?" Sally asked.

"Their stated aim is to reinstate the Natural Law, but this is disingenuous. In the past they have promised certain races a return to the old, violent ways – but they lie. And the same would be true here, too."

"So... what would they want?" Allen asked.

"What all aggressive, warlike races want – domination, complete and utter subjugation of your race. And they would be ruthless to their subjects if they ever succeeded in permanently subverting the *charea* and defeating us." She paused, her gaze distant, then went on, "Five millennia ago there was a race which the Serene failed. I was not there to witness what happened, of course, but the story stands to serve as a warning should ever we become complacent."

Sally said, "What happened?"

"The Serene brought the *charea* to this race, the Grayll; like your race, they were a technological, civilised people – but given to destructive internecine wars which, unchecked, would have resulted in their self-annihilation. The Serene intervened, bringing peace to their small world, and then made the fatal mistake, a hundred years later, of dropping our guard. We became complacent, left only a token force of self-aware entities in the Grayll's system – and the Obterek struck massively, breaching the basal reality paradigm, destroying our means of maintaining the *charea* and driving our forces from the system. For the next fifty years the Obterek used the Grayll as little more than slave labour in order to mine the solar system of precious metals and resources. They were ruthless, thinking nothing of working to death thousands of innocent Grayll at a time, of summarily executing those they deemed to be subverting their cause. After half a century the Obterek withdrew to the fastness of their own system, leaving... leaving behind not a single living creature. Those Grayll still living at the end of the period of enslavement they put to death in the most horrific fashion. And what made the slaughter all the worse was that the Obterek had promised these deluded people ultimate freedom when they, the Obterek, had finished raping the star system. The remaining Grayll were gathered together at the site of a Grayll holy temple and... and firebombed.

"When the Obterek left, and the Serene returned... they found the incinerated corpses of ten thousand men, women and children, a terrible testament to our complacency. The Serene vowed, then, that slaughter should never happen again."

After a short silence, Allen said, "And they would do the same to the human race?"

"Without question," Kath replied.

Allen considered everything Kath had said. "Might the Obterek threat have some bearing on your decision to terraform the outer planets of the solar system, to promote our migration outwards? This way, spread across the system, we present a target difficult to locate and destroy?"

Kath smiled. "That is certainly one way of looking at the problem, yes. The other reason is simply that the natural evolution of a race is ever outwards, pushing into space and exploring new habitats, spreading the gene pool in a diaspora that will thus engender a greater chance of species survival."

They were silent for a time. "It's a big commitment you're asking of us," he said at last. "I mean, it's difficult enough to think about emigrating to Australia, say, not to mention Mars."

Kath smiled. "I know, and I do not ask lightly. But let me assure you that you would find Mars conducive to a happy life. The brochure I gave you sets out in detail everything you might need to know. Browse through it at your leisure. There is no real hurry..."

Allen caught something in her tone. "But..?"

Kath frowned. "But... we are eager to set up a vital, viable colony on Mars before the Obterek find new and potentially more lethal ways of going about their goals. We are recruiting colonists daily, and we need people like you to join us." She finished her tea and checked her watch. "My train for London is due at twelve. I'd better dash."

Allen smiled to himself. The banality of human concerns after such mind-stretching issues as galactic conflict...

Kath stood and hugged Sally.

"Look through the brochure, and consider what I've said. If you have any questions, don't hesitate to contact me. If I don't hear from you in a couple of weeks, I'll be in touch."

Allen embraced Kath and murmured goodbye, and Sally saw her across the garden and down the front path.

She returned a minute later, smiling to herself. "Well..." she said.

He tapped the softscreen into life. "Let's take a look, Sal. But we can't do this without a cup of tea."

"Good idea," Sally said. She sat down on the bench and took up the softscreen.

Allen picked up the tray and retreated to the kitchen.

CHAPTER NINE

JAMES MORWELL STARTED work at nine that morning and by eleven he was through with his duties for the day.

He sat at his desk and considered the appearance of the blue figure last week, its pronouncement that he and the Obterek were working towards the same end, and its gift of the shimmering blue discs. For a few days he had allowed himself a flicker of hope. He had contacted Lal and demanded the latest information regarding the suspected Serene representatives... And the news was not good. The two latest suspects had vanished days ago without trace. Lal assured him that he was working personally to track down other suspects, and promised that within weeks he would be able to present Morwell with a dossier of likely candidates.

The news had dispirited him, and for days he'd sunk into a depressed state, where nothing he did mattered at all and no hope glimmered on the horizon.

His life, of late, was becoming meaningless.

Three days a week he and four other once eminent businessmen, all of them self-made millionaires, met for a round of golf and dinner at their club on Long Island. But he was becoming jaded with the game of late; he detected that his passion to win was not matched by that of his colleagues, and what was victory against apathetic opposition? He blamed the Serene, of course. Their *charea* had affected not only humanity's ability to commit violence, but also robbed the human spirit of something vital, the spark of life, of fight, that made individuals, tribes, nations, want to *win*.

So golf accounted for three afternoons a week, and sex – such as it was – the other three. On Sunday he rested by taking his yacht out to sea and losing himself in the blue immensity for hours on end.

Increasingly these days he enjoyed the luxury of being alone. On his yacht he cut all communications, deactivated his softscreen, and simply sailed.

It was while out on the ocean just a week ago that the idea had occurred to him, and he had greeted its sudden emergence in his head with uproarious laughter.

Along with other forms of violence, suicide was a thing of the past. These days, no one was allowed to kill himself. You spasmed if you tried to slice your jugular, or insert a rifle into your mouth and pull the trigger; you were unable to jump off buildings, or under trains. He was sure, idly thinking about it, that people must have found ways around the self-harming edict. But, if so, they had not survived to pass on the information, and Morwell himself could think of no way to subvert the Serene's *charea* – which was a pity as, these days, he was increasingly wondering what was the point of being alive.

He had been out on his boat, staring into the clear blue sky and day-dreaming about possible suicide methods: somehow infect oneself with a lethal botulism, or lay oneself open to a fatal disease... but he suspected that at some point in the process one would begin spasming.

Could he purposefully allow himself to be pitched over the side when the boat yawed, and so drown – to all intents an accident...?

The next time he'd taken his yacht out, he'd tried to do this, and spasmed well before he got anywhere near the safety rail.

Then a few weeks later, while lying on the deck under the full might of the sun, he'd had his brainwave.

Rather than do *something* to kill oneself – perhaps the answer was simply to do *nothing* to stay alive?

So excited was he by the idea that he sat up and almost punched the air in elation.

He would board his boat with no provisions, no food or water, with his emergency radio left at home, lifebelts and safety jackets jettisoned; he would set the tiller and point the yacht east and simply... sail into the vast unknown.

He would starve to death – a protracted, painful death, no doubt – or the boat would find itself in a storm and, if he did nothing to steer it through, would capsize and take him with it. Surely then he would achieve his desire to end his life?

But always a niggling doubt remained: before he even set off, would he begin the involuntary spasming that would thwart his dreams of putting an end to himself?

His softscreen chimed, interrupting his reverie.

He answered the call. Lal's sleek Indian face smiled out at him.

"I wonder if I might come up and see you, sir?"

"Is it really necessary, Lal? I was just about to leave."

Lal's smile widened. "If you could spare me just ten minutes, sir."

Morwell sighed. "Very well. Ten minutes." And it had better be good, he thought as he cut the connection.

A minute later Lal strode into the office and lounged in the seat across the desk from Morwell.

"You look, Lal, if you don't mind the crudity, like a dog that's learned how to fuck itself and suck its balls at the same time."

Lal smiled. Morwell was sure his frequent vulgarisms offended the man's deep-seated Hindu puritanism, but if so he didn't let it show.

Lal said, "Did I ever tell you that I had a sister, sir?"

Morwell sighed. "No, Lal. No, you didn't. And I don't think I ever enquired, either." Don't tell me that you're fucking her, he thought to himself, but refrained from asking.

"Ana," Lal went on. "I was parted from her at the age of sixteen, when Paul Prentice found me in Kolkata."

"That part of your life story, Lal, I am aware of."

"We lived on Howrah station, and it was hard enough looking after oneself without taking into consideration a puling kid sister. I found Ana a millstone." He paused. "I never said goodbye to her when Prentice enrolled me at the business school..."

Morwell smiled to himself and said, "With the greatest respect, Lal, why the hell are you telling me all this?"

"Because, sir, yesterday Ana tracked me down."

"And should I be delighted that the Devi siblings are at last reunited?"

Lal smiled. "Not at all, sir. But I think you will be interested in what I have to tell you."

"Go on, Lal," Morwell said with heavy forbearance, "but make it quick, hm?"

"Very well." Lal crossed his legs and leaned back even further in his seat. "After she'd shed her recriminations at the manner of my leaving, we shared a little history. I excused myself by saying that I'd not wanted to hurt her by telling her I was leaving – and that it was an opportunity I couldn't pass up. I think she was mollified. She told me what she was doing these days – working at the Andhra Pradesh wilderness city as a production manager. She's done very well for herself."

Morwell interrupted. "And I'm delighted for her, Lal. But I don't quite see..."

"She told me that she is also," Lal said, "a representative of the Serene."

Morwell stared at the Indian. He felt as if his innards had been scooped from his torso, stirred up and returned. "Go on."

"We chatted for a couple of hours yesterday, and I met her again this morning. She told me what she does for the Serene – not that she knows exactly what that is. Every month she leaves India for various cities around the world. She travels aboard what she calls a Serene jet – though it is interesting that we have never detected the flight of one of these planes. For the past five years the cities visited, she has noticed, have always been those that are occupied by Serene obelisks. There is obviously some link, sir."

Morwell nodded, his pulse racing. "Well done, Lal."

The Indian smiled. "There is more. This morning she told me about an incident in Fujiyama, Japan, which occurred a few days ago. Apparently there was an attack by extraterrestrials opposed to the Serene. Many humans were killed, though Serene self-aware entities apparently restored them to life. My sister was one of these people, along with two other Serene representatives." Lal smiled at this point. "She mentioned their names in passing, and later I checked their identities. I have all their information here, sir." He held up a memory stick. "One is a citizen of Italy, the other of the UK."

Morwell nodded, letting Lal's information percolate slowly through his consciousness.

At last he said, "This might be the break we've been waiting for, Lal."

"The discs?" asked the Indian.

Morwell laughed. "The discs indeed, my friend."

"I was wondering, as I have arranged to see Ana tomorrow, might I have the honour of..."

"We need to plan this carefully, Lal – but yes, I see no reason why not."

He sat back and stared out at the vista of Manhattan. Suddenly, life did not seem to be so lacking in purpose.

In fact, for the first time in years, Morwell felt optimistic.

CHAPTER TEN

SALLY AND GEOFF did not mention Mars for a couple of days after the meeting with Kathryn Kemp.

The softscreen brochure remained on the kitchen table, waiting to be either considered or discarded along with all the other detritus of family life: notices of local events, bills, flyers from Hannah's school...

Sally went back to the surgery the day after seeing Kath, and Geoff worked in his study editing the shots he'd taken at the Fujiyama arboreal city.

At dinner that evening Hannah chatted about school, who was friends with whom, and what Miss Charles had said about the forthcoming Serene Party, marking the tenth anniversary of the alien's arrival on Earth. Mars was not mentioned until after dinner when, Hannah tucked up in bed, Sally opened a bottle of red wine and they sat in the garden and enjoyed the clement summer evening. She said, "Have you...?"

He glanced at her. "Mars?"

"Sometimes I think we're telepathic." She reached out and took his hand. It was good to have him back.

"Well, I suppose we really should look at the brochure... I'll fetch it."

While he was in the kitchen, Sally refilled their glasses and looked around the garden. It was, she thought, idyllic, with the wisteria in bloom and filling the air with its heavy scent, and the roses banked against the cottage wall. She would miss the house, the garden, their friends in Wem and London, if they *did* agree to the move.

She laughed, and looked above the horizon at the faint red pin-prick that was the planet Mars.

Geoff came back and activated the softscreen, and for the next half hour they sat side by side, the screen propped on Geoff's lap and angled so they could both see it.

A series of images showed a terraformed Mars, a greened and rolling terrain under a blue sky streaked with brushstroke clouds. A vast area of land in the southern foothills of Olympus Mons, so they were informed, most corresponded in geographic aesthetics to rural southern England, and it was to here that the Allen-Walsh family would be located if they agreed to the migration.

There was a section showing artist's impressions of towns and villages on the red planet, and they were not unlike towns and villages here, a combination of old architecture and new poly-carbon dwellings, with the odd dome thrown in for the sake of ultra-modernity.

Sally laughed. "They're going out of their way to make us feel at home. Look, that building there..."

Between a poly-carbon tower and a silver dome nestled what looked like a Tudor inn.

"Looks like some American theme park," he grunted.

Aloud she read a little of the blurb, "The settling of Mars is the first step from planet Earth, the first small step in what is hoped will be the diaspora of humankind to the stars..."

They came to the end of the brochure as the sun was setting. The air was still warm. Sally sipped her wine and looked across at Geoff. She could tell, without asking, that he was in favour of the move.

"Well?" she asked at last.

He pursed his lips. "Well... there is that line about the move not being permanent. A minimum stay of two years, and if we don't like it for whatever reasons..." he shrugged, "we could always come back. What do you think?"

"I... I must admit I'm attracted to the idea."

"I'll tell you what, let's sleep on it. Let's go to the Horseshoes for lunch tomorrow and talk it over, okay?"

She smiled at him. "Let's do that, Geoff."

They sat side by side in companionable silence as twilight descended and Mars twinkled above the horizon.

THEY WALKED ALONG the tow-path hand in hand.

Sally recalled coming this way with Kath just the other day, and what had happened a little later. The sun beat down and butterflies jinked above the surface of the canal.

Sally selected a table in the beer garden while Geoff went to the bar and ordered beer and food. There were only three or four people in the garden beside herself. She watched the koi navigate the confined waters of the pool, occasionally nudging the surface for food.

"You're miles away." Geoff set the beers down on the table.

She smiled. "Just thinking about the past ten years, and how different it would have been if the Serene hadn't intervened."

He watched her as he sipped his drink.

She said, "I'd be dead, killed by Islamic terrorists back in Uganda."

The silence stretched. Geoff said, "I'd be alone, no you, no Hannah. And the world would be plagued by wars, murders... the same old routine of mindless violence and not so mindless violence – which was probably worse. When you think about it, all in all, we are a pretty despicable race."

"Are?" she asked. "Or were?"

He shrugged. "I don't know." He frowned, considering. "I mean, if the Serene lifted the *charea*, then it would be back to square one, wouldn't it? We'd be killing each other, invading countries, bombing."

She took his hand. "It will take more than just ten years for us to be able to turn our backs on violence," she said. "Perhaps in centuries... perhaps then if the *charea* was lifted we might have become civilised to the point where the need, the desire, to do violence would be no more."

He looked at her. "Do you think it is a need, a desire? Or just a response to circumstance?"

She considered this, then said, "I'd like to think the latter. Maybe violence was the end result of our inability to work things out in any other way. And with the influence of the *charea*, we'll learn over time that there are other ways to resolve conflict and settle differences."

"I'm sure you're right," he said.

Their food arrived, cheese soufflés and salad, and Geoff ordered two more halves of Leffe. "Right," he said, "Down to business, Sal. Mars. Pros and cons."

"Cons first," she said, puncturing her soufflé with a fork.

"We'd miss England, Wem, London, our friends. Nothing would be familiar – and that counts for a hell of a lot. Also, Hannah would miss her school, her friends."

"As you said the other day, children are adaptable. She'd soon make new friends."

"And..." he said. "And I think that's it. No more cons."

She nodded. "And the pros?"

"The pros," he began. "Well, we'd be *living on Mars*." She smiled at the big grin on his face as he went on, "We'd be experiencing life on another planet, part of humanity's first outward push from Earth. We'd be... and I know this sounds corny... but we'd be pioneers. And it needn't be forever. If we don't like it, we come back."

"And we can always return to visit friends."

He nodded, looking at her. "The thing is, do you want to go?"

"Yes, Geoff, I do. And you?"

"Me too. I'm ready for a change, a challenge."

She laughed as if with relief, squeezed his hand. "I'm glad that's settled, then. We'll talk to Hannah about it later. There's bound to be tears."

She stopped and looked up, aware of something in the air.

"Sal? What is it?"

"I don't know... Don't you feel it? Like before a thunderstorm, a charge in the air."

He shrugged. "Sorry..."

She looked around the garden. It seemed to have filled suddenly with a dozen well-dressed drinkers, but she thought the sudden odd atmosphere had nothing to do with the newcomers. She looked beyond the garden, as if searching there for the answer.

She shivered. "I don't know... for a second there I certainly felt something."

The people on the next table, two men and two women Sally had never seen before, drank and chatted amongst themselves. As Sally's gaze passed over them, a woman happened to look up and catch her eye. She looked away quickly, and Sally felt uneasy.

"Sal, are you okay?"

She had the strangest feeling of premonition, as if something was about to happen that should concern her – the strange intimation she'd had once as a student when Kath Kemp and other friends had thrown a surprise twenty-first birthday party for her.

Now she felt suddenly panicky. "Geoff, let's get out of here, okay?"

"Sal?" His expression was a strange mix of concern and amusement.

"No, I mean it. Something's not right."

At the nearby table, the woman who'd caught her eye briefly stood and moved towards their table. Sally watched her. The woman was heading for Geoff. She seemed to be moving in slow motion, or Sally's perception had been somehow retarded. Later she recalled thinking what a beautiful blue ring the woman was wearing...

A dozen figures appeared on the periphery of the garden. One second they were there, a golden enfilade of self-aware entities surrounding the startled drinkers, and then they were rushing inwards towards the woman who was approaching Geoff.

He looked up, startled, as a golden figure flashed by him, and Sally watched it collide with the woman who was reaching out with her right hand towards Geoff, her blue ring resplendent.

The golden figure slammed into the woman, seemed to absorb her. She noticed a man run towards Geoff, only he too was intercepted by a self-aware entity.

Screams filled the garden and innocent drinkers caught up in whatever was happening cowered behind tables or ran towards the pub. Geoff was on his feet, tugging at Sally's arm.

He turned as someone said his name, a bearded man who smiled and reached out. He carried a small blue disc – which was inches from Geoff's chest when a golden figure slammed into the man. One second he was standing there, reaching out, and the next second it was as if he had been replaced by the self-aware entity who spun in search of other attackers.

Calmly, two golden figures walked towards Sally and Geoff, and she was startled to hear a voice in her head. "*Do not be alarmed...*"

The golden figures approached and did not stop, and Sally cried out as one of the self-aware entities came face to face with her and enveloped her in its warmth. She felt a sudden jolt of energy, a heart-stopping surge of power that made her gasp and cry out again.

Then she was moving, and before she knew it she had left the garden and was travelling at speed; trees and bushes passed in a blur. She tried to cry out for Geoff, and was aware of another figure at her side.

She had the impression of covering vast distances in an instant, and seconds later she passed out.

SHE CAME TO her senses and she was enveloped in blackness. She no longer felt the energy of the golden figure surrounding her. She was alone again, or rather not alone... She felt someone nearby in the darkness, reached out and with a thrilling sense of relief found a hand she knew to be her husband's.

"Geoff!"

"Sal. We're okay. As the golden figure said, don't be afraid."

"But where are we?"

It was a blackness she had never known before, total and unrelieved, and she felt nothing beneath her feet. She had the sensation of floating.

She repeated her question, and Geoff responded.

"I think I know..."

"But where?"

"Just walk."

"How?" she almost wept.

"Move your feet. Lean against me and just move your feet."

As she did so she had the strangest sensation of something gaining solidity beneath her shoes, as if the very action of walking had brought the ground into existence.

Light appeared ahead, an undefined brightness that suddenly exploded dazzlingly in her vision. She exclaimed and threw an arm across her face to protect herself, and she stumbled as solid ground came up to hit her feet.

Geoff steadied her and laughed aloud.

She lowered her arm and, when her vision adjusted to the sunlight, stared around her.

They were in the back garden of their cottage, beside the gate. Before them was the cherry tree and the bench. At the end of the garden the old rectory stood, mellow in the sunlight; Sally thought it had never looked so beautiful.

She stared at Geoff and whispered, "What happened?"

He shook his head in wonder. "We were saved. The golden figures saved us."

She recalled the men and women bearing blue discs. "From what?"

"I don't know, Sal. I honestly don't know. All I know is that they saved us, brought us here – home... but not home."

She stared at him. "What do you mean?"

In reply he pointed to the sky, and Sally looked up.

Only then did she see the gourd-shape of a silvery moon tumbling erratically through a sky that was a deeper blue than any she had ever seen on Earth.

Geoff took her hand and almost pulled her towards the house. They hurried down the side path, then down the garden path to the front gate.

There they came to a halt, and stared.

Their house, their one hundred and fifty-year-old rectory, was perched on an escarpment overlooking a vast rolling green plain, at once alien and yet oddly familiar. Gone was Wem; gone was the rest of Shropshire.

She turned and saw that their house was one of a dozen lining the very lip of the escarpment, each one of a different design. She made out domes and poly-carbon villas, A-frames and things that looked very much like giant snail shells.

No sooner had she cried out, "Hannah!" than a golden figure appeared on the path from the back garden, a sleeping child in its arms.

The figure approached, halted, and held out the small girl. Sobbing, Sally reached out and embraced her daughter.

The golden figure stood before them, silent, and slowly its swirling depths took on the appearance of a human being.

Kath Kemp smiled. "Welcome to Mars," she said.

CHAPTER ELEVEN

ANA ARRIVED AT the coffee shop on 34th Street fifteen minutes early.

She ordered a mocha and sat in the window seat, staring out at the passing pedestrians. She had the feeling that she had closed a door on the old part of her life, and a new door was opening. She had found Bilal at last, and in that she felt a sense of accomplishment. She believed what he'd told her about not wanting to hurt the little girl she had been, and accepted that he'd had to take the opportunity of an education when it had been offered to him. What still rankled a little was that in the intervening years he had never really attempted to seek her out. She understood that, in a way; he had his new, exciting life, and as the years passed he must have looked back on his old life, and his sister, and thought them perhaps too painful to resurrect.

Whatever, now she had found him.

A big disappointment to her was finding what kind of person he had become. While most of the human race saw the great benefits of the Serene, a tiny minority still held out. And it was just her luck that her brother belonged to this defiant minority.

It was an aspect of his character she was determined to come to understand; only when she fully comprehended his mindset, and how it had got that way, could she even begin to work out how to show him that he was wrong. He would need educating, and Ana had resolved that her long-term project would be to show her brother how right the Serene were. She would invite him to India; they would revisit their childhood haunts together, and she would show him the wonders of the wilderness city.

It would take time, but she had plenty of that.

"Ana..." Bilal smiled down at her.

She stood and they kissed cheeks a little awkwardly, like strangers. While he was at the counter, she took in his sharp black suit, his white shirt and long ponytail. She knew she shouldn't criticise his style of dress – especially as she was wearing Western jeans and a blouse – but in these less formal times she saw his business attire as a uniform harking back to former, pre-Serene days.

He sat at her table and smiled at her. He appeared today, unlike at their first couple of meetings, a little nervous. He gestured to his coffee. "Old habits die hard. I always liked my coffee milky and sweet in India."

"You had coffee in India?" It was a luxury she had never tasted until ten years ago.

He shrugged. "In college," he said.

"They must have looked after you well. Quite apart from giving you a good education."

He shrugged again. She noticed that his hands, as he stirred his coffee, were shaking. He saw that she was looking at his hand, and self-consciously slipped it into his jacket pocket.

She smiled. "I was thinking... it would be lovely if you could come to visit me in India soon."

He nodded but did not look her in the eye. "I'd like that."

"You haven't been back for fifteen years?"

"I don't cover India now, just the US. I've had no reason to go back."

She sipped her coffee and asked, "So... what's it like working for the Morwell Organisation?"

"It pays well, and sometimes the work is interesting."

"And your boss... What's his name, James Morwell?"

"I think we understand each other. We share the same views, the same philosophy..."

She winced inwardly, and said, "He indoctrinated you, Bilal?"

"Now, isn't that a big word, sister?"

"Don't patronise me."

"And don't call me Bilal, please. I left that name behind when I got away from Kolkata. I'm Lal now."

She stared at him. The café was filling up, people queuing at the counter, others standing and eyeing their table as if suggesting they drink up and leave.

Ana felt an uneasy tension in the air, but knew it was all in her head. This meeting with her brother wasn't going well.

He said, "I prefer to think that I was 'educated', Ana. The Serene are... wrong. I was educated –"

"Please, let's not argue..."

"Just," he said, taking his hand from his pocket, "as you one day will be educated."

For some reason his fingers were glowing blue. She looked up, into his eyes, and tried to fathom what she saw in them.

Someone was moving towards her table, and a light had been switched on nearby, a dazzling golden light which intensified...

Bilal reached out for her hand, but before he made contact the golden light resolved itself into the shape of a self-aware entity and slammed into her brother. He vanished, absorbed into the form of the golden figure, which rolled with the impact of slamming into Bilal, stood and moved from the café in a blur of light.

Ana screamed.

She looked up at another approaching light and, for the second time that week, felt the life-force of a self-aware entity hit her.

She came to her senses and found that she was surrounded by darkness. She felt the energy of the self-aware entity cocooning her.

"What happened?" she asked.

A voice sounded in her head, telling her everything.

She sobbed as she recalled the look in Bilal's eyes as he reached out to her, the light of the betrayal he knew he was committing.

"What happened to him?" she asked – but the voice in her head chose not to reply.

Ana stepped forward, from darkness into dazzling light.

She was standing before her apartment in India... but something was wrong with the light. She looked up, into a bright blue sky streaked with impossibly high clouds. And overhead, tumbling end over end, was what looked like a huge, yam-shaped moon.

She turned suddenly and gasped at what she saw.

Her apartment was on the edge of a long ridge which overlooked a rolling green plane, at once exotic and idyllic. Other dwellings occupied the margin of the ridge; next to her apartment was an A-frame, and beyond that an ivy-covered, typically English house.

A small group of people were gathered before the English house, two of whom Ana recognised.

A golden figure stood before her, and Ana asked, "Where am I?"

"For your own safety, you are on Mars. Do not worry. We have contacted Kapil Gavaskar and he will soon be joining you."

Before the English house, Nina Ricci said something to the Englishman, Geoff Allen, and a tall woman Ana did not know. Nina looked across at Ana and waved.

Smiling to herself, pushing the thought of Bilal's betrayal to the back of her mind, Ana stepped from the shadow of her apartment and joined them.

THREE

2045

CHAPTER ONE

ALLEN LEFT HIS office, took the elevator down to the busy atrium, then strolled out into the sprawling gardens that surrounded the Mare Erythraeum administrative centre.

He bought a coffee at an open-air café overlooking the plain, selected a table and admired the view. He wondered if this was the finest panorama in the solar system. Once he would have said that the countryside of Shropshire provided the finest unspoilt rural views in the world, but that was before he had travelled to Mars, and beyond. Now he knew that the Mare Erythraeum, the methane plains of Titan, and the equatorial jungle zones of Venus all vied for contention.

The administrative centre was situated five kilometres along the escarpment from where, ten years ago, he had first fetched up on the planet. From the café on the lip of the drop he had an uninterrupted view for a couple for hundred kilometres across rolling farmland, shimmering canals – a conceit that proved the Serene possessed a sense of humour – to the mountains on the horizon. It was a combination of the dozen pastel shades, he decided, and the hazy quality of the air which gave the panorama such an idyllic atmosphere. There was little noise, too; the quiet trilling of parakeets high in the elms which lined the escarpment, and the distant buzz of the electric carts that beetled across the farmland far below.

He glanced at his watch. Ana was late, which was unusual for her. He drained his coffee and decided, as he was finished early for the day and the temperature was climbing, to order a cold beer.

Sipping it, he sat back and considered his situation. He was sixty-two, and he had been on Mars now for ten years; he had often wondered of late which was the more remarkable: the fact of his age or his residency for a decade on the red planet. He felt well for his age, though his hairline was receding and he'd put on a few pounds.

In the early days he, Sally and Hannah had returned to Earth every few months to see friends and renew their connection with all that was familiar about their home planet. Then, after a few years, their visits had become less frequent; it was as if they did not need to quench the nostalgic urge, as if Mars provided everything they required. Certainly most of their friends had now relocated here, and the landscape of the planet was becoming familiar and sustaining. They had found themselves spending more and more holiday time on far-flung outposts of the solar system – Venus, the asteroid resorts, and Ganymede.

And three years ago Allen had finished his last commission for the photo-agency he had worked for for over twenty years and begun work as a 'social administrator' of the Mare Erythraeum region of Mars. He was, in effect, a glorified civil servant, sitting on government committees that oversaw the smooth functioning of all aspects of life on Mars. A few years ago he'd found himself increasingly interested in the political set-up in the area, and it had seemed the natural thing to do, little by little, to move from the photo-agency and into local administration, first on a part-time voluntary basis and then, as he gained experience, on a more permanent footing.

Now he was not so sure that the decision had been wholly his own. He had fallen in with a set of people working in local admin, and they had suggested that he was just the type, with his broad knowledge of politics and people – they were flattering him, he thought – to work as a social administrator. He often wondered if he detected in his vocational shift the discreet, manipulative machinations of the Serene. But, he often wondered, to what end?

"Sorry I'm late!"

Ana Devi beamed down at him, stroking a long strand of hair from her face and bending down to kiss his cheek. He half-rose to facilitate the greeting, then sat back and watched her as she ordered an iced coffee.

Ana was thirty-six, tall and self-possessed, and had been one of Allen and Sally's best friends for the past seven or eight years. The flesh of her forearm pulsed with an incoming call, which she killed and turned the flesh-screen to the shade of her dark, Indian skin. Discreetly, not wanting their time together to be interrupted by business calls or any others, Allen tapped his own forearm-screen into quiescence.

"Kapil and Shantidev?" he asked. It was a couple of months since he and Sally had last invited Ana and her family round to their cottage on the escarpment, and a fortnight since Allen had last seen Ana.

"They're well. Kapil seems happy down at the farm and Shantidev has decided he wants to drive a tractor for a living when he grows up."

Allen laughed. "You make Kapil sound like a gentleman farmer."

She regarded him over her glass. "I often admire Kapil for his... *centredness*," she said, and shrugged, "his contentment. He keeps my feet on the ground."

Kapil managed the production output at the vast Ibrium farm, a logistical nightmare of a job which Allen knew just enough about to realise that it was demanding and high-powered.

"There's nothing like having children to make you realise how old you're getting," Ana said now.

"You don't need to tell me that. I'm sixty-two. Hannah's fifteen, going on thirty. The last ten years have gone by like that..." He snapped his fingers.

"It seems like just a few weeks ago that I was working on Earth."

"And speaking about the last ten years..."

"Yes?"

He shrugged, wondering how to broach the subject. Ana, practical, down-to-Earth Ana Devi, would tell him he was imagining things. "We both left our old jobs and moved into admin around the same time."

She sipped her iced coffee. "Mmm..."

"Well... have you wondered how much that was, on your part, a conscious choice?"

She pulled a face and stared at him. "Of course it was a conscious choice," she said. "You don't think I was ordered by my subconscious one day to pack it all in at the farm and apply for the government post?"

"Of course not. I mean... I was thinking back to when I left the agency, and it came to me that it was a combination of factors out of my control: dissatisfaction with shooting the same old things, the opening that just happened to be there in admin."

"Just what are you trying to say, Geoff?"

He shrugged, suddenly unsure of his footing. "I sometimes wonder how much we're being... propelled – I nearly said manipulated – by the Serene."

Ana twisted her lips into a frown. "I think that's something we'll probably never know."

"But you admit that it's a *possibility*?"

"I... Maybe, I don't know. But to what end?"

He considered her question. "Not long after we joined the admin team," he said, "our work for the Serene increased."

From doing the bidding of the Serene on a monthly basis, he, Ana and all the other 'representatives' of their acquaintance were informed that they would now be required to travel around the system for two days every fortnight – and most of their work would be centred on the giant obelisk situated on Saturn's largest moon, Titan.

Ana nodded. "That's right. So...?"

"So... it occurred to me that it was a bit of a coincidence."

She pointed at him. "And that's all it was, Geoff. A coincidence. Nothing more."

"Maybe you're right. But I'd still like to know what it is we actually *do* for the Serene in the obelisk every two weeks."

"I think that, Geoff, might remain a mystery for ever."

They sipped their drinks in companionable silence for a while, and then Ana said, "I've been thinking recently about the past twenty years, the arrival of the Serene and how things have changed. You?"

"Just a bit," he said.

"You don't see much spasming these days, do you?"

"Sally said the same thing just last week, and I hadn't realised – but you're right. You don't."

"Have you wondered why not?"

"Sally suggested that it's a conditional thing. Collectively, on some psychological level, we know that violence is futile so the brain is inured not to initiate the impulse."

She nodded. "She's been reading the psychology reports. That's roughly the thinking. In the early days you saw instances of spasming all over... remember all the comedians telling jokes about politicians dancing like marionettes?" She smiled. "Then... over the years... the instances of people spasming grew less and less."

He looked at her. "Did you spasm in the early days?"

Her expression clouded as she recalled something, he guessed, from her childhood. She was sixteen when the Serene arrived, though she had not spoken much about her life as a street kid in Kolkata. Now she nodded. "Once or twice, just after they came... It was a strange sensation, a kind of powerlessness, and yet a great urge to carry out the act."

"Do you recall," he went on, "how some psychologists were predicting terrible consequences of the human race being unable to fulfil what they saw as an elemental desire, the desire to commit violence? They said there would be unforeseen repercussions of the sublimation..."

"They got it wrong, which I suppose isn't that surprising when you think about it. I mean, the way some people were going on it was as if violence and the need to commit it was something that the majority of us felt and did on a daily basis. But how many times have you spasmed in the past twenty years?"

He thought about it. "I think just once, a year after the Serene arrived. I was debating with a colleague about the politics of their arrival, and he was against it. For a second, the briefest second, as he goaded me..." He shrugged. "I don't even know if I really spasmed – he certainly didn't notice anything, thankfully. I just felt a tremor, a sense of impotence."

"And I think that goes for the majority of the human race," Ana said. "So how would the inability to do violence have any long-term, or short-term, come to that, consequences for most of us?"

"And for the tiny minority, the psychopaths amongst us?"

"I rather think that they were... healed by the Serene self-aware entities among us," she said.

People like Kath Kemp, he thought; yes, that would make sense.

She sipped her iced coffee, staring over the escarpment at the pacific vista. Phobos tumbled, end over end, across the far horizon – and its rapid transit contrasted with and pointed up the serenity of the land beneath.

She said, "Do you know what the most shocking thing was, ten years ago?"

"You mean, when the Serene fought off the attack and brought us here?" He shook his head. "I don't know... The fact that the Serene were not... invincible, that they had enemies?"

She nodded. "Yes, all that. You're right. I was being selfish when I asked the question. That was shocking, too. But for me, on a personal level... I told you about my brother, didn't I?"

"Bilal?"

"Bilal. Right."

"You said he worked for the Morwell Corporation, and that he was opposed to the Serene."

"And how," she said, her expression hardening. "But what I've never told you... never told anyone other than Kapil... was that it was my brother, my big brother, who tried to attack me that day on behalf of the Obterek. He set me up, was willing to use me as a pawn to undermine the Serene." She stopped, her lips compressed as she fought with the notion. "He felt nothing for me."

Allen said, "I'm sorry."

"At the time it hurt more than I cared to admit. You see, until the age of six he and me were..." She shrugged. "We lived rough on Howrah Station, and Bilal looked after me. Then one day he just vanished, and I thought for a long time that he'd died. Years later, after the Serene came, I found out he was still alive and I tracked him down. And I found that he'd changed. He was shallow and mercenary... someone I should have despised. But he was my brother, after all... and I wanted to get to know him again. I suppose I wanted... I know this sounds silly... but I think I wanted him to love me."

She fell silent again, and Allen said nothing, but let her wrestle with her emotions. At last she said, "After his betrayal, in the years that followed, I often wondered how – or even if – the Serene had punished him."

He said, "I don't think that that's their way."

"Nor do I. But I wondered what had become of him."

"You never found out?"

She shook her head with vehemence. "No. I didn't want to. I tracked him down once, and look what happened then. But recently..."

"Yes?"

She gave a long, heartfelt sigh. "You'll think me silly, but recently I've been... curious. I suppose I look at Shantidev, and he so much reminds me of Bilal... and I can't help myself thinking back to those days. Anyway, recently I've wanted to go back to Earth, find him, discuss what he did ten years ago... find out what I really mean to him, if anything."

He nodded, considering her words. "It might be... painful."

She held his gaze. "I know that," she said, "but I've got to do it. Anyway, I've discussed it with Kapil, and next week I'm taking a few days off and going to Earth, to New York."

"I want to hear all about it when you get back."

"Oh you will, Geoff. I'll bore you and Sally to tears about what I did."

His forearm tingled, signalling that a priority incoming call had overridden the quiescent function. He apologised and accepted the call.

A familiar face expanded in the screen on his forearm. Nina Ricci smiled out at him. "Nina... this is a welcome surprise. It's been months."

"Six," she said with her customary precision. "I'd like to see you, Geoff."

"Great. When are you next over our way?"

Nina Ricci was a high-level politico with administrative duties that extended over the entirety of Mars's southern hemisphere. "How about the weekend?" she said.

"Wonderful. Stay at our place for the weekend. I'll get a few people together and we'll make a party of it on Saturday."

"That sounds like a good idea, though I would like to see you alone at some point."

He nodded. "Fine... But what about?"

She pulled a face. "About many things, but principally about the Titan obelisk, our increased duties... I have an idea."

"What a coincidence. I was just talking about those very things."

"With whom?"

Allen lifted his forearm and directed it across the table at Ana, who smiled and waved her fingers. "Hi, Nina!"

"Ana, good to see you. I take it that you will come on Saturday too?"

Ana nodded. "I'm sure Geoff will invite me," she said.

To Allen, Nina said, "Midday Saturday, then. Ciao, Geoff."

He cut the connection, sat back and smiled at Ana. "Now, I wonder what all that was about?"

Ana laughed. "That," she said, "was Nina, being all conspiratorial again. You know her!"

"And I know that when she has ideas they can often be very interesting."

They ordered more drinks and chatted as the Martian afternoon mellowed towards evening.

A COUPLE OF weeks after their arrival on Mars, as they sat in the garden with a bottle of red wine, Sally had said to him, "Do you know what's wrong with this house, Geoff?"

He looked at her. "Isn't it perfect? That's what you always said – it's perfect." He paused. "Okay, is it because it's on Mars?"

"Of course not. I like it here. And Hannah has settled in wonderfully."

"So what's wrong with the house?"

"It's the wrong way around."

"Come again?"

"The garden," she said, indicating the lawn,

"should be on the other side, overlooking the escarpment. The Serene didn't get it right."

"I think, if you recall, it was rather a rushed job. They had other things to think about, after all."

She hit his arm. "I know that! It's just... I wonder if we could get them to turn it around?"

"Tell you what, next time I see Kath, I'll mention it to her."

It was said in jest, of course, as it was a week later when he met with Kath Kemp and mentioned Sally's criticism of the Serene's architectural prowess. She had smiled and murmured an apology – but a few days later, on arriving home with Sally, he had braked their buggy before the house, stared at Sally and laughed aloud.

The Serene had turned the cottage around so that now the back garden overlooked the escarpment and the five-hundred-metre drop to the plain below.

It made a great venue for the parties and get-togethers that he and Sally hosted every month.

Now thirty friends and neighbours thronged the garden, setting up a pleasant hubbub of chatter; Martian tablas played in the background, and somewhere one of Hannah's friends was attempting – not altogether successfully – to coax a raga from a sitar.

The majority of the guests were workmates of Allen and Sally's, professionals in their forties and fifties and their teenage children. Ana had come early and with Sally had cooked up an Indian feast, which they were carrying with triumphal pride from the kitchen to trestle tables set up at the end of the garden. Shantidev, Ana's six-year-old son, was dangling contentedly from the rope-swing that Allen had made, twelve years ago, for Hannah. The sight of the child penduluming back and forth beneath the sturdy branch of the ash tree brought back a slew of pleasant memories.

He knocked back his fifth beer and listened to Kapil and a colleague at the farm talking shop.

It was six o'clock, and the sun was setting on a short Martian day. It was warm – as it was all the year round at this equatorial latitude – and the party was set to go on quietly until midnight, when the last of the guests would wander off home until next time. As Allen sipped his beer and stared around at the happy revellers, he realised that he had not felt so contented in years.

Nina Ricci had arrived a little after midday, tall, elegant and regal as ever; if anything, the passing years had done something to mature and deepen her Latin beauty. She was in her late forties now, with the poise and gravitas of an emeritus ballerina, and a restless, questing intelligence.

A murmur had passed around the gathering on her arrival; she had risen from being a nondescript journalist ten years ago, to her current, elevated position as one of the leading political thinkers on Mars.

Allen had introduced her to various friends and then, later, they had chatted about nothing in particular, catching up on each other's recent exploits – Allen realising, as he recounted council meetings, how humdrum his life had become of late, at least relative to Ricci's hectic lifestyle.

He had been eager to hear her latest theories, but it was evident from the line of her conversation that that would be saved until later.

Now he saw her in earnest conversation with a professor at the local university, a man known for his trenchant views who, on this occasion, seemed to have found his conversational match.

Allen looked around the gathering but could not see Sally.

He moved back into the house and found her in the kitchen. He leaned against the door-frame and watched her putting the finishing touches to three vast bowls of trifle. He was overcome with a strange sensation; it came to him from time to time, unexpectedly, surprising him with its power. It was an upwelling of love for this woman who had shared his life now for twenty years. She was sixty-two, upright and slim, her face lined, her hair grey, and he realised that he had never found her as beautiful as he did now. The emotion almost choked him.

Sensing his presence, Sally turned quickly. With the back of her hand – her fingers sticky – she brushed away a strand of hair and smiled at him. "What?" she asked. "You're staring at me very oddly, Geoff."

"I know you're probably sick and tired of me telling you this, but you're very beautiful."

"Give over, you."

He crossed the room and took her in his arms, thrilled by the feel of her. He pressed her to him and kissed her lips. "I came in to see if you needed any help."

"Typical. Just as I've nearly done in here."

"Sorry."

Someone ran into the kitchen with a clatter of shoes, stopping short. "Ugh! Do you have to, at your age?" Hannah stared at them. "Anyway, the beer's running low and Professor Hendrix sent me in for more."

Sally said, "You'll find it in the cooler."

Their daughter hauled open the door and dragged out the beer. As she left the kitchen, she called back over her shoulder, "And when you've quite finished in here, you should be sociable and circulate."

Allen said, "Maybe she's right."

"Help me out with these and then get me a drink, would you?"

They carried out the trifles to applause, and Allen opened a bottle of Sally's favourite white wine – a locally grown Chardonnay – and later they sat under the cherry tree with Ana, Kapil and a few other friends and drank and chatted as an indigo twilight rapidly descended.

He stared across the lawn at Nina Ricci, watching her holding forth to a group of scientists from the nearby research lab.

Sally leaned against him and murmured, "I wonder why Nina invited herself, Geoff?"

He smiled. "No doubt she has some wild theory to regale us with. You know Nina."

She looked at him. "The strange thing is, I don't think I do. I've known her for... what, ten years now, and I don't really think I know the real woman, what she feels or thinks on a personal level. Oh, I know what she thinks intellectually – she never tires of telling me that! But emotionally..." She shook her head. "She gives nothing away."

"That's Nina. I'm not sure she has an emotional life."

"If I didn't know better, if I didn't know Kath – to prove to me that self-aware entities can be imbued with just the same emotions as we humans... I would have said that Nina was an SAE."

He shook his head. "I know what you mean, but I think not. She's too critical of the Serene to be *of* them. And I don't mean critical in her being opposed to their regime... I mean critical of their methods, their lack of – as she sees it – openness."

"She still not married?"

"No. But rumour has it that she has a long-term lover, a woman twenty years her junior."

"You should ask Nina to bring her along to one of our soirées."

Nina disengaged herself from the knot of scientists and strolled past the cherry tree. She stepped onto the terrace which the Serene, when they had thoughtfully turned around the house, had cantilevered over the drop. She walked to the far rail and leaned against it, a study in isolated elegance.

Seconds later Allen's forearm tingled, and he accepted the call. He glanced across at Ricci. She was staring at her own forearm.

She looked up at him from the screen. "Geoff, why not join me? Bring Ana."

He said, "I'd like Sal to come too."

A hesitation, then Nina Ricci nodded minimally. "Very well, but bring only four chairs so that people know that we are not to be interrupted."

He cut the connection and said to Sally, "We have our orders."

Sally spoke to Ana, and between them they carried four wicker chairs across the lawn and over to the rail. Allen ventured out onto the cantilever as little as possible – he found the vertiginous drop to the plain below too reminiscent of the view from the Fujiyama city tree, all those years ago.

He recharged their glasses and proposed a toast. "To life on Mars," he said, "almost exactly ten years on."

Nina Ricci looked around the small group and said, "And have you settled down, all of you? Are you liking life on Mars?"

They nodded, to a person. Allen said, "It couldn't be better. We were a little homesick at first, weren't we?" He looked across at Sally, who smiled. "But that soon passed."

"And you, Ana? Do you miss India?"

"I don't. I have... outgrown the country of my birth. I like to think of myself as a citizen of the solar system."

Allen smiled as she said this, and thought of the street kid Ana had been.

Nina said, "Do you ever consider what the Serene might want with us, their 'representatives'?"

He shifted uneasily, wondering why her question unsettled him. Ana said, "I no longer question the Serene, Nina. They have brought unlimited good to humankind. Who am I to question what they want with me?"

"Or what they do to you, in that mysterious obelisk on Titan?"

Allen said, "*Do* to us?"

Nina shrugged. "We go there every two weeks

now, we and thousands upon thousands of other human representatives... and we walk out a day or two later with no memory of what occurred in there. And don't you think it strange?"

Sally spoke up. "The whole thing about the Serene is 'strange', if you're inclined to phrase it like that."

The Italian smiled. "We no longer travel to the obelisks on Earth or elsewhere. Almost everyone goes exclusively to the obelisk on Titan, the vastest manufactured object in the solar system. I wondered at first if it served as a device like the other obelisks—"

"A matter-transmitter," Sally said.

Nina inclined her head. "That's what I wondered. But why have one of that size situated so far out? For what purpose? And why have every representative go there every two weeks?"

Ana was doing her best to hide her smile. "And you have a theory, Nina?"

Nina Ricci allowed a silence to develop. Instead of assenting, which was what Allen had expected, she said, "I have one more question, Ana. And it is this: what are the Serene doing to our solar system?"

This was met with blank looks all round. "What do you mean?" Ana asked.

Ricci tapped her forearm, then typed in a command. From the olive skin of her arm was projected into the air before them a cuboid, three-dimensional screen.

Allen made out a representation of the outer solar system, with Saturn and Jupiter in the foreground, and the outer planets tiny dots behind them. Beyond, far stars twinkled.

Ricci said, "This has been suppressed by the various newsfeeds. I suspect SAEs in high places don't want us to know, quite yet."

Allen said, "Know what?"

"I was talking to the scientists from the university, among them a couple of astronomers – and even they are not aware of what is happening."

"Which is?" Ana asked.

"Observe." Ricci tapped her screen again and the scene hanging before them shifted. Gone were Jupiter and Saturn, to be replaced with the tiny, ice-bound orb of Pluto. "Do you see the stars immediately behind Pluto?" she asked.

Sally said, "Yes, but faintly."

"Yes!" declared Ricci. "Exactly. Look, the stars in a quadrant – imagine an elliptical section of orange peel, if you will – appear faint, compared with those to either side."

Allen peered more closely, and saw that she was correct. So..." he said.

"This appeared three weeks ago, for no more than an hour. A colleague – an amateur astronomer – brought it to my attention. When he checked again, the quadrant of faint stars was back to normal. When I saw Kathryn Kemp a week later, I asked her about the diminution of stellar luminosity."

"And she said that you were imagining it," Ana smiled.

Ricci stared at her. "On the contrary, Ana," the Italian said, "Kathryn told me that on my next visit to Titan, she would be able to answer some of my questions, and specifically she would be in a position to tell me what the Serene were doing on the outer edges of the solar system."

Allen stared at her. "So they are doing something?" he murmured.

Sally said, "Knowing you, Nina, you have an idea, yes?"

Nina smiled. "Would you believe me if I told you that I had no idea at all?"

They laughed, and Nina tapped her forearm. The three-dimensional screen in the air before them vanished in a blink.

She looked around the staring group. "In ten days," she said, "we'll meet up, as usual, following whatever it is that we do in the Titan obelisk. I have arranged for Kathryn Kemp to join us then. We might at last, my friends, find out what truly motivates the Serene."

Allen sipped his wine, and stared up at the sector of stars way beyond the icy orbit of Pluto. Beside him, Sally took his arm and shivered.

CHAPTER TWO

In the eight years since James Morwell stepped down as nominal head of the Morwell Organisation – 'nominal' because over the course of the previous two years he had been nothing more than a powerless figurehead – he had set himself on a course of merciless self-destruction.

It had become an obsession, a desire that filled his waking hours and often carried over into his sleep: he dreamed of oblivion, of finding a means to end his life in some spectacular and Serene-defying manner. Always he awoke with a new method of killing himself flittering elusively on the edge of his consciousness, and when he did recall the means bequeathed by his dream he often found that he'd tried it before, or that it was patently impossible. He dreamed of throwing himself off a tall building, of stepping out in front of a speeding truck; he dreamed of manufacturing a purposeful 'accident'...

He'd lost count of the number of times he had tried to take his life. He was determined to show the Serene that there was at least one human being on the planet who did not intend to kow-tow to their imposition of *charea*, who would attempt to defy their edict on self-annihilation. Even if he failed to carry through his suicide, the very fact that he was constantly trying and would go on doing so was an act of defiance satisfying in itself.

Satisfying, but not wholly so. Only in oblivion, he told himself, would he find true peace of mind.

In 2040 he took up downhill skiing, and off *piste* in Switzerland swerved towards a stand of pine trees at a speed, he calculated, a little over seventy miles an hour. In the seconds before impact he knew the elation of imminent self-annihilation... Except he never hit the tree. Instead he impacted with something soft, something which cushioned him in slow motion and sent him skidding sideways harmlessly into a bank of snow.

A year later he tampered with the brake lining of his Ferrari, and set off on a jaunt into the Appalachians. On a downhill stretch of road he allowed his speed to mount until he was screaming along at ninety miles per hour with a tight bend looming, and he laughed like a maniac and cursed the Serene...

Until his car mysteriously slowed, seemingly of its own accord, and eased itself to a halt beside the curving crash-barrier. He'd set off again, more than once attempting to spin the wheel and send himself over the edge... he spasmed, and could not complete the manoeuvre – and this gave him an inspired idea.

He would incorporate the very act of spasming into a series of actions which in themselves would bring about his death.

If he spasmed in the course of attempting to shoot himself in the head while climbing a sheer rock-face... then surely he would achieve his aim and fall to his death?

Three days later he drove into the Catskills and found a likely looking cliff. Armed with a pistol, he climbed for fifteen minutes, a frantic, suited businessman wholly out of place clinging to the side of the cliff. He laughed at the thought, then raised the gun to his temple and tried to pull the trigger. He spasmed and lost his grip on the rock, and fell, thinking in the brief seconds of his descent that surely now he had succeeded in killing himself.

He should have known. As with the attempt on the ski-slope, he found himself mysteriously cushioned, his fall decelerating as if he'd impacted with a mattress... And he lay uninjured on his back, staring up at the wispy cirrus high in the blue sky, weeping in rage and frustration.

That same year he had become a drug addict. He tried heroin at first, injecting prescribed doses enough to get him high, and found the resultant euphoria a balm. Over the weeks he increased the dosage, and sourced pure heroin which should, by rights, have killed him outright. Every time he injected himself he slipped into welcome oblivion, praying on the way that maybe this time he had succeeded.

And every time he came to his senses, alive and unharmed. He persevered, thinking that surely his addiction must have some long-term cumulative effect. But the fact was that it was as if his metabolism became inured to the effects of the drug. The more he injected, the less effect it had. He talked with other one-time addicts and found that the drug now had no effect on them, and so they had ceased taking it; the work of the Serene, they said, and gave thanks.

And then, just two weeks ago, while drinking himself senseless in front of a wildlife documentary – a binge which had lasted the better part of a week to little deleterious effect – he had an epiphany.

He watched in amazement as a cobra leapt towards a wild boar, struck and killed its prey.

The following day he booked a flight to Venezuela.

HE STAYED A few days in an Indian village on the edge of the Amazonian jungle, a thousand miles south of the capital of Caracas, and then bought from the tribal headman a dugout canoe and paddled it upstream. He set out without provisions or even water, much to the alarm of the tribespeople. Half a day later, when he judged that he was far enough away from the village, and from civilisation in general, that his corpse would not be stumbled upon and brought back to New York for burial – he loathed the idea of his funeral attended by colleagues crying crocodile tears and later laughing amongst themselves about what a bastard he had been – he paddled to the bank, climbed out and pushed the dugout back into the current. He watched it drift away, spinning lazily, and smiled to himself.

Then he set off into the jungle, towards the oblivion which awaited him.

There were, he had read before setting off, at least a dozen types of poisonous snake in the Venezuelan jungle, as well as half a dozen varieties of toxic spider and many other wild animals eager, he was sure, to carry out their biological mandate to protect their territory or attack him as nourishing prey.

He walked into the sweltering jungle, falling again and again, laughing like a maniac, swearing at the Serene and at his father and frequently weeping at the mess his life had become.

He fell and slipped into unconsciousness, and woke hours later to find that he'd spent a night propped against the bole of a tree overlooking a narrow gulch sparkling with a twisting, silver stream. The water looked so fresh, inviting, but he ignored his raging thirst and willed himself to die.

He passed in and out of consciousness in the hours that followed, and was visited by a series of hallucinations.

At one point Kat came to him and knelt, reached out a solicitous hand and mopped his feverish brow.

He stretched out a hand, eager to touch her pale skin. She smiled at him. "I want to help you," she said now, as she had said many times in the past.

He had met Kat ten years ago, just after the abortive attempt to 'mark' the Serene representatives. He had been at his lowest ebb, reconciled to humanity under the yoke of the alien invaders and powerless to do anything about it. He had begun to dabble with suicide, although it had not yet become the preoccupation it now was. In retrospect he thought that the arrival of Kat into his life had slowed his downward spiral, and invested his life, for a year, with some semblance of happiness... though he had hardly realised that at the time.

She had been working as a psychologist for a government run scheme helping recovering drug addicts – this was before his attempts at pharmaceutical oblivion – and he had met her at an uptown party which, he recalled, he had been loath to attend. It was only on the insistence of Lal – that greasy, betraying bastard – that he had shrugged off his apathy and gone along.

Kat had homed in on him, talked to him with warmth and understanding, and a day later they had met for dinner and something within him had succumbed and allowed this dumpy, homely woman – ten years his senior and with a penchant to mother him – into his life.

For a year he had enjoyed an easy, affectionate relationship with this calm, meditative English woman; he would never have admitted that he loved her, and she never vouchsafed the same to him, but they were close, and she helped him confront his past, his relationship with his abusive father, and helped him overcome his desire to be dominated and demeaned... But he had never, for all their intimacy, both physical and psychological, told her of his deep-seated distrust of the Serene, nor of his occasional desire to kill himself. For all he held her in respect intellectually, he could not reconcile this with her avowal that the coming of the Serene had been beneficial for the human species. He had ventured once, when drunk, that perhaps their *charea* edict had robbed humankind of its primal urge, its genetic manifest destiny to conquer and rule – but playfully she had laughed and called him a caveman... and had never mentioned his outburst again.

They had drifted apart after a year, seen each other less and less. They remained friends for a time, and then lost contact altogether. Kat had called James her 'reclamation project', helping him to find his feet so that, from then on, he could make his own way in the world... Or perhaps he was being unfair.

Now she came to him in his fever dreams, bending over him and saying, "Let me help you, James."

He awoke with a start and stared about him. The sun was coming up, sending slatted glints of gold through the jungle foliage. He wondered how long he had been here, propped against the tree, and wondered how long it might be before he died.

He saw a snake slither by a foot away, and lashed out with his foot to kick it, provoke it into striking him. But the snake ignored his boot and slithered on, vanishing into the undergrowth.

Next to visit him in the cinematic, hallucinogenic rerun of his life, was Lal Devi, and the sight of the slimy Indian bastard brought him upright and lashing out at the slim, sneering figure.

They had been so close, for so long – over a dozen years – that Lal's betrayal was all the more devastating. It was after he had drifted away from Kat, and the desire to kill himself had returned. He had tried a couple of times to throw himself, spontaneously, through the window of his office on the hundredth floor, only to go into a ridiculous fit of spasms on every occasion. Then he had climbed onto the roof, and up the Morwell logo, with a bottle of Jack Daniels and the intention of drinking himself into oblivion.

That time loyal Lal had talked him down, carried him back to his suite and put him to bed.

It had been the very last thing Lal had done for him, before his betrayal.

Lal had found a woman, the whore responsible for changing the puppyish, subservient yes-man into an opponent.

A few months after the logo incident, Lal had strode into his office and handed in his resignation. He told James that he no longer wished to work as his PA, that he found James's opinions, indeed everything he stood for in his opposition to the Serene, odious in the extreme. James had tried to argue his corner, question this sudden *volte face* from the man he considered an ally, a loyal servant whose opinions regarding the aliens mirrored his own exactly... But Lal was adamant. He had met someone, he said, who had made him face his past, his present, and look forward to a future filled with hope rather than a corrosive, stultifying resentment of the Serene.

James had exploded, and the ensuing argument had been bitter in the extreme, with both men at one point spasming in their thwarted desire to do the other physical injury. In the end Lal had turned and strode from the room, with James yelling curses in his wake – and in retrospect James cited the confrontation as the beginning of what he hoped would be the end.

A week later he had given himself wholly to finding a way to end his life.

Now he came awake again. Thirst was an acid pain in his throat and hunger clawed at his innards like cancer. He laughed, then wept, and wished for a swift end rather than this eternal, drawn-out suffering.

He saw something move on the periphery of his vision and swivelled his head painfully.

A scorpion...

It regarded him from the vantage point of a tree root beside his head, the question mark of its tail pulsing with intent.

He smiled and reached towards it, then lashed out – aiming not to kill the creature but to provoke it into attack.

He should have known... The scorpion danced forward, hesitated, then began to... *vibrate*... It was, he realised with incredulity, spasming.

Laughing in despair, Morwell sank back against the tree and closed his eyes.

HE CAME AWAKE suddenly, knowing that he was still in the jungle, sitting against the tree, and that the scorpion had been no more than another hallucination.

He stared about him in disbelief.

He was in a hospital bed in a bright, shining room, and through the window he could see the skyscrapers of lower Manhattan.

A nurse was leaning over him, and she smiled brightly when he turned to her.

"Ah, Mr Morwell... You're back with us at last."

He wondered, then, if he had truly taken himself to Venezuela – or had that too been no more than an illusion?

"How...?" he croaked.

"You were found by natives and brought down-river to a port. The Morwell Organisation arranged for you to be airlifted back to New York. The odd thing is, Mr Morwell, you were found by a tribe who, but for the coming of the Serene, wouldn't have had second thoughts about killing you there and then. Now aren't you," she went on, rearranging the pillow beneath his head, "a lucky man?"

Morwell laughed at the very idea and then, as the nurse left from the room, his laughter turned to tears.

CHAPTER THREE

IT WAS NOON when Ana arrived in New York.

She stepped from the obelisk into bright summer sunlight, hotter and brighter than the light back on Mars. She should have remembered and brought her sunglasses, but it was almost eight years since she'd last been on Earth in summer.

She crossed Times Square and made her way to the café where, almost a decade ago to the day, Bilal had attempted to infect her with the Obterek device. She had a ghost to lay: when the idea of coming to New York to track down her brother had first occurred to her, a month ago, she had known that she must return to the coffee house.

It was still there, a narrow premises with chrome chairs and tables set outside on the sidewalk. She entered the café and saw that the table in the window, where she had sat ten years ago, was vacant. She ordered a mocha and was immediately flooded with a slew of memories. She found herself fighting back the tears at Bilal's betrayal. She stared through the window at the crowds passing by oblivious outside and wondered what Bilal was doing now.

She had adapted quickly to life on Mars. Of course she had had Kapil with her, which made all the difference. They had married within a year of settling in the city of Escarpment, and had soon found themselves with a network of friends, the core of which was Geoff and Sally Allen. She had always been a survivor, but had always needed to have the safety net of friends – in the early days the children who lived with her at Howrah Station and later on at the wilderness city. The first few years on Mars had been eased by Geoff and Sally's warmth, which had gone a long way towards banishing the pain she felt at what her brother had tried to do to her.

At first it was as if she had excised the incident from her memory; she had not allowed her thoughts to dwell on New York and Bilal, had not even discussed the incident with Kapil.

Then, shortly after the birth of her son, all that had changed; it was as if she had reached a place of safety from which she could look back with impunity and consider what had happened all those years ago.

And, surprising herself, she found that she did not hate Bilal for what he had tried to do. Despite the hurt that she still felt, she pitied him. He had been driven by motives unknown to her, motives imparted no doubt by the organisation for which he worked. Slowly the idea of tracking him down and confronting him had taken root and grown, to be dismissed at first and then, latterly, to be considered as a very real option if she wished to move on. She wanted to put the incident behind her, find out just why he had done what he had done, and perhaps learn if he'd had time to regret his actions. She thought that that would be unlikely, but she was curious to find out nevertheless.

She was curious, too, about how the Serene might have censored, or even punished, her brother. He had committed a crime directly opposed to the Serene's regime on Earth, had sided with the Obterek, and she wondered what punishment, if any, the Serene might have seen fit to mete out to Bilal.

She finished her mocha and realised that the anguish she thought she might experience here, a recapitulation of the confusion and fear she had gone through ten years ago, had failed to transpire. Smiling to herself, she left the café and walked south towards the rearing skyscraper where the Morwell organisation had its headquarters.

She strolled in the sunlight with crowds of smiling New Yorkers. There was a carnival atmosphere in the air, and she might have been forgiven for thinking that there was some special event towards which the citizens were heading, a concert or arts festival.

She stared around her at the smiling faces. Many people here were so young that they had never known a world without the influence of the Serene; others were old enough to recall the old times, and to cherish the new.

As she turned along the street on which the Morwell tower stood, she thought back to what Nina Ricci had told them at the Allen's party. It was odd, but she had never really questioned the motives of the Serene; she had seen the beneficial effect of their intervention in the affairs of humankind, and felt disinclined to ascribe any motive other than altruism. So she had no idea exactly what she and thousands of other human representatives did in the obelisks, but so what? And as for what the Serene were doing on the outer edges of the solar system...? Again, she felt disinclined to enquire; she trusted the Serene, and left it at that.

But, she wondered now, shouldn't she feel just the slightest curiosity?

She recalled an argument she'd had with the prickly Nina Ricci. Ricci had just been elected to the legislative assembly of Mars and was understandably full of herself. They had been at one of the Allens' monthly parties, and Ana had said something about the effect of the Serene being wholly good. Nina, whose clinical intelligence and thick skin inured her to the criticism of her peers, had turned on Ana and snapped, "What an ill-considered statement, Ana. How can you say that when you are not in full command of all the facts?"

Ana had blinked, surprised at the vitriol in the Italian's tone. "But I'm basing the statement on what I have experienced of society and how it's been affected by the arrival of the Serene. Anyway, what facts might I possess that would make me think otherwise?"

Nina had smiled her insufferably self-satisfied smile and said, "Until we understand the motivations of the Serene, we can only make partial and ill-formed judgements. Stating that the effect of the Serene has been wholly good is dangerous."

Others at this point had entered the argument, and Ana had taken the opportunity to slip away from the group.

Since then, she had wondered increasingly at the motives of the Serene – but for the life of her could only discern the benefits of their intervention.

She stopped on the sidewalk and craned her head to take in the enormity of the tower before her. It rose dizzyingly, and she experienced a kind of vertigo as she strained to see to the very summit of the glass-enclosed needle. At the top, tiny at this distance, was the rotating Morwell Organisation symbol, an entwined MO surrounded by laurel leaves – a touch which Ana thought either crass or ironic.

She wondered if she would find her brother unchanged in ten years; would he still be the same brash, materialistic, Serene-hating businessman she had encountered last time? Or might the intervening years and his experience of the Serene have worked to mellow him?

She stepped through the sliding glass doors and crossed an atrium the size of an arboretum – which it resembled, with its overabundance of potted palms and leafy ferns.

She found the reception desk and approached a smiling, uniformed woman in her twenties with the beauty and hauteur of a catwalk model.

"I wonder if you might be able to help me? I'd like to make an appointment to meet Bilal Devi, Mr James Morwell's –"

Smiling the woman interrupted, "I'm afraid that

James Morwell is no longer associated with the Morwell Organisation."

Ana blinked. "And his personal assistant, Bilal Devi?"

"One moment, please..." She turned to a softscreen on her desktop and played long fingers across its surface.

She looked up, her smiled fixed, and said, "My records show that Mr Devi left the Organisation almost nine years ago."

The information surprised Ana. "He left? Ah... do you have any idea where he might be found?"

The receptionist's smile became sympathetic. "I'm sorry, no, Ms...?"

"Devi. Ana Devi. You see, Bilal Devi is my brother and I am trying to find him."

The woman appeared sympathetic. "Perhaps..." She glanced at her screen again. "What I can do is refer you to Personnel. There is a chance that they might be able to help."

Ana thanked the woman who stroked her screen, tapped her fingers in a blur, then looked up at Ana and said, "If you go to the Personnel office on the fiftieth floor, Helena Lopez will see you at once."

She thanked the receptionist again and made her way to the elevator pods.

On her ascent to the fiftieth floor, Ana wondered why Bilal had left the Morwell Organisation. It was too much to hope that he had seen the error of his ways, she thought; more likely that he had been sacked – a demotion organised by the Serene?

The head of Personnel turned out to be a motherly

woman in her sixties who listened to Ana's story with a sympathetic smile, then referred to a softscreen.

"Here we are... Bilal Devi. He resigned his post as James Morwell's PA in August 2037, just after James made an attempt to kill himself."

"Do you have any record of where my brother went, or might be now?"

"That kind of information is not kept on our records... But I know someone who knew Bilal around the time of his resignation. If you would care to wait while I...?"

"Of course."

The woman murmured something into a throat-mic, waited for a reply, then smiled across at Ana. "Ben will be down shortly. Can I get you a coffee?"

Ana thanked the woman but refused the offer of a coffee; she was feeling hyped enough at the idea of speaking with someone who knew her brother at the time of his resignation.

She looked at the woman. "You said that James Morwell attempted to kill himself?"

"More than once, I'm told. Of course he didn't get far... but could you blame him, with a father like Edward Morwell?"

Ana shrugged. "I don't know anything about..." she began.

"He was a tyrant, believe me. I worked here when Edward Morwell ran the ship. Ruthless? And the way he treated his son... Rumour is that he beat James daily. The poor man never recovered. Ah, here's Ben."

Lopez made the introductions and Ben Aronica hitched himself onto the desk and nodded at Ana.

"I knew Lal. Not that we were close, but we worked on various projects. He was driven, and worshipped James. When the boss tried to jump off..." Ben raised a forefinger above his head... "the company logo, Lal brought him down. We were all watching. James began spasming well before he reached the plinth. It was... pathetic is the only way to describe what happened." Ben shrugged. "James stood down after that, then vanished not long after. I've no idea where he is now."

"And Bilal?"

"He resigned a few days after James attempted to kill himself."

"Do you know why he resigned? Did he give you a reason?"

"I'm sorry. He never said."

Ana took a breath and said, "Do you know where I might be able to find my brother now, Mr Aronica?"

Ben smiled. "He went back to India, to Kolkata." He rolled up his right sleeve and accessed his softscreen implant. "And I might even have his address."

Her heart beating wildly, Ana watched him stroke the screen.

India... she thought; he went back to Kolkata!

Ben said, "Here it is. We were in contact for a while, eight years ago. He sent his address, though of course he might have moved on since then. He was at 1025 Nanda Chowk," He looked at Ana. "I hope that'll be some use."

Ana beamed. "I can't begin to thank you..." she began, before something caught in her throat.

She thanked them again and made her way from the Morwell Organisation skyscraper, elation filling her chest. The sunlight greeted her as she stepped onto the sidewalk, and the people of New York seemed to be smiling with her.

She made her way to the Times Square obelisk and booked transit to India.

CHAPTER FOUR

IN MIAMI, JAMES Morwell purchased a Porsche 600 horsepower speedboat, moored it at the exclusive Simmons' Marina, and stocked it with provisions sufficient to last a week. He wondered, while ferrying the cartons aboard the boat, what might have happened had he attempted to set off without food and water: would the boat refuse to start, or would he find himself going in circles and arriving back at the marina, his bid to end his life thwarted once again?

He recalled considering this form of suicide many years ago. He even wondered if, in the year lost to drug and alcohol addiction, he might have made a similar bid, and failed.

He wondered how the Serene would quash his attempt to end his life this time.

He set off at midday and headed south, then set the boat on auto-pilot and retired to the galley. There he cooked himself what he hoped would be his last meal, chicken kiev with roast potatoes, washed down with a bottle of champagne. He carried the tray to the foredeck and, as he sailed steadily away from the Florida coast, sat in the sunlight and ate.

By the end of the meal, and the bottle, he was a little drunk.

As the sun went down he returned to the galley and carried his provisions, box by box, to the foredeck. There he stacked them on top of each other until he had every scrap of food, and all the canisters of water, waiting to be despatched.

The question was, would the Serene allow him to jettison the provisions?

He stood beside the rail and considered the darkening ocean, then reached out and pushed the topmost carton. It tumbled over the side and splashed into the sea. Smiling, he pushed the second box and, encouraged, lifted the third and fourth and pitched them over the rail. Then the last box went over, and the final canister of water, and he laughed aloud in triumph and staggered below-deck to his berth.

The following day he sat in the light of the sun and stared at the horizon as the boat carried him south.

He wanted to die, but he had no desire to suffer the painful effects of starvation. To this end he had brought a supply of heroin, and when the first hunger pangs griped him, he injected himself and slipped into oblivion.

He had no recollection of how many days elapsed; one day phased into another, a long stretch of stupefied euphoria. His world consisted of the dazzling sun and the scintillating sea, the up and down motion of the boat as it rode the swell. At some point he must have switched off the engine, or the boat must have run out of diesel, as it sat becalmed on the ocean, laved alternatively by sunlight and moonlight while he sprawled on a mattress on the foredeck and laughed insanely to himself.

Kat came to him in his dreams, and in his waking hallucinations, offering a solicitous hand – and Lal showed himself too, always sneering.

He passed in and out of consciousness, in and out of periods of clarity, and during the latter he wondered if, truly, this time he might have beaten the Serene.

He was a thousand miles from civilisation and any hope of succour; he had no food and water... He must surely now be close to death?

Had a week elapsed, two? He was weak; he could hardly move from his prone position on the mattress. It was all he could do to raise his head and stare out across the calm waters of the ocean.

He saw flying fish glint in the air, and porpoises arcing from the sea in graceful parabolas.

The same day he made out another silver-blue glint across the foredeck. At first he thought that a flying fish had flopped aboard, but as he raised himself onto his elbows and stared, the glint expanded.

He wondered if this were yet another hallucination. A featureless blue figure sat cross-legged before him on the foredeck, serene in its motionlessness. He smiled at his choice of words. Serene? Very far from... But what did it want?

He sat up, his head spinning, his vision blurring. The figure stared at him; at least, its smooth, featureless headpiece looked in his direction. At last a voice sounded in his head, calm, neutral, soothing. "We want, James Morwell, exactly what you want."

He blinked. He certainly was hallucinating – but, unlike the other visions that had haunted him, this one was welcome.

"And what is that?"

"An end to the regime of the Serene in this solar system, and... your annihilation."

He stared at the pulsing blue figure, its depthless innards swirling with a dozen shades of lapis lazuli. "My annihilation?"

"Is that not what you have been attempting for ten years? Is that not why you are here, aboard this boat, in a futile attempt to end you life?"

He bridled. "Futile?"

The Obterek sat like Buddha, calm, unflappable. "Futile, because the Serene would not allow you to kill yourself."

He laughed. "But how could they stop me this time?"

"You would be found, rescued, brought back from the brink of death. In fact, as we speak, a liner has been diverted and will arrive to effect your rescue in a little under three hours."

He felt pain and despair well within him. "No!" he cried pathetically. "No, not this time!" He shook his head. "I want to die! You can have no concept of what it's like to be denied..."

He hung his head and sobbed. He tried to stagger to his feet and pitch himself overboard, but he was far too weak to even climb to his knees.

The Obterek sat silently, watching him.

He said, almost pleading, "What do you want? Why are you...?" He stretched out his hand to the being.

"We want to help you, James Morwell. We want to assist you in your desire to kill yourself."

He stared at the blue creature, not daring to laugh for fear of insulting the Obterek and sending it away.

He whispered, "You can do that? You can help me kill myself?"

The being inclined its head. "We can do that."

He leaned forward, eager. "Then do it! Now! Kill me... I've had enough. I want nothing more than to be allowed to die."

The Obterek sat impassively, staring at him with its featureless face.

"What?" Morwell whispered, fearful now that the creature would not carry out its promise.

"We will help you die, James Morwell, but in return we require your assistance."

"My assistance? What could you possibly want from *me*?"

"We want you to help us assassinate someone – and in so doing bring about the beginning of the end of the Serene in the solar system."

He stared, open-mouthed, and it was some time before he marshalled his thoughts and asked, "How would this be possible? Kill one person, and bring about the end...?" He shook his head. "And what of the Serene *charea*?"

"It is possible if we use you, James Morwell, if we – if I – inhabit you, take you over. If I became one with you, a tiny part of you, I would go undetected by the Serene. Then we would be able to approach the subject, and inhabit her. We would for brief second be in control of the subject, and be able to guide it into what the Serene call the *takrea*..."

Morwell repeated the word, excited by what the Obterek had told him.

The blue being said, "The *takrea* is the obelisk on Titan. It is the... quantum engine... if you like, that powers the *charea* in the solar system. I carry within me the means to destroy the *takrea*, and so cease the rule of the *charea*, and so free the human race at last and set it on its true course."

"And in so doing," Morwell said breathlessly, "grant me oblivion?"

"Precisely so."

He recalled the last time he had had dealings with the Obterek, and how that had failed spectacularly. "And you would be more successful than the last time...?"

"We had... limited resources then, limited access to the requisite power. We have had ten years to plan our next move, to wait until the time was right... The power drain will be great, but it will be required for seconds only. We know we will succeed."

Morwell thought about humanity released from the slavery of the *charea*, humanity allowed to fulfil its true, evolutionary destiny, to expand and conquer... He would not be around to see this happen, of course – but he would be the catalyst for the change, the martyr who sacrificed himself for the sake of humanity.

He flung back his head and laughed at the idea.

He reached out his arms as if seeking to embrace the Obterek. "Inhabit me."

"In time. First, I must tell you about the subject."

Morwell assented, and wondered who they might use in order to gain access to the *takrea*. One of the human representatives, no doubt.

"Who?" he asked.

The figure said, "You knew her as Kat Kemp."

He stared, rocked. He mouthed the name, "Kat? But... but why Kat?"

"Because, James Morwell, she has constant access to the *takrea*–"

"But why should I kill...?"

"Because she used you."

Morwell shook his head, confused. "Used? We... for a year we were lovers. She *helped* me, not used."

The creature stared at him in silence. He received, then, the distinct impression that the being pitied him. It said, "Just after our abortive attempt to plant certain representatives with the transmission devices, the Serene deemed that certain people should be... monitored in order to assess the level of their threat in future."

He shook his head. "Kat? The Serene used *Kat*...?"

"James Morwell," said the blue being, "Kat Kemp was... is... a Serene self-aware entity."

He felt as if he had been hit an invisible blow in the solar plexus, an impact both physical and mental.

"She was charged with monitoring you, of assessing your threat, of being with you during the period that the Serene thought we might contact you again. After a year, she was discharged of this duty, and she brought about the end of your affair."

He felt a sudden surge of anger at the idea of her betrayal... No, not *her* betrayal: *its* betrayal...

"She used me..." he said.

"As the Serene are using the human race to infect you with their own unnatural edicts, their own perverted ideals."

He leaned forward. "And when you inhabit me, and then inhabit Kat Kemp... and we walk into the *takrea*?"

"Then I, we, will detonate, and Kat Kemp will die, and the *takrea* disintegrate, and the *charea* in the solar system break down... Then the Obterek will be able to supplant the Serene."

He would be dead, then – he would have achieved that which, for ten years, he had sought relentlessly. It was only a small regret that he would not then be around to witness the liberation of humankind, the return to the old laws of the universe, the true way...

He was taken then with the urge to lash out, to commit violence, to kill.

An idea grew in his head, and he smiled as he said, "I agree to help you, but first... There is someone I wish to kill. You can allow me that one last wish? I will not be around to see my people returned to the old ways, so let my last voluntary action on Earth be to *kill*."

The very idea excited him more than he had ever imagined.

The blue figure bowed its head. "First, I must consult with my peers. The execution might serve as a... test-run, as you would say... before the real thing."

It felt silent, and very still, as it communed with its kind.

Seconds later it looked up, and said, "It is granted. For the briefest period, for a matter of seconds only, you will have the opportunity to contravene the Serene *charea* and kill." The Obterek paused, then said, "And who will be your victim?"

Morwell smiled to himself. "Lal Devi," he said.

"PLEASE," SAID THE blue figure, "stand up."

With difficulty, James Morwell pushed himself to his feet and stood facing the Obterek, swaying.

The blue being rose and faced Morwell, exuding power. It stepped forward, moving faster than he had expected, and slammed into him. He gasped; it was as if an electric charge had passed through his body, galvanising him, filling him with energy.

He closed his eyes and felt the essence of the being inhabit his body, his senses. He had never felt as alive as he did now.

He heard a voice in his head. *Open your eyes, James Morwell.*

He did so, and found that he was no longer aboard his boat on the ocean. He was standing in a hotel bedroom. He stared across the room, saw a neatly dressed young man staring at him – and only then realised that it was a reflection of himself in a mirror.

He raised a hand and stared at the flawless skin.

You, said the voice in his head, *but a younger, more vital version...*

He smiled to himself. He felt powerful; for the first

time in twenty years, he had power and the ability to use it.

He stared through the window at the city of Kolkata sprawling far below.

Somewhere out there was the man who had betrayed him, Lal Devi, and he was about to die.

Smiling to himself, James Morwell left the hotel and crossed the teeming city.

CHAPTER FIVE

TO GET FROM the Serene obelisk in the centre of the
city to the address which Ben Aronica had given her,
Ana had to pass the railway station and the warren
of alleyways where Sanjeev Varnaputtram had made
his home all those years ago. As she negotiated the
potholes and roaming, khaki-coloured cows, she
thought back to her last encounter with him. He
had been a sad, fat, pathetic figure, deserted by
his followers, self-righteous and self-piteous. She
wondered if she would find him alive still. If so he
would be in his late seventies now – but she doubted
he had survived for long after their last meeting.

She came to the pale green timber door in the
crumbling wall. It stood ajar, and the riot of
vegetation behind it formed a resistant pressure
against the gate as she pushed it open.

She battled her way through the jungle and came to
the house. The door stood ajar, its timbers rotten. An

aqueous half light prevailed within, and Ana stepped cautiously over the mossy tiles of the hallway and approached the double doors to Sanjeev's bedroom.

She reached out a tremulous hand and pushed open the door.

She had expected to find an empty room, stripped of all possessions, with little evidence of its former occupant and little to remind her of the crimes committed within.

She gasped as her eyes adjusted to the gloom and she took in the contents of the room.

Garish movie posters adorned the walls, moulded and ripped, and a table stood beside the charpoy where, when Ana was ten, Sanjeev Varnaputtram had...

She shut out the thought.

Lying on the bed was a skeleton.

Ana took a step forward, and then another, and stared with disbelief at all that remained of the monster, Sanjeev Varnaputtram.

She recalled him as vast – larger than life – with an attendant malignity that had seemed, to the child she had been, to make him all the bigger. Now, astoundingly, he had been reduced to a skeleton, and Ana found it hard to believe that his bones were no larger than any others.

His skull had slipped sideways, its orbits regarding her lop-sidedly. Its lower mandible hung comically open. He had been dead for so long, she thought, that there was no longer any smell or any sign of the putrescence that must have attended his death.

She considered his death – and the fact that he had lain like this ever since, his remains forgotten and unmourned, a fitting end to a life spent persecuting those less powerful than himself.

She was about to turn away when she saw, pinned to the flaking plaster of the wall beside the charpoy, the photograph of a young girl.

Her breath caught and she gave a small sob of shock.

The image of herself as a girl of fifteen or sixteen smiled out at her – the photograph of her on the station platform all those years ago. To think that he'd had it with him to the very end... The idea almost made her sick, as if the evil man had possessed some small part of her down all the years.

Now she reached out and pulled the picture from the wall, and stared at the girl she had been.

She raised the photograph to her lips and kissed the faded image.

SHE LEFT THE house for the very last time and made her way through the tangle of creepers and vines that choked the pathway. She was about to reach out and pull open the gate when someone on the other side pushed it towards her.

She stood back quickly, expecting to see an aging Sikh or another of Sanjeev's erstwhile minions.

A Buddhist monk in a bright orange robe stood smiling before her.

"Oh," she exclaimed in surprise.

The beaming, bald-headed man – a diminutive figure she guessed to be in his eighties – gestured with palms pressed together at his chest and said, "Namaste, child."

"Namaste," Ana responded, raising her hands in a shadow gesture.

"May I ask what brings you here?"

In response, before she realised what she was doing, she raised the photograph of her younger self and showed it to the monk. She murmured, "When I was a child, one day the owner of this house..."

The monk raised a hand. "I have been told about what Mr Varnaputtram did here."

She smiled and, emboldened, asked, "And what brings you here, sir?"

"You have heard of the Buddhist concept of contemplation, the practice of beholding the act of bodily decay?"

She nodded. At least, in death, the corpse of Sanjeev Varnaputtram had served some use.

"Sanjeev Varnaputtram died eight years ago, and since that time I come here every month and look upon his remains... There is a chai stall along the alley. Would you care to join me?"

"That would be lovely," she said.

They sat on rickety wooden chairs in the alley, while children and rats played around them, and Ana said, "My name is Ana Devi, and now I live on Mars."

"Mars!" exclaimed the old man, as if the fact of her residence so far away was a miracle. "Mars... but as a child you lived here, in this city."

And she found herself telling the old monk all about her life on the station, her beatings at the hands of Mr Jangar, the station master, and Sanjeev Varnaputtram's abuse of her and her friends.

"I last came here ten years ago, sir, and confronted

Varnaputtram, and told him what I and the other children had achieved in life, and I thought that was the end of the affair."

"And you were mistaken."

"I think so. I realise now that this is the end, to have seen his bones, to have reclaimed this from his possessions." She showed the monk her photograph again, and he took it in fingers as brown as cassia bark.

"I can see that you were a kind child, and strong, and you have grown into the woman this child promised to be. Tell me, what do you do on Mars?"

"I work in administration for the Martian legislature, and also... I am a representative of the Serene."

"Ah, the Serene..."

Ana hesitated, then asked, "I would like to know what you think of the Serene, sir."

He smiled, and nodded for so long that Ana thought he might never stop. At last he said, "I think the Serene were at one time like ourselves, child – that is, they were Buddhist."

"And now?"

"Now, they have achieved satori and they have brought their ways to our world."

They sat in silence for a time, drinking their sweet, milky chai, and Ana asked at last, "And Sanjeev Varnaputtram, sir? What of him?"

"Mr Varnaputtram was not enlightened, child. He was driven by ignorance, and a lack of empathy. He was also a very unhappy man."

"I hated him for many years."

"But no longer?"

She looked into her heart, and said truthfully, "No longer."

"That is good." He reached out and clasped her hand. "I am so happy for you, for hatred is corrosive; it sours the heart; it achieves nothing. You are wise beyond your years, child."

Ana smiled, and wanted to tell him that she was thirty-six years old, but the truth was that, sitting here in the presence of the ancient monk, she did indeed feel like the child she had been.

"And now?" he asked.

"Now I must search for my brother." And she told the monk all about Bilal and what had happened ten years ago.

"I feel that you will find him," he said. "And then?"

"I don't know. I... I would like to tell him that I forgive him what he did to me, but to do that I think I must first try to understand why he did what he did."

"Understanding, empathy, is always enlightening. Only he who understands can forgive."

She finished her tea and smiled at the monk. "I must be going..."

"I have enjoyed our conversation, and have learned something."

She stared at the man, and wanted to ask what he might have learned, but felt that it might be impolite, or immodest, to ask. She pressed her palms together and murmured, "Namaste."

"Namaste," said the old man, and then. "But one more thing. If I may ask... in what do you believe, child?"

Ana thought about it for long seconds, then said, "I believe in the Serene, sir," and turned and walked away down the alley.

SHE TURNED ON to the main street and walked towards the station. She would take a short-cut over the footbridge across the multiple tracks, where as a child she had perched on the girders like a station monkey.

The station was not so crowded as it had been in her childhood; more people owned electric cars now, and scooters, and consequently the platforms were almost deserted. She crossed the footbridge, noting that the nimble grey monkeys still cavorted through the girders on the lookout for unwary children with bananas.

She left the station and strolled down the busy streets, passing Bhatnagar's restaurant. She had half a mind to stop and eat a masala dosa, but the desire to find Bilal's address drove her on. Maybe later, and maybe accompanied by Bilal, she could stop and eat... or was she being too hopeful? Who was to say that her brother would still be at the same address? And even if he were, would he anything other than angry and resentful at her sudden reappearance after all these years?

She came to a residential area that in her childhood had been a slum but which was now an affluent district of poly-carbon apartments on wide, leafy streets.

Heart hammering, she consulted her softscreen implant and read the address she had entered there. 1025 Nanda Chowk... She summoned a map of the area, which showed her present position in relation to her destination. She was fifty metres from the turning, and her chest felt fit to burst as she hurried to the corner and turned down Nanda Chowk.

1025 was a small, neat weatherboard building with a lawn and a flower-embroidered border – not the type of house where she had imagined her brother might live.

She pushed open the gate and walked up the path. She stood before the white-painted door for a minute, working to control her breathing and marshal her thoughts. She recalled the time she had confronted Bilal in his office ten years ago, when despite all her determination not to accuse him she had done just that, and regretted it.

This time, no accusations.

She touched the sensor beside the door, stood back and waited.

She heard a sound from within, footsteps approaching the door. She was sweating. She fixed a smile in place and stared at the door where she expected Bilal's face to appear.

The door opened and a portly Sikh in his fifties smiled down at her. "How can I help you?" he asked, suspiciously.

She began to speak, her words tripping up over themselves, then took a breath and began again, "I am trying to find my brother, Bilal Devi. I was given this address..."

"Ah, Bilal. Yes, yes. But I am afraid that Bilal moved out just last year."

"Moved out?" Ana repeated as if she failed to comprehend the meaning of the words.

"Yes, yes," said the Sikh. "He took up residence in his place of work."

"And where might that be?"

"Bilal worked in the new Gandhi State Orphanage on Victoria Road, beside the river. Your brother is a fine man and does good work there." Smiling, he reached out and took Ana's hand in a prolonged shake. "It is a privilege to meet Bilal's sister. When you find him, please convey my compliments, ah-cha? I am Mr Singh-Gupta, and for many years my wife and I had the honour of having Bilal lodge in our family home."

Ana smiled and promised to convey these sentiments to her brother when she found him. Thanking Mr Singh-Gupta, Ana took her leave and hurried across the city towards the river.

Bilal worked in an orphanage? Her brother, the trendy, materialistic, Serene-hating businessman... he now worked in a state-run orphanage, doing good work with needy children?

As she hurried along the busy street, Ana wondered if the person in question was indeed her brother, or someone else entirely – then chastised herself for the thought.

Was it too much to hope that Bilal had indeed seen the error of his ways?

The Gandhi State Orphanage was an ultra-modern poly-carbon building more like a rearing ocean liner than a government building, all curving sleek lines and convex silver planes.

Taking a deep breath Ana paused before the sliding doors, counted to ten, then plunged inside.

She asked a young man at reception where she might find Bilal Devi.

"And why do you wish to see Mr Devi?" he asked.

Over her surprise that he was indeed here, she said, "I am his sister, and I have not seen my brother for many years..."

The receptionist regarded her with wide eyes. "Mr Bilal never said anything about a sister. Ah-cha. He is off duty at the moment, and you will find him through there." He pointed to a door at the far end of the foyer, and Ana thanked him and made her way across the carpeted floor.

She pushed open the door and blinked as she found herself dazzled by sunlight. She had expected another plush room, but was standing before a big courtyard surrounded by flimsy timber shacks with swing doors like bathing cubicles. She counted twenty such cubicles and wondered which one might be Bilal's.

She was about to return to the foyer, and ask the receptionist where precisely she might find her brother, when she heard someone speaking.

She recognised the voice, and it was coming from a shack to her right. She moved into the shadow, stood by the open window, and listened.

Bilal was saying, "... and then Mahatma, with his followers, left Sabarmati Ashram and walked to the coast..."

Through the window Ana saw six boys and girls sitting on the floor in a semi-circle, staring with rapt expressions at the man who sat on the bed, an open book on his lap.

She stared, hardly able to credit that this was indeed her brother. He seemed to have aged more than just ten years since the last time she had seen him; gone was the suit, the long hair, and the earring. His hair was cropped short, and he wore a faded pair of jeans and a bleached green t-shirt.

His voice was gentle as he told the children the story of Mahatma Gandhi's trek across Gujarat in 1930.

He paused, perhaps sensing that he was being watched, and looked up.

Ana did not pull back, but stared in through the window at her brother sitting cross-legged on the bed. He appeared thinner in middle-age, almost starved, and his expression was dumbfounded.

His lips moved, shaping her name. He spoke in rapid Hindi to the children, telling them to remain where they were; then he unfolded himself from the narrow bunk, crossed the room to the door, stepped out and confronted her.

They stared at each other in silence for what seemed like a long time before he spoke. "What do you want, Ana?"

His tone was neutral, gentle.

She said, "Just to talk, Bilal."

He uttered a sound, a low moan, pushed himself from the doorway and to her surprise hurried across the compound. He slipped between two shacks on the far side, and it was a second or two before Ana moved herself to give chase. "Bilal!" she called after him.

She turned sideways and inserted herself between the timber lean-tos. Ahead she saw Bilal turn right. She followed him and found herself on the eastern bank of the Hoogli, its vast expanse surprising her after the confines of the compound.

The bank sloped steeply at her feet, comprised of concrete walkways, piers and timber moorings.

Bilal was sitting at the very end of a timber jetty, regarding the muddy waters far below, his legs dangling. He could run no further, and Ana took her time before approaching. Her sudden appearance after so long, she realised, must have come as something of a shock. He needed time to adjust to the idea of seeing her again... She stared at him, and was reminded, in his almost abject, little-boy-lost posture, sitting there swinging his legs, of the fifteen-year-old she recalled from so long ago.

She moved from the shadows, into the blistering heat of the sun, and walked along the jetty towards him. Further down the river a dozen young boys, as naked as monkeys, were hurling themselves from a pier and crashing into the water with delighted cries and shrieks.

She sat down, a metre away from her brother, and said, "Remember when we came here to jump in and swim? And sometimes we came to fish, though I can't recall ever catching anything."

"Back then the river was polluted, Ana. Nothing lived in it. Now, the river is full of life."

She murmured, "The Ganges is like the world, come to life again."

A companionable silence came between them, but there was so much that Ana wanted to say.

Bilal showed no inclination to say anything more, so she said, "I did not expect, when I went to New

York in search of you, to find you in Kolkata, working in an orphanage."

He hugged his right knee and stared into the river. His crew-cut hair was greying. Lines radiated from his eyes. She wondered where the slick businessman had fled to. He said, "Why did you come here, Ana? To accuse me again, to point the finger and blame me?"

"No, not this time, Bilal. I came... to see you. To talk about how it was when we were young. I just wanted to say that what happened ten years ago..."

"Stop, please. I don't want to be reminded of..." His face was twisted bitterly at the recollection.

"Then let's not talk of that, Bilal." She paused, then went on, "The children back there were entranced by your story-telling."

"They are young, and love stories. For many of them, it is the first time that anyone has read to them. Would you believe, Ana, that many of them had never even heard of Mahatma Gandhi?"

"Had we, at their age? I don't know what is more surprising, Bilal; to find you here at the orphanage, or to hear you reading stories about Gandhi-ji. He was a man of peace, after all. The Serene would have loved him."

For the first time her brother turned and looked at her.

"I am not the person I was, Ana. I have changed."

"What happened?"

He gave a long sigh, staring out across the wide river to the far, crowded bank, and it was a while before he replied.

"I lied when I saw you ten years ago, Ana. I lied

about the time I left you when you were six. I... never had any intention of coming back to find you. I was thinking only of myself, of my survival. I'll be honest, though it pains me to say this... I thought then that you were a burden. I wanted nothing more than to get away, to better myself, but how could I do this when I had a sister hanging onto me, dragging me down?" He stared at her. "I'm sorry if these words hurt, but they are the truth."

"I guessed as much, Bilal." Though that did not make the truth any less painful.

"I wanted to get away from the poverty, the beatings. I was sick of being hungry, of being treated like a rat, of being a nobody. And then I had my chance, and no one and nothing was going to hold me back. Ana... I want you to understand this, to understand the boy I was then. I wasn't a good person, but there were reasons why I wasn't."

She said, "I'm not blaming you."

"Our uncle beat me daily, which is why we left his house and fled to the station. Not because he threw us out, but because he beat me for not bringing in enough rupees to pay our way."

She shook her head. "I didn't know. You never told me."

He shrugged.

She said, "But you did come back to find me, like you said, five years after you left? You told me that you came back to the station, but I was not there. I knew you were telling the truth because then I was in Delhi... so I knew you had come back for me."

She stopped as she saw him shaking his head. "I

was lying, Ana. I never came back. That you were in Delhi then was just a coincidence."

She nodded, taking this in, dismantling the memories that she had erected over the years of Bilal caring enough, once, to come in search of her.

She smiled to herself, and was not surprised that she felt no anger. His admission fitted with who he had been, back then, and who he might have become now.

"So the Bilal I met ten years ago, the champion of the Morwell Organisation, the hater of the Serene..."

"Was the person I had become because of the person I had been, the boy who had nothing one day, and then was suddenly offered the world. Please understand how that kind of promise can make a person... inhuman."

"And now?"

"As I said, I am a different person now."

"And I asked, 'What happened?'"

He lodged his chin on his knees and regarded the water. He said at last, "Shortly after I... did what I did, tried to infect you with the Obterek implants... I expected retribution from the Serene. I expected some form of punishment. I don't know what, but I lived in constant fear. James Morwell too, I know. But the strange thing was that nothing happened. We were not punished, or even admonished."

"The Obterek never contacted Morwell again?"

"Not to my knowledge. Perhaps six months passed, and then I met a woman, an incredible woman who changed my life, little by little. I... until that point I had never been in love. I'd... I suppose, looking back, I'd used women for my own ends. But with her...

things were different. She opened my eyes, made me confront my mistakes, look upon what I had done wrong, face my shortcomings and my humanity, or lack of..." He stopped, then said, "She also made me understand all that the Serene had done for us."

"She sounds wonderful. Are you still...?"

He shook his head. "We were together for two years, and then..."

To her surprise, Ana saw that he was crying.

She reached out, found his hand and squeezed.

He said, "She died in a car crash back in '38, a head-on collision with a tanker."

She let the silence stretch, before saying, "So you left Morwell, started work at the orphanage?"

"Oh, I'd left Morwell long before that, perhaps a year earlier. How could I go on working for a man I knew to be insane, as well as immoral? I handed in my resignation to him personally, told him what I thought of him and his organisation. We parted, you might say, on bad terms. And I've worked here ever since, paying for my sins."

She smiled. "Not sins," she said. "You've become a good man, Bilal."

He asked in almost a whisper, "Can you see your way to forgive me?"

"Who said that to understand is to forgive?"

He laughed. "It might have been Gandhi," he said. Along the bank a small boy whooped, cartwheeled through the air and landed with a smack in the river.

"And you, Ana? What are you doing now?"

So she told him about her husband and son, and her life on Mars, and her work there and even her work as a representative of the Serene, and for a while as they sat on the banks of the river, with the cries of the children playing in their ears, it was as if she were five again, chatting to her brother about life and the strange world around them.

At one point she said, "You should come and live on Mars, Bilal. I would be able to find you work."

"And leave the orphanage? I like to think I'm needed here. At least, I need the orphanage. But I will visit you one day, I promise."

"I'll look forward to that," she said.

He rose to his feet, reached out and pulled her upright. "How long before you go back?"

"I'm here for a few days."

"Then let's meet again. Tonight? I know a wonderful restaurant by the park. If you drop by here at eight..."

"I'll do that." They came together in an embrace, and Ana thought that her heart was about to burst.

"I suppose I must get back to work," he laughed. "There's a story to finish..."

They made their way back to the compound, and Ana remembered to convey Mr Singh-Gupta's best wishes.

They said goodbye outside his cubicle, and when he passed inside she lingered within earshot and smiled as she heard him say, "Ah-cha. Now, where did we get to...?"

She passed into the orphanage and crossed the foyer, emerging with a light step and an even lighter heart into the afternoon sunlight. She recalled the words of the old monk she had met in the alleyway earlier, and she felt like finding him and telling him all about her meeting with Bilal.

As she was crossing the car park a young man in a sharp blue suit passed her, heading for the entrance of the orphanage. For as second she thought that the man was familiar, but she could not place the face.

She made her way to Maidan Park, sat in the shade with a sweet lassi and contemplated her good fortune.

THAT EVENING, A little before eight, Ana caught a taxi from her hotel to the orphanage. As the car carried her through the crowded streets of the city, she sat back and contemplated the meeting with her brother and how their relationship might develop. One thing was certain from that afternoon's meeting: Bilal had changed, become a better person, and Ana looked forward to getting to know this new, reborn Bilal. They had a lot to catch up on, a lot of memories to share, and many years ahead of them in which to do so.

The taxi pulled up outside the orphanage and Ana climbed out as the sun was setting over the Hoogli.

A police car was drawn up ahead of the taxi in the parking lot, and before it an ambulance.

Ana crossed to the sliding doors and passed inside, to find the foyer a mayhem of activity. Police officers, paramedics and suited officials milled back and forth, and through the rear door Ana made out a crowd of children assembled in the courtyard.

She pushed her way to the reception desk and smiled at the same young man she had spoken to earlier. His expression, on seeing her, was odd: he appeared at first shocked, and then uncertain, and he turned quickly and spoke to a woman in a smart navy blue suit.

The woman looked up, at Ana, and it was then that she knew that whatever was going on here concerned her: the woman's expression slipped into a mask of compassion.

"Ms Devi, if you would care to accompany me..."

She ushered Ana around the desk and into a small side room, an office equipped with a single desk and two chairs.

The woman sat down behind the desk and Ana remained standing, facing the woman. "What is happening here?" Ana asked.

"I understand that earlier today you saw your brother, Bilal Devi?"

Ana found herself slumping into the chair opposite the woman. "What is happening? Is Bilal...?"

"Can I ask you why you were visiting your brother, Ms Devi?"

Ana laughed, despite the fear building within her. "Why do you think? He was my brother, and we hadn't seen each other for a long time."

"And how did your brother seem when you met him?"

"Seem? Look, just what is going on here? Will you please tell me?"

The woman said, "I am Director Zara Mohammed. I run the orphanage. Your brother worked here for nine years, and we became very close..."

Panic seized Ana; she was having difficulty getting

her breath. "It's Bilal, isn't it?" she almost shouted. "What's happened to Bilal?"

The woman surprised her by standing and coming around the desk, kneeling before Ana and taking her hand.

"I'm sorry, Ms Devi. Your brother, my respected colleague Bilal Devi, passed away earlier today."

Even though she knew it was coming, the fact rocked her. Her heart thumped and she felt its pulse in her ears, deafening, drowning out whatever the woman was saying. Director Mohammed's lips moved, but Ana heard nothing.

"How?" she heard herself asking.

The Director squeezed her hand, her eyes slipping away from Ana's.

"I want to see him!" Ana cried. "I want to see my brother!"

Then she was on her feet and rushing out of the office. She crossed the foyer to the rear door and burst through into the courtyard. She was aware of the faces of surprised policemen, and the tear-stained faces of a hundred boys and girls, as she pushed through the crowd and made her way towards Bilal's timber shack.

Three policemen, as many paramedics, and half a dozen men and women in suits crowded the entrance to the rude dwelling. They turned, startled, as Ana attempted to push through them to the door.

Director Mohammed had caught up with her. "Ms Devi! Please, I would not advise..."

"I am Bilal Devi's sister!" she cried into the face of a policeman who barred her way, "and I want to see my brother!"

Shocked, the man stepped aside and before anyone could move to prevent her she pushed open the flimsy wooden door and crossed the threshold.

She stopped dead in her tracks, a cry stilled on her lips.

The sight of her brother hit her like a physical blow to the sternum. She gasped for breath, mouthing, "No, no..." over and over again.

Bilal sat on the narrow bunk where, earlier that day, he had told a story to the orphans in his charge. He had been thrown back against the wall, his head hanging forward, the very book he had been reading that afternoon cradled in his lap.

It was open to a photograph of Mahatma Gandhi, and Bilal's fingers lay upon the great man's face as if in benediction.

Ana stared at her brother, at the massive gunshot wound in the centre of his chest, and cried in disbelief.

"No!" she cried, and Director Mohammed slipped into the room and held Ana as she wept.

CHAPTER SIX

IT SEEMED TO Sally that, in her sixties, her life had entered a period of calm and quiescence that had its analogue in the collective demeanour of the human race in the middle period of the twenty-first century.

She was no longer ambitious as she had been when young; she was no longer as concerned about what people thought of her. She was happier in herself and in her dealings with others, had fewer worries, and if she thought of the future at all it was with positivity and confidence.

It seemed, likewise, that humankind since spreading from Earth and inhabiting the solar system had entered a period of maturity, of co-operation and tolerance. The human race teemed across terraformed planets and moons, inhabited vast spaceborn dwellings hollowed from asteroids. They worked together increasingly without the boundaries of nations to impede progress with concerns of petty national interest, freed from the malign influence of multinational business corporations. Religions had mellowed, even the more radical sects of Christianity and Islam which in the past had threatened head-to-head conflict; millions still believed, but without the self-righteous fervour of old. New cults had sprung up, many with the Serene at their core. Of the old faiths, Buddhism was increasing in popularity, as citizens drew parallels between the ways of the Serene and the philosophy of Siddhartha Gautama.

All in all, Sally reflected as she stared out through the dome of her surgery across the Mare Erythraeum, it was a good time to be alive.

She had seen her last patient of the day and had the afternoon to herself. Geoff, on some administrative tour of a farm in the south, wouldn't be back until later that evening; she'd dine that night with Hannah and her new boyfriend. Before that, she had a lunch date with Kath Kemp.

Her old friend was a frequent visitor to Mars, and particularly to Escarpment City. The obelisks made interplanetary travel no more difficult than stepping from one room to the next – once the traveller had reached the embarkation obelisk, of course, which often took hours by conventional transport. Sally saw Kath perhaps once a month, when they caught up with each other's work and reminisced about old times. She had gone through a period – on learning what Kath Kemp was, ten years ago – of not exactly mistrusting Kath but questioning everything about their relationship. She had wondered if she had been manipulated, if Kath had had ulterior motives for fostering their friendship – but for the life of her Sally could discern no such motivation on the part of the Serene self-aware entity. They were, she genuinely felt, two like-minded woman with a shared past in common, and even similar temperaments – even if one of them just happened to be an alien construct.

Trust, Sally thought as she switched off her com and left her surgery – that was what it boiled down to. She trusted Kath Kemp and the Serene, despite Nina Ricci's increasing frustration at what she saw as the Serene withholding information from their human representatives.

She caught an electric buggy from the business core of the city to the Lip. It was a warm autumn day on the red planet and the plain was basking in hazy sunlight. Her favourite café was almost full, but she'd taken the precaution of reserving a table by the rail.

She was early, and admired the view across the flat, patchwork farmland as she waited for Kath to arrive.

A minute later the small, dumpy woman – she had thickened in old age, Sally thought – crossed the patio towards her table. Sally stood and they embraced, and then ordered coffee and salad.

Kath asked about Sally's recent work, enquiring about the efficiency of new anti-cancer drugs trialled on a group of her patients – and for the next fifteen minutes they chatted about this and other aspects of Sally's practice.

Sally had no doubt that the enquiry was part of a gathering of information which the Serene would collate and use to refine and direct future policy – but at the same time, she thought, Kath was genuinely interested in her work on a more personal level.

As they ate, Sally's thoughts turned to Geoff's forthcoming trip to Titan, and what he hoped Kath Kemp might reveal to him, Nina Ricci and Ana Devi, there.

"You do realise," she said at one point, "that your promise to Nina has made Geoff uncharacteristically restless? He's talked about nothing else for days."

Kath laughed, wrinkles creasing around her kind eyes. "Nina is one inquisitive and perceptive woman. One in a million. She keeps us on our toes."

"Every class needs an *enfant terrible*," Sally said. "I suppose what you'll tell them is confidential?" She was fishing, and smiled at Kath's mischievous expression.

"It is, but won't be in a couple of days." Kath regarded her coffee, then looked up. "As we'll be making it public anyway in a week or two, why don't you come with Geoff to Titan? Make a holiday of it. Can you get time off?"

Sally felt a rising excitement. "I'm due a little leave, and I've only seen Titan on film. From what Geoff tells me, it's beautiful."

"One of the wonders of the solar system. Prepare to be amazed. We'll also be going onward, outward, from Titan."

"We will? But I thought..." Sally faltered. As far as she knew, Titan was the outer extent of human habitation in the solar system. Then she recalled what Nina Ricci had said about Serene work on the very perimeter of the system.

"You don't mean...?"

"I can't say, especially now, with security tightening as it is."

"It is? I thought everything was going well on that front, what with the Obterek..."

Ten years ago, for a few weeks after their evacuation from Earth to Mars, Geoff and Sally, Ana and Kapil, had lived in fear of what course the Obterek opposition to the Serene might take. Despite constant Serene reassurances that they had nothing to fear, they had indeed feared: Sally and Geoff had discussed the situation, and Geoff had summed it up well when he described feeling that the human race was a tiny, insignificant and ignorant life-form caught in a battle between two vast and incomprehensible armies.

Then, as the weeks lapsed and turned to months, and the threat of Obterek action never materialised, their fears eventually receded. It must have been years, now, since Sally had last considered the Serene's galactic opponents.

Kath was regarding her empty plate as if wondering whether to tell Sally something. At last she said, "There have been worrying developments lately."

"The Obterek?"

Kath nodded. "We wondered when they might next make a move. It was too good to be true that this period of quiescence, which had lasted for almost a decade, would continue indefinitely."

"What happened?"

"An incident on Earth just yesterday. You'll hear about it soon enough. A breach in the *charea*. A tiny breach, but nevertheless very worrying, as even the tiniest, briefest breakdown in our systems is a reason for the alarm bells to start ringing..." She laughed and said: "Listen to me, spouting platitudes like some jaded news hack."

"You think it might just be the start of..." Sally let the question hang.

Kath sighed. "That's our fear, but you can never tell with the Obterek. We're monitoring the situation, stepping up security..."

At that moment Sally's softscreen chimed. She moved to cut the call, but Kath leaned forward and said, "No. I think you had better accept it."

Nodding, a sick feeling in her chest, Sally rolled up her sleeve and tapped her forearm. Instantly Ana Devi's face stared up at her, unusual in that the woman was not smiling. "Ana?"

"Sal. Can I see you?"

"Of course. Are you... is everything okay?"

"Yes. No. No, it isn't. Can I see you? I just want to talk..." The Indian woman smiled up at her, but Sally could tell that she was close to tears. "I'm back on Mars. Will you be at home this afternoon?"

"All afternoon. I'll be back in... say an hour. Drop by at any time, Ana."

Ana nodded, thanked Sally, and cut the connection.

Sally looked up and stared at Kath. "That was Ana. She seemed..." She shook her head.

Kath said, "You'd better be getting home, Sally. Be there for Ana, and give her my condolences."

Kath stood and made to leave.

"Kath?" Sally said.

"Ana will tell you all about it. I really must be going."

They kissed cheeks, and Kath said, "I'll see you in two days, Sally, on Titan."

She watched her friend hurry from the café, then made her way home with a feeling of dire expectation in her chest.

SHE SAT BENEATH the cherry tree in her garden and waited.

The sun was going down and birdsong filled the warm air. If she closed her eyes she could imagine herself back in Shropshire. When she opened her eyes, however, the quality of the light – somehow hazier and less intense – told her that she was no longer on Earth, and the tumbling shape of Deimos gave the game away.

But the back garden and the cottage were as restful as ever, a piece of England transplanted, which Sally found a refuge from the pressure of work. She knew that Ana loved the cottage and the garden, and thoughts of Ana brought back what Kath had said. "*Give her my condolences.*"

Had something happened to Kapil or to Shantidev?

She started as she heard the squeak of the gate at the side of the house, and a second later Ana came into view along the path.

Sally stood and faced Ana down the length of the garden, and something in the Indian woman's posture made Sally run to Ana and hold her as she sobbed on her shoulder. She inhaled the woman's scent – rosewater and shampoo.

She led Ana back to the cherry tree and sat her

down on the bench, then sat beside her and held her hand. "Ana? Tell me..."

"I hadn't seen him for ten years... and I expected to find the man I had last seen. Brash. Arrogant... If I succeeded in finding him at all... But I found him. Against all the odds. Found him... I didn't really expect to. But I did!"

"Ana. Take it easy. Slow down. Does Kapil know you're back?"

"He's... he's on Venus. I contacted him. He's on his way back. But... but he won't get home until later tonight. And I just had to talk to someone..."

"Of course, of course." She gripped her friend's hand. "Tell me."

"I went to Earth especially to find him."

She recalled Geoff telling her last week that Ana was going to New York to try to find her brother, Bilal.

"Ana, what happened?"

The Indian woman stared at her, stricken. "Someone murdered my brother," she said.

Sally wanted to say that that was impossible, that people were not murdered anymore. The coming of the Serene had seen to that...

"But who...?"

"I know who, Sally. I saw him. You see, when I was leaving the orphanage that afternoon, I saw someone. I didn't know who it was at the time, only later... It was Bilal's old boss, the businessman James Morwell. Only... only this was a different, younger version of James Morwell."

"But why would he want to murder Bilal?"

Ana shook her head. "I don't know. I can't

imagine. But... later I was questioned by a Serene self-aware entity. It... it entered me, just as ten years ago it saved me from the Obterek at Fujiyama, and when it came out it told me that I had been correct. I *had* seen James Morwell, and he was working for the Obterek." She looked up, into the sky, and said, "And the self-aware entity told me, Sally, that they feared this was merely the start of a new, concerted Obterek onslaught."

Sally held her friend as the day darkened towards evening and a chill crept over the garden.

CHAPTER SEVEN

To ALLEN, THE process of stepping into the obelisk on Mars and stepping out again on Titan seemed instantaneous.

He knew intellectually that a day, perhaps two, had elapsed, but always as he completed his stride through the black wall and stepped out on the other side, he found it hard to believe. He always had to check the calendar on his softscreen to confirm how much time had passed, and always he felt renewed respect for Serene science. This time, thanks to Nina Ricci, he also experienced curiosity at what the Serene might be doing with the human representatives in the Titan obelisk.

The sight that confronted him on emerging from the obelisk never failed to halt him in his tracks. He had seen many an artist's representation of the rings of Saturn as seen from the moon of Titan, spectacular landscapes of methane plains with the mighty ringed planet canted at varying angles above the horizon, but the reality stunned him. It was the colours, he thought. Saturn itself was a vast pastel swirl and the rings, tipped so that they presented a great multi-stranded girdle encompassing the planet, ranged the spectrum. In the foreground the moon's electric-blue plains provided a vivid contrast.

The city itself was situated on a plateau on the moon's southern pole, a collection of what looked like blown-glass habitats occupied by scientific teams huddled around the rearing tower of the obelisk, and all protected from the moon's hostile hydrocarbon atmosphere by a bell-jar dome.

For the past five years or so the routine had always been the same. Allen, Ana Devi and Nina Ricci, sometimes accompanied by other representatives, would meet at a café bar across the plaza from the obelisk. There, while admiring the views across the plain far below, they would chat for an hour or two before entering the obelisk again and finding themselves back on Mars. It was a time to catch up – if they hadn't seen each other on Mars for a while – though oddly they never speculated about what they might have undergone in the day or two that had elapsed within the obelisk.

Allen crossed the plaza and made his way to the table beside the far rail, where Sally, Ana and Kapil were seated. Ana was subdued, far from her usual voluble, talkative self. Kapil was gripping her hand beneath the table, murmuring something to her. Ana stared out across the jagged, frozen plain, but looked up and smiled briefly as Allen sat down next to Sally.

He ordered coffee and, to break the ice, commented that the sight of the southern polar plain never failed to excite him.

Sally said, "I didn't think it would be so... vivid. The pictures I've seen failed to do it justice."

"Vivid and inimical," Kapil put in, ever the scientist. "It might look beautiful, but it's one of the most hostile environments known to man."

Ana said in a small voice, "I wonder why the obelisk is this far out – I mean *this* obelisk, the biggest in the system, the one every representative now goes to? Why couldn't it be situated on Earth?"

Kapil shrugged. "Security?"

Sally said, "But secure from whom? The Obterek, presumably? Surely they can access anywhere in the system, always assuming they can breach Serene defences in the first place?"

"Perhaps the defences are harder to breach this far out?" Ana suggested.

"Or maybe," Allen said lightly, "the Serene just like the view."

Sally looked up and said. "Here are Nina and Natascha."

They rearranged themselves around the table and pulled up a couple of chairs. Natascha was tiny, blonde, quiet and undemonstrative – a complete contrast in every respect to her Italian lover. She worked as an engineer on the Martian atmosphere plants, and had been a regular at the Allens' monthly soirées, gracing the gatherings with her quiet, deadpan wit. She and Nina had been together for almost ten years, as unlikely a pairing intellectually as they were physically.

They sat and ordered white wine and Allen said, "We were just wondering why the obelisk was situated this far out from Earth, Nina. I was about to say that no doubt you'd have a theory."

Natascha smiled into her glass. "Nina has a theory for *everything*, believe me."

Nina listened to what Kapil had suggested about security, then dismissed the idea with a wave. "The entire question as to why the obelisk is here is redundant, my friends. It could be here or anywhere – it would be equally as vulnerable on Earth as it would be here, or on Mars or Venus. The concept of distance, to Serene minds habituated to the idea of teleportation, is irrelevant. More important," she went on, "is its function. It's in some way more important to the Serene, because of its size and the fact that the human representatives come here now solely and far more often than we ever visited the other obelisks."

Natascha said, "But do you have a theory for that, my darling?"

"For once, you'll be surprised to learn, I do not. That's what I hope we'll find out from Kathryn, when she deigns to turn up."

Nina turned to Ana and murmured her condolences, touching the Indian woman's hand.

Ana smiled and said, "I have had time to think about it, Nina, and perhaps it was meant to be. Bilal had come to a peaceful period in his life, a period of contentment, I think. He had left behind the person he was, and was helping others. It was better that he die now than before, when he had not realised his... his potential."

Allen looked at her, wondering how much this was Ana rationalising the tragedy for the sake of her grief – or perhaps, in some way known only to the Hindu mind, she really believed this. To Allen, Bilal's death was an unmitigated tragedy, a murder made all the more horrible because of the fact that no one, these days, met intentionally violent ends.

Ana went on, "What frightens me is that it might be the start of more violence from the Obterek. It's bad enough that Bilal is dead, but let it be the last."

Natascha said, "And you are certain that you saw Bilal's old boss, Morwell, enter the orphanage as you left?"

Ana smiled. "His old boss, yes – but he was in some way younger. As if the Obterek had made him so."

"You said that a self-aware entity told you that Morwell was working for the Obterek?"

"That's what I was told."

"But it didn't say why Morwell was doing this?" Nina Ricci asked. "Why, in other words, the Obterek might want your brother dead?"

Ana shook her head. "It said nothing about this, and I was too shocked to ask."

Into the following silence, Sally asked quietly, "But why would the Obterek want Bilal dead?"

Nina Ricci cleared her throat, and heads turned to her. "In my opinion," she said, "they didn't specifically want Bilal dead. I know this might be hard to accept, Ana, but I think that anyone would have sufficed."

Natascha looked at her lover. "I don't follow..."

Nina went on, "The Obterek used Morwell as a tool to see if they could succeed in breaching the

Serene's *charea*, however briefly. To see if it could be done again."

They sat in silence for a time, digesting the corollary of this idea.

At last Ana said, "You are right, I do find it hard to accept, even though it might be the truth. Bilal told me, when we met three days ago, that he and Morwell had parted on bad terms. Perhaps it was Morwell who suggested to the Obterek that it might be Bilal who... who should serve as the... the test case." She stopped, Kapil gripping her hand, then looked up bravely and said, "He was reading a book about Gandhi when he died, which would have been hard to imagine him doing ten years ago."

Allen ventured, "Perhaps, if his death served to warn the Serene that the Obterek have returned to the fray, then it might not have been in vain?"

Ana nodded. "Yes, that would be a nice thought, wouldn't it?"

Nina Ricci sat up and said, "I think this is Kathryn, if I'm not mistaken."

Allen turned and watched Kath Kemp approach from the obelisk across the plaza.

Nina was in the process of pulling up a chair for her, but Kath said, "That won't be necessary, but thank you. We won't be stopping here. I have a more... secure venue for our meeting. Please, if you would care to follow me."

Exchanging glances, they rose and trooped from the café area.

* * *

KATH LED THEM across the plaza to a section of the flooring marked with black and white squares like a chess board. When they were all standing upon the 'board', Allen felt the ground give beneath his feet.

Ana let out a small gasp of surprise and reached out for Kapil. Kath smiled and said, "An elevator. We will be travelling only a short way."

"Where to?" Nina Ricci asked.

"Beneath the surface of the moon," Kath replied, "and then out again."

Her answer provoked a murmur of surprise amongst the group, and Sally caught Allen's eye and smiled tentatively. He slipped an arm around her shoulders as they dropped.

Seconds later the elevator halted, and Kath Kemp stepped from it and led the way along a lighted corridor. They arrived at a black door, not dissimilar to the surface of the obelisk. For a second Allen thought that it might indeed be a subterranean extension of the obelisk, then had second thoughts: if his orientation was correct, then when they stepped off the elevator they had been heading *away* from the obelisk, towards the face of the cliff overlooking the plain. This was confirmed a second later as Kath palmed a sensor and the black door slid aside to reveal the frozen methane plain stretching ahead to the horizon.

For a shocking second Allen thought that they were stepping onto the very surface of the moon. Then he made out, perhaps thirty metres away, an arrangement of loungers and foam-forms, surrounded by what looked like the inner membrane of a dome. Clutching Sally's hand, he followed Kath through the entrance and found himself in a long bolus of what appeared to be glass extruded from the wall of the cliff.

They came to the loungers and Kath invited them to be seated.

Allen sat down and looked up through the ceiling at the stars twinkling high overhead. If he looked back, he could see the domed city arcing above the lip of the cliff-face, and the summit of the obelisk. Ahead, high above the horizon, Saturn cast its light across the methane ice plain.

"Very spectacular," Ricci commented, "but I'd like to know just why we have been brought down here?"

Kath Kemp stood before them, silhouetted against Saturn's light. She inclined her head. "Despite its appearance of insubstantiality, this is a secure area. We cannot be overheard or observed."

"This gets better and better," Ricci smiled. "So you're really going to divulge..."

Kath held up a hand. "It has never been the policy to keep from you the information you needed to know. We had, and have, and will continue to have, the best interests of the human race at heart."

Ricci interrupted. "But it is you, or rather the Serene, who decide what we 'need' to know – which begs the question..."

It was Kath's turn to interject. "We told you everything which was necessary for your understanding relevant to an ongoing and unfolding situation."

Allen smiled to himself at Kath's convoluted politician's spiel. She went on, "However, due to recent developments in the Serene's management of the situation, it has been deemed necessary to inform, little by little, the human representatives, and their loved ones, of their larger role in the scheme of things."

She fell silent and looked around the group, and Allen was aware of the increasing tension in the room. Sally squeezed his hand as she stared at her friend.

Ana said quietly, "Does this have something to do with what happened to Bilal?"

Kath shook her head. "Not directly, no. But indirectly, yes, everything is linked."

"Would you mind explaining what you mean by that?" Ricci asked.

Kath paused, staring down at her feet, then raised her head and looked around the group. She said, "Twenty years ago the Serene came to Earth and changed everything. The Serene stopped you harming each other – in effect, we saved you from inevitable self-destruction, just as we'd saved many other races across the millennia. In order to do this, and to facilitate the changes that would inevitably eventuate, we required the help of the human race itself to work as our representatives, on Earth to begin with, and then across the solar system."

"Yes," Ricci said, "but what actually did we do – or rather, what did you *do* to us? Just what went on – goes on – in the obelisks?"

Kath paused, looking from one to the other of the six humans seated before her, then said, "You must consider that the Serene's concern is the long-term welfare of the human race. Not only did we wish to save you from yourself, but from the attention of our opponents, the Obterek. To this end we deemed it necessary to take a sample of the finest human beings your race had to offer and... study you."

Natascha sat forward. "Study us?"

"It was a long and laborious process. Within the obelisks, every month, we..." She paused, then said, "I will resort here to brutal terminology, but there is no other way of explaining what we did. Very well, in order to study you we had to take you apart, strip you down, and then build you back up. But in doing so we... we incorporated several fundamental changes in your molecular and genetic make-up."

Allen sat back, heart racing. He said, "Changes...?"

"We made alterations in order to improve you, to give you capabilities that will serve you, the human race, in the decades and centuries to come."

Ricci sprang to her feet and paced to the curving glass wall and back. She stopped and looked at Kath Kemp, and Allen was unable to work out if her expression was one of anger, resentment, or excitement. It seemed that all three reactions passed across her face in the seconds that followed, before she said, "You've *changed* us? Changed *me*? But into what?"

"To someone who will be better able to serve your race in the years to come," Kath said.

Kapil glanced at Ana, then said, "And how will that be?"

Kath Kemp smiled. "To answer that, I must first answer a question that Nina asked me a month ago, about the diminution in the stars."

Sally laughed. "But how can that be related...?"

"Please believe me, Sal – it is," Kath said. "You

see, it is all tied in to the need to protect you from the Obterek, and to do that we need to protect your habitat – the solar system."

Nina Ricci cried, "You're talking in riddles!"

Kath stared around the group, and seemed to be considering what she said next. "Very well, I think a practical demonstration is required. What we are about to do you might find shocking, unbelievable, but let me reassure you that you are at no risk whatsoever during the process."

Several of them began to speak at once, but Kath held up a hand and said, "Please follow my instructions. Now, Ana, Nina and Geoff... If you would kindly stand and move into the centre of the room."

Allen glanced at Sally, shrugged, and did as instructed, curiosity intermingled with a slight sense of foolishness; he was a schoolboy again, manipulated by the teacher in order to demonstrate some scientific principle.

He stood between Ana and Nina, and looked to Kath for further instructions.

She said, "Stand a little further apart, so that you are separated by about one metre."

Ricci protested, "Just what is all this about?"

Kath ignored her. "Now, Sally, Kapil and Natascha, please join your partners and hold hands."

Sally climbed from the lounger and joined him. Her hand found his and squeezed.

"Ana, Nina and Geoff, your softscreens are activated. I have initiated a program that will allow you to hear my instructions mentally."

"But how the hell did you do that?" Nina murmured.

Kath said, "In five seconds, you will hear me 'think' a set of co-ordinates. You will repeat them to yourself, mentally. And that will initiate the procedure..."

Allen watched as Kath stepped forward and took Nina Ricci's hand.

Before he could even begin to wonder what was going on, he heard Kath's voice in his head. "75-438-779... Now repeat."

Allen did so. He felt a split-second of disorientation, and then something flashed in his vision and he was forced to close his eyes.

He staggered, as if the ground beneath his feet had shifted, and then opened his eyes.

And he saw that he was no longer on Titan.

HE WAS STANDING in a sunlit vale or meadow, a warm breeze lapping over him. He was still gripping Sally's hand, and turned to her.

Her face wore an expression of enraptured wonder that was beautiful to behold.

Then he saw that the others were alongside Sally and himself. All of them were staring around in awe, open-mouthed; they looked at each other and could not help but laugh.

Allen turned to Kath, who was watching them with amusement

"What the hell," Nina Ricci said, "is going on?"

"Where are we?" asked Ana.

"This simple demonstration," Kath Kemp said, "should answer your first and fundamental question: what was it that the Serene were doing with you representatives for twenty years, every month initially, and then every two weeks. We were, little by little, installing you with the ability to shift, as we call it – or perhaps you would prefer the term *teleport*."

Allen felt dizzy and sat down on the grass. Sally flopped beside him and found his hand. Ana and Kapil were embracing. Nina and Natascha stared at each other and laughed.

"You're kidding, right?" Nina said.

"I think," Allen said, "that what we just did proves to us that this is no joke."

"Let me explain," said Kath. "We have invested in over ten thousand individuals – you human representatives – the ability to shift to any point within your solar system instantaneously. The science, the mechanics, of this we need not go into now; suffice to say that we have employed the same laws of quantum mechanics to effect this ability as we did to enable the *charea* edict. Programmed into your softscreens is an almost limitless cache of co-ordinates that will enable you, at the speed of thought, to select a destination and shift yourselves there. To access this cache you merely have to 'think' of your destination; for example a certain street in a certain city. Instantly the program will decode your thought and supply a destination code, which you will repeat. A nano-second later, you will find yourself there."

Sally was shaking her head. "But how did I... and Kapil and Natascha...?"

"The shifter will have the ability to take with them a maximum of three other people, and will do so by the simple expedient of ensuring that all three are physically connected."

"Right," said Nina with determination. She was staring ahead, at a stand of trees some five hundred metres away.

Allen then had the disconcerting experience of seeing a human being vanish from before his eyes. Nina appeared, instantly, beside the trees half a kilometre away. She lifted a hand and waved.

A second later she was back beside Natascha, shaking her head in wonder at what she had just done.

Allen heard his heartbeat hammer out his shock and elation. He closed his eyes, and into his head came a vision of a pub garden, millions of miles away; the Three Horseshoes in Wem, Shropshire, where many years ago he and Sally had spent many a pleasant evening.

A string of co-ordinates entered his head. *32-779-043...*

He opened his eyes and stared at Sally. "Hold my hand," he said.

Tentatively, she reached out and took his hand, and Allen repeated the co-ordinates.

He heard Sally gasp, and then he was in the garden of the Three Horseshoes, seated beside the fishpond. It was early morning in England, and the sun was rising over the elms which bordered the garden.

"I'm dreaming this," Sally said, "Please, Geoff, tell me I'm dreaming..."

"Then so am I," he said, and reached out and hugged his wife.

"The thing is," she said, "do you know your way back to the others?"

That was a point. He closed his eyes and recalled the grassy vale, and immediately the program responded with a string of co-ordinates.

Sally said, "Do you realise what this means, Geoff? In the wrong hands..."

"Shall we go back?" he said.

"The silly thing is that I'd like to stay a while, have a stroll around, explore again... But there will be plenty of time for that in future, won't there?"

He smiled. "We can explore everywhere you've ever wanted to explore," he said, and squeezed her hand.

He repeated the co-ordinates mentally, and a split-second later they were seated on the breast of the meadowed vale, Nina and Natascha staring at them in amazement.

Seconds later Ana and Kapil popped into existence before them, and Ana gasped, "We were in India, revisiting the farm where we first met. Oh, it was..." She turned to her husband and wept on his shoulder.

Nina said to Kath Kemp, "You do realise that if the wrong kind of people...?" she began.

Kath looked at the Italian with all the forbearance of a wise school-teacher. "Nina, we have invested the ability *only* in you representatives. We know you, on the most fundamental level. You are not the kind of people to abuse the gift bequeathed to you. Look into your hearts, each of you, and ask yourselves if that is not true."

Allen smiled to himself, overcome by the weight of trust the Serene had granted him. Then again, he asked himself, how could it be trust when the Serene knew him, and the other representatives, intimately? He felt not so much trusted, then, as blessed.

Nina Ricci stared across the greensward at the diminutive Kath, and said, "You have graced us with a power beyond our expectations, an ability none of us could have dreamed of... But – and far be it for me to sound suspicious, or ungrateful – but why have the Serene done this? What exactly do you want from us?"

Kath gestured, raising both her hands candidly. "As I told you, our desires are the continuance of the human race, the protection of your species, initially from yourselves, and then from the threat of the Obterek. With your ability, you can assist the Serene in this."

Ana said, "In what way? I don't understand how our ability to... *shift*... can help protect us."

"Your ability will not protect you, but it will help towards setting up a system, an environment, in which the human race will be safe."

"Again," asked Nina Ricci, "how?"

"To answer that," Kath said, "I need you to ask a question. And the question is this: where are we now?"

All six humans looked around them. Natascha said, "It looks like a meadow in Georgia where I went on holiday as a child."

"The hills of Tuscany," Ricci laughed.

Ana said, "Or the vale of Kashmir."

"It could easily be somewhere in Shropshire," Sally said.

Kath smiled. "You are all wrong, but right in that it is a place of surpassing beauty. We are not on Earth; nor are we on any planet or moon in the solar system."

More to himself, Geoff said, "The dimming of the stars..." And aloud, "Then where?"

"Look into the sky," Kath said, "and tell me what you see."

Allen looked up. The sky was cloudless. "The sun," he said.

"How many?" Kath asked.

Allen laughed. "One..."

"No!" Nina Ricci said. "Two..."

"Three... four!" Kapil exclaimed.

Allen saw that they were right; high above, a series of small, bright yellow suns marched across the heavens.

He shook his head. "But that's impossible, isn't it? Where are we?" He had a sudden, explosive thought, and said, "On the home planet of the Serene?"

Kath shook her head. "We are still within the confines of your solar system, but only just."

Nina Ricci pointed to the sky. "But the suns?"

"The dimming of the stars," Allen said, but aloud this time. He had the inkling of an idea. "On the edge of our system, Kath? On some kind of... of artificial platform?"

She smiled. "Almost. We are on the edge of the solar system, but the structure is somewhat more impressive than a mere platform. Imagine the skin of an orange, or rather a more oblate satsuma, cut into sections. Imagine the sections reformed into an oblate whole."

The idea was dizzying. Allen laughed. "And this... this is one of those sections?"

Kath Kemp nodded. "It is. From point to point

it measures one astronomical unit, and the same across at its widest point."

Nina Ricci was shaking her head. "But it's... vast."

Kapil said, "That's the distance from the sun to the Earth!"

"In surface area," Kath said, "it equates to forty million Earths."

"And you say that this is just *one* section?" Kapil asked.

"The first," Kath said. "Soon, others will join it, and in five of your years, the entire solar system will be enclosed."

Kapil was shaking his head in wonder. "And the number of sections it will take to do this?" he asked.

"The Serene estimate approximately two million," Kath said.

Allen laughed. "My maths isn't up to it..."

Kapil said in awed tones, "So there will be the equivalent of eighty trillion planet Earths on the inner surface of the shell, give or take a handful."

"How?" Sally asked. "The energy required, the material..."

Kath said, "We beam the energy from the far stars of the core, and utilise *takrea* technology to transport the rock and iron of distant planets. Surrounding the solar system are thousands of vast quantum engines, fabricators, which take the energy and reconstruct it." She gestured about her. "Forming the shell, which is in the region of fifteen thousand kilometres thick."

Natascha asked, "But why, Kath? Why are the Serene doing this?"

Kath nodded, as if the question were entirely reasonable. "Think about it," she said. "Think about what is happening to the human race. There are no more wars, no more crimes of violence, no more murders. Also, with the coming of the Serene and the advance of pharmaceutical sciences, many deadly diseases are no more. The human race is expanding, hence the outward push from Earth, the establishment of colonies on Venus, Mars, and the moons of Jupiter and Saturn."

Kapil finished for her. "And we need space into which to expand," he said.

Kath looked around the astonished faces of the humans before her. "This is not the first time the Serene have built a habitat shell around a solar system," she said. "It is one of the corollaries of saving a race from itself."

"But will there come a time, in the far, far future," Nina Ricci wanted to know, "when the human race will expand to fill all the available land within the shell?"

"That is very doubtful," Kath said. "It has not happened so far with any of the other races the Serene have assisted; they have instituted measures to curb their populations."

Beside Allen, Sally opened her mouth with an exclamation of understanding. "Ah, I see now..." she said.

The others looked at her.

"I understand why the representatives have been granted the ability to... shift," she said.

Kath Kemp was nodding. "When the shell is complete, the distances between areas of population across the inner surface will be so vast that we will need people, individuals, to travel back and forth, as envoys, messengers – couriers, if you like. To create and sustain a system of obelisks to perform this function would be an energy drain beyond even the resources of the Serene, hence the creation of a cadre of *shifters*, as you will come to be known."

Allen slipped an arm around his wife's shoulder and smiled at her.

"Of course," Kath went on, "as twenty years ago when the Serene recruited the representatives, we gave you the option of withdrawing, without fear of prejudice. We offer you the same option now; if any of you do not wish to enjoy the facility of shifting, or do not wish to carry through the work of the Serene, please say so and you will be returned to Mars with no memory of what has taken place here."

Allen laughed. "You are," he said, "joking, right? As if I could turn my back on the ability to..." He shook his head, suddenly speechless at the thought of what the Serene had granted him.

Kath turned to Ana Devi. "Ana?"

She smiled and clutched Kapil's hand. "I agree with Geoff," she said.

"And you, Nina?" Kath asked.

"I would not turn my back on the ability to shift for all the world," she said.

Kath Kemp smiled. "Thank you all," she said. "You have made me very happy."

Allen asked, "And the other representatives? Have the Serene told all ten thousand of us?"

She smiled. "We are in the process of doing so,"

she said. She gestured around her at the meadow. "As we speak there are groups of representatives, with their attendant self-aware entities, being told just what I have just told you."

She paused, then went on, "In celebration, I suggest we return to the plaza at Titan. I've had the presumption to order a magnum of champagne in readiness for our return."

Nina Ricci said, "But won't our sudden arrival, out of the blue, cause a little consternation?"

"Until a formal announcement is made regarding the shifters," Kath said, "the Serene have ensured that your arrival, anywhere, will go unnoticed by those in the vicinity."

Allen smiled to himself; the Serene had thought of everything.

She stepped forward and held out her hand to Allen, and he understood then why she had taken Nina Ricci's hand on Titan.

"You can't shift?" he said.

She smiled. "We can do many things, Geoff, but the Serene have not endowed us with that ability."

She looked around the group as the representatives linked hands with their partners. "If you visualise the plaza..."

Allen did so, and the co-ordinates entered his consciousness.

Gripping Sally's hand, he closed his eyes and repeated them.

And when he opened his eyes again he was on the plaza beneath the dome on Titan, and the others were already making their way to the café bar.

CHAPTER EIGHT

JAMES MORWELL LOOKED at his reflection in the mirror of his hotel bedroom and liked what he saw.

It was entirely appropriate, he thought, that as in a matter of hours he was due to annihilate himself he should take on a new visual identity. Gone was the Morwell of old, the pale, weak-chinned failure, to be replaced with this young, tall, blond vision.

It is necessary, said the voice in his head, *to disguise you...*

"I understand," he said aloud, then laughed at himself.

In one hour you will leave your planet forever. Are you ready?

"I am ready... though I can hardly bring myself to believe that soon I'll be..." He did not say the word, as if by doing so he might curse himself. He had tried for so long now, for so many years, to end his life that the idea that soon he might achieve his goal

– with some help, admittedly – seemed impossible to imagine.

A blessed cessation of the anger that haunted him; oblivion. Nothingness.

And in bringing about his own end, he would be helping to end the tyranny of the Serene in the solar system. The old ways would be restored. Humanity would be handed back its true destiny, no longer yoked to the pacifist ideals of a faceless alien race.

Thanks to me, he thought, the human race will be free.

He wondered if his sacrifice would be remembered, and exalted.

We will ensure that your name lives on, said the voice in his head.

In time he would be even more famous than his father had been. He laughed at the idea. His father was little remembered now, the long-dead tycoon of long-dead business concerns. He closed his eyes and saw his father advancing on him with a baseball bat, and cursed his memory.

Look at me now, you bastard...

Are you ready? said the voice.

"I'm ready," he replied.

He left the hotel and took a taxi to the Kolkata obelisk, where he had transit booked for Titan.

He sat back and stared out at the crowded streets as the taxi carried him towards his destiny. They passed within half a mile of the state orphanage where, three days ago, he had taken the life of Lal Devi.

The killing had not proved as satisfactory as he had hoped. He had imagined that Lal would grovel, would plead for his life, would apologise for betraying Morwell all those years ago. But when Morwell had walked in on Lal in his crude timber shack, he found a man changed from the slick businessman he had been. Lal seemed calmer, more reflective, centred.

He had smiled up at Morwell from where he sat cross-legged on his bunk, and said, "I did wonder if I would see you again, one day."

Even the sight of the automatic pistol in Morwell's right hand had failed to faze him.

"I want an apology," Morwell had said.

Lal had merely smiled and said, "Go to hell, Morwell..."

"You'll regret that, Lal."

"I regret nothing, least of all leaving you, the Organisation. It was the finest thing I ever did."

Morwell shook with suppressed rage. "I gave you everything, Lal. I saved you from a life of squalor. I educated you, gave you opportunities beyond your wildest dreams."

"You inculcated me with the same corrupt ethos that you yourself had been infected with from your father."

"No!"

"You filled my head with greed and gain, with concepts of power at the expense of others. Your ideals were against everything that is good and right, Morwell. But then how could they be anything else, handed down as they were from a father as monstrous as yours...?"

"Take that back!" Morwell cried.

"I take nothing back," Lal said gently. "I pity you, I really do."

And Lal was still smiling when Morwell pulled the trigger and shot him in the chest.

He pushed the incident to the back of his mind as the taxi pulled up in the shadow of the obelisk. He climbed out and paid the driver, then approached the sable, unreflective surface. He paused and looked around him at the teeming streets of Earth.

Proceed, said the voice in his head.

He stepped into the obelisk.

AND STEPPED OUT onto the plaza beneath the sloping rings of Saturn.

Cross the plaza and take a seat in the café bar by the edge, said the voice. *There you will see a group of seven people, among whom is your target, Kat Kemp.*

Heart thumping, Morwell stepped from the shadow of the obelisk and moved to the café bar. He sat down a few metres from the group, ordered a beer from the waiter, and stared across at Kat Kemp.

The years had been kind to her, he thought. She must be in her sixties now, but she had changed little from the woman he'd known nine years ago. A few fleeting memories of their time together came to him, but they were few, and they provoked no sadness or regret.

The only emotion the sight of her did provoke was the bitterness of betrayal. She was a self-aware entity, who had targeted him on behalf of the Serene. She was not a human, who had felt affection for the person he had been, but a mere robot fulfilling its programming.

He smiled to himself at the thought of the delicious revenge he was about to take, and he wondered if Kat Kemp would have time, before she died, to realise fully what was happening to her.

The group appeared to be celebrating something. They raised champagne glasses and laughed like fools.

To the Obterek in his head, he thought, "And nothing can go wrong, now?"

Nothing. We have everything planned, down to the finest detail.

"And I will die?" The very idea quickened his pulse.

You will die.

"And the destruction of the obelisk, the *takrea*...?"

The annihilation of the takrea will be a blow from which the Serene will not recover, said the voice. *The quantum engine at its core, which maintains the functioning of* charea, *will be annihilated. The human race will be freed from the shackles of the Unnatural Way.*

"And the Serene will be unable to re-establish control?"

Without the quantum engine to maintain charea, *the Serene will be unable to defend themselves. We will invade, establish outposts across the solar system. We will re-establish the Natural Way of the universe. Your name, James Morwell, will go down in history.*

He sat and drank his beer and smiled at the thought. He stared out through the wall of the dome at the massive beauty of the ringed planet above the horizon. Such magnificence, and his ability to perceive it, to perceive anything, would soon be no more... Soon his singular viewpoint on this universe would cease to be, and he felt nothing but satisfaction at the idea.

Very soon now the seven will leave the café bar and make their way to the obelisk. When they move, you will follow them. I will give the word for you to approach Kat Kemp. You will briefly inhabit her, through my agency, and we will be in control of her. Then we will step into the obelisk.

And then, Morwell thought, oblivion...

He stared across the café at the group, at Kat Kemp who was laughing and smiling at something a tall, grey-haired man was saying... Morwell recalled making love to her, all those years ago, and he felt absolutely nothing at the recollection. You are the enemy, he thought, and felt anger welling at her betrayal. No, not *her* – he reminded himself – but *its*.

Five minutes later they made their move. The grey-haired man took the hand of a tall, thin old woman and led the way from the café bar, followed by a younger Indian couple, and then Kat Kemp, a handsome dark woman and a tiny blonde.

Go, said the voice in his head.

Smiling to himself, heart thudding at the thought that everything in his life had led up to this moment, James Morwell stood and followed them from the café.

CHAPTER NINE

GEOFF ALLEN PAUSED in the shadow of the obelisk and turned to Sally. He stroked her cheek. "Strange to think that we've no longer any need to be using the obelisks."

Sally shook her head. "It's impossible to imagine, Geoff. I still can't take it all in."

"To go anywhere, anywhere at all... No, I still can't get my head around the idea. It'll certainly make holidays that much easier!"

"Where should we go first?"

"Oh... How about back to the Three Horseshoes at opening time, to celebrate with a bottle of Leffe?"

She made to punch his ribs. "Where's your sense of adventure, Geoff!"

Kath called to them. "It's all very well for you people..." she indicated the obelisk, "but I've still got to use this old, outmoded form of transportation."

Nina Ricci asked, "Where are you going?"

Kath looked at her softscreen. "I have a meeting on Venus this afternoon."

"Give me the co-ordinates," Nina said, "and I'll whisk you there."

Kath smiled. "Very kind of you, Nina. But my transit is already booked, and I have things to do within the *takrea*. I'd better be getting on my way."

Things to do... Allen thought in wonder.

He said, "How about a party at our place next week, to celebrate?" He looked around the group. "Everyone can make it?"

Ana and Kapil consulted and nodded; Nina and Natascha too.

Kath Kemp smiled across at him, and he was struck by the sudden fact of how lovely she was. "Try keeping me away," she said.

Sally said, "That's a date then. Bye, Kath."

Kath Kemp waved, then turned and strode towards the sable face of the obelisk.

ALLEN WAS ABOUT to ask Sally where in the solar system she would like to go now when a sudden movement beyond Kath caught his eye. A tall, fair-haired young man was approaching the obelisk as if to pass through its surface, but at the very last second his course veered and he moved towards Kath Kemp.

She stepped backwards, exclaiming in surprise at his proximity, and the smiling young man kept on walking as if intent on knocking Kath from her feet.

Then, in the blink of an eye, the man vanished and

in his place was a blue figure – an Obterek – and a split-second after that the Obterek slammed into and merged with Kath Kemp.

Geoff stared at the grotesque amalgam that the blue man and Kath Kemp had become; they flickered – like the visually fleeting images on a spinning coin – as one attempted to gain mastery of the other.

Allen looked around him at his friends, a frozen tableau of shock as they watched the conflict taking place before their eyes.

Then Kath Kemp/Obterek moved like a jerking marionette, step by painful step, towards the surface of the obelisk.

And in his head Allen heard Kath's tiny, desperate voice, "*Help me...*"

Sally cried, "What's happening, Geoff?"

"*It's taking me over...*" Kath's words were desperate within his head. "*I... I cannot let it enter the takrea!*"

Kath was putting up a terrible fight. The amalgamated figure before them fluctuated between Kath and the Obterek, its forward progress impeded when it became Kath; when the Obterek gained mastery, however, it staggered forward as if leaning into a headwind.

Allen heard screams in his head, a tortured moan from Kath and an even more horrific, bestial cry from the alien creature. He held his head in his hands, mentally deafened by the psychic fallout of the fight talking place before him.

As he watched, horrified, Kath seemed to gain the upper hand. She managed to turn away from the *takrea* and take laboured steps back towards the café, stopped each time the Obterek gained control of her body but progressing when she gained ascendance.

"What can we do?" Ana yelled at him.

"Just..." he began, not really knowing what he was about to say. Then it came to him. "Ana, Nina... all we can do is put ourselves between... between it and the *takrea*."

Nina stared at him. "And then?"

"Then we do our best to stop the Obterek."

The hybrid figure was perhaps ten metres from the *takrea* now, a visually discordant, ever-shifting optical illusion – one second the bent, tortured image of Kath Kemp, and the next the straining, far larger figure of the Obterek.

Allen stepped forward. He felt a restraining hand on his arm. "Geoff."

He turned. Sally stared at him, her features contorted with fright, eyes pleading. "Geoff, please..."

"Sal, I've got to..." he began, choking on a sob.

He pulled away, moved hesitantly towards the Kath/Obterek figure. Ana was to his right, perhaps three metres away, Nina to his left.

"It's... *winning*," Kath called out mentally. "*It's much stronger... There's little I can do, the pain...*"

As he watched, the figure flickered and the instances of its appearing as Kath Kemp became less and less frequent. The Obterek was gaining mastery.

He glanced at Ana, reassured by her expression of determination.

"*Kath!*" he called out the thought, "*how can we stop it?*"

The Obterek remained for long seconds. Then briefly Kath appeared, and a fraction of a second later vanished. The Obterek seemed to expand, to become visually larger as it dominated, sensing victory.

Slowly, step by step, Allen approached the terrible figure. Beside him, Ana and Nina kept pace.

The Obterek faced them, something almost arrogant in its stance. It was without facial features, so Allen was unable to apprehend the victorious expression he was sure it would have worn. But its body language, its swagger as it drew itself to its full height, convinced him that it was relishing the end game of its conflict with the self-aware entity.

For a fraction of a section a bowed, shrunken Kath Kemp appeared, and in that instant her small voice uttered a string of numbers. Beside him, Nina Ricci repeated them as if in triumph.

"What?" Ana Devi asked.

Allen knew full well what Kath Kemp had given them, knew full well what he might in seconds be called upon to do.

But, he asked himself, would he be equal to the challenge; would he be able to sacrifice himself, and everything he had gained, in order to stop the Obterek?

But what, he asked himself, was the alternative?

On the concourse of the plaza in the shadow of the rearing Serene obelisk, in Saturn's bright ring-light, three tiny humans confronted the pulsing blue figure.

And the Obterek made its move.

It lowered its head and mighty shoulders and charged like a bull towards the *takrea*.

The confrontation was over in a matter of seconds, but even so Allen had time to wish that the alien would head towards Nina or Ana rather than towards himself... a treacherous, terrible thought that he banished as soon as it appeared.

Because he was better than that, and anyway the Obterek was heading directly towards him – and he knew exactly what he had to do.

Behind him, as he began running to meet the alien, he heard Sally's desperate cry – and for all the world he wanted not to go through with this; he wanted to turn to Sally and tell her that he loved her so very much... but he consoled himself, as he came within metres of the alien figure, with the knowledge that Sally already knew this.

The Obterek dodged him, jinked to his right and sprinted for the *takrea*. Allen dived and managed to trip the creature, which leapt to its feet with amazing agility and sprinted towards the obelisk.

Allen ran and in desperation dived after the figure as it hit the surface of the *takrea*. He fastened his arms around its muscular midriff and held on. The Obterek screamed, a terrifying war cry which Allen interpreted as acknowledgment of its defeat.

He felt a searing pain, and before it overwhelmed him he repeated the figures Kath had bequeathed him...

And then he was suddenly *elsewhere*...

And he felt no more.

* * *

IT HAPPENED SO fast that Sally was unable to scream – and at the same time it seemed an age between Geoff's leaving her side and his reaching Kath. Sally stepped forward as he ran towards the figure, wanting to prevent what he was about to do; it was as if she knew, even now, what was about to happen, and while a small part of her wanted to scream aloud in denial, another part of her realised the inevitability of events.

Geoff slammed into the Obterek, seemed to merge with it, and then vanished, taking the Obterek with him.

Sally wept.

Ana came to her side, holding her upright, and Nina joined them and uttered soothing words. She held onto them desperately like the survivor of some terrible shipwreck.

As one they looked up as a blinding white light – like a supernova high above Titan – exploded silently in the dark, star-flecked heavens.

CODA

2055

SALLY WALSH SAT on the bench beneath the cherry tree as the guests mingled on the lawn, chatting and laughing and occasionally glancing into the sky. There was a sense of anticipation in the air, a charge of expectation. Sally had feared this day for a long time but, now that it had come, she realised that she had known all along that it was something that had to be lived through, and that in doing so she would be stronger.

She examined the grain of the wood beneath her wrinkled fingers, then the cherry blossom above her head, and then looked along the length of the crowded lawn to the house. It was hard to imagine that it was not the same garden where, almost thirty years ago, she and Geoff had sat out on summer nights drinking red wine and chatting. The house and garden were identical in every respect to the ones that she had left behind on Earth, and then on Mars; she had always accused Geoff of being a stick-in-the-mud, but she realised that she was just as guilty, to drag this shibboleth of old times across the solar system to this place, the first section of the Shell to be inhabited.

She watched Hannah playing with her daughter Ella; and nearby Ana and Kapil laughing with their teenage boys; Ana had aged well. In her mid-forties now, she was still handsome, with a streak of grey in her hair. She too had migrated to the Shell with her husband, together managing the vast farm that fed the colonists of the sector. Nina Ricci had moved from Mars and Natascha had made the trip with her.

Other friends from down the years had accepted her invitation to the party: Ben Odinga from Kallani, Uganda, in his eighties now and frail, and Yan Krasnic, the same age but still as massive and robust. Even Mama Oola, rubicund and ageless, had made the trip and smothered Sally in her laughing, all-consuming embrace. She wished that Geoff could be here to witness this gathering of friends old and new, but of course if that were possible then this gathering would not be...

The first few years of her life without Geoff had been harder than she could ever have imagined. Her friends had rallied round, and without their love and support she might not have made it through; she had wished herself dead on more than one occasion, then hated herself for submitting to such negative, selfish emotions. Geoff himself would have chastised her for such maudlin introspection, and anyway – even if suicide had been possible – how could she have consigned those she loved to a similar grief to that which she was enduring?

And down the years the burden of his absence had become a little easier to bear; she recalled the good times together, and they sustained her, along with her family, and the extended family of Ana and Kapil. She was, all things considered, a lucky woman... even if she was almost seventy-three and slowing down reluctantly, a grandmother now – how hard that was to believe! Inside, she often thought in amazement and regret, she was still the thirty-six-year-old who had gone out to Uganda with such hopes and high ideals.

She turned away from the house and stared across the rolling grassland that stretched towards the nearest township. A narrow lane crossed the meadow, and along it beetled a small electric car: a late guest, come to join the festivities.

She watched it pull up a hundred metres away, and stared as a small, female figure climbed out and regarded the house. Sally stood quickly, her pulse accelerating. Surely that was impossible, could not be... She made a few faltering steps in the direction of the figure, who was climbing the incline towards the garden now, and they met at the wooden gate.

"I'm sorry for surprising you like this, Sally," said Kath Kemp. "Perhaps I should have called ahead."

Sally opened her mouth, but the words would not come. At last she managed, "You... But you –"

Kath smiled. "Technically I am Kathryn Kemp's... 'iteration' – a copy, if you will. Essentially I am the same person, with all her thoughts and memories."

"But... ten years," Sally managed.

Kath led her back to the bench and they sat down. "It took that long for the Serene to rebuild me, install all my old memories. I would have come sooner, but that was impossible."

"They brought you back..." Sally said, her thoughts spinning, "in which case...?"

It was as if Kath were reading her thoughts. She shook her head, gently, and took Sally's hand. "I'm afraid that some things are beyond even the capabilities of the Serene." She paused, then went on, "His sacrifice was ultimate, which is why we celebrate his life."

Sally smiled and squeezed her friend's hand. "You will stay? I mean... not only for the party, but as a guest here for a while?"

Kath laughed, the warm chuckle Sally realised she had missed all these years. "I am coming to live and work in this sector, Sally. If you would like, we can resume where we left off, all those years ago."

"I would like nothing more," Sally said. "We have a lot to share, and a lot to catch up on."

She stared into her friend's laughing, human eyes. So what, she thought, that the being before her was but an iteration of the Kath Kemp she had known and loved. *That* Kath Kemp had revealed herself to be not human but a construct, and even that had failed to undermine the affection she felt towards the woman.

"But I'm being a terrible host!" Sally said now. "Can I get you a drink?"

"An orange juice would be lovely."

Sally caught the attention of a passing waiter, who fetched Kath a juice.

She sipped the drink and said, "I came here to celebrate with you, Sally, to be with you – and to tell you a little more about the Shell."

Sally stared at her. "I sense... *something*," Sally said. "A revelation, a 'the Shell is not all that you thought it was' moment."

Kath laughed. "You're sharp, Sally Walsh! You're as sharp as ever."

"Well then..."

Kath said, "We told you the truth in that the Shell is necessary for the future of the human race, as a place of domicile for an expanding population. But it is something more."

She touched the softscreen on her forearm, and in the air before them appeared a rectangular image of deep space, flecked with stars, and at its centre a great grey sphere. Towards it moved a hundred dark shapes, slow but relentless.

Sally looked questioningly at her friend.

"Upon sealing the Shell, five years ago," Kath said, "we effectively prevented the Obterek from subverting the underlying reality maintained within it. The Shell acts as a shield, denying the Obterek access to the solar system. We have done this with many other systems across the universe, and always it is a race against time."

Sally shook her head. "I don't understand."

Kath said, "Many decades ago, when they discovered that we were planning to assist the human race, they sent off a war fleet of destroyers from their home-system across the galaxy, in the hope of arriving here before we could install the shield. Their ships are equipped with, for want of a better word, disruptors, weapons which would help the Obterek undermine the *charea*..." Kath gestured at the screen in the air. "This is not a true representation of the reality out there. In fact, the Obterek ships are many light years distant."

"And when they arrive here?" Sally asked. "Do you, the Serene, have the means to..." She had been about to say 'attack,' but stopped herself.

Kath smiled. "To defend ourselves? The Shell will do that, Sally. We need not respond to their hostile advance with hostility of our own. We are adequately protected within the Shell, and the Obterek will realise this and, in time, after a token attack, will desist and move on."

She paused before continuing, "And the human race, along with the Serene, will work to expand the *charea* beyond the confines of the Shell."

Sally stared at her. "That is possible?"

"Your finest scientists, guided by the Serene, are working on it as we speak," Kath said. "It is our hope, in a hundred years or two, that we will be able to spread the *charea* to link other races, across the face of the galaxy."

Sally smiled at the thought, and realised that tears were rolling down her cheeks. She backhanded them away. "Look at me..."

"I know," Kath Kemp murmured, "the idea makes me feel like weeping with joy, too." She touched her softscreen, and the image of the Shell vanished.

Where it had been, across the lawn, Sally made out a hesitant figure, staring at her.

She half stood, unable to believe her eyes, and laughed.

Kath looked at her. "What...?"

"I don't know if I can take much more of this," Sally murmured. "Two surprises in one day. Please, excuse me one moment. I'll be back."

She stood slowly and made her way across the lawn to where the small, bowed man stood, looking at her with uncertainty and maybe even fear in his eyes.

Sally said, "It is! It *is* you..."

"I have found you at last, Dr Walsh. It has taken me a long time, but at last I have found you."

Something caught in her throat, and she shook her head in lieu of words.

She stared at the old man's face, his hooked nose, his hooded eyes. She would have recognised him even if it had not been for the jagged scar that ran like a wadi from his temple to his jaw.

"I have come to say that I am sorry for what I did thirty years ago, Dr Walsh. I have come to apologise. Perhaps later, on another day, we can talk a little more?"

Sally bowed her head. "I would like that, yes," she said.

He reached out a tentative hand, and Sally smiled and, slowly, reached out her own hand and gripped his.

"Thank you, Ali al-Hawati..." she murmured, and watched him as he turned and moved slowly through the crowd and left the garden.

When she returned to the bench beneath the cherry tree, Kath Kemp had been joined by Ana and Kapil, Hannah and her husband and Ella.

"Who was that?" Hannah asked.

"Oh," Sally said, sitting down beside Kath. "Just someone I knew, many, many years ago..."

Sally's granddaughter tugged at her dress and said, "Nana, why are all these people here?"

Hannah hoisted the three-year-old onto her hip and explained. "We've come here to celebrate, darling. You see, ten years ago today, your granddaddy did a very, very brave thing, and today all humanity, across the system, will remember what he did for us."

"What did granddaddy do, Mummy?"

Hannah jogged her daughter and looked into the

sky. "He stopped someone destroying everything that was good," she said.

"Who did he stop?"

Hannah shook her head. "We don't know his name, darling, but he was working for the bad aliens, the Obterek."

Sally smiled and caught the attention of a waiter. When everyone had taken possession of a full champagne glass, Sally looked around at her friends.

Somewhere in the garden, a man was counting down and the guests joined in, chanting, "Ten... nine... eight..."

Sally said, "I would like to propose a toast." She smiled at Ana Devi, who returned her smile; then she turned to Kath Kemp and said, "To humanity..."

"To humanity," her friends replied.

And seconds later, high in the sky above them, something exploded like a supernova and bathed the land with light.